SWEET
BITTER
CANE

GS JOHNSTON

An Italian–Australian World War II saga

www.gsjohnston.com

Follow on Facebook at @GSJohnston.author

Follow on Twitter at @GS_Johnston

Published by MiaRebaRose Press

Paperback: ISBN-978-0-9925484-3-8
ebook: ISBN: 978-0-9925484-4-5

Typeset by Green Avenue Design   ·

Cover Design © Ian Thomson

Cover photographs © John Bortolin

PART ONE

1920–21

Love's gentle spring doth always fresh remain
Venus and Adonis – William Shakespeare

CHAPTER ONE

The Madonna flew from Jerusalem. Like a gyre she rose, wingless, from the Church of the Holy Sepulchre, passing over the sea, over Crete and Sicily, between Capri and Vesuvius, close to the sun, amongst the starlings and swifts and the shrieking seabirds. She swept along the coast of conquered pasts, above the dusty aqueducts, the chipped and crumbling buildings, olive groves and grain fields and winter-gnarled vineyards, never once losing her way, full of grace.

She glided over the cobblestones of Tovo di Sant'Agata in far northern Italy, past the stirring baker and the sleeping cobbler, through the village square, over the water well and barking dogs and prowling cats and shivering rats. She touched down, crimson and sapphire robes fluttering, her lips and cheeks a healthy rose, at the end of Amelia Durante's bed.

For the first time in many years, this vision returned to Amelia uncourted. While staring at the Madonna to the side of the altar in the parish church, blood pulsed the statue's white marble to flesh, her lips alive, her weeping robes the same deep colours. The questions came again to Amelia: What did this vision mean? That she was blessed? That she would travel? Or that she would never leave the village? The Madonna cared for her? What else could it mean? The Madonna beckoned her.

Taken over, she extended her right hand, splayed her fingers. They hung in midair, a featherless wing. The air, heavy with frankincense, scorched her eyes. Amelia gasped, snatched back her hand and raised her left. What kind of fool gave the wrong hand? She swallowed her doubts and watched the gold ring slip over her knuckle. How innocent it looked, this self-joined circle, and what power it held. Even through the white film of her veil it shone, sun-gold.

The priest began. '*Confírma hoc, Deus, quod operátus es in nobis.*'

With her free hand, she rotated the ring, just a single turn, this key to freedom.

'*A templo sancto tuo, quod est in Jerúsalem,*' the small congregation responded.

Amelia looked beyond the priest to the white-lace altar and the risen god above. She inhaled the incense.

'*Et ne nos indúcas in tentatiónem.*'

'*Sed líbera nos a malo,*' she said.

Had she made the right choice? So much was still to be resolved.

'You may kiss the bride.'

Giuseppe turned to her. So strange to see him in a suit, with a tie and white shirt. With infinite care, he gathered the bottom of her veil as if raising the curtain on a theatre performance. His eyes didn't leave hers. He leaned forward, moving his mouth towards her lips. She pressed up on her toes, as far above her mere 150 centimetres as she could muster, but turned so his lips touched her cheek, then the other. It seemed natural to kiss her brother like this. He was just her proxy groom.

She relaxed to her soles and smiled. He returned the gesture, then took her ringed hand in his clammy palm and turned her towards those assembled. Above, the bells clamoured their silver celebration. He walked her along the central aisle, towards her family.

Her mother and father, Velia and Emilio Durante, were in tears, but they gathered smiles as best as they could. After all, this church ceremony was for them, though they could ill afford the expense. All that was legally necessary to complete her marriage to Italo Amedeo could have passed in a notary's office.

To her left, Italo's mother, Signora Pina, stood glaring at the altar. She was painfully thin, fierceness etched into the lines on her face, her greying hair oiled and pulled to a tight bun at her nape. In the row behind her were Italo's aunts, Zia Fulvia and Zia Francesca. Amelia smiled at them, and they dabbed their eyes and bowed their heads and nodded in fervent supplication. Neither woman had married, the Great War, poverty and their hesitations rebuffing the few available suitors.

Outside the church, the humid air prickled Amelia's skin, unusually warm for February in the far north of Italy. Wreaths of olive branches entwined with white roses and lilies – peace, transience and purity – lay wilting in the sun, after a morning funeral.

'You're married,' Giuseppe said, smiling.

She smiled but felt no difference.

Her mother rushed from the church, squinting in the harsh light. She was in her mid-forties and still a proud woman. She smiled but her lips trembled. She embraced Amelia. 'Don't ever regret this,' she whispered.

Her handsome father and her elder brother, Aldo, nodded as Zia Fulvia and Zia Francesca hurried to her.

'You make such a beautiful bride,' Zia Fulvia said.

'If only Italo were here,' Zia Francesca said.

'Soon I will be in Babinda with him,' Amelia said.

She liked the word – Babinda – the bold play of vowels sounding Italian even though it was far away in Australia.

The gay party started towards the Durante home. The villagers smiled and waved, every heart so easily drawn by a wedding. Even the uniformed officers left over from the war – who, two years later, still spilled from the town's cafes – raised their open hands high above their heads in celebration. The war had left them idle. Each bomb and bullet and bayonet had torn the fabric of the village to ribbons, killed the youths, left only scarred old men and babies. But they all smiled, dulled and weary. Who were they to know all wasn't as it appeared? Her marriage rebutted everything they'd fought for – she'd married to leave rotting Italy.

In the main piazza, a man sang a nursery rhyme, his voice unsure and quavering.

> Garibaldi was wounded,
> He was wounded in the leg …

Signor Gregorio slept under the lip of the main fountain. Amelia often brought him food and, in winter, without her father knowing, ushered him into in their barn to sleep. Every piazza in Italy had an eccentric, a religious zealot or political conspirator, and he was theirs. She unlinked her arm from Giuseppe's and went to him.

'It's my wedding day,' she said. 'Why do you sing of Garibaldi?'

Gregorio looked at her, his face crushed and wrinkled, an oval frame of wild hair and wiry grey beard. She'd no idea how old he was, but it was said he'd fought for Garibaldi.

'He commands us to be one,' he said. He raised both arms in an arc, his hands aloft as if about to conduct an orchestra. He blinked both sparkling eyes. 'He brings all to all.'

He'd a large tear in his coat's side.

'What have you done?' she said, pointing to the hole. Clearly, the magnanimous legacy of Garibaldi hadn't made provision for its repair. 'Take it to my mother. She'll sew it up.'

Deflated, he lowered his arms and nodded. She smiled at him. She'd always appreciated his views of the world, which ran counter to most people's. She turned back to the party. Gregorio began to sing again.

> Mamma, don't cry that it's time to leave
> I go to war to win or die.

Amelia's family home was small and typical of the village, built many years ago of roughly hewn limestone with small windows to the world, no shutters. It was kept as well as poverty would afford, the terracotta tiles in strict rows and plumb lines, the sills buffed and whitewashed, the path stones free of weeds. The ground floor consisted of a stable and a low-ceilinged living room, with a kitchen and a chimney. They all slept in this main room, below a hay-filled loft. For this special day, they'd moved the table to the street so there was room for their guests.

'To those who were,' Amelia's father said, raising his glass. 'To those who are.' He smiled at his daughter, his eyes bright with tears. 'And to those who will be.'

Tonight, Amelia would leave her family and her village, as a bride should do, and return to the hamlet of Bovegno with Italo's mother, some hundred kilometres to the south. But it would be Signora Pina who'd share her wedding bed, not her husband, who was on the other side of the world in a small town in Far North Queensland, Australia.

Signora Pina snored all night, whistling on the inhalation and whining out. She lay on her back but, as if to taunt

Amelia, occasionally rolled to her side and ceased snoring. In these moments of quiet, Amelia imagined Italo's breathing, firm and regular, water lapping at a lake's shore. But the peace was a momentary aberration. Signora Pina would growl pungent farts, slump to her back and begin snoring again. Signora Pina had slept far too many years on her own. When the first cock crowed well before light, Amelia rose.

The prior evening, Signora Pina had given her a wooden spoon, a traditional gift from a new mother-in-law. Amelia took it from the table but wondered at the sincerity of the gesture. How many hours had she dreamt of her wedding day? It was over, so quick it hadn't really begun. She rekindled the fire and made coffee, the oily brew in a tiny cup. She hardly ever used sugar, such was its price, but while Signora Pina continued to snore, Amelia stirred in a heaped teaspoon, taking the bitterness away.

In Australia, Italo grew cane. Was this his sugar?

From her diary, she took her one photograph of him. Although fifteen years older than her, he had dark hair and in unison his aunts had said, with a dreamy air, 'His eyes are as blue as the sea.' Hers were like her brothers', plain hazelnut, but she'd seen eyes like Italo's in the faces of Bovegno. She searched the photograph again to find something new, something she'd never noticed. He was seated in a Savonarola chair, in a studio, stiff and dressed in a vest and a jacket, a light collarless shirt to fight against the Australian heat, with a white bow-tie.

How was your wedding night?

But a photograph can't reply, and she knew Italo had had no ceremony. Only a woman's virtue was at risk, only a woman's family honour. A man would laugh out loud at such a suggestion, but such was the world. Now a married woman, she could travel to Australia, but even a married woman couldn't travel alone. On the boat, she'd have a chaperone, the only demand her father had made, to be paid for by Italo. Italo owned his land. Imagine that. She'd never even heard of anyone she knew owning land—

'You think it will be different there.'

Signora Pina's hoarse voice made her jump. The death of a husband soon after the birth of an only child had cheated Signora Pina, each year harshening her tone, frightening off any man who may have been interested. And when Italo was only twenty, he emigrated to Australia. For fifteen years, Signora Pina hadn't seen her only child, her only son, her only notion of family.

'I've made coffee,' Amelia said. 'It's still fresh.'

Signora Pina continued to stand in the doorway, glaring at her.

'You're right,' Amelia said. 'It's grown bitter. I'll make some fresh.'

She poured the older coffee for herself and began again, but under Pina's scrutiny what was second nature became foreign. She concentrated, ground only the beans needed, watched the water to assure it would remain just off the boil. The silence rang.

Signora Pina, stern, harsh and angry beyond belief, annoyed her. Amelia was forced to live with Pina and had no choice but to honour her elder and Italo's mother, but she didn't understand her. All she could do was hasten the remaining immigration paperwork and count the days until she could leave. Amelia fought not to show her discomfort and, without a tremor, placed the fresh coffee on the table. Signora Pina made no move to acknowledge it, less still any intention to drink it. Amelia sat opposite. Pina lit a cigarette, the first of the day's chain. They remained so, silent.

'Why would you marry someone you've never met?'

Why would she ask this now? Was this the heart of Signora Pina's resentment?

'Other girls have married this way. Travelled to Australia, some to America ...'

'And what were their fates?'

'Zia Fulvia and Zia Francesca assure me ...'

'Two spinsters.' She spat the words. 'They've never even tasted love. What do they know?'

Perhaps her judgement was that Amelia Durante, the daughter of a peasant apple farmer, wasn't good enough for her son.

'What are you running from?' Signora Pina's voice was tight. 'A mother who'll never be pleased? A father who beats you?'

'Signora ...' Amelia breathed deeply to choose her words. 'The facts of this courtship—'

'What courtship? A few letters ... You put too much confidence in words.'

'But the facts remain.' Signora Pina recoiled at Amelia's force. 'Two years ago, Zia Fulvia and Zia Francesca approached my parents. The delay wasn't mine. My parents begged me to forget this, forced every delay.' She steadied herself. 'I am *not* running away.'

Signora Pina was silent. Perhaps Amelia had won some ground.

'I love Italo ...' Amelia said.

'You've never met him. You don't know him.'

'We will learn to love—'

'You don't even know what love is.'

'I'm not a foolish girl.'

'Do you think he's not loved? He's thirty-five. If you think this is true, you're more foolish than I first thought. Look around you. He has no fortune.'

'We will make one together. It's possible in Australia. A peasant in Italy can never hope for such a thing.'

There. She'd called herself what she was.

Signora Pina sighed and looked away. 'Men think only of themselves.' Signora Pina stopped. 'He's only married you because there are no suitable women in Australia.' She sighed. 'What's done can't be undone, but you'll promise me one thing.'

Amelia breathed out. 'Of course. Whatever you wish.'

'No doubt, God willing, you'll soon have children. You must bring them back to me.'

What did she think? To reach Australia was months and months of travel. Did she think they could travel like the Madonna flew from Jerusalem?

'I'll not die alone. You must return to care for me.'

And then Amelia understood. Pina resented the marriage as it was another statement, perhaps the firmest statement yet, that Italo wouldn't return for an even longer time. He would now have a wife, and an Italian wife, and soon a family in Australia.

'Promise me. Or I'll curse you.'

Amelia resented this corner into which she'd been forced. She stood, picked up her cup. She had no choice. 'All right. I promise.'

How was Amelia to bear this? If only Italo were there. He would know what to say, what to do.

'Can't you be happy for me?' Amelia said. The words fell from her mouth, too late to catch them.

Signora Pina's face hardened further.

'In Italy, people toil for more poverty,' Amelia said. 'I've escaped.'

Signora Pina blew smoke at the untouched coffee. Amelia had spoken out of turn, had rubbed her nose in her own lack of courage to follow her son to a new land with greater expectations. The unification of Italy and the Great War had brought huge waves of change. Amelia knew men who were unemployed. Italo had left for this reason. She could see the villages destroyed. And yet there was no will to rebuild them, no-one who could see what had to be done.

She thought of a line in a letter from Italo that had won her heart.

> In Australia, the sky is so large and clear and blue. Nothing can hinder a man, and anything is possible.

It wasn't just the sentiment but the play of words. He put them together with a poet's measured touch. But she wouldn't tell Signora Pina about his letters. She'd said too much. Though in many ways she hadn't said enough.

She had to leave the confines of this hot kitchen. She'd go to the water well. She picked up the wooden pail. Signora Pina made no move to stop her. Outside, the morning was still cool, and she grasped her shawl at her chest, tightly around her shoulders. The sun, low in the winter sky, came down the street. She was amongst strangers, something she had to get used to. She exhaled her frustration. Did Pina have no consideration for her? She'd taken a great gamble and now the dice were thrown, spinning in the air. She was married but had never felt so alone. Through the sun's rays, she caught a person's silhouette, something familiar and heartwarming. She squinted.

'Mamma,' she said. 'What are you doing here?'

'Aldo went to the market in Ghedi. I wanted to see you.'

Amelia threw her arms around her, and although she exerted all control, she started to cry and then to sob. How would she bear life without her mother? She inhaled the scent at the base of her neck, as soothing as warmed milk. After some moments, Velia took her hand, pulled back from her, smiled and led her away, through the square towards the church. They sat in front of the Madonna, Pina's empty bucket at Amelia's side, and she poured out what Pina had said.

'She's small-minded,' Velia said. 'Don't reduce yourself to that.'

'She should be happy.'

Her mother said nothing. What an insidious position Amelia had put her in; for Velia to say she was happy would be a lie.

'You've never said anything about Italo,' Amelia said.

'It's not for me to judge, but from what you've told me from his letters he sounds a fine man.'

'But you think it's foolish to marry someone I've never met.'

Her mother said nothing, just kept her eyes fixed to those of the Madonna. Amelia pushed back the quick of her thumbnail to make it hurt.

'I'm so scared,' Amelia said. 'Isn't that silly, now that it's all done?'

Velia squeezed Amelia's hand, and they were silent. 'My parents didn't want me to marry your father. He was only a farmer, and they'd worked hard in their shop for so long. They knew a farmer's life ... They wanted a better life for me. But every morning he came to the bar next to the shop before he travelled out to their land.'

'So far out of his way.'

'I know.' Velia smiled. 'And when I saw him ... When he looked at me, I felt something so strong. I couldn't describe it.' Her eyes shone. 'He was so handsome. What hope did I have?'

Amelia had never heard her mother speak of this. 'Do you regret it?'

'I married him for this feeling, despite everything my mother said. But with time, the feeling faded. Those things weren't so important anymore.'

Amelia swallowed hard. 'Don't you love him?'

'Of course I do. But there was a time … It lasted for many years. Even with all of you children and all the work, I felt very lonely. As hard as it is for me to say this, in my heart, I feel you have made the right choice. Your father doesn't understand, but I do. But I'll miss you. You're my child.'

Amelia looked away, into the face of the Madonna, so open and tranquil.

'I've brought you a present,' Velia said.

From the bag, she produced two packages wrapped in brown paper. One was flat and the other rectangular, a small box. Amelia smiled and opened the flat, softer one. Inside was a silk shirt, a light mauve.

'Mamma, it's so expensive.'

'You'll need it, to make a good impression.'

She pulled it free from the wrapping.

'So beautiful. Your stitch is so fine—'

'It's not my stitch. I bought it.'

Amelia gasped. Such extravagance.

'Open your other gift.'

She pulled back the thick brown paper. Inside was a book, an Italian–English dictionary, large with a strong binding of red leather and the pages with gilded edges, the paper as thin as tissue.

Amelia laughed. 'Where did you get it?'

'I had your uncle send it from Bologna. Despite all our poverty, I always bought you any book you needed.' She stopped herself. 'Your reading has led you to this marriage.

It carried you away. Your brothers don't see the point of it but from the moment I started to teach you, you read everything anyone gave you, newspapers, even pamphlets on the street. You're like me – you believe it.'

'Do you remember, years ago, my vision that the Madonna flew from Jerusalem to me? I think the vision was about being carried by reading.'

Her mother smiled. 'Despite our lifetime of hard work, your father and I are no better off than when we first met. I'm bone-tired. But we were lucky – your brothers were too young for the war.' She turned and looked at Amelia, grabbed her forearm, her nails digging into the flesh. 'Go.' Her eyes widened, the black discs at the centres flared. 'I give you my blessing to fly. Break this cycle. But don't just fly – soar, as close as you can to the sun.'

Her mother said goodbye, demanded she not follow her. She watched her walk the aisle, the tap of her sole uneven on the marble floor. Once she was gone, Amelia turned to the Madonna.

'Please, Holy Mother, keep me safe.'

But the Madonna remained, calm and impassive.

For now, Amelia would fill and empty Signora Pina's buckets.

CHAPTER TWO

Plans hardly ever go as willed. Despite Amelia's rush, spurred by her dislike of Pina, the final stages of the bureaucracy took months. And once all the document leaves were in place, booking a steamer proved full of headaches. The closest port was Genoa, but these boats travelled only to Sydney. Italo couldn't be away from the farm the length of time required to travel to meet her in Sydney. And her father disapproved – it wasn't possible for a young woman to make her own way from Sydney to Brisbane and then to Cairns.

But spring unfurled some good news. In July a British ship, the *RMS Orvieto*, would leave London but passing through Naples, sailing to Brisbane. Brisbane was closer; Italo could meet her there. And then Zia Francesca found a married woman who'd also make the voyage and act as a paid chaperone. And so all parties agreed, and the ticket was secured.

In Amelia's rush to say hello to Italo, she'd pushed from her thoughts the final goodbye to her family. In early July they left the cooler air of the north. In a last-minute gesture, Italo paid for the whole family to take a train south along the Adriatic coast and then overland to Naples, into the parched heat. Bologna, Pesaro, Ancona – such cities flew past the window. Amelia's head spun. Those last moments together, the heat in the train, the uncharacteristic silence that would just not remit, the scratching for the last few words so she could hold the sound of their voices in her heart. Her brothers made no attempt to tease her. But even the knowledge she'd finally see Italo did nothing to quell the running tide of anxiety pulling and releasing in her belly; what had she done? This was folly, this was folly, complete, miserable and unanswerable folly.

Finally in Naples, they stayed in a pensione near Piazza Dante, on the fringe of the oldest part of the city, the thick walls so high no sunlight graced the narrow streets. They could understand nothing of the Neapolitan dialect, which bore little resemblance to standard Italian and even less to theirs. They ate pizzas covered with tomato and mozzarella and basil and olive oil. She'd never tasted something so rich. Her brothers ate three each.

And the next morning, in a single file, they walked towards the port. They passed the church of Gesù Nuovo, the austere façade protruding grey pyramids. She excused herself and went to the church's centre door. An old man, his clothes tatty and soiled, his scent rancid, sat on the portico step. He raised his shaky palm. It lacked the two central fingers.

'Signorina,' he said. 'Just a coin, just a coin.'

Amelia stared into his eyes. He opened them wide. His left leg was missing. She opened her bag, found a few humble *centesimi*. She had no need of this money anymore and didn't stop to count it – her last Italian transaction.

Inside the church, her eyes burned with the thousand colours of inlaid marble, the gold and frescoed ceiling forming another sky, held high by square pillars that dwarfed men. She walked towards the altar, massive gold candlesticks and apricot marble columns pointing to heaven, past row after row after row of low wooden pews. At the centre, the Madonna stood, massive and white and bold, her clasped hands held to the side of her chest, her face and eyes lowered in diffidence. Amelia knelt on the cold marble and prayed – Hail Mary, Mother of God.

Once she'd finished, she moved into the Holy Mother's gaze. She gasped. This was the face she'd seen in her vision, so many years ago. She bowed, pressed her heated cheek to the cool marble floor. She'd not made a rash decision. Her path was long and slow, unromantic perhaps, but it was her own.

'It's time for me to go,' she said.

She raised herself, walked the central aisle, out into the powerful Neapolitan sun. Her mother smiled. In silence, they continued to the port. These were her last steps with her family, her last in Italy. She could find no words. Perhaps none were needed. The voices on the street, the clatter of traffic, rang too loud. She cowered, covered her ears. But Aldo took her arm, his strength encouraging her. This just had to be endured.

Amelia guessed the salty tingling in her nostrils was the sea. They followed a chicane of signs, joined long lines, heard the babble of immigration. This was real. This was happening. And then they were there, on the dock, standing near a tower of metal that somehow floated. The black hull, scored with rows of portholes, gave way to the white upper decks, crowned by two white funnels with lazy trails of dark smoke. The hull bore patched sections of paint, rust and brown stains, old, worn, almost uncared-for. Two masts and booms bookended the vessel, should the steam motors fail.

Single men danced to the gangplank, whole families waddled like ducks, and young women on their own or in pairs, pulled themselves free of their parties. The moment had come. Monday the twelfth of July, 1920.

First, she hugged her brothers, tall Aldo and then Giuseppe, who always smiled but now wept. They were good brothers. What more could she have asked for? Then her father.

'Don't go,' he said, his voice cracking. 'You'll have to work so hard. You can't speak the language. You don't know him. I'll miss you. I love you.' He broke into open cries, his lips trembling. She'd never seen him so and searched for words to allay him but could find none. 'You'll see things I can't even imagine. I can't protect you.'

She couldn't look into his eyes, still so filled with confusion. And lastly her mother.

'You carry my dreams,' Velia said. 'I will miss you.'

She held her mother's warmth. 'I will miss you too.'

Would she ever see her again? Italo was her fate.

She stepped away, but her mother held onto her hand; her father cried. She pulled, but her mother's grip was tight. She opened out her fingers. Her hand began to slip and then jolted free. Her mother wailed. Although her portmanteau was hardly heavy, she carried it with both hands – no brother now. Her steps on the gangplank, the bridge between the land and the sea – all these moments she etched on her brain. She turned to her family, still on the dock and now so small and far away. The ant-like figures waved, and she waved her hand above her head, stretched it as high as she could so they could see. Another group arrived on the deck and she moved into the shadows, gave her papers to a uniformed man who glared at the information. She had tears now, her vision blurred, her cheeks hot and wet. When she looked back to the dock, her parents and brothers were nowhere in sight. Their pain had been too great, and she exerted incredible effort not to drop her portmanteau and run through the crowd to find them. Cries rose in her throat, but she swallowed them whole.

Her third-class ticket sent her to the lowest deck, each step along the long corridor heavy. In all the strain she'd given up trying to stem the tears. She found her cabin. Already there were two women, the cabin cramped. The elder, a squat woman of at least sixty years, came to her with open arms. Amelia raised her portmanteau like a shield but allowed herself to be taken by the soft folds of flesh. No words passed between them. Amelia stayed in the embrace until the woman released her and held her by the shoulders. The woman's eyes were blue and soft, her flaxen hair now mainly grey.

'Are you all right?' she said, in Italian but with an accent, heavy, German. Her large eyes changed expression constantly.

Amelia nodded.

'I am Frau Gruetzmann.'

Amelia could find no words.

'And this is Clara Sacco.'

She recognised the name. This woman was her chaperone. She was only a few years older, taller than her with a fine figure, her nose straight and proud. Amelia offered her hand, but Clara embraced her.

'This needn't be formal,' Clara said, and smiled. 'And this is my son, Cristiano.'

Amelia looked around the small cabin. A little boy of only five or six, his dark hair cut short and his eyes fine and inky, sat in the shadows on the lower bunk. He walked to her, stretched out his hand. The prim gesture made her smile and pushed at her gloom. She took his small hand. The three women and the boy stood together, Amelia still holding her portmanteau but now at her side.

'And who are you?' Frau Gruetzmann said, and smiled.

Amelia laughed. 'I am Amelia Durante …' She stopped herself. 'No … I'm no longer her. I am Amelia Amedeo.'

With this error, she'd told this woman not only her name but her position, the purpose of her travel, where she was going. She felt the ring on her finger.

'You're from the north,' Frau Gruetzmann said. 'Your accent.'

'Tovo di Sant'Agata.'

The Frau narrowed her eyes and nodded.

'Cristiano can move to the top bunk,' Clara said.

There were two sets of bunks. The top bunk seemed its own world, and after sharing a sleepless bed with Signora Pina for nearly three months, its privacy was appealing.

'It's easier for him to stay below,' Amelia said. Clara made to protest but Amelia cut her off. 'I insist.'

Clara nodded. Under Cristiano's watchful eye, Amelia raised her portmanteau to the upper bunk and unpacked her few clothes into a small cupboard at the bunk's foot. He was most impressed by her Italian–English dictionary, though the book brought thoughts of her mother and fresh tears. Frau Gruetzmann smiled and chatted away, soothing the pain. She was from Innsbruck, which explained why the Frau had noted Amelia's accent. She'd joined the boat in Toulon, two days before, and already knew where everything was. She was travelling to join her son, who lived in Melbourne. He'd been interned during the war in a prisoner of war camp in Victoria but was quite free now and making his way. Amelia felt the pathos – just two years ago Austrians and Italians were sworn enemies, and yet here they were, sharing a cabin, leaving Europe behind, a heavy underscore to the futility of war.

Frau Gruetzmann spoke of Clara as if she weren't in the room. She was to join her husband, Paolo Sacco. They lived in Bologna and had married in 1914, just before the war. He left for Australia and eventually settled in Brisbane. Amelia reckoned the years – Clara hadn't seen her husband for six.

'Cristiano, how old are you?'

'I'm six.'

Amelia nodded. 'You're a man now.'

Cristiano nodded. His earnest face warmed her heart, but she doubted he'd ever met his father. She couldn't imagine the full weight of the sorrow accompanying such separation. Suddenly her path seemed common.

The ship's horn blew, three times. They looked at the ceiling of their cabin. Cristiano grimaced and covered his ears. No-one said anything. The departure hour, the moment inscribed on all their documents, had become real. They were leaving Italy.

'You two go to the deck,' Frau Gruetzmann said. 'I'll mind the boy.'

'I want to go too,' he said.

Clara reached out her hand to him. Amelia didn't want to watch Italy fade and craved solitude. But Frau Gruetzmann wasn't going to leave the cabin. As much as she appreciated her distracting talk, she felt a great need of peace. Clara smiled. Cristiano offered his hand. They were kind. Perhaps the fresh air would lift her spirits.

The three walked together, the floor rippling under her feet. The ship's horn blasted three more times. At the deck's railing, Amelia took in the bite of brine. Below, men ran to the gangplank, raggedly dressed peasants waving hands and papers above their heads, their belongings wrapped in newspaper in their other arms. They were no better off than Signor Gregorio.

'It would appear they too have missed Garibaldi's promises,' Amelia said.

Clara glared at her. 'Careful – you sound like a Bolshevik.'

Amelia had read this word in a pamphlet but had no clear idea of what it meant, except people spoke of it in harsh tones.

'The rising fascists,' Clara said, 'would strike you down.'

Clearly, Clara was better educated, and Amelia should learn to hold her tongue.

Finally, the gangplank was hauled away, the thick ropes unleashed, withdrawing like snakes into their holes. Amelia checked the dock one last time but there was no last glimpse of her family. The *RMS Orvieto* was dragged from the port by two tugboats. Italy began to slide away. With the other passengers, Clara and Amelia and Cristiano walked to the rear deck. Fishermen in their two-sailed boats bounced across their wake. Clara looked back towards the shore. Her face bore no clear emotion, neither pleased nor sad to be leaving.

'You must be excited,' Clara said.

The tension rose again, lodged bitter cries in her throat. Amelia raised her hand to her mouth. Clara raised a comforting hand to Amelia's shoulder. She nodded, though she felt no sense of excitement. But Clara was trying, and she shouldn't be ungenerous.

'Your husband must be excited,' Amelia said, wincing at her awkward deflection.

Clara exhaled. 'If it weren't for Cristiano, I'd be like you. The truth is I don't know him.'

'Then why did you marry?'

Clara narrowed her eyes. 'The truth?'

Amelia hadn't meant to pry. But she nodded.

'Yes, I'm tired of deception. Let's start this voyage with the truth,' Clara said. Her voice had a soft, wooden register. 'I was pregnant.'

Amelia sucked her bottom lip. She turned her eyes from Clara to the Bay of Naples. Only then she saw, to the side of the bay, brooding Vesuvius, a plume of dark smoke lazing in the sky as from a sleeping winter house.

'And a piece of paper and a ring made everything all right?' Amelia said, glancing back at Clara.

'In some eyes....'

'But why did Paolo leave you in Italy?'

'When we met, he was about to emigrate. He couldn't – well … wouldn't – alter his plans. I was to join him in a month, two at the most. Naively, I hoped I might even get away with no-one knowing I was pregnant. But then the war came, and we thought it was unsafe to travel, especially with the baby.'

'But the war's been over for two years.'

'Once it was clear I was pregnant, I couldn't work—'

'You worked?'

'I was a teacher. So without work, there was no money to live, even less to travel.'

Amelia looked back to the smoke from Vesuvius and then the two trails from the steamer's funnels. How often hopes crashed without money.

'We've lived with Paolo's parents for six years in Bologna. Paolo found work with a building company and started to send some money. But it wasn't much, especially after I paid for our living. It took years to save for our passage.'

'Paolo and Cristiano have never met, have they?'

Clara turned to Amelia. 'You're smart.'

A comfortable silence fell between them.

'And you?' Clara said. 'You've taken a larger gamble. At least I've met Paolo. There must have been someone in Italy?'

'In my village and the next village and the next, there are hardly any men left. Those the war hasn't picked off, immigration has won. There are just frail old men and babies.' She shuddered, breathed in the enormousness of what she'd done, tried to shake it off. 'Perhaps it's better to marry someone like this. My friends in the village … The men failed them.' She stopped, aware of Clara's scrutiny. 'I've taken a great risk. And I'm frightened. I've no idea how this will end.'

Clara turned to dimming Naples. 'But there's something far more dreadful that's made you leave.'

Amelia looked back towards Vesuvius, unsure what she wanted to say to this woman she'd only met. Her honesty unnerved her.

Clara searched her face. 'Why are you so scared to tell the truth?'

Clara had trusted her with a story she doubted many knew. So Amelia would tell a story she hadn't even told her mother.

'I had a friend, Emma Veronesi,' Amelia said. 'She was a very beautiful girl. We'd known one another all our lives. She only had to smile … But that's not fair to her. She was so much more than just her smile.

'During the war, the son of the feudal lord came home on leave. Each day he rode through the streets on his fine horse in his fine, fine uniform. How could Emma not notice him, this Raffaelo Mancuso?

'One afternoon she was filling the water buckets at the fountain. He rode by and she stared at him. The next day, he met her eye. He stopped, dismounted and came to the fountain. She stepped back to allow him to drink, but he wasn't thirsty. He talked to her. And I've no doubt she smiled her smile.

'Each day he'd come and dismount. Until one spring day, he asked her to meet him, in the early evening, in the forest. I begged her not to go. But she went. And they met. And he told her he loved her, and kissed her, and had his way with her.

'And of course, she believed all his promises, as did I with each passing day. Raffaelo returned to the war but said once it was over he would marry her, and she would have everything. What fools we were. The fighting against Austria in the Veneto was fierce. She feared he'd not return. But she was pregnant. And when she told him, when he finally returned, he denied knowing her. Before anyone else knew, Emma threw herself from the church spire.'

'My God.' Clara breathed deeply. 'How awful. I'm sorry for you.'

'And the day she died, when I stood at the well, he rode past. He raised his buttocks from the saddle, took the horse to a canter, but I knew what he was showing me. His ass. And he knew that I'd say nothing. What lets them take whatever they want?'

'*Jus primae noctis* – the right of the first night – medieval laws.'

'Beautiful Emma. He threw her away as if she were muck.' Amelia looked out at the dark, breathed in the sea air. 'The priest refused her a funeral mass. She burns in hell, he said.' The priest was wrong. Amelia knew. Emma was with the Holy Mother, who saw and felt and understood everything. 'I don't want to die poor while someone who owns the land I work is made wealthier. I want something more, free from the stain of poverty, free from fief.'

'And this is it?'

'Italy is barren with its old ways. Australia is new. New ways.'

Clara was silent. 'You're right; Australia is a young country. Let's hope it has new ways.'

The deck vibrated below their feet.

'I've never told Emma's story to anyone. People think Emma was possessed by the devil or there was madness in the family. Only Mancuso and I knew the truth. And no-one would believe me ...'

'I do.' Clara took Amelia's hand.

'Will we ever return home?' Amelia said.

'Italy isn't our home anymore.' Clara continued to look to the horizon.

Amelia observed her. She had warm eyes and an open face. All that was left of Italy was the dark trail of Vesuvius, cutting through the salt air and the blackening sky. She would miss her parents and her brothers; just to think of them squeezed her heart. What were they doing now? How long until they returned home? Would they go that evening with the others of the village to Veronesi's large stable for *la veglia*, the evening party? The men would play cards, the women's never-idle hands spinning wool and their voices telling stories to the young. Shouldn't she be there with them?

She breathed in her last glimpse of Italy. Signora Pina had made her promise they would return. She shook her head. The sea was black, capped here and there with white peaks, not a drop of blue to be seen. She felt pulled apart, as if she'd shed an old skin. She made a promise to herself: from now on, she'd go only forward.

The *RMS Orvieto* had no second class, just first and steerage. A steerage ticket restricted the passenger to the lower decks, a mix of Italians, Germans and Irish. Amelia listened to all the voices she didn't understand, but the Irish – their hefty rhythm, their broad smiles and laughing – she liked the most. The first-class passengers, a mix of English and

Scots, were free to range to the lower decks, but Amelia and Clara's daily walk was restricted to the lower.

'Why can't they stay on their own deck?' Amelia said.

'There's space for everyone—'

'They just want to ogle us.'

In an effort to tire themselves, they repeated circuits of the decks many times, but the crowds slowed them. Amelia linked her arm through Clara's. Whilst they kept to one another's company, they saluted the other walkers and passed small amounts of information. Some were families, some single men and even two others brides by proxy.

'Do you speak any English?' Clara said.

Amelia winced. 'There are many Italians in Babinda. Italo said I don't need it.'

'You won't have any independence without it.'

Amelia thought. 'Do you speak it?'

'Not a word.' Clara smiled. 'Let's start together in the morning.'

And so each morning after breakfast and their walk, they studied. They made lists of every item in the cabin, and Clara found each word in Amelia's dictionary. Every morning all four of them would repeat the words – bed, porthole, floor, ceiling, chest of drawers (three words where they had one). Amelia was years from her schooling, which had been snuffed by her work on the farm and then the war, snuffed by her just being a girl. She swam in a head-aching confusion, but her love of Italian words soon carried over into an interest in these clunky and abrupt ones, sounds that had no rhythm or rhyme she could find but that somehow made meanings. Clara was a steady teacher and mixed the work with much laughter and courage. Three days later, when they'd crossed the Mediterranean to Port Said, they'd all, even Cristiano and Frau Gruetzmann, made headway with the nouns of their cabin.

Each evening the Italians ate at one long table, the men at one end and the women at the other. The noise – plates and cutlery, the men's opinions and counters, glasses knocked together and over – made eating vibrant. The wives kept an eye on their husbands' plates and, if they finished their food, a stodge of potatoes and meat, they would hurry to replenish it.

'And you wonder why I want to leave Italy,' Amelia said.

Clara regarded the wives and their husbands. 'What would you have them do?'

'Serve themselves. Serve their wives, God forbid.'

Clara laughed. 'I wish you luck.'

Would Italo expect her to wait on him? Surely, a man who'd lived on his own, far away from Signora Pina, would be able to serve himself food. She looked at the other unmarried women. They too watched the wives, but they watched as if learning how to be, rather than how not to be.

'I'm glad you're teaching me English.'

Each day brought more heat, landscapes she could never have dreamt of seeing. There was an excitement to this, but at the same time she wished the voyage would end. The land of the Suez Canal was ceaselessly flat, and each hour the air became hotter and drier. Along the shore camels toiled, carrying goods, carrying people. They passed steamers returning to the Mediterranean, so close they could see the passengers on the deck, waving and smiling. And on the shore, trains passed them effortlessly.

Five young boys, dressed in what appeared to be long white shirts that brushed the ground, waved to them from the canal's edge. Amelia and Clara waved back. In unison, the boys turned, pulled up their shirts to reveal their round, bare bottoms, which they proceeded to wiggle. Clara and Amelia gasped in shock and then bent over with laughter, drawing the scowls of those on deck who'd not seen the show.

Each day grew more stifling, as much as forty-two degrees Celsius by midday. To avoid the heat, they took their walks earlier and earlier in the morning. Soon they'd left the calm waters of the Suez Canal and were moving through the long Red Sea, a place from the Bible, where Moses had parted the water – and she, Amelia, was seeing it.

With only a taste, Amelia was now keen to further her English studies. Clara began the verbs, starting with the conjugations of 'to be'.

'There's so little difference between them,' Amelia said.

Clara patted her hand. 'Don't listen to the end of the verbs. Listen to the beginning.'

'This language is upside down.'

They added new verbs – to eat, to sleep, to want, to feel, to hear, to touch. They made small sentences, peppering them with the nouns they'd learnt. She would listen to those who spoke English, concentrating on the sounds. How flat they all seemed, how lifeless, as if everyone who spoke English were sad. In her sleep, verb conjugations pounded like galloping hooves. By the time she'd memorised the verb 'to eat', they were free of the Red Sea, moving into the Gulf of Aden, the horizon free of land.

On the first morning in the Gulf, the blue sky washed over with fierce dark clouds. A storm was coming, the tail end of a typhoon, and the passengers were asked to secure their cabins and remain below decks. They hoped it would last only a few days, not all the way to Ceylon. The winds picked up, the dark water rose, the crest broke open, sounding like shovelled gravel, white spilling over the slope of the wave. The ship rolled. Amelia gripped the railing. The wind moaned through the decks and open passageways. She turned back to the cabin.

Clara and Frau Gruetzmann had put themselves to bed. Clara lay flat on her back, her face pale but heavy about her eyes, staring at the ceiling. Cristiano sat on the top bunk. Amelia took his hand to relieve his fear and to assess what she could do. Both women had vomited into buckets, the stench nauseating. Amelia drained one into the other and took it to the deck. The engines strained up one side of a wave, but then the propellers broke free of the sea, whining high as the ship slid down the swell.

Day and night, this pendulous action remained. Luckily, both she and Cristiano remained unaffected. Cristiano worried about his mother and helped where he could. The cabin reeked of vomit, but it sat so low in the water it was impossible to open a porthole. The ship surgeon, McCausland, examined Clara and Frau Gruetzmann and instructed Amelia to give only small amounts of water. Amelia held Clara's head from the pillow to sip from the glass, but whatever she managed to swallow soon returned to the bucket. After two days, despite the unrelenting motion, Frau Gruetzmann recovered a little, enough to sit and drink some weak black tea.

Amelia had reports; they would see Ceylon in three days, if they were lucky. And the reports were good to their word. They sailed into Colombo on Monday, the twenty-sixth of July. With each metre they advanced, the sea calmed and the sky brightened until there was full sun. The port was busy, all manner and size of craft crisscrossing. The boat was surrounded by a sea of black hair as the native boys yelled to the passengers from rafts, trying to sell trinkets, diving for the coins the passengers threw into the blue sea. For the first time in days, Clara, weak and shaken, came to the deck.

'The nausea won't stop until I'm on dry land,' she said.

And so they arranged their passes. On land, Clara's legs wobbled, drunk from the sea. They walked her to a shaded bench. Amelia looked at this strange place. The men, lithe and tall, wore long swathes of fabric, almost dresses, white turbans covering their dark hair. Some women wore rings through their noses. Men, indentured like beasts, pulled small single-seat vehicles, tooted at by cars, swerving past long carts drawn by oxen. Others, their heads shaved, were swathed in orange or maroon robes. Amelia tried to take it all in, but her eyes saw things she didn't know how to understand. The ground was covered in gobs of red, the droppings of some exotic bird, and she instructed Cristiano to avoid them. But the men chewed something and then spat it to the street, leaving their mouths and the street stained red.

Once Clara felt less nauseated, Frau Gruetzmann and Cristiano walked ahead towards the steamer. Clara smiled for the first time in days, which warmed Amelia's heart. A heavy squall came over. Clara took Amelia's arm, and they walked the long portico to the ship.

Now they'd reached the equator, their morning walk was accompanied by a humidity that became higher and more oppressive until it broke into rain. And even then, the cool relief from the closeness, the exhaustion and the sticky skin was only brief as the steaminess rose again.

'You'll need to get used to this,' Clara said. 'Babinda isn't so far from the equator.'

The thought of such sultriness was unpleasing.

This was the last leg of their journey to Australia. Each morning they would stop at a map that charted the ship's progress.

'Is Brisbane near Babinda?' Amelia said.

Clara pointed to Australia. 'Brisbane is here.' She ran her finger north, along the coastline, higher, higher and higher. 'There's Babinda.'

'It's not so far …'

'Look at Italy. It's the same distance as …' She opened her thumb and her forefinger. 'From Munich to the heel of the boot.'

'That far …' The distance flattened Amelia. Her only friend in Australia would be so far away.

'We can write,' Clara said.

'But it won't be the same.'

Clara smiled. 'Nothing is ever the same.'

Amelia looked out to the clear horizon. What an irony – to have wished these days of travel to pass quickly. She wanted to pitch the ship's anchor overboard, halt any more progress. In Clara, she'd found the friendship she'd had with Emma. She looked at the distance between Babinda and Brisbane.

'Come,' Clara said. 'We've many verbs to master before Fremantle.'

CHAPTER THREE

Australia rose on the horizon, shone at them. The passengers crowded the decks, two, three deep at the rail, jostling for their first glimpse of the port town of Fremantle at the mouth of the Swan River. It was a Friday morning, the sixth of August, 1920.

'It's so small,' Clara said with a note of disgust but couldn't take her eyes away.

People started to yell to their loved ones, who were so far below Amelia doubted anyone could understand.

'I'd be happy with a single hut,' Amelia said.

Clara continued to stare at the shore but raised her lips to a smile. 'What have we come to?'

Amelia bent next to Cristiano. 'What do you hope to see first in Australia?'

He looked to the shore. 'A kangaroo.'

She smiled. Men walked along the dock in time with the ship, beyond them carriages for coal and rows of warehouses. There was industry. Clara was too harsh.

Frau Gruetzmann packed a small day bag and they joined the long immigration queue. The day was indifferent, neither hot nor cold, but the sun shone, the sky a profound blue. They watched huge cranes haul the cargo from the hull. Cristiano had it on good authority there were three British automobiles to be unloaded. A mix of people of all ages stood at a distance.

'What do you suppose they're looking at?' Clara said.

Both the men and women wore hats, the women dressed in lightweight fabrics. And then Amelia remembered. It was no longer summer, as it was in Italy. In Australia everything was upside down; it was now August, almost *Ferragosto*, the celebration for the height of summer, yet it was the middle of winter. But the women dressed like it was summer.

'They've come to see the "new chums",' Frau Gruetzmann said. 'I was told about it. That's what we are.'

Frau Gruetzmann used the English words, and Amelia had no idea what they meant. But once Clara explained the term, it was evident to Amelia that 'new chums' was what they were. From the stern looks on the mob's faces, Amelia was unsure what favour that classification afforded. Everywhere was English, all the signs and all the people speaking it.

They began to walk. Amelia sucked the air deep into her lungs, fresh and clean but dry. Cars moved along the street, but there were also horses pulling drays. They passed a café and Clara asked for a table but couldn't make herself understood, so Amelia took her coat sleeve and pulled her back outside, and they erupted into laughter. The streets were wide and bore so few people. They walked into a park and found a bench, part shaded by a tree. Even Cristiano was without words.

Men and women lay on the grass, some seated. A noise, almost human, roared in the treetops. Cristiano covered his ears. Frau Gruetzmann's eyes bulged. Clara looked to the canopy.

'It must be a kookaburra,' Amelia said. She looked at Cristiano. 'It's laughing at you.'

They continued to look up but couldn't spot the bird. What a wondrous sound, so different from a nightingale's. But what had amused it? The other people paid it no heed.

They were drinking from tall brown bottles. Italo had written of the Australians' love of beer, and she presumed this was what they were drinking, the empty bottles left lying on the grass. But in a park and at this hour of the day?

A man stumbled towards them, saying something. Amelia looked at Clara, but she hadn't understood his meaning either.

'I not know,' Amelia said to him, in her brittle English.

The man stopped walking and glared at them. He smelt of alcohol.

'He's drunk,' Clara said, in Italian.

The man's red eyes swelled.

'Dagos!' He yelled the word, spat it. 'Dagos. Dagos. Dagos.'

Clara pulled Cristiano to her and they moved away. The man repeated the word and many more with much the same tone again and again until he began to laugh, leaving them to retreat towards the boat.

Amelia felt unsettled; why was there a need to drink in such a manner? And why were there no police to stop such behaviour? And the man appeared angry with them. Why was he yelling? She'd not challenged him. But what could she say? Every defence she had was in Italian. She had no power. And with no common language, nothing would ever be understood. She vowed she'd never retreat again, and she'd master this upside-down tongue.

Their voyage along the southern coast was without incident. At Port Adelaide, more cargo was unloaded. Melbourne was a true metropolis, its gateway a large working dock. Here, Frau Gruetzmann left the boat. Her son, a middle-aged man with her large eyes, came to meet her. Amelia cried as she remembered Frau Gruetzmann's first kindnesses, and they promised to write long letters with every detail of their new lives. Without her, the cabin seemed large and excessive. They lost sight of the coast again until they passed Botany Bay and then moved north, entering the magnificent headlands of Sydney Harbour, which Clara thought missed only the Colossus of Rhodes. They were only a few days from Brisbane.

'Zia Amelia,' Cristiano said. 'Will you and Zio Italo stay with us in Brisbane?'

It was the first time he'd called her his aunt, and she felt she should correct him, but she liked the sweetness of his thought.

'Only for a few days.'

A gloom came over his face, and he withdrew into his thoughts.

'Zia Amelia,' he said again. 'How will you know what Zio Italo looks like?'

She smiled. 'I have a photograph.'

'Will he be with my father?'

It warmed her heart that, to Cristiano, his father and Italo were already friends. She couldn't bring herself to tell him the truth. 'I'm sure your father and Zio Italo will be there together.'

They sailed into Moreton Bay through a series of small islands on Friday, the twentieth of August, 1920. She wore a dress saved for the day, but it was woollen, too heavy for the heat, yet she had to make a good initial impression. The few remaining passengers crowded onto the deck, each having a position at the rail and a clear view. Amelia kept her eyes to the shore, her small portmanteau over her belly. Clara and Cristiano stood next to her.

'You won't be able to see him yet,' Clara said.

'Aren't you excited?'

Clara was silent. 'I don't know ...'

Amelia breathed deeply. 'I'm scared, more than anything.'

'Why fear?'

'God knows what will happen. You'll be so far away. I never thought to have another friend like Emma.'

Clara's eyes teared. 'You're a strong woman. You'll overcome everything.'

Amelia swallowed her tears. And the two embraced.

Once the boat was tied, they made their way to disembark. Amelia walked but felt she was gliding. Once her papers were processed she waited for Clara and Cristiano. And there the three were, in a large arrival hall that thundered with names and benedictions and oaths, and replete with the smell of brine and the dust of travelling. Amelia looked at the crowd. Surely, Italo would be at the front and rush to her. She strained to hear her name. She should yell to him, 'I am here. I am Amelia.' But even her heightened condition couldn't summon such disinhibition. There was no familiar face in this sea. And even so, as Cristiano noted, his face was unfamiliar to her.

Clara moved forward, a few paces at first, and then stopped. A man was standing still, just staring at Clara. Amelia put her hand to Cristiano's shoulder. Clara looked back at them, her face drawn tight, and Amelia urged her on. Clara stepped and then stepped again. As did this man, the sinewy man with dark, tight-curly hair who moved with grace and who could only be Paolo Sacco. They embraced, tight as they could, and stayed so for a long time. Amelia moved back from them, her arm resting on Cristiano's shoulder. Clara's body shook over and over. Cristiano called out to his mother, but she didn't respond.

'Zia Amelia,' Cristiano said.

Amelia knelt beside him.

'Is that my father?'

'That's him.' Together they looked. 'He's rather handsome, like you, don't you think?'

Cristiano stared at the face with closed eyes resting on his mother's shoulder, at the large hands dwarfing her back, and then nodded.

Amelia looked away, not just because the moment was too intimate but also to find Italo. It was so noisy and full of people, and hot. And the air stirred, full of dust that caught the streams of light from the high casement windows. How was she to find Italo? Suddenly, Paolo released Clara and came forward. He reached out his hands and Cristiano withdrew into the folds of Amelia's dress.

Clara knelt to him. 'This is Papa.'

Cristiano buried his face in her chest.

Paolo smiled, broad and generous. 'He doesn't know me from anyone,' he said, his eyes moist and hurt.

'It will take time,' Clara said.

Paolo smiled, a little dejected. He turned to Amelia.

Clara stood and took her hand. 'This is Amelia Amedeo. She's travelled to meet her husband.'

Amelia smiled at Paolo and nodded.

'Can you see him?' Clara said, drying her own eyes with a small handkerchief.

Amelia looked from face to face, the near and far, the old and young, all the hall. She walked a few paces, returned and scanned the crowd the other way.

'I can't see him,' she said.

'I'm sure he's here. We'll wait for the crowd to thin.'

Amelia smiled and looked away. Clara, Cristiano and Paolo moved closer together, and she distanced a few paces. There were many men, but most had found who they were looking for. She thought she saw him, his thick, dark hair. She knew his height, 175 centimetres. She knew how tall that was and had drawn a spot on the wall and looked for men of that size. There were many, but some had grey hair and some were clearly not Italian, and Italo just didn't seem to be there. Her belly gnarled. What could she do if he hadn't come? He must come. It was all arranged. For months. *Years*.

'Something's delayed him,' Paolo said.

Amelia flashed a glance at him. Her panic was written on her face as the same expression ignited on Paolo's.

'He's had a long time to prepare,' she said.

'We can wait with you,' Clara said, looking at Paolo, who nodded.

'You can stay at the hostel with us,' Paolo said. 'We can telegram him. But he'll come.' He smiled. 'We can wait.'

A wave chilled through Amelia. She recalled all of Signora Pina's judgements – that she didn't know Italo, that they'd never met. Was this the first of her curses? Did she know something of Italo that Zia Fulvia and Zia Francesca hadn't admitted to?

'He should be here,' Amelia said, the scold clear in her voice. 'Why has he abandoned me?'

Tears came to her eyes. She closed in on herself, raised her hands to cover her face. Clara placed her arm around her shoulder and motioned for Paolo and Cristiano to walk away. Clara held her, pulled her to sit on her trunk.

'Signora Pina was right. I have no idea who this man is.'

'Please don't say such a thing. There are a thousand good reasons … You're just anxious and tired. You've come so far. Don't doubt him now.'

Amelia placed her chin on Clara's shoulder, pressed her head closer to feel her warmth. She breathed in. Clara's scent – homely, like spun wool – and the dark of her closed eyelids brought a dash of calm. Clara was right. He was likely late for one of a thousand good reasons. It was a large country. She shouldn't feel abandoned. She'd asked to stand on her own feet, and so she should stand. She'd courted this adventure. Thank the Lord for Clara.

She opened her eyes, cast them around the emptying hall. There was no-one who fit his photograph, the few remaining people surrounded by trunks and tears. Clara made to pull away, but she grasped her. She wasn't ready.

Where *was* Italo?

Perhaps she'd missed him. In her mind's eye, she conjured his image and scanned the hall again. Everyone was occupied, all but one man who slouched against a metal pole to the far side of the hall. He had fair hair, almost blond but almost red. She'd never seen such a colour, almost giving off light. Even though he slouched, his weight thrown over to his left hip, he was tall, a smoking cigarette resting at his thigh. He wore short pants, khaki, cut to the knee, his solid calves bare. Despite his casual stance, his eyes darted about the hall as if he too were looking for someone. He looked at the hall clock. He looked back at a paper he held.

'That man,' Amelia said.

Clara pulled away and looked at her. 'What man?'

'Over there.'

Clara looked at him. 'I can assure you that isn't Italo.'

'He's the only person who hasn't met someone.'

Clara looked. She nodded. 'But ...'

Amelia stood. With each step, she felt odd, woozy in her thoughts but not quite faint and yet somehow quite alive. He saw her and straightened, a little more with each step, until she stood in front of him, about thirty centimetres shorter. He pulled on the cigarette, rolled thick, so unlike those her brothers smoked.

'I am Amelia Durante.' Why did she still think of herself as that? 'I am Amelia Amedeo.'

His eyes were dark, strange pools that absorbed all light. He said something in English, his voice thin and sad. She couldn't make it out. He repeated it. His hair, the soft wave curved over his brow, the colour, as if the first morning light of a day rested there. Clara came to her.

'I can't understand him,' Amelia said.

The man looked from Amelia to Clara and back, and again said something. Clara shrugged her shoulders. Amelia turned to him and smiled.

'What's happening?' Paolo said, coming across the hall towards them, carrying Cristiano. Paolo said something in English, and the man raised his open palms. He handed Cristiano to Clara. The women stepped back.

'Who is he?' Amelia said.

Paolo said more and he replied. He fumbled for something in his jacket pocket and handed an envelope to Paolo.

'He's Fergus Kelly. The letter's for you.'

Amelia stared at Paolo as if he too were saying things she just didn't comprehend. The letter hung between them. She lifted her hand to it. Her name – Signora Amedeo – was written in Italo's hand. She finally summoned the courage to open it.

> My dearest Amelia,
>
> Welcome to Australia. Your new home. Our home.
>
> I'm sorry I can't be there. This is not the meeting we'd planned. The cane is ready to cut and must be delivered to the mill on time. I've sent Fergus for you. I'm sorry I cannot be there. But it's only a small delay. You'll be here soon. Fergus will travel with you.
>
> I must go now. The harvest calls. We'll be together soon.
>
> Your loving Italo.

She held the letter to her belly and her hand to her mouth. She felt faint. Her eyes welled with tears. Clara stepped towards her.

'What's happened?' Clara said.

She managed to smile and handed her the letter. The lilt of his words was familiar. The anxiety lifted but her relief was rapidly salted by disappointment.

'How could he do this?' Amelia said. 'Our plans are destroyed.'

Paolo spoke more to the man, this Fergus Kelly.

Clara returned the letter. 'He's a good man. He's sent someone.'

'You have to hurry', Paolo said, 'to catch a boat to Cairns. From there you'll go to Babinda.'

Fergus left to find a trolley for her trunk. It was happening so fast. She didn't want to leave Clara, not now, not like this, in such a hurried and forced manner. She fought for breath. Clara embraced Amelia, held her tight. Cristiano wrapped his arms around her legs.

'Everything will be all right,' Clara said.

'Will it? This wasn't how it was meant to be. This isn't what I want.'

Clara pulled away from her. 'Don't despair. It's only two more days till you'll see him.'

What was there to say? She'd no choice but to go with this man whom Italo had sent. She knelt to embrace Cristiano, but her legs shook in such a manner she thought she would topple.

'Is this Zio Italo?' he said.

'No, darling. It's a man who'll take me to him.'

'When will I see you?'

Amelia hugged him again to soothe her uncertainty. 'Soon.' She stood up.

'I'll write a letter,' Clara said.

Fergus said something to Paolo, who urged her to hurry.

'Keep busy,' Clara said. 'It keeps ill feeling at bay.'

With one last glance, she followed Fergus from the hall. He pushed the trolley. There were no words, just gestures and glances. After a long walk to another part of the port, they arrived at a boat, a small ferry with a huge funnel. She was taken to a cabin.

She'd had no luxury to find her land legs, let alone soothe her heart.

CHAPTER FOUR

The engine strained. The boat vibrated and lurched. From the deck, Brisbane was fading before she'd even had a chance to know it. They were headed further north. This was no large ship, and it pitched and wandered, though they stayed within sight of land. Fergus was nowhere to be seen. She felt flints of anger and disappointment. Four men from various regions of Italy spoke in Italian, canecutters returning to Far North Queensland. She withdrew to her cabin. The disappointment at not seeing Italo was a physical blow, as was saying goodbye to Clara in such a hurried manner. Who knew when they would meet again? She curled to a ball, touched her wedding ring to remind herself this was real.

She took her evening meal in the small dining room. There was no sign of Fergus. Perhaps he'd missed the boat, but he'd come on board with her. Perhaps he was taken ill by the motion. Dinner was a large piece of mutton with potatoes and carrots. After she'd eaten a small part of it, she retired to her cabin. She had no need of company. The engines throbbed all night.

She woke early. She'd never slept in a room on her own before and liked the solitude. She dressed and went to the deck, the day fine but already humid. They were far from the coast, although she could just see it on the horizon. She saw Fergus, standing in the aft, staring at the boat's wake. He was smoking, each exhalation swirling around him until it was no more. Her spirits lightened.

'Good morning, Fergus,' she said, in English.

He turned to her. While his features were generous, his lips full and almost red, his cheekbones high and carved and proud, he appeared stern. Dark circles rimmed his eyes. She doubted he'd slept. He raised his hand to the wide brim of his hat, made of some type of felt. The cigarette shook in his hand as if he were nervous. Without meeting her eyes, he turned and left. She watched as he walked away, dressed again in his khaki shorts hemmed at the knee, his legs spread wide to counter the boat's motion. Perhaps he was uncomfortable they couldn't speak. Perhaps the boat's motion made him unwell. Perhaps he just didn't like company. But whatever he felt, it was definite.

She looked at the boat's wake. How was Clara? Her first night with Paolo. Poor Cristiano had looked so lost and confused. A tide of despair pulled at her. If Clara were there she'd have walked the deck, so Amelia completed one circuit in less than a minute and then another till she was bored. The minutes clicked slowly, the vessel small and noisy. She passed time in her cabin, studying her grammar and reading a novel Clara had given her by Federigo Tozzi.

The following morning was hotter and more humid. She put on a long-sleeved white cotton dress, the only one she had. They were to arrive in Cairns around nine that morning. Italo would be waiting for her, and the white dress would provide coolness and a hint of their wedding day. She stood on the deck. Though it was only morning, the light was harsh. If Clara thought Fremantle was small, she would have laughed out loud at Cairns. They approached the wharf, and Amelia could barely see a building amongst the thick vegetation hugging the shoreline. The air was clammy. The sun bit. People on the wharf waved at the boat.

She searched for Italo and hurried down the gangplank to the wide wooden wharf, her heart beating hard and her breath short. There was a whirl of voices and movement, but no-one came to her. The heat dried her throat and she dusted flies from her face. The sea churned under the wharf's slats. People peeled away until she was standing on her own. Where was Italo? Her heart hollowed. The anxiety welled to tears, but she bit down on them. Only then did Fergus appear with another man, who helped carry her trunk while she carried the portmanteau. He said nothing, his face stern. He began to walk.

With no words, she followed him to an old truck, with a large cabin and a long tray, some distance from the pier. What had happened to Italo? How could she ask? And even then, how could she understand? She took stock. Clearly, Fergus hadn't been expecting him. Only she had. How foolish. The wrack of anxiety crushed her. The two men lifted her trunk to the tray, and Fergus opened the passenger's door, on the other side of the vehicle compared to Italian cars. But then why the hell wouldn't it be? Everything else was around the wrong way. The truck had no colour, save the baked-on layers of red dust. Fergus made no salutation to the man who'd helped him, leaving her confused. She had no words to offer him except to dip her head in appreciation. Fergus looked drawn and tired.

They drove away from the coast, away from the rising eastern sun, through a patch of low buildings, the small dash of civilisation quickly snuffed out. He drove the truck on the left side of the road, and the sensation was vertiginous. They moved through a valley between two parallel rows of mountains. Those on her left gave way to the coast. Those on the right, more substantial, rose on the inland. The land between was flat, as if it had been made just to grow sugarcane. The plants rose, higher than her, a row of tan near the earth topped by green reeds and feathery white crowns.

49

They were tightly packed. They waved, like a gentle sea, slow in the late-morning breeze, welcoming her, she imagined. They passed neat field after field, well over an hour of them, occasionally a straight path leading away from the road into the labyrinth. All so planned. She saw a bird, large and lazy in the sky, and imagined its view, this tile of green fields. This was her new home.

Ahead, a locomotive ran on tracks along the roadside. Slowly, they overtook it, car after car of cut canes lying neatly across the trays. When they passed, the men in the engine waved but Fergus made no motion back, nothing to indicate he was even aware of them. But she smiled and raised her hand.

She turned to the oncoming road. Though the truck's windows were open, Fergus emitted a sharp odour, that of a working man, pungent over the cigarette smoke. They passed a sign at an obtuse angle on a pole – Babinda. There it was, simply written, although it hastened her heart. Nothing save a few splayed wooden buildings, a train station but no church spire. There was no-one about, no life at all. Fergus didn't slow the truck. And quickly they were between the fields again, Babinda just a sign.

Up ahead, from the middle of a field, thick black plumes of smoke spiralled into the sky. She looked at Fergus's impassive face.

'Fire,' she said.

Fergus pushed his hat back and nodded. He appeared unconcerned, but nothing had cast emotion on his face since she'd met him.

The smoke hung heavy. Without warning, Fergus slowed the vehicle and turned from the main road towards the fire, closer and closer. Did he intend to help? She panicked. She had no handkerchief to cover her mouth. Was Italo's farm on fire? The smoke hid the sun, the light tinted orange, and yet they drove closer, the fields blackened, smouldering, those ahead still burning. Why had he turned into this? The fire was dangerous, and so much cane had been lost.

In a small clearing, a group of men stood about with trucks and other machinery. What could they do against such a fire? All that could be done was to pray for rain, but despite the pressing humidity the blue sky gave no sign. There was a sense of calm. Fergus slowed the truck and stopped. He said the first word he'd said since they left Brisbane.

'Italo.'

The word had an odd sound, the stress all wrong. Amelia turned towards the group of blackened, indistinguishable men. Fergus came to her door. She stepped to the ground. The earth was covered in a hard type of grass, which had been scythed. She walked around the front of the truck, towards the men. None of them moved. No-one came to her. No-one said a word. They held large metal cups in their hands. The hot, smoky air made it hard to breathe. To the side, a small train engine with several trays like those she'd seen on the open road stood half loaded. No-one came to greet her. How could there not be alarm with fire?

Three men came out of the burning field, from between the rows of cane, stopped and stood, looking at her. Then one man advanced, his pace slow at first. He was tall and thin, the sleeves of his once-white shirt rolled, and his thick forearms and hands black.

'Amelia,' the man said, his front teeth glowing against the char. 'I'm Italo.'

She looked at him. Her heart beat harder. He was indeed the height she'd expected but she was hard-pressed to link him to the photograph. His sooted face ... Sweat had run clean rivers down his temples, onto his cheek, only for them to be darkened again. But even through this camouflage, he was much older than his photograph. And his head, with that thick black hair, was almost completely bald. This couldn't be him. This was some trick. But his eyes were blue. And she'd seen the ocean now and could agree with his aunts, but the black skin made the contrast shocking.

'This wasn't how we planned,' Italo said.

'No,' she said, her first word to Italo.

'You're dressed in white. I can't touch you.'

He smiled, then looked back at the other men and said something to Fergus. 'We must finish here. Fergus will take you home. I'll be home this evening—'

'Did the field catch fire?' she said.

This distracted him. 'We set fire to it. It's controlled. Safe. Perhaps we could discuss it this evening.'

Italo smiled, lingered, his gaze intense. But he turned away to the men, who all went back to whatever they'd been doing. He was lean. Behind her, Fergus opened the passenger's door. Still walking away, Italo stopped and picked up a rod of cane. With a knife, long like a machete but far broader at the extremity, he slashed at the end, the blade an extension of his hand. The rod fell to the earth. He started towards her, slow at first but then with some pace. He held out the few centimetres of cane. It was a yellow-green but its skin was black. She reached out, touching Italo's fingers as she took it. He smiled, let go of the cane and skipped back a step. He looked into her eyes and smiled again. He turned, waved his hand above his head.

She couldn't move. Was it the heat? The lack of air? Were her feet stuck? She looked down at them. She just had no will. She watched him. Without turning, he disappeared into the smouldering cane rows.

In the truck, she held the cane between two fingers. So that was it? That was all? She'd come all this way and he gave her a damn piece of burnt cane, a charred bouquet, and disappeared. Blue eyes. He was fifteen years older than her. What a fool she'd been to believe the photograph, probably taken before he'd even left Italy. But it irked her that after all this travel and all this time and all this planning, he chose to harvest cane rather than care for her. She understood the pressure of a harvest; when her father's apples were ready all hands were pressed to service. But there were many men here. Surely, he could have been spared. Even for just a day. Today. In a real sense, his wedding day.

At the main road, Fergus said something. She looked at him, and he motioned to the piece of cane and then lifted his fist to his mouth, a cigarette trapped in his finger, and flicked his tongue about it. The gesture was obscene but despite her shock, he motioned again. She looked at the blackened object in her lap. He nodded. Slowly, she raised the cane to her mouth, flicked the tip of her tongue across the cut surface. She winced. It was surprisingly sweet. Fergus smiled and turned back to the road. She raised the cane to her mouth, but he swerved the truck, jolting her hand, and her tongue caught the burnt edge. It was bitter, exceedingly so. Had he done that on purpose? She clamped her expression to conceal her discomfort. She rubbed her tongue against the roof of her mouth, swallowed the unpleasant spit. Why would they burn something sweet to bitter?

After a broad curve in the road, Fergus pulled off to a track that led along the base of a small hill, one of the few such interruptions to the flat valley. They passed a long, low wooden building. On the other side were the endless fields of cane. Fergus stopped. She looked around her. The only building was a small house, rough wooden shingle walls and an iron roof, a wide verandah with a metal awning curving over at the outer edge. Fergus was out of the truck and hauling her trunk from the rear tray.

Was this Italo's home? She walked towards the building, raised from the ground, five wooden steps to the front verandah, which seemed most curious. Why bother with such an arrangement? Above the steps, interrupting the curve of the roof, was a large semicircle piece of wrought iron filigreed three smiling sunflowers. Such artifice amongst so little. She mounted the steps. The verandah was covered in leaves and other debris, the boards with gaps between them, the wood grey and splintering. This hadn't seen a woman's hand.

'Thank you,' she said.

He nodded, remained, his eyes lowered to the ground.

'Thank you,' she said again, more because she had nothing else she could say. The humidity was absolute, as if the air itself was wholly water. She raised her hand to loosen her collar and then extended it to him. He pulled back but then raised his eyes to hers, raised his hand to hers. The skin was wrought, glazed hard. Timpani thunder rolled in the distance, across the plain. He pulled his hand from her.

'Signora Amedeo?'

The voice was a woman's and came from the dim recess of the house. When she looked to Fergus, he'd turned away, already down the front stairs and towards the truck. She heard footsteps on the hall's wooden floor: a woman in her mid-forties, her light brown hair cut close. She wore a loose dark-grey dress with no apparent style, made from light cotton.

'Welcome,' she said, holding out both hands. 'I'm Maria Pastore.'

Amelia could find nothing to say.

'Didn't Italo tell you I'd meet you here?'

Amelia shook her head.

'Typical.' She sighed. 'I'm your neighbour. Come in. I'll make you some tea.'

Whilst this woman spoke Italian, her accent was odd, and Amelia couldn't place it. She heard Fergus's truck start.

'Who's that man?' she said.

Maria came out onto the verandah. 'He's the son of your other neighbour. Nice boy – well, he was, before the war.'

Amelia's expression curled in confusion. 'But the war was in Europe.'

She smiled. 'Many Australians fought, for Great Britain. Fergus was in France, I think. Come, let me make the tea.'

Amelia stood in the doorway and watched Fergus's truck move off.

'You should change that pretty dress,' Maria said.

The truck disappeared behind the small hill, but she could still hear it. She looked out at the cane fields running from the bottom of the hill to the rim of the next forested hill. How odd to live and work in the same place. Her father's orchard was some distance from the house, and they'd lived in the village. Here, the house was surrounded by nothing but cane. And what an expanse. She moved a pace or two into the hall but could still hear the drone of Fergus's truck. A patter began. She looked to the ceiling. Rain. Perhaps the humidity would break.

CHAPTER FIVE

The air inside the house was close and musty. Fergus had placed her trunk in the hall between the two front rooms. Both were bedrooms, Maria explained.

'Yours and Italo's is on the right.'

Maria leant forward and pushed the door. The bed had a metal frame, above which hung a large white veil.

'It's to keep the mosquitoes out,' Maria said. 'I made the bedspread for you.'

She'd never seen such a thing, small patches of blue silk sewn to large swathes of vivid green wool, together in a ragtail map, no regard to suiting one piece to another. She hated it – ghastly – but hated more she'd be forced to live with the gift. She coloured, averting her eyes, but smiled.

'You're too kind,' she said.

And across the hall was another room. Two bedrooms.

'Does someone else live here?' Amelia said.

'Just Italo. And yourself.'

Maria moved a few steps down the hall. All this space to just the two of them? The front section of the house then stopped, connected to the second by what Maria described as the 'breezeway', an area floored and roofed but partly open on both sides, the rain demarcating a sharp line of wet and dry, dark and light, on the rough-wood floors.

'I don't know the Italian word for that,' Maria said.

'*Loggia.*'

Maria nodded. Across this area, two more steps led to a doorway that entered a large rectangular room, midway along the long wall. A fireplace stood at the left-hand end, surrounded by three armchairs in a horseshoe. In this heat, how could a fireplace ever be necessary? And at the other end of the room stood a table and four chairs.

'The kitchen's through here,' Maria said.

She walked to another doorway, up two more stairs. A large wooden bench stood in the middle. There was no stove, a fire on a slab in a chimney being all there was for cooking. The floor was bare, dark earth, the walls papered with layer after layer of old newspaper, a small window interrupting the wall opposite the fire.

'There's a washroom out the back.' Maria pointed to the back wall of the kitchen. 'And up the hill is the toilet.'

Amelia looked at the wall.

'You'll get used to it,' Maria said. 'Outside, you have a water tank, filled by the rain. The tap's here.'

In the corner of the room, a dulled pipe thrust through a rough-cut hole in the wall. A brass tap shone at the tip.

'In all the years Italo's lived here,' Maria said, 'it's the only thing he's done to the house.'

Amelia continued to stare at this wonder. The hours and hours she and Emma had spent carting water from the village well, each with two buckets balanced on the ends of a long rod held on their shoulders. This tap brought water directly into the kitchen.

'It's no great wonder,' Maria said. 'If there's one thing we have in Babinda, it's water. We pride ourselves with the highest rainfall in Australia. Let me make you some tea.'

The rain beat the metal roof. Maria stoked the coals and moved a large kettle into the embers. She chatted on. Her parents left Italy in 1882. They came from the north, Udine, in the Veneto, and first settled in Sydney, where Maria was born. That explained her; she spoke Italian but with an odd accent, an Australian accent, and peppered it with words and sayings used by older people in Amelia's village, like Signor Gregorio.

'They came to work in the cane fields in 1901. They brought a lot of Italians here then, to replace the Kanaka people. They were natives, brought from the islands to work the fields. But they sent them back.' Maria faced her, lowered her voice as if someone were listening. 'They didn't want the same problems as in America, with the blacks. So they shipped in Italians and other Europeans. That's how we came to be here.'

Amelia bit her underlip. How harsh to send a group of people away because of the colour of their skin. And in many ways, they'd imported the Italians purely *because* of the colour of their skin. She shouldn't judge what she didn't understand, but it seemed heartless.

'I've prepared your dinner,' Maria said, her tone turned light. 'It's just a stew.'

Maria mixed in confusing English words. Maria lifted the lid on a large metal pot at the side of the fire. Inside were vegetables and some kind of meat in a thick sauce.

'It's mutton,' Maria said.

Amelia smelt the stew – good, wholesome cooking. 'So much meat,' she said. 'We only ate it two or three times a year.'

'A year! I didn't know that.'

'Is there polenta?' Amelia said.

Maria laughed. 'Lord, no. It's damper and dripping.' She walked to a small wooden box on the sideboard. 'I made it today.' Maria opened an earthenware pot. 'It's the meat fat, collected after cooking.'

The odour was unsettling. Amelia strode from the room with the excuse to change her dress, its hem already quite blackened. Her trunk was still locked, so from her portmanteau she took the same dull blue-grey skirt she'd worn most days on the boat, and a darker-coloured shirt. The wool was too heavy for the heat, but there was no other choice.

Maria brought a tray with the tea to the main room. Amelia stared at the pot, which wore a knitted cover, made of many coloured wools, a similar mix to the quilt, its spout and handle protruding from holes. Maria helped her set the small table for the evening meal. Like the verandah, the floors of the main room were wooden and bare and rough but worn smooth in patches, gaps between the planks. But they'd not been scrubbed for a long time. A small dark rug lay under the table. Amelia stared at them. At least the rough limestone walls of her parents' house were impervious to wind. Maria came to her side.

'He'd hoped to build a new home before you arrived, but you'd like to have some say in how it's built, I said.'

Building a new house? How could such a thing be possible? Italo must have more money than either his aunts or his mother knew. Perhaps she would like some say in how it was built, but the cracks in the floor were a high price for such a voice.

'I've two chickens you can have,' Maria said. 'We'll just have to get a coop built.' She gestured to a clock on the mantelpiece. 'Look at the time. Mine will want to be fed. I'll come in the morning, to see how you're getting on.'

Amelia thanked her for everything and, from the verandah, watched her walk towards the main road. She hadn't asked Maria anything of herself – where she lived, if she had children, even her husband's name. But Amelia could tell Maria was an honest soul.

The rain cleared, cooling the air. What words did she have to describe this landscape to her parents? The ones she'd brought from Italy – flat, blue, plain, green, hill, cane

– somehow failed. Of one thing she was certain: there were new words. The wind rustled the cane. There were birds with unknown calls. But there was no other sound. No-one's voice. She'd grown used to the drone of a ship's engine and close contact with people and had quite forgotten quiet. But she'd never heard such silence before. At home, there was always noise of some nature. She listened. Not here. It made her shiver.

She needed to relieve herself. At the back of the kitchen was another small room with an outside entrance. Beyond that, some distance up the hill, a privy, built of greyed, splintering wood. The seat was rough and suspended over a dark pit. In the kitchen, she turned the bold brass tap, which required some force but eventually yielded. The water spluttered and streamed. She passed her hands in and out and into the cool ribbon and then shut it off. The tap dripped large, slow tears. Such innovation. She turned it on again and then off. Water, any time she wanted.

She looked at the newspaper pages stuck to the wall, the writing in English. The date in the corner, the twenty-fifth of March, 1902, a Tuesday. She looked closely, tried to read the sentences, only understanding a few odd words. How would she ever comprehend this? On another part of the wall was another day's newspaper. Why would you decorate a room like this? She put her flat palm to the wall, which buckled under her slight pressure. The wall was little more than a weather break.

She had no idea where to unpack her things, but when she opened the wardrobe in the main bedroom, it was completely empty. The house was like the bedspread – pieces were pleasing but the whole wasn't. She found the key to her trunk, undid the straps and then the lock. She lifted the top layer and placed the carefully folded silk blouse on the bed.

Under it was a small blanket, embroidered with wandering cherry blossom. Her mother had packed it; it had been hers and was now intended for her first child. She tried to smell her mother. Tears came to her eyes. What had she done? She would have a child without her mother's help.

Heat coalesced on her forehead, above her lip. These damn flies. This dust on everything. And although it had rained, it was humid again, syrupy on her skin. Unpacking had upset her and she returned the items and closed the trunk.

She heard steps on the front verandah and poked her head from the room into the hall. Italo stood. She pulled back into the room, dried her eyes and went to him. He'd washed his face, although it was still smeared with soot. She walked the few paces to the door, looked at him, as he did at her, through the veil of the metal-mesh flyscreen. Now his face was almost white, she could see he wore a thick moustache that hung down the sides of his mouth. This too hadn't been in her photograph. And his thick dark hair really was gone, his pate shiny. And what was left of his hair, a thin band on top of his ears, was grey, but the cane soot lessened the effect.

'The mills know no clock,' he said. 'The cane has to be delivered or there's no end of problems.'

Amelia smiled with her lips and nodded.

'Why don't you come in?' she said.

And then he looked at the screen door. He opened it, the hinges crying in pain. But he remained outside, on the verandah, looking at her from his great height.

'You're as beautiful as my aunts said.'

Her eyes moistened again, and she did all she could to clamp the tears. She turned into the house, resting in the hall near the bedroom door. She heard his steps and the closing flyscreen.

'You must be very tired,' he said. 'Let me go and wash and we'll eat.'

For some small moments she regarded him, as he did her. What did he see? But what was she hoping to see? For over two years, she'd stared at his photograph. Now she tried to see him. But he wasn't really there, covered in this veil of soot and sweat. And what was there to read of a person in their physique?

He stepped towards her. She braced herself. She didn't want him to kiss her. Not here. Not like that. She stood her ground. He remained close.

'If I could get by,' he said.

She looked behind her. She and her trunk were blocking the hallway. She half smiled and stepped aside.

Italo walked through the house, out the side of the breezeway to the washroom. She went to the small kitchen. At least the roof didn't leak, and the floor was dry. She'd never cooked on an open fire. Maria had told her how, but she was at a loss to remember and stirred the embers on the slab, moved the pot with the stew to a hook over the embers. With all of Italy's poverty, at least her parents had a stove.

She heard him moving in the washroom. What did she make of him? He was softly spoken, as Zia Fulvia had maintained, but not as expressive as his letters had suggested. Signora Pina knew of the photograph's deceit and must now be laughing. Well, he may be older but at least he owned this large stretch of land. And the cane grew tall and strong. And he was tall and strong and healthy, although a little thin. The rich red land was good, not some marsh or barren hill.

Italo came into the kitchen. He wore just a towel at his waist, dark hair in the shape of a crucifix on his chest. But the underside, along the ridge of his chest, was greyed. Like her brother Giuseppe's, the hair trailed to his towel. She looked away.

'I'm too used to living on my own,' he said.

But he didn't move away or seek to find something else for cover. She turned back to him. What was she meant to do? Go to him? She'd never seen a man before, not like this, just her brothers or father, but they were different. His shoulders were wide, at least twice hers. And his body so long and flat and without a skerrick of fat. His arms were of another type to hers, long and rangy with bulges and depressions, as if bands constricted and released the muscles. Despite all her work in her father's orchard, hers had no such signs of strength. His lower legs, his calves and ankles, were so large, as were his feet, some extra grip on the earth.

What did he want? What did he expect?

She swung to the fire. She heard him leave the room. Was he disappointed? Had she done the wrong thing? Were they to have fallen into one another's arms? She stayed in the kitchen, took the lid and stirred the pot. The fire was too hot and, as Maria had warned, the stew had caught. She removed it from the heat and spooned it onto the plates.

He returned to the main room and stood near the table, dressed in a white collarless shirt and grey serge trousers held with braces. He stepped back as she placed the plates. He'd lit a curious type of incense, a coil held on a metal tray, the odour strong and slightly unpleasant.

'For the mosquitoes,' he said.

Without words, she returned to the kitchen for the damper and pot of dripping. He uncorked a bottle of wine and took two glasses from a sideboard. The bottle had no label or tax stamp. He smelt the cork and left the bottle to rest. She felt her nerves and moved to seat herself. He moved quickly to take her chair. Once he was seated opposite, he poured the wine. Even then they didn't speak. As if acting some practised part, they lifted their glasses, touched them together and sipped the wine.

'A little young, perhaps,' he said.

Then it was perfect for their first meal.

'You've cooked on the open fire,' he said.

'Maria did.'

'That's right. She said she would.'

She ate some of the stew. It was simple but tasty. He tore the damper. It was heavy like cake but not moist, quite unlike bread. He smeared the dripping on it.

'Have you finished your harvest?' she said.

He shook his head slowly. 'Many more days of work.'

'Your land is large.'

'Large?' He raised his brow, which caused his shiny pate to ridge. 'Oh … The field you came to this morning isn't mine. It's Manny Pellegrino's. His crops were due at the mill.'

So, she'd been left in Brisbane for some other man's crop, not even his own.

'We work in gangs,' he said. 'Harvest each other's crops. We share the tools, the trucks and the labour. We just have to get the work done. No matter what.'

And his land didn't spread as far as she first presumed. 'How far *does* your land extend?'

He looked from his meal, his face set in questioning. 'From the road to the hills, a hundred and forty acres, but about a hundred in use. When there's time, we can walk the boundary.'

She looked back at her meal. She hadn't meant the question to be so pointed. 'You burnt the cane on purpose?'

He laughed. 'It gets rid of the leaf rubbish. Makes the cutting quicker. And it drives out the rats and snakes.'

'Snakes?'

He looked and smiled. 'And spiders too.'

He was teasing her, as her brothers did.

'Don't you get burnt sugar?'

He laughed, sat back in his chair. 'The cane protects the pulp, but you're right, we lose a little. But it's quicker to harvest. So what we lose in the sugar we gain in time. And we can plant much closer together, so more cane per piece of land.'

She'd never considered so many things and had so much to learn.

'I'll have Signora Maria take you to the village.'

So there was a village, not just a crooked sign.

'I sense, from my mother's letters, she disapproved of our match,' Italo said.

She froze. Signora Pina disapproved of almost everything in equal measure. But she didn't want to say this, not now at any rate.

'I'm sure I felt no such thing.'

He pulled at a crust of damper and placed it in his mouth. His eyes never left hers as he chewed it slowly.

'The house isn't what you expected.'

She said nothing.

'I'm sorry there's no stove.'

'Maria said I'll learn.'

'I've plans to build a proper house, further up on the hill,' Italo said.

'She mentioned it.'

'It's the best view in the valley.'

So the evening passed, with little questions of Italy, with small comments about his aunts, about the village, even some about his mother. He asked of the voyage, and she told him of Clara and Cristiano and the wonder of the Suez Canal and the violent storm in the Gulf of Aden. He remembered the men in Ceylon who chewed and spat the red matter.

'It's betel,' Italo said. 'They chew it with lime. I thought they were spitting blood.'

He laughed and she tried to. But as they talked, Amelia felt a gulf, as large and rough as the Gulf of Aden; as unknown as the sea was Italo. With time, she told herself, with time.

When it was time for bed, he excused himself to smoke a cigarette while he checked the horses in the stable, the long building she'd passed near the fields. After she'd cleared the meal and cleaned their plates, she closed the bedroom door. What was she to do now? What would he expect? There was no drape. She undressed. She put on her sleeping clothes and climbed into the bed, swirled the mosquito veil around her, lay on her back and stared at the ceiling.

It was half an hour or more before she heard him come back to the house. She lay still, startled when he entered the room, bathed in the silvery moonlight. She feigned sleep. He shuffled about the room. She heard the rustle of fabric as he removed his clothes and opened her eyes to thin cracks. Through the veil, she saw his naked back. Two distinct ridges of muscle ran the sides of his long spine. His braces hung from his waist. He stepped from his shoes. He folded over, to pull down his trousers. His lean waist gave way to strong buttocks, his legs stretched long, reminding her of Giuseppe. He went to his side of the bed. She clasped her eyes, heard the covers move, felt his pressure on the mattress. He was naked. She stayed still, afraid to move, to breathe.

Should she speak? Should he?

How she wished she'd asked Clara what would happen. But he didn't move and soon his breathing slowed and became lapping, so unlike his mother's. Was this the reality of married life? She'd expected something else. A small draught brushed her cheek. And with it, she remembered her home, her parents, her brothers and herself all sleeping in the same room, their warmth pressed against the cold.

And a certain sadness settled on her.

CHAPTER SIX

She woke with a start. Not a sound. No light. No drone of engines.

She wasn't on the boat. She'd arrived, slept in Italo's bed. He was already gone. She lay still, but the moments stretched longer. And longer. She couldn't bring herself to move. She jittered. Until now, this had been an adventure, as if she and Clara had stretched a thin corridor from Italy to Brisbane. But that was over. The door had shut. This was it. No return.

She should rise and meet the day. But who was there to greet? No-one she knew. What had she done? This house was little more than a hut in the forest with no curtains at the windows, huge cracks in the floor. What were her family doing? Had they just woken? No. She'd no idea what time it was there. Why had she left her parents? They may have been poor, but they had a stove.

Where was her dictionary? Even to her, the thought was irrational, but she mustered her strength, rose from the bed, found her gown and house shoes and walked to the hall. The verandah door was open, leaving just the flyscreen. It had no lock. He wasn't out there. She walked through the breezeway to the main room. Her dictionary sat on the table. No-one. And no-one in the kitchen. The fire hadn't been stirred.

'Italo?'

She held her breath. The clock on the mantle said it was just past five. Some money was on the table. Maria was coming to take her to the village. He mustn't have wanted to wake her and left the money. No note. If he started work at this hour, no wonder he slept so soundly. She thought of returning to bed but felt uneasy. There were no locks. And if Italo was working, shouldn't she? But first she would make herself coffee. In the kitchen she looked on the tabletop, through all the kitchen cupboards. There was no coffee. No grinder. Nothing. Nothing of any use. What type of man lived like this?

She found the teapot, filled the kettle from the tap, stirred the fire. Where was the tea? She looked over the shelf, over those things on the mantle: King Tea, in a wrapper bag.

This strange house, so much space it was like the outdoors, so many holes it was the outdoors. Perhaps if she unpacked her things it would at least begin to feel like home. In some solemn ceremony, she placed each item of clothing on the bed: the two cotton dresses, a woollen skirt she could never wear in this heat and the silk blouse her mother had bought her. She placed the bundle of Italo's letters on the small table beside her bed.

The memories each item evoked became overwhelming, and the heaviness swelled. She took her tea to the front verandah. There wasn't even a bench to sit on, so she sat on the stair. The first sun appeared, rising on the distant field, turning the proud cane heads silver, coaxing them to maturity. Such a different field to the one that held her father's sparse apple trees, the cane so closely packed and thick like a tapestry. The morning air was crisp but with each second the light felt harsher, hotter. Small flies swarmed in the air.

She wished for Clara and Cristiano. It had been a happy time, and although Clara had been paid to chaperone her, they'd become friends. Perhaps they should have stayed on the boat and just continued their journey. She went inside to her portmanteau and retrieved a block of writing paper.

But on the step, she had the sensation of being watched. Down the slope something moved against the cut grass, grey and the strangest beast she'd ever seen. It rose, conical on its broad hindquarters, over a metre tall, and glared at her. Two stunted arms held some blades of grass. It chewed slowly while it watched her, its dark eyes large in such a rodent-like face. And then this movement started in its stomach, low to the ground and rising. And then a head appeared, much smaller but shaped like the other.

She gasped, which startled the animal. It must be a kangaroo. It must be the mother. The animal turned, fretful like a deer, slow, almost lazy and yet precise, and hopped away, her long tail beating the earth, disappearing into the brush some distance from the house. Amelia remained. If she stood still long enough perhaps the baby would tell its mother it was safe to return. But after five minutes it was clear the beast had gone.

She sat on the verandah step and wrote to Clara, telling her although things were very unfamiliar, she was all right. She implored her to tell Cristiano she'd seen a kangaroo. Then she wrote to her parents and brothers but soon realised she'd written nothing more than a list of harsh complaints: the house, the heat, the dust, the lack of anything to cook on, the flies and her dull sorrow. She screwed up the paper and started again, sticking, as she had with Clara's letter, to the factual: She was safe. Italo seemed lovely. She would write more when there was more to write. She told them of the kangaroo.

She suddenly felt restless and changed her clothes and started down the hill, trying hard to put something sprightly in her step. The grass beneath her had been scythed, but it was an incredible colour, the green so vivid it almost hurt her eyes. The humidity was thick, but the sky was blue, not a trace of cloud. At the bottom of the hill, she came to a path dividing the lower edge of the hill and the first of the fields.

She crossed over. The canes appeared to grow in bunches, as many as ten and fourteen growing from one base, splaying out. They looked most curious, fiercely straight, reaching to the sky, most much taller than her. They didn't appear to follow the sun, like sunflowers. They were independent.

She took a cane in her hand. It was a type of grass, she'd read somewhere. It had some girth, more than she would have imagined. She pulled it. It flexed, the length marked by ridges, knuckles dividing the growth into smaller sections. Reeds grew from the higher sections, making the cane look top-heavy, and she wondered if they'd adorned the lower portion but had fallen off, leaving the knuckles. She must remember to ask Italo.

She pulled until the head was at eye level. Above the hair of reeds was a type of flower, she supposed, but unlike any she'd ever seen. Rather than soft and concealing petals closed over like those of a rose or a camellia, this flower thrust itself forward, dry and brittle and bold, feathery like a duster.

So this was sugarcane. Their fortunes rode on this thin, straight plant. She let it go. It hurtled back into the bunch, rocked slightly, its feathery head waving like a national flag.

She turned to the house. In the distance, three brown-and-white cows walked ahead of a man with a pronounced limp. They moved along the ridge, away from the house. He waved to her and she returned his gesture. At the house, the cows had left pats on the grass to the side of the breezeway. But in the kitchen, the man had left a jug of fresh milk.

It was still warm and she poured herself some, the taste comforting.

She found an old broom, its bristles worn and slanted, and swept the verandah. No need for a shovel as, once prompted, the leaves and dust fell through the cracks. She set to work in the main room. For such a large chamber, there were few windows, the inside of the house dark and the light outside too harsh. She dusted the chairs and the mantle and the sideboard, then swept the floor. But each time she moved a piece of furniture it looked just the same, out of place and untidy.

There was nothing to eat in the house, save the leftovers of last night. What had she come to? Suddenly, Signora Pina's derision seemed more like fair warnings and not jealousy. This was the end of the world. In Italy they may have been poor, but they had good food and a rug on the floor her great-grandmother had made, and floorboards and walls without huge cracks. Why had she been so headstrong? Tears and cries rose. Clara advised avoiding such moments; she must keep busy.

She had to relieve herself and returned to the privy – so uncivilised, this dark room now hot inside. The lean-to on the side of the house had no window. A rectangular tin hung from the ceiling on a pulley, small holes pushed through the bottom. He must fill this with cold water from another tap poking through the wall from the tank. A sour, fusty odour, something of day-old cook cabbage and onion, emerged from a heap on the floor – Italo's blackened clothes. She bent over and gingerly picked up the acrid shirt. She was meant to clean them. But how?

'Hello.'

The call came from the front of the house. She dropped the shirt tail and walked around the outside of the building.

Maria stood on the verandah, looking into the house, down the hall.

She turned to Amelia. 'Good morning. Have you eaten? I've brought us breakfast.'

Maria brandished a wicker basket and let herself in, and Amelia walked back around the outside to meet her in the breezeway.

'There's no food in the house,' Maria said. Amelia followed her through the main room to the kitchen. 'Italo never cooks. He's over at our place most nights. But I guess he won't be now. So once we've eaten we can go into town and buy provisions.'

Amelia said nothing. She remained standing on the kitchen doorstep. Maria stopped moving and looked at her.

'Did you sleep?' Maria said.

'Yes.'

'You must have been very tired. All that travel.' She pulled back a cloth from a basket to reveal a wheel of small bread rolls baked in a round tin. She'd bought ground coffee. 'Italo loves coffee,' Maria said.

'Then why is there none?'

Maria placed the jar of grounds on the bench.

'Italo needs … help.'

Maria made the coffee. How good it smelt. They drank it in the main room and ate the small bread rolls with butter and a strange jam. Maria talked and Amelia felt so leaden, but this woman was generous, and so she too should be.

'What's your husband's name?' Amelia said.

'Dante.'

'Was he born here too?'

'He came out before the war.' Maria thought. 'About the same time as Italo, but he came straight to cane cutting.'

'So you met here?'

'There are so few women I could have had my pick … But I chose Dante.'

Amelia wouldn't advance on this note of discord. 'Do you have children?'

'Four. All boys. But they're older now and need me less.' She rolled her eyes. 'And more.'

Maria talked about people in the district as if Amelia already knew them: Pennisi, Tedesco, Lanza. She tried to concentrate but it was meaningless. After they'd finished, they made ready for the long walk to the village, the prospect of treading on dry land pleasing. But some way from the house, Maria walked to a truck.

'Can you drive?' Amelia said.

'Of course. Can't you?'

Amelia stared at her. 'Of course not.'

Maria pulled back in shock. 'Another thing we'll have to teach you.'

Once they were on the main road, Amelia appreciated the quiet. She couldn't remove her eyes from this new world of so much space, other houses built in a similar manner to Italo's, raised high from the ground.

'Why are the houses like that?' she said.

'It keeps them out of the flooding and cooler in summer, as the air moves about.'

Her parents fought to keep warmth in. This really was a world upside down. The valley was flat, framed with beautiful mountain ranges, the vegetation lush and green. The sight lifted her spirits. But soon they came to the village, the main street so wide, wider than four streets of Tovo di Sant'Agata put together. But there were few people, as if the street had been built for the future. Buildings lined the street, built on the ground but with large awnings over the footpath, held by poles flush to the curb, long colonnades.

Some of the buildings even ran to a second floor, and most had pelmets with stylised signs.

'I don't get the luxury of coming to town that often,' Maria said. 'I have a lot to do.'

First they stopped at a tailor, then a bootmaker. Amelia listened as Maria negotiated her business, all in English. How lucky she was to have both tongues. While the shop assistant went to check something, Amelia excused herself and went outside for some air.

It was still humid. If this was what it was like in spring, what would it be by summer? She looked at the other women, dressed in lighter fabric. She would need to sew something similar. She saw in the distance a familiar face. Her first sensation was that it must be Italo, and it lifted her spirits. But he was cutting cane. It was Fergus. He stood some metres away, along the street, slouched against a pole of the colonnade, much as he'd been in the arrivals hall in Brisbane, a burning cigarette in his hand at his side. She waved. At first she thought he hadn't seen her but then he turned and looked, more glared, his face stern but impassive. He raised the cigarette to his mouth, exhaled a haze. Then something came into those dark circles, some small light, calm and yet searching. He raised his brow slightly and nodded. Maria came to her.

'Looks like one of his bad days,' Maria said.

'Bad days?'

'Some days it's like there's a fog between him and the world. No-one can get through. He never sleeps. Wanders around half the night. Best left on a day like that.'

Maria put the packages on the truck's tray and Amelia looked back at Fergus.

'It's sad,' Maria said. 'Such a good-looking young man. His father's given up on him. To be honest, I'm surprised he found you in Brisbane. But there you go, people are full of surprises.'

They drove in silence. The war had reached Australia. She wanted to talk to Fergus, but it wasn't possible unless she learnt English.

'I to learn English,' Amelia said, in English.

'Good,' Maria said. 'Very good.'

They went to the butcher. Maria spoke in English, and Amelia concluded all the shops were owned by English-speaking people.

'I bought you half-a-dozen *chops*,' Maria said, using the English word. She handed Amelia a parcel wrapped in paper.

Amelia stared at the package. 'What are *chops*?'

'It's a cut of mutton. Just cook them in a pan in a bit of dripping. Boil some vegetables.'

Amelia looked at the package again. She was embarrassed to admit she had no idea what a chop was.

In the draper, Amelia found some heavy material, a brown colour, to make curtains for the bedroom. She found a pair of nightclothes for Italo.

'You'd better buy some needles and thread too,' Maria said. 'There'd be none at the house.'

Maria introduced her to some Italians on the street, all men, and there were too many faces for her to remember. There were no Italian women. That was why Amelia was there.

In the general store, Amelia found some coffee beans and a small hand grinder. Maria bought them for her, along with the basic provisions for the house: oil, more tea and a sack of flour. Amelia asked to mail her letters, so they walked to the post office, the entrance up a small number of stairs. Maria ordered the stamps and Amelia floundered around to find the correct money. *Lire* and *centesimi* were so much easier.

How many pence made a shilling, and how many of these made a pound? The man behind the counter said something to Amelia, and Maria nodded. He went back to a wall of small slotted shelves and handed Amelia a letter. She recognised the handwriting – dear Clara's – and placed it safely in her bag, to savour later.

When they returned to the street, a man was yelling, mainly at a group of men. That much Amelia could understand. Perhaps he was just the Babinda village eccentric, their Signor Gregorio. The men were dressed like Italo, and she presumed they were canecutters. They said things back to the man, just humouring him, but they did their best to ignore him. Maybe this man was drunk, but it was only midmorning, though this was a country with many strange habits. Maria took her arm and led her away.

'Is he drunk?' Amelia said.

'No.' Maria's reply was sharp, her grip firm.

'What's he saying?'

'I'll tell you.'

Once they were at the truck, Maria let go of her arm. She heaved the goods onto the tray and lassoed them in, and they drove out of the village.

'That man was accusing those Italian men of working for less money than the union's rates.'

'Is that true?'

'There may be some, but the majority don't. And he knows that. So they accuse the Italians of other things: not expecting a weekly wage and just taking their money at the end of the season, working longer hours than they should, on and on it goes. To listen to some of them you'd think the Italians have put every British Australian out of work. And if it's not that, it's that Italians are buying all the land.

And they don't stop at that – apparently, we only buy the best land.'

'They must be selling it to them.'

'They don't consider that.'

Amelia sighed heavily and looked out the window. Italo had said anything was possible under Australia's blue skies. But in Babinda the morning had already clouded, grey and darker-grey streaking the horizon to the zenith.

'They call us the olive peril,' Maria said.

Amelia looked back to Maria.

'Maybe it doesn't translate,' Maria said. 'Before, during the gold rush, it was the yellow peril, that Chinamen would take over the country. Now we've moved here, it's the olive peril.'

Amelia pulled up the sleeve of her shirt. Indeed, the skin on her hand was olive from the sun, her forearm whiter. But didn't everyone's skin colour in the sun?

'Truth is they're scared of anything that's not them,' Maria said. 'They want us all to work for nothing, say nothing, do nothing, like the Kanaka.'

They'd now cleared the village and were back on the wide plain, and a cooler breeze swept them along.

'They're annoyed the Italians are successful,' Maria said. 'If the Italians hadn't helped one another, worked together, they'd never have been able even to buy land, get loans from the bank, lawyers, let alone work it. The British Australians are just too lazy to get organised.' She was silent for a while. 'I dare say you were annoyed Italo didn't come to meet you in Brisbane. I know you mightn't see it this way – he had no choice. Nothing will stop the mill. They just have to get the cane there in the time that's allotted. Not even a new wife can stop that, I'm afraid. Take comfort in that. Despite all his faults, Italo's dependable.'

They drove in silence.

'I shouldn't be so critical,' Maria said. 'God knows, I was born here. Technically, I'm one of them.'

'Have you ever thought to go to Italy?'

Maria laughed. 'I've never imagined that. What's it like?'

'It's upside down to here. It's beautiful – everything is old, everything has a story. But in many ways, this is its greatest problem. And the war destroyed so many things. My father doubts Italy will ever recover.'

'It's always been a part of me that's missing. I'm told about it, I speak the language, but I don't know what it is.'

'Italo said anything is possible in Australia. I believe that.'

'And it's not in Italy?'

Amelia turned to Maria and smiled, shrugged her shoulders. She wouldn't criticise Italy.

They'd arrived back at Italo's farm and brought the supplies into the house. Amelia stoked the fire and made them fresh coffee, which was surprisingly good.

'If we start in Italian,' Maria said, 'we'll stay in Italian. If we start in English, it will be hard and slow but it's the only way you're going to learn. And you need to learn.'

Amelia smiled. Despite Italo's claim there would always be someone close by who spoke Italian, the morning's outing had shown she needed to speak English. It would be hard work, but she would enjoy it. A new land needed new words.

CHAPTER SEVEN

Amelia took Clara's letter to the verandah, pleased just to
see her firm hand. The letter was written and mailed the day
they'd parted. She had no real news, just hopes Amelia was
all right. Cristiano had settled, but he talked of her and Italo
constantly, although he thought Fergus was Italo, despite
her corrections. Paolo worked on a huge construction site
in the city, to be some government building. It was strange
and lovely to see Paolo. The hostel was dreary, but once she
found some work they would rent a small house. She had a
million questions of Italo and expected her to write immediately. Again she urged her to keep busy; it would drive all
homesickness and loneliness away. It heartened Amelia that
a letter could come so quickly.

Amelia spent the rest of the afternoon making curtains for
the bedroom, sewing a flap and inserting the rod, hemming
them at the base. She did a rough job of it, one her mother
would chastise her for, but it would do until she could do
something better.

In the late afternoon, she filled the kettle and placed it
to the side of the coals. She went back to the verandah to
read her grammar book but a short time later heard a truck
approaching from the main road. It stopped at some distance,
six or so men sitting in the back tray as if the driver didn't
want to come too close, all speaking Italian. Then Italo – at
least this blackened man she presumed to be her husband
– appeared, stood and jumped from the tray. He waved to

her and she raised her hand. The truck started again, back towards the main road. She stood from the step.

'Goodnight,' she said.

He smiled again.

'That's very good,' he said. 'But "goodnight" is at the end of the day. It's "good evening" now.'

She blushed. Of course. She knew that. But there was an infinite distance between what she knew and her mouth.

'It's a lovely evening,' he said.

He came up the stair. She stepped back to allow him space. He looked around the verandah, took the book from her.

'You need a bench,' he said.

She nodded, delighted at the prospect.

He stopped. 'If there's anything else you need, just let me know.'

She nodded again, as any word seemed inadequate.

'I'll go and clean up,' he said.

She'd forgotten to ask Maria what to do with the work clothes, still in a stinking heap on the floor. But she motioned to him, told him to take the kettle from the hearth.

'The water is warm, for the shower,' she said.

He smiled and made his way inside, towards the rear of the house.

She read more and then returned to the kitchen to prepare the evening meal. The paper parcel of chops sat on the bench. She unravelled the roll. A chop was mostly bone, a circle of red meat and a strip of white fat. *Costoletta d'agnello*. So expensive, her mother had never cooked them. What had Maria said? She needed to listen more. She filled a pot with water and hooked it to a low link on the chain to give it more heat. She cut some potatoes and carrots Maria had left. Italo hummed some tune in the washroom.

She placed the pan between two stones to the side of the fire, moved some coals in under. Once it was hot, she melted the dripping and added the chops. They spluttered as they seared. She forced a knife under them to turn them. She heard Italo walking. Was he in the main room or the breezeway? A loud whooshing erupted from the fireplace, heat slapping her cheek, flames dancing above the pan. She stood, suspended by their incongruity, their colours, their beauty. The heat engulfed her. She grabbed the pan; the metal was hot and burned, but she managed to lower it to the hearth then waved her hand in the air. The flames rose high; the fat spat. She took a cloth and waved it, but the breeze gave fuel to the flame. To call Italo was to draw his attention to this failure, the kitchen choked with smoke. Slowly the flame lowered, the fuel extinguished, leaving a congealed liquid about the chops. The fumes began to clear.

She couldn't hear Italo humming. He must still be dressing. She lifted the charred chops from the pan to a plate, swaddled in a gelatinous black. They were ruined. But they had to eat something. She took them to the dining room. Italo was seated at the table. The meat smelled burnt and could only taste worse. She couldn't look at him and returned to the kitchen for the vegetables. But in all the confusion she'd left them too long, and they were almost broth. She rescued what she could and took them to Italo.

Fortunately, he'd lit another pungent incense coil, masking the malodour. She served him. He stared at the meat but said nothing. What kind of fool wasted such money? She cut into the meat, charred and raw inside. Italo cut the bone free and raised it in his hands, nibbled at it, pulled the pinkish flesh with his teeth.

The conversation came slowly. She told him Maria had come and they'd gone into town. She liked the village. He smiled. She gave him the nightclothes. He blushed. She was sure he did. Not just the heat.

'I've lived too long on my own,' he said. 'Thank you.' He looked at the meal's remains. 'Did your parents have a stove?'

'Yes.'

He sighed. 'There's no point in spending money here. I want to build a new house.'

She breathed in. 'I'll learn.' She refolded the nightclothes. 'A man left milk in the kitchen this morning.'

'Ben. He lives near the creek. He looks after the cows.'

The conversation came hard and without a rhythm. He was tired. But her mind jumped around, made more nervous by the silence. By eight-thirty, when the sun had gone, he excused himself to check his horses and smoke a last cigarette. She cleared the meal's remains. The poor man must be hungry, but there wasn't even bread. How was she to bake bread? She prepared herself for bed and lay still, waiting. The kerosene lamp cast dancing shadows on the ceiling, increasing her anxiety.

Would it happen tonight?

Italo came into the bedroom. She made no effort to close her eyes. He wore the nightclothes. Their eyes met.

'It's a very busy time,' he said.

'Maria explained.' They were both silent. 'What can I do to help?'

'There's nothing now but in about ten days, the gang will come to harvest my cane ... our cane. They'll need to be fed. Maria normally does it for me, but perhaps ...'

'Of course.' She felt pleased to be asked, but how could she cook for so many men without a stove? 'But I'll need her help ...'

'Yes.'

'She's coming in the morning. I'll speak with her.' She thought of Maria's preparedness to help. 'I like her.'

He nodded. 'I think we should marry.'

She laughed. 'We're already married.'

She raised her hand, splayed her fingers to show him the ring his aunts had bought with his money.

Now he laughed. 'I know we can't marry again,' he said. 'But … perhaps a celebration. Being together might make it more … as it should be.'

'You're too busy.'

'This Sunday.' He came and knelt by the bed. 'Will you marry me?'

She laughed, as she'd not since she parted from Clara. 'Of course I will.'

He took her hand, leant in and kissed her cheek.

'I'll wait till then,' he said.

She searched his eyes. Shouldn't that light kiss on her cheek ignite something, some ricochet of events? Emma had told of a sizzling in her spine. This was no more than Giuseppe's kiss at the altar, light, moist. But whatever the moment was, whatever the possibility was, it was gone. Italo withdrew to the door. She half resented this. And she half thanked him. Standing in the hallway with one hand on the doorframe, he drew it partly closed.

'Goodnight,' he said, in English.

He'd not noticed the brown curtains she'd made for the window. He closed the door, and she heard his steps to the other room.

When she woke, Italo had already left. She made coffee, grinding the beans and resting them in boiled water, and sat on the front step to watch the rising sun. What did she think of Italo? To find clarity, she wrote to Clara. Whilst he wasn't what she'd expected, he wasn't unpleasing. He seemed kind, considerate and thoughtful, although perhaps a little self-willed, as Signora Pina had suggested. And now they were to celebrate their marriage. Perhaps it was a nice thing to do, the first sign of romance in what had been a long chain of cold bureaucracy. She'd only agreed to the church ceremony for her parents. Italo had been shut from any celebration, from anything more than months of signing notary papers. He may as well have bought another horse. She looked at the less-than-practical house. It was impossible to describe. The prospect of feeding a gang of working men was unnerving. What would she feed them? And cooking on that damn fire.

In the kitchen she filled the kettle, and when it had warmed she took the water to the rear washhouse. By now the mound of Italo's clothes had grown, as had their odour. But she quickly removed her clothes, unwound the rope from its peg and lowered the metal can, poured in the water and raised it. The water over her head, over her body, felt nothing short of luxury. She lathered her hair, her skin, and when the streams ran dry she filled the can again with cold water that braced her against the rising heat and humidity of the day, rinsing her clean.

When she'd dressed, she heard the lowing of the cows, quite close. Ben must be moving them past the back of the house. She walked to the breezeway. The three cows stood at a distance. The door to the main room opened. At first she just saw a man, Ben, but then realised he was hunched over, turned in on himself. He wore a cap, but there were patches of hair missing at the side, the skin ruffled and marbled. His clothes were old. He made no overture to acknowledging her. He shuffled down the two stairs in the manner of an old,

old man. His face was as young as hers, but the skin pulled tight from his cheek to his neck, a braised red.

'Hello,' she said.

But he continued, half dragging one leg forward. After his back was to her, she saw one hand, the same heated colour, but the fingers were missing, just stubs. She raised her hand to her mouth to snuff a gasp. He walked away, as if she weren't there, as if he'd seen nothing. He picked up a cane and motioned the obedient cows to continue along the ridge.

The poor soul. How had he been so injured? And why had Italo not warned her? He returned no look, made no sound, followed the cows.

In the kitchen, he'd left the jug of fresh milk. She placed it in the coolest corner, near the tap, and then set to clearing the kitchen, set to push Ben from her thoughts. But he reminded her of Signor Gregorio in her village, and that brought another wave of homesickness. Would this longing ever leave? Ben laboured to walk; there must be something she could do to help him. She'd ask Italo.

She heard a truck. It must be Maria. By the time she walked through the house to the front, the vehicle had stopped. But it wasn't Maria's truck, being much larger and with timber stacked on the rear. She pulled back into the house. She couldn't see the driver, whose seat was on the far side of the truck. She heard the door open and peered out. Fergus stepped from the truck. He looked towards the house, caught her peering out from behind the door. She stepped to the verandah, pleased to see him. Ben had unsettled her.

'Good morning, Fergus.'

She smiled broadly, and he nodded, a burning cigarette drooping from the corner of his mouth. He came around the truck and took three or four great lengths of timber from the tray as if they were of no great weight and carried them towards the house. He lay them at the base of the stair. He said something. She didn't understand, and he said it again. He walked the stairs to the verandah and then reduced what he was saying to one word. This was ridiculous. She raised her open hand and turned back into the house, taking the dictionary to him. It trembled in his hands, but he found the word.

Panca. Bench.

Now she understood. Italo had asked Fergus to build a bench. How sweet of him. The consideration lifted her spirits. She nodded to Fergus. He smiled, an openness spreading to his eye.

'May I?' he said.

He motioned to the dictionary and flicked through the pages. He kept his finger under a word and turned the book slowly to her, moving closer. She caught his scent, already strong for this hour of the day, mixed with smoke.

Table – *tavolo.*

Italo had also asked him to build her a table so she could sit outside and have a place for her book and her study. She looked from the dictionary. He smiled again. Then his finger moved from the page, and his hand that held the dictionary aloft pushed it towards her. She clasped the book to her chest. He moved to return to the truck, but she was before the stair and had to step out of the way.

He brought more pieces of equipment. She found an empty bottle, filled it with water and took it back to the verandah, as the day had suddenly become warm. He'd put himself to his task with firm and definite movements, his eye moving between the bedroom window and the timber. He took a long piece and held it at knee height below the window and looked back to her.

'Yes,' she said.

He nodded. Once this was decided, he went about his job with purpose. She went back to her own work. Clara was right; she must keep busy. She tidied the main room. She heard Fergus on the verandah, the rhythm of his saw regular and pleasing. She picked up her broom and began to sweep, great long strides that synchronised to the rhythm of Fergus, continuing to the breezeway and the front hall.

She walked to the verandah, turned and stopped. He'd removed his shirt, wearing just a white cotton vest and khaki shorts. His back arched away from her, out over a piece of timber held between two trestles. His far knee rested on the piece, part to steady it and part to be able to reach further along, his other leg straight but at an angle, a large arc of muscle from his thigh. His arms forced a plane, moved like some mechanical apparatus, the arms on the wheels of a train.

She hurried through the house to the kitchen, her heart pounding as it shouldn't, as there'd been no undue exertion. The morning's humidity had risen, and she tore off a light cardigan she wore over her shirt. She filled a glass of water from the tap, drank it whole, the coolness doing nothing to relieve the heat. As much as she shouldn't look again, she filled a water bottle and returned to the verandah. He'd replaced his shirt. And then she heard Maria's truck, straining up the small rise to the house, and walked to the rail to welcome her.

Maria greeted Fergus, but he barely acknowledged her, intent on his task.

'This will be lovely,' Maria said.

He continued working as if the women weren't there. Until then he'd been quite jolly, but Maria's presence brought a change.

'You knew about this?' Amelia said.

She nodded. 'Italo spoke with Dante.'

The two women went inside. She made them tea and told her of the previous evening's culinary disaster. Maria showed her how to vary the heat of the frypan by moving the coals about, how to vary the heat for the pots by adjusting the height of the hooks on the chain. She tried to concentrate on what Maria was saying, but she could hear Fergus's saw, its unrelenting rhythm. Maria showed her the large copper stored under the house, and how to boil Italo's soiled clothes clean.

That evening, she sat at the new bench and table when Italo came home.

'Do you like it?' he said.

She smiled. 'I like it very much.'

He smiled, his teeth gleaming. He bent down, inspected the joints in Fergus's work. The memory of his saw's rhythm unsettled her.

'I saw Ben today,' she said, more to distract her thoughts than anything. Italo nodded, ran his hand along the table's surface. 'Why's he so disfigured?'

'A fire, when he was young.'

She paused. How awful. 'Is there something I can do for him?'

Italo looked at her, somewhat taken aback. Then he shook his head. 'He has everything he needs. I'll go and clean up.'

He walked around the house to the washroom. In the kitchen, she could hear the water fall from the tin can suspended on pullies. She moved the coals away from the pan and seared the evening's chops.

On Sunday morning before the dawn, Amelia heard Italo in the breezeway. They were to go to church. They ate their breakfast in silence and then rode on a small dray behind one of Italo's horses into the village. But there was no church, just a hall with seats and many people. They mainly spoke English, the service in Latin with smatterings of English words. Amelia took communion but not confession; apart from the fact she couldn't speak English and the priest spoke no Italian, she had no new sin to confess.

Outside the building, she met some of Italo's friends. In all, she counted about thirty people, with the surnames Alcorso, Pellegrino, Nanni, Sabbatini, Garofalo, Lucchesi, Pennisi, Tedesco, D'Angelo, De Francesco, Lanza – too many for her to remember. And she met Maria's husband, Dante Pastore, a fine-looking man but older than she'd imagined. The only women were herself, Maria and two others, Anna Nanni and Teresa Garofalo.

They all followed Amelia and Italo's dray back to the farm, a jumbled procession, a gypsy caravan coming to town, some single on horses, others grouped on horses and carriages, some trucks in low gear. They carried cooking equipment, even extra furniture. As far as she knew, no invitations had been sent, but clearly people knew to come. They were all Italian. She'd prepared nothing, but like a troop of well-rehearsed performers, these people went to their tasks. On the flatter side of the breezeway, a man set a metal device to turn a whole pig over a fire. Other people set the mismatched tables and a host of chairs on the verandah. How impersonal, these people she'd never met, celebrating her wedding. But how generous of them, their resplendent smiles, their help. She spread the cotton tablecloth the women had brought, but they shooed her away to prepare herself.

In the bedroom, she closed the door and the brown curtains and sat in the semi-dark on the bed's edge. The day was warming. Voices moved around the outside, the clatter on the verandah, instructions and disagreements, and the women were sometimes shrill, but there was great joy. She wished her mother was there. It was six months since the church wedding. A wave of sadness, so sudden and heavy, came over her. She had no energy for this day, a sorry consolation. But she had no choice; she must meet these people's enthusiasm. She raised herself from the bed, dressed in the white cotton voile she'd worn in Tovo di Sant'Agata. But she wore no veil, just a white hat with a small, round brim that sat proudly high on her forehead.

She walked to the verandah. At first no-one noticed her but then Anna Nanni touched Teresa's arm and motioned towards her. They stared at her, surprised initially, but then relaxed to smiles. And then the men came, swirls of them around her, their smiles and laughter and joy as inebriating as strong liquor. And then Italo was by her side, smiling like she'd never seen. But that was no great surprise; she'd only seen him for a handful of days.

They sat together, halfway along one side of the long table made from many small tables, facing the fields. There were toasts – so many she lost count of them – to her and Italo's long happiness, men welcoming her to the village. The good wine made by these men rose to ease her mind. Someone brought plates of carved porchetta, the salty skin as brittle as glass, and there was more wine and bread – someone had baked bread! – and a hot salami one of the men had made, which tasted exquisite. The men poured beer from tall brown bottles. And when the food was waning, she heard music, an accordion sighing to life, from which Dante Pastore squeezed music. Soon another man tuned a violin.

Italo raised an outstretched hand to her. She flooded with embarrassment as he held her, as they waited for the music to beat. This was the closest they'd been. She looked into his eyes but had to look away. And then they swayed, their rhythm carrying them around the small verandah. She felt the strength in his shoulders, carried by the force of his hips. She smelt the yeasty beer on his breath and she smelt his skin, the sweet of a cologne, the slight sour of a cut onion.

Maria and the other women cried, and the men clapped the simple stress of the waltz. Around and around and around they turned. She was warm from the day, giddy from the toasts, burning from the other men's eyes. Would this never end? As ungrateful as it was, she wanted solitude. She'd not sought this public display.

Finally, the music wound down. Finally, they parted. The hands came towards them, all well-wishing. At least they wanted to wish Italo well. The men were very fond of him. To a degree, she was an afterthought, a 'new chum', yet to find her place amongst these people.

The dance's stress had taken her breath. She withdrew, slipped from the men and the harsh daylight. But the house was overly hot. In the kitchen, she poured a glass of water and went to the breezeway, although the wafts of cool air here were only fleeting. She'd never imagined feeling so alone. She longed for the past, felt alien in the present and feared the future. Her lips trembled, and she fought off these emotions.

Someone appeared in front of her, as if he'd been standing flush against the outside wall. She jumped with fright. Fergus. She didn't know he'd been invited, but then she'd known nothing about the day. He towered over her, the same as Italo. She smelt his cigarette tar. She smiled. Nothing was said because there was nothing that could be said.

'There you are,' Maria said, coming from the hall.

Amelia looked to her and then back to Fergus, but he'd disappeared.

Maria came to her side. 'What's the matter?'

'Nothing,' Amelia said. 'Hot. I think Mamma and Papa.'

Maria smiled a lippy smile. 'Yes. Don't cry. Your photograph.'

Italo had arranged for a photographer from Cairns to come to the house. She nodded, and they walked to the verandah. Fergus was seated at the table, amongst the men. He was dressed, as ever, in a shirt and shorts and boots, a contrast to the other men in their serge or corduroy trousers, shirts and ties; some even wore jackets. But whilst Italo was tall, as were Dante and Manny Pellegrino, Fergus was solid. He had washed and combed his hair, the colour glossed and shining. He listened to the men, who gestured with their hands and faces to fill the void of misused or poorly connected words. He took a wad of tobacco from a small tin, rubbed it in his palm and rolled a fat cigarette. The other men's talk in Italian was all of Italy, of the stories of why they'd come to Australia. They seemed happy Fergus was there, a foreigner in this little Italy.

Someone had brought a chair, a Savonarola, the same chair in the photograph she had of Italo, taken many years ago. To her, the chair was familiar and foreign. Although the evening was only forming, the light still strong, the mosquito coils burned. Italo came to her and took her hand, led her to the chair. He sat, and she stood by his side. Even in this arrangement, she was only slightly taller than him. Maria brought a posy of white flowers. The photographer, Mr Taylor, came to her, placed her hand on Italo's shoulder, placed her right hand to allow the long trail of flowers to drape over his shoulder. She was bewildered, paralysed, a statue, yet her hand trembled.

Mr Taylor said something.

'You both have to be still for some seconds,' Maria said.

How could she be still with this thrumming in her legs and arms?

He returned to his apparatus. 'Please remain still,' he said again, motioning he was to start the process. He repeated this process three more times, with slight adjustments to their clothes and the flowers. She feared the posy shook in her hand and in the image the flowers would blur. And then Mr Taylor said he was finished.

A voice rose, a woman's, Anna's, full of melody and melancholy. With only a few words, Amelia recognised the song.

> *Mamma mia, dammi cento lire, che in America voglio andar*
> *Cento lire io te li dò, ma in America no, no, no.*

> Mamma, give me a hundred lire so I can go to America.

> I will give you a hundred lire but to America, no, no, no.

It was an old song from the north of Italy, full of longing, the hope and fear of immigration. And soon Dante began, without strain or effort, as if it had been rehearsed, the accordion gently placed under the melody. And the violin rose, so filled with sorrow it was another voice. But this performance hadn't been planned; immigration was a melody Italians had rehearsed for decades.

She looked around the crowd. How their eyes filled with memory, with longing, all traces of the day's happiness lulled with nostalgia. But most of all, Fergus sat still, between the men, his eyes, also filled with tears, fixed to the singer.

How could he know this song? How could he have felt its meaning? Did he, after all, speak Italian?

After the guests were gone, Italo came to their bed. He swaddled himself and Amelia in the white veil of the mosquito net. She lay still. This event was to happen, this thing that defined so many other actions. He lay on his side, facing her.

'Are you tired?' he said.

'Not overly. It was a lovely day.'

'The first of many.'

She smiled. 'Did you invite Fergus?'

'Of course. He brought you to me.'

She laughed and thought of this. 'Does he speak Italian?'

'Not at all.'

'Yet he had tears during the song.'

Italo exhaled. 'He's a troubled soul … He has little to do with his family. Did you mind him being here?'

'Not at all. He was the only Australian.'

Italo placed his open palm on her belly. Paralysed, she was unsure what to do, what was to pass. Her mother had told her nothing. And Emma spoke of nothing practical. Why hadn't she spoken more fully with Clara? Italo raised himself, pressed his lips to hers. And so it advanced. Italo took all control. She had nothing to do, it appeared. He lay on her. He kissed her mouth, the nape of her neck, which just tickled, but his energy increased. His hard horn rubbed between the lips of her vagina. When he entered her, slowly and thoughtfully, the sharp pain subsided. But would she describe the sensation as pleasure? And as he continued this irregular thrusting, why couldn't she erase the image of Fergus, his glistening hair, the dark, dark eyes filled so with tears?

CHAPTER EIGHT

The new brown curtains darkened the room, but a ray of light pierced a small slit in the wood. Italo had gone. She rose from the bed and walked to an oval wall mirror. She looked at her face. The light was weak. She moved closer. Scrutinised it. What did she expect to see? Her hazel eyes, fine nose, cheeks, chin. So, that was what it was all about. That was what women were sweet-talked to. A traded apple for this? These feelings weren't so great, so wonderful. She wondered at the power of it. Was that all Emma and Clara had been drawn to?

And then she thought of the consequence – would the seed grow in her? She felt warmed by excitement. Her heart raced. How she wanted children. But then she felt a sliver of cold fear. In this new land, there was much to understand. How would she cope with a child? And especially without her mother's help? She placed her hand on her belly. She remembered the tightness she'd felt in Emma's. How would she know if it grew? She prayed to the Madonna. Yes, please, many children, but not just yet.

She looked again in the mirror. Her dark-brown hair was longer. What had she expected to see? Some curious mix of innocence and self-confidence? Where Italo had known what he desired, she had not. She glared at her round face and again observed no change.

She dressed in her house gown and walked to the verandah. Any signs of their celebration were gone – the tables and chairs, the aroma of meat and especially the music and the laughter, the lamps that had flickered so beautifully into the evening. Only the new table and bench sat under the bedroom window.

She walked through to the breezeway. Even the earth where the pig had been roasted somehow looked untouched. Someone coughed in the main room. Her heart accelerated. It must be Ben. She braced herself, inched forward, listening, tiptoed towards the door, pushing it open slowly. But Italo was seated at the table and looked at her. She breathed out. She didn't know the sound of her husband's cough.

'I didn't know you were here,' Amelia said.

He stood abruptly and came to her, held her forearm and kissed her. She shied, more as it had taken her by surprise than anything. But she wasn't used to being kissed in the morning. And she felt nothing great. He let go of her forearm. He smiled.

'Change of plans,' he said. 'Enrico told me yesterday. The harvest has been moved forward a week. The gang will arrive on Thursday.'

'Thursday.'

'That gives us only three days to get organised,' Italo said.

'Organised?'

'Some of the men stay here. They sleep in the barracks. They'll have to be fed.'

'What?' She glared at him. Clearly, the blankness of her expression had had some effect on him.

'You've had no time to find your feet—'

'I need to feed them?'

'Maria will help.'

He jabbered a list that needed doing, running her mind to the point of giddiness: the barracks cleaned, menus to be planned, food stores to be bought. She grabbed some paper and a pencil and began to scribble, saying yes to tasks she didn't understand.

'I have to go,' he said. 'But I'll come back at lunchtime, see how you're getting on.'

'But ...'

'Don't worry. I'll send Ben to tell Maria.'

With that, he stood. He smiled as he left. How was all this going to be done? And in such a short time. She made coffee and sat at the bench and table on the verandah and read and reread the list. The men would be there for ten days, at least. She had to cook breakfast and lunch and morning and afternoon tea. And some of the men needed dinner. She'd never cooked for more than five people, and now she would for ten or more. And there was nothing to cook on but an open fire on a stone in a room that could hardly be described as a kitchen. And she could only cook Italian food, and there were so few ingredients.

She heard Maria's truck straining from the main road. When Maria walked onto the verandah, she could evidently see the panic in Amelia's eye.

'Don't be worried,' Maria said, the stress of the situation causing her to break their rule of only speaking in English. 'I've done it many times.' She took the piece of paper from Amelia and looked over the list and smiled. 'You're organised. Good.'

What would Amelia do without her? How blessed she was to have met Clara and now Maria.

'Just as well Fergus has made you this lovely table for us to work at. Now, go and make me some coffee.'

They began by planning the menus for each day. They'd make thick porridge for breakfast, as it staved off a day's hunger.

'But some of the men will want eggs with bacon or steak. Some will want both. We'll need a load of bread at each meal.'

For morning and afternoon tea they'd make some kind of cake. Maria recommended a rainbow cake. They could bake enough in the morning and it would do for afternoon tea. Or they could do the same with scones, which would keep fresh enough till the afternoon.

'We take this out to them in the field,' Maria said.

'We need to do this too?'

'Their time's more important than ours.'

But lunch would need to sustain the men. They worked extremely hard and needed fuel. She and Maria could roast a beast, much as they'd done for the celebration. They'd need to serve it with vegetables and roast potatoes and a thick gravy.

'Not too much salt, as it makes them want to drink.'

And they could serve some of the meat cold in the evening or use the rest for a stew the following day. They would make sweetened jelly, set in the cool lee of the water tank and served with canned fruit. Or they would make bread custard puddings with the stale bread, if there were any.

'What about a minestrone?' Amelia said.

Maria sat back in her chair.

'It would be easy for us,' Amelia said. 'I could make it the evening before. We'd just have to heat it.'

Maria considered the option. 'It's worth a try. But you won't find any beans.'

'In Australia?'

'Maybe in Sydney or Melbourne.' Maria shook her head. 'But not up here.'

Amelia felt confused. Was Maria making fun of her? How could they not have them?

'Without beans a minestrone has no heart.'

By midmorning they'd drawn up the menus, which Maria reduced to a long shopping list. Amelia felt breathless. There was so much to organise, such great quantities to buy, so much to learn. And once the harvest began, there would be just so much to do.

'We'll never sleep,' Amelia said.

'The men work hard and so do we. I'll bring my kitchen hand, Meggsy, to help.'

They went to the village to buy the provisions and by midafternoon brought them back to the house. There was no room to store anything in the small kitchen, so housed in the breezeway were the sacks and sacks of flour, bags of potatoes and carrots, a whole waxed wheel of cheese, bottles of beer and cans of fruit and corned beef, the bags of tea and oats and onions and sugar. (Of all things, they'd bought sugar.) The meat, beef and mutton, would be delivered three times a week and stored in a large meat safe covered with a damp cloth and suspended by a rope in the breezeway. She'd not been able to buy any pulses – no-one had heard of borlotti or cannellini beans – and she doubted the minestrone could be made. Maria would bring more eggs, and Ben more milk, each day.

In the early evening, after Maria had gone, she stood in the breezeway. She couldn't believe the amount of food. A hungry army was about to descend. How could she describe such a sight to her parents? She checked off the lists again, not just to be sure she had everything but also so she knew where it was. Would this be enough? Once the harvest began, there just wouldn't be time for more supplies.

'I thought it was a good omen.'

Italo stood at the side of the breezeway. She'd been so caught with the inventory she'd not noticed him and wondered how long he'd been there. He looked tired, drawn.

'When I came at lunchtime, you were already gone. It's like you've done this before.'

'I don't think so.' She went back to her master list. 'It's mostly Maria's doing …'

They ate their evening meal, cold porchetta from the celebration, the skin hard and salty, with vegetables she'd manage to cook rather than destroy.

That night, he came to bed after he'd gone for his evening walk. He lay next to her, on his side, facing her.

'Goodnight,' he said.

She looked into his eyes. He closed them. She heard the rain at the roof, soft and discombobulated, spluttering to start. His breathing slowed and was regular. She closed her eyes. And then his hand smoothed over her belly, warm as a blanket. And then it moved in slow circles, almost soothing, and soon he was on her, his weight crushing her as he moved into her, his hot lips at her mouth, about her mouth, in her mouth. She searched for her role. Should she move as he did? Counter him? Under his weight she couldn't budge, and it seemed she shouldn't. His breath rushed and sucked at her cheek. He knew what he wanted and would take it. It had little to do with her. He stretched, stiffened, shuddered. And relaxed. But she lay still. He was exhausted. He rolled from her. He said nothing and in moments his breath subsided to calm and sleep. She, though, was far too agitated to dream of sleep, the night an endless list of lists.

The following morning she went with Italo to the stable on the flat land below the house. Tacked on to the far end was a barracks, made only of timber frame and galvanised-iron sheets and a bare cement floor. Outside the door, under an awning, was a huge trough with a washboard fixed at an angle, a long line strung in the air.

'The men get prickles from the cane in their clothes,' Italo said. 'Hairy Mary, they call it. They get ash in their hair. If they don't wash, it irritates their skin and they scratch. Worse than a dog with fleas.'

Three double bunk beds were perpendicular to the wall opposite the door. There were two canvas stretchers folded against the wall, and a single hammock.

'After lunch', Italo said, 'the men come for siesta, during the worst heat of the day.'

There was only one window on the end wall. The air was close, spiked with the scent of burnt mosquito coils, and she pushed up the tin frame. On the other side, in an alcove, was a cement floor with a drain. Strung high on a system of pullies was a rectangular tin with holes pushed through its bottom, forming a shower, like the one in the washroom, no provision for modesty. There was an outhouse to the side of the barracks.

'What do you want me to do?' she said.

'A bit of tidy up.'

She nodded.

He kissed her, thanked her, and left.

She pulled a mattress from the lower bunk, dragged it to the sun and returned for another, which she pulled from the bunk to the floor. Someone had left a coil of yellow rope she reached for, but it began to move. She jumped back and screamed. The snake unravelled, its eyes fixed on her. It flicked its tongue. With all force she ran from the barracks into the sun, fought to steady her breath.

'Italo.'

She breathed again. She'd dealt with snakes in Italy. It had just caught her by surprise. She didn't need Italo. The thing was probably more scared of her. She grabbed the broom by the door. But the snake had gone. She looked along the lower reaches of the walls, its tail disappearing through a split in the corrugated metal wall. Outside, she found a rock and wedged it into the hole. In a blaze, she pulled the rest of the mattresses from the beds but there were no more snakes.

She dusted the bunks, the small table and three chairs, and then swept the floor. Once the mattresses were returned, she looked at the basic conditions. The men would have little time for luxury, working up to thirteen hours a day, seven days a week, until it was done. They needed only to clean themselves and sleep. The only comfort she could offer them was good food, and plenty of it.

She was occupying her time, but it was more than mere occupation. Since she'd stepped on to Italo's land, it was as if work now had purpose – all her effort was for herself and Italo. Every action brought satisfaction. For the first time since the wedding in Tovo di Sant'Agata, she felt she'd made the right decision. She squinted at the sun, high and burning. Her new life.

The harvest began in the early evening, the whole gang arriving at around three. They parked two large trucks on the flat near the barracks, unloaded boxes of equipment and then, in a ragtag line, walked up the hill to the house and onto the verandah. They were all Italian. Some were Italo's age and had been at the celebration, and some, younger, she'd never met before. Six men would stay in the barracks: Pasquale Alcorso, Gaetano D'Angelo, Lorenzo Nanni, Salvatore Lanza, Tullio Pesaro and Enrico Garofalo. All were from

Lombardy or the Veneto except Salvatore, who was from Sicily. They were all large, strong men who would have larger, stronger appetites. Mariano Lucchesi and Sergio Tedesco owned farms nearby and would return home in the evening – two fewer to feed. Amelia didn't know if they had wives.

She made the first huge pot of tea and carried it to them. Some sat on the benches, and others brought chairs from the house. Although they spoke of this and that, each man knew his part and went about it. Tullio filled a dozen canvas waterbags and hung them from the edge of the verandah's roof like washing. Immediately they began to seep, dripping profusely, but with refillings they'd be cured and watertight by morning. Italo brought a wooden case to the verandah. Each man drew a broad knife, those ones she'd seen in the fields. They were new, the light glinting on the metal. From the men's talk, the blade would last only one season. She picked one, judged it in her hand. They were heavy, and she marvelled at the men's strength to wield them like a but-terknife for an entire day. She returned to the kitchen and brought the scones she'd baked earlier in the afternoon. As they talked, with care and practised ease they stroked a file along the blade's edge. Some had the opinion that five or six more seasons and they'd return to Italy with enough money, as much as £500, to build new lives.

Italo neither affirmed nor negated their assertions. It was something, this idea of returning to Italy, amongst so many things they hadn't yet had a chance to discuss. But it seemed odd the men thought they could build new lives in old Italy. This was their new life. Couldn't they see that?

But then their talk turned to the job at hand and she knew to step back, as she had no part in this. And by four-thirty they decided the day had cooled and the wind had dropped sufficiently to burn the cane. The men thanked her as they left the verandah, ambling to the fields in front of the house. Italo kissed her cheek.

The other men were now far from the verandah. She drew herself to her full height on her toes and kissed his cheek, the act so quick it left her with no great sensation. When she returned her heels to the verandah, he smiled.

'Once this harvest is done,' he said, 'we'll have a few quieter days.'

He walked towards the rest of the gang. Smaller and smaller they became, until they were swallowed by the fields.

She took the tray of cups to the kitchen. It was good the men worked together, in a collective. Why wouldn't they? It made sense to share the precious resources of labour and equipment. What one gained no-one lost. They weren't competing for a price. Even she and Maria were a collective of this type, as she would help Maria cook for the gang when Dante's cane was harvested.

She was unsure what time the men would return, so she'd make a simple stew for dinner, which would keep. Despite the volume of the ingredients, she soon had it simmering, suspended high over the fire. But first she smelt it, this cloying scent of smoke in the air, and walked out to the verandah. From there she could hear it, a rushing noise, this cracking and crackling. The flames reached high above the cane heads, a rain of orange cinders. Her pulse rose. Such a sight induced fear, though she was told it was done on purpose and wasn't a concern.

Despite all these signs of heat, the evening felt chilled now the sun had gone. She returned to the bedroom for a crocheted shawl and wrapped it around her shoulders. She stepped from the verandah, walking towards the flames. She could feel the heat, hear the intense noise, hear the vermin shrieking. She could never have imagined such a thing. How could she describe it to her parents?

She stopped at a small path between two fields. Only one side was on fire, burning in a patchwork. She heard steps behind her, running, and spun around. But there was no-one. Shrieking rats streamed from the burning field, across the path and to another maze of cane. She listened for the men's voices, but there was no sound above the flame's roar. Birds circled in the dark sky, their bellies brushed golden by the firelight. Had they been driven from their nest? She heard a voice. At the fringe of the light she saw someone moving away, into the dark.

'Who's there?' she said.

She turned and could see the men at the end of the path. Again she sensed someone moving and walked towards the men.

A wind came out of the fire, sweeping the folds of her dress from her. The flames rose, arced over, a cathedral roof. She breathed but there was just heat. No air. No smoke. Heat. Nothing to breathe. And then the roof fell, as if it had never been there. But fires flared on the adjacent field. The flames rushed the lengths of cane, exploding the heads.

The men had gone. She retreated but the flame caught the scythed grass of the path to where the men had been. She advanced in that direction, and the flame caught this path, a rain of ash and ember about her. She was surrounded. Her best option was to go into the part of the field that had just caught alight. Perhaps she could beat the flame before it advanced. But as she got closer to the side of the field, the intense heat pushed her back. She fought for air – hot, choking air. She took a fold of the shawl and placed it to her mouth. The sound pounded. She felt she would fall.

'Help.'

Her throat, dry from the heat, cracked with fear, crackled the word. No-one would hear. The smoke rushed past the stars like storm clouds, the maddened birds circling. She gasped. What a waste, to have come this far, that it had all come to only this – this rush, this clamouring, this lack of strength, this beating. A white wave washed over her sight. Her knees gave way. This was her end. She crumbled to the soft, heated and inviting earth.

CHAPTER NINE

She woke.

She was lying. On a bed. The room flickered to a lamp. It wasn't Italo's house. She raised her head, perceiving a single bed with a metal frame, but immediately the wooziness made her spin. Her head ached. Where was she? It was only a small room: a table and one chair, a single door. She swung her legs to the floor. Black dots swarmed her vision. The room swung, afloat. She braced her hands on the bed. She could smell fire and held her breath to listen. She could hear the fire. Then she heard something moving outside the door. Her heart pumped. She stared at the door and heard a step, followed by another shuffle. Fergus. He stood in the flickering lamplight, holding a white enamelled cup in his hand. He smiled.

'Tea,' he said.

She relaxed her shoulders, lifted her hands from the bed and sighed. What was she doing there? He smiled and moved the few paces to her but held the tea at arms-length. The enamel on the cup was chipped. She raised it to her lips but felt the heat and lowered it to her lap.

'You fell,' he said, miming the fall.

'Yes.' He must have been behind her, working with the men. She thought of what would have happened if he hadn't. 'Thank you.'

He took a tin of tobacco from his pocket and with practised certainty rolled a cigarette. She raised the cup and blew the surface and then sipped it. It was bitter, without sugar or milk, but the beverage raised her spirits. No damage had been done. She'd been foolish. But she'd been rescued. She must get back to finish the men's dinner. And hopefully without Italo knowing what had happened. He'd be angry. She put the tea on the small table near the bed.

'I go,' she said.

She stood, but the rapid action caused white to flicker in her eyes, her head all dizziness. She sat back. Fergus came to her, to catch her again. She held a hand up to him.

'I go,' she said.

He stared at her and then held out a hand. She was unsure, but realised she'd not get to the house without some help. She placed her small hand in his. His was rough, warm, but it was large and swallowed hers. She made to stand and felt the strength come into his arm. Once she was vertical, she resisted the urge to collapse to the bed. And as she stood, holding one of Fergus's hands, the dizziness subsided.

'Walk,' he said.

She nodded. He scooted ahead of her, through the door. The cooler night air roused her spirits. She could smell and hear the burning cane and the men's voices. He let go of her hand, walked some two or three paces and turned.

'Come,' he said.

She took one step, and then another. He walked ahead. She felt unsteady, her gait laboured and heavy. Fergus trod lightly on the balls of his feet, which made his bare calf muscles tighten and round, then slacken and relax. He made for a track into the rainforest. She followed, watching the motion of his calves. He turned back to her, caught her looking.

'Are you all right?' he said, stopping. He looked at the back of his legs.

She felt hot beyond the dictates of the evening and looked away. 'Much hot.'

The land fell away at the side of the path. They were on a hill. She looked behind her. It was just a small hut with a fire outside. Through the forest, she could see the orange-glowing cane fields. The flames were low. She was relieved it was still burning; perhaps she could get home without Italo knowing.

Fergus started to walk. She followed at a distance, the path rough but not overly so. She knew where they were, the hill on the far side of the property. Fergus continued ahead, turning back to check her progress. She kept her eyes on the path. The chilled forest air was humid, filled with shrieking birds she supposed had been disturbed by the fire. But the mosquitoes shared no fear and gyred around Fergus's head. She caught his scent in the air. The path descended to the valley's plain. She would make her own way from there. She'd been foolish to bother him. She hoped not to explain any of it to Italo, and if Fergus were there she'd have no choice, which would be embarrassing.

'I go,' she said and pointed towards the house.

Fergus looked ahead and then said, 'No.'

'I go,' she said, as firmly as she could.

She searched for more words. She looked into his dark eyes and wondered if anyone had ever reached their depths. She made to move past him, and he moved away.

'Thank you,' she said.

And he remained standing, watching her. A few paces past him, she stopped. Damn this language. She had no words to explain she wanted to stay but had to leave.

'Goodnight,' he said. His face was blank, and then he forced an awkward smile.

Why couldn't she walk away? Why did she want to extend this moment? 'Goodnight,' she said.

She heard the men's voices at the fire, summoned her sense and started towards the house, only then remembering the stew and hurrying more. But the hearth fire had died, and it hadn't burnt. She took a lamp and went to the bedroom mirror. Her face was covered in black stains, ash and char. The fire had singed one side of her hair around her ear, the ends fuzzy and uneven and smelling. She cut it away, squaring it as best she could. Her clothes too were stained and smelt of fire. But everything smelt of fire. And she'd lost her shawl.

In the mirror, she brushed back the cut hair behind her ear. Her hand shook. Just the thought of what had happened unsteadied her.

The men's voices were around the barracks, laughing and joking. They'd finished their work. Once she'd changed her clothes, in the kitchen she washed her face and set to finishing the meal. Still woozy, she found the work made her concentrate. Italo came to the kitchen doorway. He was blackened. He took off his shirt, the skin of his arms and chest still white.

'The wind changed,' he said. 'The fire jumped to another field. But it's under control.'

She looked at him. 'Thank God.'

He went to wash. He'd not noticed any change in her hair. And nor did he later smell fire on her, as he pressed and pressed until he was done.

Amelia rose with Italo, well before the dawn. In the kitchen, she stoked the fire to let it burn down, prepared them coffee and took some to Italo with a piece of yesterday's bread. She stood on the verandah, staring at the slow smouldering.

She'd not slept all night – the fire closed over her, the smoke entered her lungs. How close she'd come to death. And then, in another swathe of images, she'd seen her brother Aldo's legs, similar to Fergus's, though they'd never inspired such heat in her.

'What time will the men be up?' she said.

'About six-thirty.'

She walked towards him, her tread heavy from tiredness, and raised a hand to his forearm as she passed, some small gesture of their teamwork. He made no response. She heard his steps from the verandah towards the field, and she returned to the kitchen to make the vat of porridge. She'd measured it all the previous evening and placed the oats and water in a huge pot over the fire. While this was slowly heating, she mixed a mass of flour and water and baking soda to knead damper.

Yesterday evening could have ended in disaster. She hoped Fergus would say nothing. But then she'd worried if it was wrong to keep something from her husband. And then it worried her more why she couldn't tell him. Would he be angry she put herself in peril? Her father would be. Or would Italo just be thankful? She didn't want to find out. But then it worried her why she'd want to keep her rescue by Fergus a secret, which she decided was at the heart of her dilemma. She placed the damper in the oven pot.

She remembered the sensation in the field, of someone behind her. Had that been Fergus, or one of the other men? There'd been so much noise and smoke, could she be certain it was anyone?

By six-thirty she heard the men talking on the verandah and took them the teapot. It was the first day, and she hoped all their planning would bear fruit. Some of the men wanted coffee, so she made this. She took the whole porridge pot to the table and let them serve themselves, offered them eggs and bacon, but none seem so inclined.

Maria arrived before the men left for the day, with her kitchen hand, a runt of a woman, Meggsy, who spoke no Italian. Amelia doubted she'd be much help, but in no time, she'd set the spit to the side of the house and started a fire to burn to coals. Today they would roast a calf and carve it for lunch with boiled vegetables and roasted potatoes. Maria showed Amelia how to impale the beast on the long metal pole. Every fifteen minutes she had to rotate the carcass. If she forgot, the meat would burn and spoil, but if she remembered the meat would be cooked through by eleven, leaving it tender and tasty and with time to carve it for lunch. She'd use the rest of the meat for dinner.

'What do you know of Fergus?' she said to Maria. The moment she'd spoken, she realised the question was inappropriate and turned away, to hide the flood of colour.

'Only what I've told you,' Maria said. 'They keep to themselves, mostly.'

'Are they Irish?'

'Their name's Kelly. Fiercely Irish. His grandparents came during the famine. Oisin, that's his father, was born in Ireland but Fergus was born here. He's what you'd call an Australian.'

'But that makes you Australian.'

She looked at her sideways. 'Perhaps it does. But perhaps there's a different set of rules for us.'

'Why would you say that?'

'Haven't you noticed the divide through the valley? The British Australians and the Italians? Just between us, they who were here first think they're entitled to all the land and everything they can grow.'

'Why did Italo ask Fergus to come for me?'

'I told you, since he came back from the war he's pretty useless. Shell-shocked, they call it. Italo couldn't spare any of the Italian men, so he paid Fergus to collect you.'

'I see.'

'He was such a lively lad when he was younger, always in trouble. But that look he had in his eye, and that smile; he would melt the hardest heart and get away with anything.'

She'd seen such a look. That day in the truck when he'd acted to lick the sugarcane. But it was passing, flickering and gone.

'He's turned into a bit of a hermit,' Maria said. 'He lives on his own in a small hut. You'd best go and turn the calf.'

Amelia nodded and walked out through the breezeway. She'd imagined the hut was just a place he went, but he *lived* in it. She turned the beast to the other side.

'Why doesn't he live with his family?' Amelia said when she returned to the kitchen.

'Who?'

'Fergus.'

Maria hesitated, as if she refused to gossip or she was too intent on the mound of potatoes she was peeling.

'Oisin, his father, he's a brute of a man. He never had much sympathy, and it ran out quick smart when Fergus returned. His mother, she's a sweet soul. She tries, but he doesn't seem to want any involvement with them. This used to be Oisin's land before Italo bought it. Italo took pity on Fergus and lets him stay there.'

'Does he work for Italo?'

'Just odd jobs. Italo only wants Italians. And Fergus runs hot and cold.'

Last evening, Fergus hadn't been working in the fields. Then why was he there?

'Others came back from the war with far worse than Fergus,' Maria said, 'and have got on with their lives.'

Amelia thought back to the scars of war, men left without limbs, men without eyes, men with broken minds. Maria was too hard. She'd never seen the war. In Australia, it was a word, a world away. Fergus bore what had happened. And he had no-one to share this with. No-one had seen what he'd seen.

'It's time we took them morning tea,' Maria said. 'Then we'd better get a move on with lunch.'

Once they'd made the tea, they loaded the truck and drove to the field. Amelia saw the narrow path in which she'd been caught. How foolish she'd been. The cutting was well underway, a large swathe of the first field toppled. The men waved to the women and downed their broad, particular knives, stretched out their backs and came to the truck. They all wore trousers to protect their legs. Shorts would have been cooler. Some had removed their shirts, wearing just their cotton undershirts. And they wore the most bizarre array of hats, some round and pulled down about their face, others with the side turned up like Fergus wore his, yet others with wide brims. All were blackened.

The women filled enamelled cups with tea, and the men picked up huge pieces of Maria's cake and sat in the rubble, the debris they'd cut from the cane. They talked and joked amongst themselves, ignoring the women.

Once the men had finished, the women gathered the cups and took everything back to the house. Meggsy disappeared into the washroom. They put the potatoes on to roast and took the calf from the spit to the kitchen bench. Maria carved it with precision and speed.

The lunch was a blur. The men came to the house, having washed to remove the Hairy Mary from their skin and changed their clothes. The table was set in the main room. One minute the food was there, the next it was gone. They drank wine, tea, water. They talked. And another sweet cake Maria had made vanished. And then the men were gone, to the barracks to sleep until the day cooled. When they were leaving, Italo came to thank her and asked how they were getting on. She had no words, just that she'd see them in the field for afternoon tea.

The women had no siesta. Meggsy cleared the table to the washhouse. Amelia and Maria cleaned the pots and all the other parts of the kitchen. By three, she heard the men's voices at the barracks. They took tea and the remainder of the morning cake to the field, an even greater swathe of the cane now cut.

After this, Maria and Meggsy left but would return in the morning. Amelia started the evening meal. But while she mixed damper, she thought of Fergus. Her first impression had been he was withdrawn merely due to their lack of a shared language. She placed the damper in the oven pot and then in the coals. She turned the rest of the morning's meat to an evening stew. But the more she heard of Fergus, she could see he'd suffered in a way perhaps people didn't understand. She owed him her life.

Once the damper was cooked, she made a parcel of food: some meat and damper and a piece of the morning's cake. She wrapped it in brown paper and string. She left through the breezeway and found the path that rose steeply and then flat along the ridge. When the hut hadn't appeared after some time, she thought she'd lost her way or had dreamt the hut. And then she saw it ahead, the single grey square in the clearing.

'Fergus?'

She waited but could hear nothing save the wind moving through the trees. She called again, edged closer to the door and knocked. When there was no response she looked around for somewhere to leave the food. But he might not be back for some time, and the birds or a kangaroo may come and take it. She pushed on the door, which opened, without any latch.

'Hello?'

It began to rain, the drops penetrating her clothes, heavy and large and warm. She pushed the door. There was no-one inside. She looked back to the clearing. No-one was coming, traipsing through the rain. She stepped into the hut, walked the few paces to the table and placed the food package on it. She looked for some paper and a pencil, thinking she should leave a note to explain where it had come from. There was a calendar on the wall, a single sheet of paper, the months printed in a grid. 1914. Six years ago. On the bench below, neatly stacked, were as many as thirty tins of Capstan Tobacco. She picked one up. It was empty. She replaced it to the order. The bed was made, the blanket drawn tight across the metal frame, the white sheet a starched collar. A folded shirt lay on the pillow. He slept in this shirt. Water dripped from her hair to the fabric.

Tacked to the wall was a photograph. She rose on her toes to it. Three men were seated on a mule, the animal controlled by a man with dark skin, dressed in a tight white cap with no peak and a long white shirt, like she'd seen on the young boys along the Suez Canal. In the background were canvas tents. They stood on sand. The men wore wide-brimmed hats, but the brim pulled up on one side. One man, at the rear of the beast, made as if he were falling, a large smile on his face. She looked closer. It was Fergus, as she'd never seen him, smiling and happy, overflowing with foolishness. All three were just young boys, not really men at all. But he was as Maria had described him, delight high in his eye.

A noise at the door startled her. Fergus. She coloured. She should have left straight away. Now she'd been caught prying. Fergus, his lips pulled tight, no trace of a smile, nodded.

She turned to the photograph. 'You.' She pointed to the man at the rear of the beast.

Fergus nodded. He was dressed as always, a shirt and his shorts cut to the knee, his dark green socks poking over the top of his working boots. In fact, he was almost dressed as he was in the photograph. What words did she have? She needed to walk past him, but he blocked the doorway. She looked away to the table, to the small chest of drawers, but when she glanced back at him his eyes were riveted to her.

'I must go,' she said.

And then she remembered and pointed to the parcel of food. But his dark eyes remained fixed, despite the insistence of her outstretched finger. He had no other interest or concern. She was absurd. She stepped to the door. But it would appear he read this move of escape as something else. He remained fixed and then stepped forward, met her, raised his hand to her shoulder. They stood so, connected.

Suddenly, the hut's air was laden as if about to burst. It was a matter of metres to the door, but she didn't want to leave. She leant forward, infinitesimally small. He reached to her. Their lips met. She felt his breath. It shuddered, cooling his lips. Tasted sweet. Honey. He moved, kissed her cheek, the nape of her neck, which sent shudders through her, and she twisted but he held her. He breathed out and she had to close her eyes.

Something rose, some tingling that she supposed to be her heart. Her hands hung limp. Should she meet this? She should run. But she raised one hand, stroked his hair with her open fingers, fine and soft and yet strong. He kissed her closed eyes. She shook, a noise caught in her throat, and he lifted her then, and she fell as she had in the fields, her head resting on the plates of his chest. She inhaled him. But she should rise and run from this flame. Instead she pulled at the buttons of her blouse, no shame in it at all, and in one motion he pulled his shirt free, hurling it to the hut's corner. And in such frenzy, they unfurled.

Under his great weight she twisted, writhed, murmured cries she couldn't control. She ran her hands over his back, his skin like silk. He reared from her, sitting back on his haunches between her legs. Their eyes met, his so large and dark. Where Italo was long and lithe, he was a solid, tight girth. He withdrew, slid from her, his hot mouth and tongue hungry between her thighs. His hands shook as he held her breasts. At points, the intensity was too much and she begged him to stop. But he couldn't understand her. And she had no words for this in English, this pounding rise of pleasure. And she thanked him for that. And then begged him not to stop.

And he: a week ago he'd slumped against a pole in Brisbane, half lifeless. Now he grew to greater strength, pressed to her. And his hands, rough as they were, slid tender down her hip, tender on her thigh, tender prising apart her lips. Fire rose and fell to the waves of pleasure, his voice caught between groan and whimper, in time with his hips, in time with her rise. This was this call, this call of Eden. She couldn't fall. Her hands clutched about his free ribs. Surely, his was the hand of God.

Fergus slept on his side, facing her, his lips slightly apart. She brushed his hair from his brow. What colour? What words to describe it? The skin on his chest, on his loins and large thighs was so white, gleaming, no hint of pink, the blue veins visible on his thigh, the rivers that they were. The fingers and palm of his right hand were stained with tobacco. His chest was hairless, as were his thighs. His forearms were tanned, browned and angry, but nowhere near as dark as Italo's, the light hairs sun-bleached almost clear. His Irish heritage. This skin was too white, not made for this country.

He opened his eyes as if he too had forgotten where he was. But then his eyes softened and ripened. He liked this moment too. She closed her eyes, to hold this, because this moment was all this could be. His breath caressed her cheek. She opened her eyes and he was still there. She looked to the window. The afternoon had turned the corner towards evening. Italo and the gang would soon be back at the house. She rose from the bed. Naked, she found her clothes. He watched her, didn't lower his eyes from her, eyes that scorched. She dressed as quickly as able and walked to the bed and sat near him. She took his hand. They stayed so.

'Goodbye,' she said.

He raised himself and kissed her lips. His tasted of honey, yet again, although none had been eaten. Her desire flared, but before it took hold she stood, her hand still to his.

'Come again,' he said. 'Tomorrow.'

Could he mean this?

'No,' she said, one of the few words they had in common.

She pulled her hand from his, turned and walked the steps to the door. She must go back to her life. Her new life. There was too much risk in this. This was a dalliance, wrong. She closed the door without looking back and made her way along the ridge. Unseen beasts thrashed in the forest – feet drummed the earth, wings beat the air, mingled cries of distress and sadness and joy. Her pace heated. She whisked across the open field. It was only five-thirty – still time to gather the evening meal.

How could she live with such intensity? How could she now live without it? Such pleasure existed. The thought caused her to skip three steps. How could this be borne?

What had she done?

No-one could know.

CHAPTER TEN

In the evening she easily avoided Italo, working in the kitchen to prepare for the following day while he too prepared. And she worked to keep her thoughts free of Fergus, but they returned and lingered – his fiery tongue, such strong sensations. And then she chastised herself. What she'd done was a sin. How could she have let herself be seduced? But that was unfair to Fergus. She'd urged it on. Should she visit a priest? The local one was Irish and spoke no Italian, and she couldn't express what she'd done in English. So that was hopeless. But she needed penitence.

It was after eleven when she went to bed. Thankfully, Italo was exhausted and had fallen asleep. She made certain not to wake him, but she lay awake. This shouldn't have happened. What if she became pregnant? She couldn't ask the Madonna not to let this seed grow. How long till she'd bleed? She reckoned the dates. It would be soon.

In her half sleep, she remembered Emma's smile, the morning after she'd first met Raffaelo Mancuso in the forest. They were at the village well. Emma wouldn't allow her smile to beam; it remained muted, her lips held tight.

'What's the matter with you?' Amelia said.

Emma raised her eyes and the edges of her lips. Other women waited for the water. Emma shook her head and said, 'Later'. But Amelia understood what had happened, at least to the extent of the little she knew of such matters. Once they'd filled their buckets, shouldered the poles, they moved away from the well.

'It was like nothing on earth,' Emma said.

Amelia couldn't believe the things Emma recounted. That her whole body tingled just at the touch of his lips. That they'd taken off all their clothes. That he'd said she was the most beautiful thing in the world.

'Then he must love you,' Amelia said.

'There is no question of that.'

'And do you love him?'

Emma smiled her usual smile. 'There's no question of that.'

Amelia felt envious that Emma should feel such a thing. But it was sinful, what they'd done. Yet how could joy be wrong?

'If you love one another,' Amelia said, 'there can be no harm in it.'

Emma Veronesi had been so young. Amelia was older and a married woman. But she understood the joy Raffaelo Mancuso had placed in Emma.

At the first hint of the day, she rose before Italo. In the cramped kitchen she made coffee, began to heat the vat of oats. Italo came to the doorway, dark rings under his eyes, his body slumped from lack of energy, and she wondered how he'd last another ten days. But she'd had no sleep at all and wondered how she'd make it through that day. They both knew what had to be done. Without speaking, they sat together on the verandah. In the morning light, the fields were a patchwork – not unlike Maria's bed quilt – blackened in part, some cut to the ground, some with white, ferny heads still waiting. And in truth, she appreciated the silence more than he could ever know and had no desire to challenge it. She had to forget what she'd done with Fergus. That was her intention, her only path. If not spoken of, it would recede into the past.

Should she speak with Maria? No. She hardly knew her, and this was too much to speak of. No. She wouldn't approve. And if Maria knew, she'd feel implicated if she didn't tell Italo. Amelia had no desire for that. And there was enough to do. But she needed to speak with someone.

Once breakfast was done, the men went to the field, already scented with sweat and liniment. She and Maria and Meggsy began like madwomen. Never had she seen so much food eaten so often by so few. The women cut, stirred, swirled, baked and set. She was pleased to be busy; it took her mind away, in pieces, from Fergus.

'I'd give my right arm for a stove,' Amelia said.

Maria looked at her. Did she look as bedraggled as Maria? Maria looked shocked too, as if she'd looked in a mirror. They stayed so for some seconds and then began to laugh.

Meggsy came into the kitchen in some distress and said something.

'We've run out of wood,' Maria said.

Maria and Amelia looked at Meggsy and laughed again, which left Meggsy looking confused.

'It's true,' Maria said. 'We forgot to have extra wood split.'

Italo laughed when Amelia told him, when they took the morning tea to the men in the field.

'If that's the worst of it,' he said, 'you've done well. I'll send Ben to find Fergus. He can split the rest of the woodpile this afternoon.'

'No,' she said. The word was instinctive. Perhaps abrupt. 'I can split some.'

'You've enough to do.'

'I did some this morning.' It was a lie. 'I can do more each day.'

The men started back to the field. Italo walked a few paces and then waved his hand to acquiesce to her wishes.

If Fergus came near the house there was no telling what he might say. What he might do. She should never have gone to the hut. She knew that now. But now she knew what it was she'd gone for. Before it had been some feeling, some instinct, below her level of detection. The worst of it was she'd no idea what she'd do if she saw him. Once she'd returned to the house she closed the bedroom door, knelt at the side of the bed and prayed to the Madonna for guidance, forgiveness and penitence. She said ten Hail Marys but soon realised there was too much work to be done for this.

If only she could see Clara; she would understand and have some salving words. She could write to her. No. It was far too dangerous to put this on paper. No. Should she confess it to Italo? From what she'd seen of him, he was a good man. What would he think of this? What would he think of her? What would he do to Fergus? And he was too busy and stressed with the harvest to deal with anything more.

She had to endure this – no-one to share her burden. She must carry the weight. This was her penance. She knew neither man. She'd chosen between them before she'd met either. But as dangerous as it was, she must see Fergus, impress on him to never speak of this with anyone. It was a mistake. He would see that. But she couldn't risk seeing him. Even the simplest thought of him, as she prepared the lunch for the men, and that same heat, that flame, ran to her face, across her body.

The bone-grinding toil of each day blurred into the next. Every second evening the men would burn more fields, and she would stay in the house. Each day the men came from the field for lunch. While they ate, she boiled water and made pots of tea that she took to the table. But six days into the cutting, Italo stood away from the men, looking out at the field.

'We're running behind,' he said.

'How can that be?' she said. 'You can't work any harder.'

'Each year the mill puts more pressure, tighter and tighter, shorter amounts of time to get the cane to the mill.'

'Can't you stop and then cut it later?' Amelia asked.

'We'd never get the men. They're booked for the whole season.'

'Then cut it at the rate you can and store it until the mill can crush it.'

'It will rot.' He looked out at the field. 'We need more men.'

'Then employ them.'

'They work in other gangs. And the more men we have, the more we have to pay.'

'Why don't you ask ...'

She stopped herself. How could she think to suggest Fergus?

Italo looked at her. 'Who?'

'Me.'

He smiled, placed his hand on her shoulder. 'It's very hard work.'

'I'm strong.'

'You have work here, in the house.'

She thought. 'I can organise the meals in the early morning, some in the evening. Maria and Meggsy could take over.'

The other men began to laugh. She hadn't realised they'd been listening.

'Of course,' she said. 'Everything I do is so bloody easy.'

She left the verandah with haste, but Italo followed her to the kitchen.

'Even in Australia a woman has a place and she should stick to it,' she said.

Meggsy scuttled from the kitchen.

'I did harvest my father's apples,' she said.

'I've no doubt. But apples are light.' He ran his hand over his forehead. 'Would you be able to bundle the canes together, get them on the transports?'

'I don't see why not. Each cane is light.'

Italo considered the suggestion.

'And the best thing of all,' she said. 'You won't have to pay me.'

She caught Italo's eye.

'All right,' he said. 'But you'll have to wear something else.'

He found some work clothes, his pants and a shirt. His waist was bigger, so she tied them with a belt. The work would be sweaty – she pulled her hair high, away from her neck and face, and secured it under a large hat. She went to the kitchen.

'You look the part,' Maria said, but her tone was curt.

'Don't worry, I'll prepare things here in the evening and the morning.'

'I'll wager you'll be too tired to lift a finger, but anyway, we'll get by.'

Amelia turned to leave. 'Leave me a list of what you want done.'

She walked with Italo to the field. The men jeered but good-naturedly, and she took a deep bow. In these clothes, a curtsy seemed inappropriate. The small engine and tray were brought as close as possible to the field on portable tracks.

The men waded into the field, drew their odd-shaped knives from the backs of their trousers, stooped to grab the cane with one hand and sliced at the base. Such was the sharpness of the blade, the strength and skill of the men, within two or three cuts the cane came away. With some poetry, they straightened their backs, swung the cane in the air, their blades countering through the air to remove any remaining tops, the stripped cane falling to the ground. She watched Dante – he forced his boot under the canes, his foot at a right angle to his leg, holding and gathering as many as a dozen canes to a bunch. Once there were enough, he leant over, forced his hand and forearm under the canes, jostled them slightly to greater order, then slipped his other arm under to the lee of the first. Then in one great movement, the entire bunch, like a mere feather, ascended to his shoulder, and he stood, the middle of the bunch resting on the shoulderblade, and moved immediately towards the transport, wasting not one overburdened second, upending them onto the open tray.

'Don't lift as many,' Dante said.

She nodded, breathed deeply, raised her boot under the canes, but they wouldn't behave and gather on the instep. She slipped one arm under the canes she had, fewer than a half-dozen, and then the other, and lifted them to the air. In the moment, a memory took charge of her muscles. She was with Emma at the water well. She knew the subtle moves to balance the load on her shoulders to cart water.

'Good,' Dante said.

She stepped, staggered at first but then gained the load. But once balanced, the load lightened. With clean steps, she walked to the transport, leaning to flip the bunch over to the tray.

Dante continued. She watched him, his strength and expertise outstripping hers. But she gained fluidity with her boot and grace with the lift. Emma shared the weight. It would take her twice as long, but she would clear the canes. Once Dante was sure she knew what she was doing, he took a blade and started cutting, glad at the vital pair of extra hands.

Within a single hour, sweat stung her eyes. She hurled the canes into the air and, feeling she had no more power, gritted her teeth to find it. Her feet ached. She felt a dull pain in her lower back and belly. She'd already strained herself when she twisted, her hands blistered, despite the canvas gloves. She felt sharp cramps in her belly. These she recognised. Her period had come. She raised her eyes to the sky. A wave of relief washed over her. She couldn't be pregnant. This part of her sin would remain secret. She excused herself and returned to the house to take care of this change.

Once back in the field, she looked to the heavens; the Madonna had answered her call for penitence. And no seed grew in her. But she wouldn't show her pain, her tiredness. It burnt her anxiety. And her guilt.

Towards the end of the day, as the shadow of the western mountain stretched lazily over the plains, she stood up, arched to stretch her back. Her hands were black. She raised a cloth to wipe her face. It too was black. Black-faced Dante laughed at her. She must look like all the other men. Beyond him, over his shoulder, she saw someone move in the forest. She looked but there was no-one. She'd imagined it. But then she saw the familiar colour of Fergus's shorts. And then he stepped out from behind a tree. He stared at her. She returned his glance. And then he turned away, and in two or three steps was lost in the dense forest. How long he'd been there, she had no idea. Was he following her?

In the coming days of work, the only thing running against her was time – just never enough. Nothing was too hard, Amelia kept telling herself. In the evening, once she came in from the field, she finished the meal Maria and Meggsy had started and served the men. They complained about the successions of stews, but she knew they only joked.

'Perhaps you'd like to cook tomorrow evening,' she said to Lorenzo Nanni, who was young and still cheeky. Her comment silenced him.

She prayed to the Madonna for a deal; if she could not sleep for the next week, then, when all the work was finished, she would sleep for a week. But she'd already asked too much of her, and by eleven in the evening she was drunk with exhaustion and fell into bed.

Each morning she would rise at five and have breakfast ready for the men. She would leave with them, having only eaten quickly in between. Maria and Meggsy would prepare the morning and afternoon tea and lunch. But even then, in the field, she helped serve the men, made sure they had their share of cake or scone and a full enamelled cup of tea before she'd have her own restoration from the beverage.

And each afternoon after her work, she would see Fergus. If they were in the fields further out, he'd be in one of the windbreaks of trees in the middle of the fields. If she was working at the edge of a field, he would lurk in the rainforest, as close as he could. He remained, part of the forest, looking at her.

One afternoon she went to the skin bag of water in the shadow of the transport. Fergus stood to the lee, less than fifty metres from the men. If the men noticed him (how could they not?) they made no sign to acknowledge it. She wanted to run to him. She wanted to run from him. In such contradiction with herself, she couldn't stop her pleasure at seeing him, and smiled. He stretched out a hand, repeatedly clasped his fingers to his palm, his face imploring her to go with him. She clasped hers together, over her belly.

Her heart stopped, a body blow, a punch in the stomach, winded. Her senses flared. She shook her head, as violently as she could.

'No,' she said. 'Never.'

Before he could speak, before she could ask him to keep her secret, she turned back to the field, her mouth dryer than it had been. How easy it would be to down her work and walk to him. How joyous to ignore all the glances and the words of the men around her. But these things were stronger than her heart and held her in place. And as jubilant as it would be to touch him again, in silence she thanked the men for their presence.

On the last evening of the harvest, they cooked a special dinner. Maria mixed flour and water and eggs to pasta, rolled to even sheets by hand and cut to the long, flat ribbons of pappardelle, topped with braised salami and roasted tomatoes. But the flour wasn't the correct hard type, another thing unavailable, and the pasta wasn't quite right, but everyone ate it coated with a sauce that evoked rich memories in all. But the men brought bottles of beer and some wine, and Dante brought out the accordion and a violin, and they sang their old songs. The men raised their glasses to the women, for their cooking, but also for the hard work Amelia had done in the field. They knew of this work, and from that could judge her mettle.

And the next morning, except for the burnt and rutted fields, it was as if the harvest had never been. All the tasks were done, the carnival rolling on to the next set of fields. She had no planning, no buying, no cooking or cleaning and no canes to bundle. The men were gone from the barracks. But Italo went out to the fields. He had a few 'free' days before he and the gang would start on another farm. He had to turn what was left of the cane into the soil to rot and nourish the earth, preparing it for the next planting.

That evening, after they'd finished dinner, as was usual, Italo prepared to go and check the horses and smoke a final cigarette in the last of the day. He came to the kitchen doorway.

'Come,' he said, smiling. 'Walk with me.'

She hesitated, and he felt it.

'Leave your work,' he said. 'There's something I want to show you.'

Slowly, she lowered the towel to the bench, pulled the cord of her apron free, pulled it over her head. He reached out his hand to her. She smoothed her hands over the front of her dress and then over the loose strands of hair. Despite her profound weariness, she thrust her hand to him.

His hand was warm and roughened, like Fergus's. But she must stop this, school herself to forget this man, not allow this continual judging. They walked to the breezeway and then out to the open evening air. Italo carried his caning knife, stuck down his belt at his rear. They followed the path she'd taken towards the bush and the ridge. Italo said nothing, occasionally pulling the blade free and slashing at the scrub on the path. And she had no words, the air alive with the night sounds of waves of rattling cicadas and drumming frogs.

They went in the direction of the rainforest, where the path led off to Fergus's hut. She tightened. Where was he taking her? Had he seen Fergus looking at her in the field? She hesitated, and her hand slipped from his. Some bird retched high in the canopy, loud and intrusive. The damp, the ever-present moisture, filmed her skin and hair. She stopped and he did too, ahead of her. He looked at her.

'Where are we going?' she said.

'I want to show you something.'

'What?'

He extended his hand again. But she didn't want to take it.

'You walk ahead,' she said. 'I'll follow.'

He lowered his hand and moved slowly into the forest.

'When I first came here,' he said. 'I didn't like the forest. Compared to the forests at home ...'

She looked out into the dimming light. They were now well along the path to Fergus's hut. Would he be there? Surely, he wouldn't say anything? But she didn't want to see him. She could smell smoke. Fergus had a fire burning. Her heart began to drum. What could she do? She looked ahead, over Italo's shoulder. She couldn't yet see the hut. But they were close. She stopped walking. Should she turn back? Why had he brought her there? He knew what had happened and meant to confront them. What excuse could she offer?

'Italo,' she said, the word shrill and unguarded. The forest lulled.

He stopped, some metres ahead of her. They were in a small clearing, the earth flat but rising behind them.

'There's something I must tell you,' she said.

'Later.' He smiled. 'What do you think of it?'

She looked at him, her face knotted in pain. He raised his hand, the knife pointing at the view. Through the trees, she could see their house and the stable and the fields beyond, almost a bird's view.

'Would you like to live here?' he said.

He confused her. She looked from him to the aspect and then back at him. She bit on her tears. What was he talking about?

'We *do* live here,' she said.

He laughed and his blue eyes smiled.

'I want to build a house, here, for us. We can get access from the main road and come around the back of the hill.' He pointed in a large arc to mimic a new road. 'We'll get the breeze.'

She turned from him to the view. What a thing to wake to every morning. But it was too near Fergus.

'But it's in the forest.'

'I can clear the forest.' He walked away. 'All this land was covered only a few years ago. It's one of the reasons Kelly sold it to me. He thought it was unusable. But the first ten years I was here, I cleared acres and acres in Chillagoe to earn the money to buy this land. These people leave the stumps in the field and plant around them, which makes harvesting even harder. They can't even lay the tracks for the transports. We dynamited the massive stumps out. All that beautiful wood went to fire a smelter. But we can use it to build.'

But what about Fergus? They couldn't build near him. Was he to be evicted?

'I don't know …' she said.

He smiled, coyly lowered his eyes to the ground. 'You've brought good fortune,' he said. 'The harvest was very good.'

Colour came to her face. 'I don't know of that.'

'I can put some money aside. We can start to plan the house.'

This man. So simple. So direct. What had she done? To tell him now, at this moment, was brutal. Did everything have to be said in a marriage? How could she know?

'We've not really had a chance—' he said.

'I was pleased to help.' She lowered her eyes to the ground. 'It had a purpose.'

'Purpose?'

These feelings, even in Italian, flopped and floated and evaded expression. But Italo had been honest with her, and she should try with him.

'In Italy,' she said, 'everything I did was for someone else. All the work we did for my father, of all the money we earnt, the major part went to the feudal lord.'

'That much I remember of Italy.'

'Do you know how I met your aunts?'

He thought for some moments and then shook his head.

Surprised he didn't know, she recounted the fateful day, two years before they'd married, when she'd travelled with her brothers, Giuseppe and Aldo, to this distant village of Bovegno.

'We'd lost so much during the war,' Amelia said. 'The Austro-Hungarian army took the cow and the few chickens, the apples, really anything they wanted. Once it was over, we had to … find ways to recoup the losses. But it was impossible, when so much went to the lord. Until Aldo had an idea: we'd sell some apples away from Signore Mancuso's and his accountants' sight.'

Just hours after Aldo had conceived his plan, a Bovegno market vendor had insulted him with a stupidly low price. Could this imbecile not see quality, in contrast to his own rotting produce? How much Amelia would have liked to bypass these damn fools and heap their father's apples, six or seven shiny varieties, onto a trestle table and sell them directly to the public. The markets had eyes, willing to report to the feudal lords those stepping up from their low stature to such enterprise.

'Have you tasted the sweetness?' Amelia said.

The vendor turned to her. She could read him – how dare a woman bargain? She reached to the cane pannier strapped to her back and handed him an apple. He took it, sniffed it, and bit.

'You feel the firmness,' she said. 'And is it not ... juicy?' Amelia held his eye. She knew these words – sweetness, firmness and juicy – would work an incantation on the vendor.

At a small distance, two slight women watched her. She strengthened her performance, leant into the vendor, held his eyes while he savoured the apple, her blouse at her chest. Her brother raised his price higher than even she'd hoped. In a daze, the vendor agreed. While her brothers closed the deal, the women approached her, commended her skill and asked her name and provenance.

A week later, a letter had arrived for her father, who couldn't read; her mother read it. Italo's aunts had liked the look of this eighteen-year-old girl, doll-like as she was but still with fine proportions. She'd had the fire to argue. They had thought her a fair match for their nephew, Italo Amedeo. And there'd been no talk at all of a dowry.

Now Italo remained, his gaze intense and unflinching. Finally, he said, 'Such a flirt to know your power over a man.'

'One must cut a coat with the available cloth.'

He continued to stare. She'd revealed too much – this didn't speak well of her, that she knew so much of men; their impulses were so plainly read, though. But then he threw his head back and broke to laughter, and she joined him by smiling.

'This work with the cane,' Amelia said, 'was for you. And me.' She looked him in the eye. 'Us.'

Italo was quiet. He looked towards the view. 'Do these mountains remind you of home?'

She remained looking at him until he motioned to the view, the Bellenden Ker Range. Slowly, she turned her head. Mount Bartle Frere was the highest peak. These mountains were nowhere near as rugged. And they had no buildings, no signs of civil life. And the forest, the trees and the ferns, were nothing like those of home, growing in cold, dry air. Had he forgotten? Or did he just try to view this place as home? Did that make it more acceptable? But perhaps he was right; she did see something, maybe just the play between the flat plain and the sharp rise to the mountains. She nodded to him, slowly.

'Then you mean to stay here?' she said.

'Stay?' Some of the joy left his face. He breathed out slowly. 'What does that mean?'

'Then why build a house?'

Italo remained still. Her argument had turned too quickly.

'To hear the other men talk of going back to Italy …' she said. 'Why? They'll go back to flaunt their new money to old ways. Nothing's changed.'

'I'm pleased to hear it.'

'Here, you can build a house where and how you like. Who can build a house in Italy?'

'I might own the land,' he said. 'But I don't belong to it.'

'All those songs they sing aren't known anymore in Italy.'

'Then something has changed.'

She looked at him and he started to laugh. 'They'll still be peasants toiling for masters.'

'You don't want to go back?'

She swallowed hard and looked out at the view, breathed in the endless expanse. 'I thought I would … I don't know. I can't say. Your mother made me promise we'd return.' She turned to him. 'With children.'

'She's alone.'

'Already, I feel … free. I don't want to lose that.'

They were silent, separate, looking together to the north and the future.

'I know you don't love me,' he said. 'I can just imagine what my aunts told you.'

'They said you had blue eyes.'

'And a full head of hair, I'm sure.'

'And I can imagine what they said of me,' Amelia said.

'You don't even know me ...'

When she thought of what had happened with Fergus, she thought she didn't know herself. 'Love takes time.' She drew in her breath. 'When do we start to build?'

He smiled. He pushed a wisp of her hair behind her ear. He leant forward and kissed her, his thick moustache prickling her lips. Did her heart drum? Did her face flush with heat? She checked all these signs. She felt none. Perhaps a person only felt these things once in life, and once they were done, all other kisses were just pale reminders.

The daylight was nearly gone. They started back along the ridge, back into the forest. Italo had confused her. He wanted to return to Italy and build a large house in Australia, a contradiction. In the dark damp, she smelt smoke laced with mutton fat, Fergus's dinner.

'What was it you wanted to tell me?' he said.

'Oh ...' She blushed again. 'I forget.'

Later that evening, Italo carried her through the breezeway to the bed. Fergus's face rose in her mind, his soft, hairless thighs silk to her touch, his soft skin pearl to her eye. She conjured these memories again, more to counter this pain she'd not felt at all with Fergus. His name came to her lips, but she sucked it back and swallowed the word. Italo took this as a sign of encouragement, emboldening his efforts, forcing harder into her. No appreciable, pleasurable sensation or release came to her as Italo quaked and shuddered.

CHAPTER ELEVEN

Now the earth was bare, a new rhythm came to the farm. Italo rose each morning, and after she'd made him coffee he'd walk out to the main road to be collected by Manny Pellegrino. They were now harvesting Salvatore Lanza's property, to the north of Babinda. Amelia's days became her own. She didn't mind. It was months since she'd been alone. She wished her mother would write, and she may have, but it would take at least six weeks or more for the letter to arrive. On the verandah table, she wrote another letter home, a long study on every aspect of the harvests, from their mounds of food and her labour in the field to how, despite the exhaustion, she'd enjoyed it. She wrote of the lack of beans and good flour, and the abundance of meat and how much Australians liked mutton.

And she decided to clean the whole house, as it evidently hadn't been cleaned for a considerable time. She opened all the windows but doubted she'd ever clear the mosquito coils' odour. She dragged the dining table and chairs from the main room into the breezeway. On one side of the room, closer to the fire, Italo had a desk, covered with pieces of paper. They appeared to be invoices and payments. But they were higgledy-piggledy over the desk, no order to the dates. Those at the top appeared to be closer to the present date, those lower were older and then older still. She shuffled them to a single stack, found some string, tied them and placed them in the empty drawers and carried the table and the chairs outside.

She rolled back the rug and scrubbed the boards with a stiff, purpose-bought brush. She took the rug and hung it over the side fence and beat it with a wide plank. Once she'd returned it to the room, returned all the furniture to their stations, a thin layer of dust already covered the dining table. She sighed. She was never going to win this war. But she would fight.

And since that day in the field by the tractor, she'd not seen Fergus. In the early evening she looked for signs of him – a trail of smoke from his fire, him walking along the edge of the forest – but found none. Even in the village, she'd not seen him. Somehow, the lack of him, although it was what she'd asked for, worried her. Perhaps he'd accepted the impossibility of the situation and avoided her out of grace.

Since she'd arrived she'd intended to plant a small garden. She'd collected some seeds, and Maria and the other women gave her more. Now there was time to plant. The lightly sloped patch of soil to the west of the breezeway had all-day sun. Italo had some free time and built a wire-mesh fence to keep out the kangaroos and possums and bandicoots and hosts of other animals she had no names for. She turned the sods and dug some of the cow manure into the soil.

She planted pumpkin, cabbage, beetroot, carrots, potatoes, rhubarb and silverbeet. In a corner, she'd try a bay tree, thyme and basil. With the rain and the humidity and heat, she had no idea what would grow and what would perish, but trial and error would soon educate her.

And on the other side of the breezeway, part shaded by the house, Italo built an enclosure for the two chickens Maria had promised.

'Do the chickens need to be hemmed in?' she said to Italo. 'Are there foxes?'

'I don't think so, but a snake can eat a chicken whole.'

He opened his mouth wide and flicked his tongue. She winced. He started to laugh and she threw a sod at him. But she'd keep the chickens in their pen.

And Italo proved a patient teacher as she kangarooed the truck along the paths between the fields. But she proved herself a willing student, and within weeks could drive the truck into the village with Maria. And the Italian women at church talked of the coming wet season ('Just you wait for that') when already it rained nearly every day, and not just a shower but long, heavy falls. The next major task in the new year was to plant the new season's cane. Italo had stored lengths of cane to cut to small sections, setts, which they buried in the earth to sprout. At first she thought he was making a fool of her by saying you could grow new cane from this without seed, but Maria confirmed this method.

And slowly over these months the bits of this new language, bits gathered from any book she could borrow, came together, from the daily *Cairns Post* newspaper and the *Queenslander* magazine, a weekly summary of the *Brisbane Courier*, or gathered ad hoc on the street. She fluttered across the pages of her mother's dictionary. Always there was another word. Often there was another meaning for a word she knew. Often a single sound was written in different ways with different meanings – rain, rein, reign. And then there were sayings, like 'beyond the pale', and it would take her weeks to find someone to explain that pale was a social boundary, not just a colour. English was designed to keep the migrant out.

But after three months, she and Maria could pass the whole day in English. Sure, she stumbled and often fell, and often took three attempts just to get the subject and verb to agree, but she was managing, always jumping back and forth between the two. Yet speaking with Maria was one thing; her accent was familiar, and she spoke slowly and, Amelia suspected, used words Amelia knew. Each Sunday, Amelia would sit through the church service and could only understand the Latin. She still hadn't taken confession. And so her sin rested in her.

Despite Italo's constant affections, there was no sign of pregnancy. Part of her felt dismayed, but a greater part felt relief; as much as she wanted a child, she had so many new things to deal with. There would be time. The children were in the future.

And she wrote back to Clara and Paolo and Cristiano, who, from their cheery letters, were all doing well in Brisbane. Clara had found work as a seamstress in a small factory, which meant they had a little more money and hoped to move from the hostel. Amelia urged them to come to Babinda as soon as they could, for Christmas, even. She received a reply. Clara too hated the heat and humidity, far worse than Bologna's. Cristiano would start school in the new year but was finding life hard without English, although at times she felt he'd picked up more than her. And they'd moved from the hostel to a small, run-down house they rented in New Farm, a suburb of Brisbane. She doubted they could afford the travel and the time off work to come to Babinda, but it was a lovely idea.

The remnants of the year pushed forward to Christmas. She'd always loved Christmas evening, when her mother had prepared special foods. But what could she buy here? She would try to save some money, but without aunts and uncles and family, and with the heat, the holiday seemed broken.

And in Babinda she would shop on her own. The shop-keepers, busy with their day, would grow impatient as she pointed to items she wanted, and her confusion stripped all her courtesy away to craggy nouns. One afternoon she left a shop particularly downhearted. With the keeper's frustration, every word and phrase she'd polished became dulled and fell from her. And he'd snarled at her. No disguising that. He was busy, but his anger made her lunge at English worse.

Outside the Babinda State Hotel, a group of men were talking. One of the men was overly loud, and she veered to avoid them. But as she passed, the group went quiet. She could feel their eyes. At first she quickened her step but then realised this only showed her fear and slowed it. She heard some words – nice, pretty; one of them even badly pronounced *bella* – but she kept walking.

'Do you know why Italy's shaped like a boot?' yelled one of the men, the older one, who stood apart from the mob.

She turned but realised the question hadn't been directed at her. But in a way, she knew it had. Now the men all looked at this man. His red eyes glared at her. Every part of her said to leave. But she wanted the answer.

'Because they couldn't fit that much shit in a shoe.'

The men laughed. The one who'd told the joke staggered slightly, and she guessed he was drunk. But then the men realised she'd stopped and was looking at them. Some of them returned her gaze, their expressions blank and fixed, and then turned away with what she hoped was embarrassment. Other Italian men, who must have heard what he'd said, just continued to walk, offering no reaction at all, as if he'd just said it would rain. But the man, a tall, strong man in his late fifties, met her eye.

Many retorts came to her: Why is Australia the shape of a cowpat? Didn't he know of the Roman Empire? The Renaissance? She looked the man in his burning eyes. She mustered all the defiance she could find.

'And a boot is better to kick with than a shoe,' she said.

The men were silent. A woman had spoken. Then they erupted in laughter, huge bolts. Although her heart beat fast and she could only draw breath to the top of her lungs, she kept the eyes of the man who'd spoken, not looking away. And then she realised all these thoughts had come to her in English, and she hadn't moved back and forth and back and forth. It didn't matter what this man did. She'd won. She thought in English.

Slowly, his expression changed from sneering joy to concern. She nodded to him and walked away, into Mellick's Draper and Mercer. Once clear of his view, she collapsed into a seat.

Maria came to her. 'Who's that man?' Amelia said. 'The tall one. Standing at the front.'

Maria looked at the group. 'That's your neighbour, Oisin Kelly.'

Amelia held her breath. Not only was he her neighbour, this man thought he'd swindle Italo with bad land at a high price. And he was Fergus's father.

She told her what had happened, and Maria was unsurprised.

'Why didn't the Italian men say something?' Amelia said.

Maria laughed slightly. 'Most speak English poorly. I doubt they understood.'

Amelia pulled back. She'd just assumed they spoke and understood English. 'How well does Italo speak?'

Maria scrunched her mouth and her shoulders. 'He's okay …'

But still, these men had no right to assume they were better than the newer immigrants. Oisin was born in Ireland and came to Australia with his parents after the Potato Famine. How was his circumstance different to theirs, except by a handful of years? Where was this superiority or this entitlement seated? What made him a kind of lord of the land?

So it all poured out that evening to Italo.

'How can he run a successful business being drunk in the street in the middle of the day?' she said.

'I'm not so sure he does.'

'How much more successful are we?'

'What do you mean?'

'If they're so resentful, we must be earning more money.' Was it wrong for a wife to ask such questions? 'How much did the last harvest earn?'

Italo looked away. 'I've not really done the accounts yet, but enough ...'

Amelia felt herself heat. How could he run a business without knowing? Her mother did her father's accounts; they had no choice but to try to stay ahead of the landlord's accountants. Amelia went to the desk, opened the drawer and took out the pile of papers.

'Then I'll do them,' she said.

'You don't have time for that.'

'I'll make it.'

'But you don't know how to do them.'

She thought for some seconds. Her mother had never shown her. 'How hard can it be? We either earn money or pay money.'

'It's a bit more than that ...'

A voice, a man, yelled out 'hello' from the verandah. Italo looked at her and she followed him. Oisin Kelly stood framed by the flywire door. She stopped, still in the dark confines of the hall. She felt her heartbeat, her skin prickle. What the hell was he doing there? Had he come to tell Italo she'd spoken against him?

'I'm sorry to disturb you,' Oisin said.

If he recognised her, he made no sign of it.

'Come,' Italo said, motioning with his hand to enter.

'I'm just wondering if you've seen Fergus?'

'Fergus?' Italo said.

Amelia tightened.

'We've not seen him. Over a month,' Oisin said. 'Probably closer to two.'

'I no see him,' Italo said. 'Some time.'

Italo turned to Amelia and asked her in Italian if she'd seen Fergus.

'I've not seen him,' she said, in English. She wouldn't be less in this man's eyes.

'Do you mind if I go to the hut? Have a look around?'

'No,' Italo said.

Neither man spoke.

'I come with you,' Italo added.

'I'll find my way.'

'*Certo*,' Italo said. 'As you like.'

With that, Oisin turned and left the verandah. They watched him stride along the ridge of the hill in the direction of the hut and then returned to the main room. Italo went to the invoices.

'Where would he be?' she said.

Italo looked from the pile of invoices. 'Who?'

'Fergus.'

'He's taken off. He does it all the time. His mind's a mess.'

In the morning, after Italo had left for the day, she walked to the hut. From the fringe of the clearing, she called out Fergus's name. There was no response, save the calls of the birds and the wind moving through the forest. She edged closer. The coals of his fire, a circle of stones on the ground, were covered in leaves and twigs. The fire hadn't been struck for some time. She knocked, which caused the door to open slightly and then close. She pushed it, just a notch, and said his name again and again. When there was no sound, no response, she pushed the door further.

The room was darker than she remembered, the curtains pulled over the window. The small table was cleared. She ran her finger over it, dusty, untouched for some time. She pulled back a hessian curtain that cordoned off a small corner storage area. None of his clothes, not that he ever appeared to have many, hung there. He'd disappeared.

She suddenly felt chilled and implicated, even attacked. What part did she have in this disappearance? Was he safe? She allowed the curtain to fall and turned towards the bed, the blanket pulled tight. But his nightshirt wasn't on the pillow, as it had been the first time she'd come to the hut. She remembered the passion they'd shared. But the bed held nothing, mute folds of fabric.

A small book lay on the bedside table. It hadn't been there before. *The Poetry of William Shakespeare*. With all care, so as not to disturb the bed, she lay on her side, rest her head on the pillow, crisp and clean. She breathed in, searched for his scent but could find little trace of it, echoes at most. This was foolish. What did she want? Something material, some mark or stain or hair, some element of proof of his existence. But these were remote, flushed, brushed from the room. He'd not left on a whim. His leaving was calculated and planned.

She scanned the room. His calendar, jammed on 1914, was still pinned to the wall. Still the neat stack of empty Capstan tins, silent, waited for a new task. To the side of the bed hung the photograph of him in Egypt on the back of a mule. She wanted that moment, the slice of time where he was smiling and happy despite the torment the war would bring. What did this mean that he'd left these things? That he'd return? She raised herself from the bed. With one hand she held the edge of the photograph, with the other pulled the pin from the wall. The joy on his face reminded her of the heights of Emma's joy. She had no photograph of Emma. But this was her happiness. She stole the photograph, these organised shadows and light of him, these mere marks on paper. She hurried back to the safety of Italo's house and pressed the photograph into the folds of her dictionary.

CHAPTER TWELVE

Her silk blouse lay heaped at the bottom of the wardrobe. She grabbed it, but as she raised it the fabric flowed through her fingers like granulated sugar, the remnants falling to the floor. She looked up at the hanger – the shoulders and collar still hung, pressed and buttoned, the cleave across the chest ragged and torn, the long, disembodied sleeves unable to raise a protest.

Had Italo done something to it? Some mistake? No. He never opened this wardrobe. The mauve fabric had dark spots, like ink had been flung at it. She smelt her fingers. Mildew. The humidity had soured the silk.

She sat on the bed. She couldn't stop herself and started to sob. She'd only been here ... How long was it now? A little less than four months. The shirt had cost considerable money and was a gift from her mother, and she'd never even worn it. She couldn't stop the weeping. Had she been reckless, not cared for the shirt? But she couldn't have known this would happen. These fine threads connected her to her mother and to home, and now they were gone. And she had no clothes with any hint of refinement.

She raised a hand to her mouth, drew and held her breath. This was irrational. The blouse was Italian. She'd left Italy. Babinda, with all its heat and humidity, had eaten it. Babinda was her home. She should stop her crying.

That afternoon she drove to the village and at the draper bought enough plain white cotton to make herself and Italo new shirts. She went to the butcher, the general store and then the post office to mail three letters and retrieve their mail, which included the first letter from her mother. She opened it there, quickly read it, filled to overflowing with small news of her brothers, her father, and everyone else in the village who had done something that had come to her mother's ear. They were all well; they missed her; the economy was worse. There was no real news, nothing of her mother's feelings. All she needed was to see her mother's hand. But most importantly, the letter contained seeds, three cranberry-swirled borlotti beans. How precious. Not enough for a crop, but enough to grow the seeds for a crop. Once she was home, with great happiness she pressed them into this foreign earth.

She spent the next day making patterns from an old shirt of hers, and one from the shirt Italo had worn to their celebration. She cut the cotton fabric, stitching the sections together, both a plain design, no artifice save an embroidery of two, small-crossed sugarcanes at the outer edges of the sleeves. She hung hers in the wardrobe, dusted out the remains of the silk. She folded Italo's, placed it in a drawer. Christmas was only a few weeks away. She'd keep the shirt a secret for a present.

The new shirt brought a lightness, marking the end of her journey. She was no longer at sea. She'd found her home, her purpose, her place. With this spirit, she prepared the evening meal. She told Italo of the silk shirt, of what she thought it meant. He didn't seem prone to see it as symbolic, but he smiled and laughed at her story.

'I forgot,' she said. 'There's a letter for you, from Melbourne.'

Italo picked up the letter. 'Who do I know in Melbourne?'

She turned to him, shrugged her shoulders. She picked up the dinner plates and took them to the kitchen. When she returned to the main room, the letter lay on the table, still unopened. Italo had left. She cleared the rest of the table.

'Aren't you going to open it?' she said when he returned.

'What?'

'The letter.'

'Oh ... maybe later.'

'Italo ...'

It was only then it occurred to her. When she'd arrived, there wasn't a single book in the house. The only ones were those she'd bought or borrowed from Maria. And he never looked at the newspapers she bought. She'd never seen him read. But how could she ask such a question?

'Would you like me to open it?' she said.

He looked at her. 'If you like.'

She put the plates on the table, brushed her hands across her apron and took the letter.

'It's from Angelo Rada.'

Italo looked at her. 'Angelo Rada ...' He repeated it again. And then his face opened with happiness. 'Angelo ... I've not heard of him since I left Italy.' He came to look at the letter. 'And the letter is from Melbourne?'

She checked the return address and the stamp and nodded.

'What does it say?'

She opened the envelope and unfolded a single page. The writing was sparse, the hand rigid and slow, childish. To herself, she read the letter.

'Your mother gave him your address. He's arrived in Melbourne and he's having trouble finding work and wants to know if you'd go and see him in Melbourne.'

'In Melbourne?'

'He says he's in some trouble with the law.'

'The law? What kind of trouble?'

She read over that paragraph again. 'He doesn't really say. He just asks you to come.' She read the whole letter again. 'Melbourne is a long way.'

'It is.'

Italo retreated to his thoughts but then prepared to leave on his nightly walk.

She breathed in. 'You didn't write your letters to me, did you?'

'Of course I did.' He met her glance and then turned away. 'I would say them to Dante, and he'd write.'

She felt a wave of embarrassment. Dante knew every intimate hope, every desire, every grievance. Dante knew the moves of their courtship. He'd penned those two special letters in which Italo asked and she agreed. And then an even worse thought flicked into her mind.

'How do you know he wrote what you said?'

'Of course he did.'

'How do you know he read what I wrote?'

He raised his hand and dismissed her, opening the door and leaving. She stood still as the ramifications rained down on her. Signora Pina would have known Italo couldn't read or write and would have known the letters were written by someone else. Was she still laughing at foolish Amelia? No wonder the farm's accounts were in such a mess. Nothing had ever been done. But the worst, the most awful thought, was that Dante had tailored Italo's words, sculpted whatever he'd said into writing. The beautiful lilt of his language, this thing that had exerted such an effect on her, wasn't his at all.

Had Dante won her heart? Or at the least cajoled her consent to this life? She'd fallen in love with someone else. Not Italo at all. And how would she ever be able to face Dante again, knowing now what she knew? This was unbearable. She felt brittle. And Maria knew. She was involved in the deception.

Having fed the horses, Italo came back to the room.

'I will go to Melbourne,' he said.

'What?'

'It sounds urgent. There's not much work now. In the next week or so, I suppose.'

'It's nearly Christmas,' Amelia said.

'It would cost a lot for the two of us to go—'

'I'll be left on my own.'

'Someone has to stay to look after the farm.'

Her face flushed, not just with anger but with disappointment. She'd been planning Christmas. She'd made him a present. But she wouldn't fight. She wouldn't give him that satisfaction.

'Angelo has only just arrived,' Italo said. 'You know what that's like.'

'It's our first Christmas.'

'If it's as urgent as you say it is, I must go. He must be in trouble.'

For days, she seethed. She couldn't look at him. She couldn't speak to him and kept her words to the most basic. At night when he touched her, she shrugged her shoulder from him, told him she was still bleeding though it had finished two days ago. At least he had the grace not to press himself to her. How could he choose to spend Christmas with someone else? For days she entertained the idea that she too would leave the farm and go to Clara in Brisbane. But he pointed out again they couldn't both be away, as someone must tend the farm. She ground her teeth to stifle her anger.

CHAPTER THIRTEEN

With Italo gone, despite his insistence on her needing to mind the farm, her days were her own. She still rose before dawn and made coffee. She waged her war, dusting the tables with an old shirt, sweeping the hall, the breezeway, the verandah and all the rooms. She had no need to go to Babinda for supplies, as without Italo there was little need of food. And her garden had started to produce, thinning the first baby carrots, as sweet as sugar, and the first lettuce, and she lifted some small potatoes from the rich earth. One of the borlotti beans grew, a coiling vine she trellised on an improvised system of poles. After all these weeks there was no sign of the other two. But one plant was all she needed. Already it had flowered. Next year she'd have more seed.

She avoided Maria and Dante, unsure what she would say to them of her embarrassment, anger and sorrow. Ben came and went, noticed only by the jug of fresh milk left in the kitchen, the distant cows' lowing and their cold pats along the trails, which she dug into the vegetable patch. But the lack of another soul gave an expanse of free time. She read and wrote letters, but they took so long to be answered that all semblance of conversation was lost. She worked on the farm's accounts, devising her own system of simple debits and credits, well aware it wasn't completely accurate. She needed help. But who was she to ask? In the *Cairns Post* she saw an advertisement for an accountant. She'd contact them in the new year.

And wells of disappointment opened when she least expected them. How could Italo have left? Was it true he'd always do whatever he wanted without thinking how that affected her, or anyone else, for that matter? Except for the men he worked with: he would never fail them in whatever work had to be done. She couldn't say Signora Pina hadn't warned her. Clara and Maria were wrong. Answering this call to responsibility didn't mark Italo as a responsible man if he didn't answer hers.

To keep these thoughts at bay, she made herself busy. At the back of the vegetable patch, higher on the hill, she planted a mandarin, an orange, a lemon and a papaya, hoping they would like the humidity.

When Italo had been gone three full days, when she looked out across the fields, she thought the seasons had little effect on the vista. Unlike at home, where in a year leaves came and went, the rainforest retained the same blend of greens. Only the canes were gone, the green and tan and white waving heads replaced by the rich red earth. Did these English words she'd acquired do any better job of describing it? She looked closely at the verge of the field and the rainforest. How do you describe such a border? In many ways, the verge was unnatural, as just a few years ago the thick forest heaved (the word seemed apt) over the plain. Italo had cleared the 'unusable' land. No doubt his success was yet another source of envy and suspicion from the British Australians.

Something moved. She looked closer. Someone walked out of the forest. It was a man wearing khaki shorts, a billowing white shirt and curious slouch hat, the brim raised on one side. She walked to the verandah rail. Fergus. He'd seen her, she was sure, but he walked uninterrupted, almost marching, his step showing no ripple of the excitement she felt. She remained at the rail, her heart and interest piqued. Thank God he was all right. No harm had come to him. He marched on, straight across the furrows of the fallow fields.

He was on the rise now, the small hill past the stables, on the path to her steps. A cigarette burned in his hand. She remained fixed, stolid, but then a smile bloomed across her face. He stopped at the base of the steps. His slouch hat cast a shadow across his face, but his dark eyes were dulled.

'Good morning,' she said. She tried to make her voice indifferent, but she didn't know how to in English, and it tumbled out as it wanted.

He nodded.

'Where have you been?' she said.

'Clearing forests. Up north.'

He'd cleared forests, blown out the huge stumps from the earth, but for someone else. Yet neither Fergus nor his family had worked this hard to clear Italo's land before they sold it to him. The first farmers had had the choice to use the more easily cleared land. They were savvy, leaving the more difficult terrain to the gullible newcomers. She could almost imagine their snickering.

He'd lost weight, but the loss didn't disquiet him, his cheek and jaw carved sharper. She waited for him to speak, but that wasn't in his nature. Then a fear he might leave gripped her.

'Would you like some tea?'

He drew his breath and paused. 'Yes.'

She nodded and turned back into the house. The still-warm water took little to reboil. She placed cups on a tray with the teapot, some sugar and a small jug of milk. She returned with the tray, the cups rattling in their saucers. He sat at the table, said nothing as she approached and made no move to look at her as she served the tea.

'Italo is away,' she said.

Why would she say such a thing? Her mind rattled. Her hold of English loosened. She thought in Italian.

'I know,' he said, momentarily meeting her eye.

'Is that why you returned?'

He shook his head. 'You speak English now.'

'Is better, but still with problem.' She poured the tea.

He sat in silence, defiantly looking at the view. 'You took my photograph.'

'Oh …' She put down the tea and looked at him. 'I am sorrow.'

'Sorry.'

She stood, turned back to the house, carried the dictionary to him, ran through the pages until she found the photograph.

'I knew you'd taken it,' he said.

'You left it.'

He reached for the photograph. It remained held between them. Though he'd come to retrieve it, he displayed no anger she'd taken it. And she held on, not wanting to give away that thin slice of happiness. But it belonged to him. After some long moments – in which his eyes, cast to the side, wouldn't meet hers – she let it go. He pulled back his hand, placed the photograph in his breast pocket. She flinched at his uncaring, his disdain for something so precious.

'You must not tell anyone,' she said.

His face remained impassive, and she feared she'd not said what she'd set out to.

'What do you think I am?'

Her heart raced. She took this phrase back into Italian: *Cosa pensi che io sia?* He reached out his hand and covered hers. A glove of warmth. Their hands remained so until his warmth bit like a naked flame. She pulled back.

'I don't want,' she said.

A question came to his face.

'I do not feel for you that.' She looked at her lap. 'I sorry what happened. But no again.'

Slowly, he removed his hand from the table. The silence hugged them. There seemed no answer to the humidity that clung to her, pasted her clothes to her skin, took all her energy. He too was heated, a layer of sweat shining his face.

'Let me take you somewhere,' he said.

'What?'

'I want to show you a place.'

The thought of turning him away left her unnerved. In that moment, more than anything, she wanted some time with him.

'All right,' she said.

Fergus rose from the table and walked from the verandah. A few paces from the house he turned back, nothing gleeful on his face, and waved to her to follow. She stood, skipped the stairs and followed him all the way to the stable.

With great ease he chose a horse and saddled it, leading it outside. He mounted, swinging his right leg over the horse's back with grace. He lowered his hand. She hesitated, but he took her arm and pulled her from the ground as if she were a doll. She sat behind him. She placed her hands on the back of the saddle, but he took her forearm and placed it around his waist. She pulled away, but he jiggled the reins and the horse jolted, and she grabbed at his waist with both hands, the practicality of the gesture absolving the indecency, but not his warmth. He raised his buttocks from the saddle, took the horse to a canter, a practised rider.

They started towards the west, towards the early afternoon sun. The breeze felt fine on her face. But the warmth, sticky as it was, between her chest and his back felt finer. Mingled with the scent of the horse, she found Fergus's and inhaled deeply. Once they'd cleared the edge of the field they took a small path, cut between two sections of the rainforest, continuing for a good half-hour with no need to speak.

When they finally stopped, she could hear the rush of water. In one forward kick of his leg over the horse's neck, he dismounted. He reached to her, grabbed her waist and lifted her to the ground. He'd not let go, their faces within centimetres of one another, and she twisted to free herself. He took the horse and, without a word, walked off down a path. And she followed. Once clear of the forest, the water ran over large, smooth grey stones, pooling in places, small pockets worn in the rock, in which water eddied and twirled and spilled. In other places it opened to shallow beds, surging through small apertures from one higher pool to a lower.

He tethered the horse near some calm water. They sat separate and, with no words, watched the river pass, always changing and the same. The river had met its match, the stone, whatever type it was, resistant to its wearing action.

He untied his shoes, removed his socks, placed them to the side and shuffled forward to let his feet drop to the water. And after some silent while, he stood on the rock, and in one motion pulled off his shirt, folded it and placed it on the rock. And he turned his back to her and removed his shorts, folded them and placed them on his shirt. She couldn't help but look at his pearl buttocks and ridged back, the outer reaches of his four limbs stained that odd red-brown. He walked, stepped into a pool and then leant forward, his thighs doubling in size, pushing off into the water. His momentum carried him forward until he rolled onto his back.

'Come in,' he said.

'No.'

She'd not take off her clothes. There might be people. And she couldn't swim, and in places the water rushed deep. But he moved to a small pool to the side, a weak spot in the rock, a hollow, ground round and smooth. It wasn't deep – nothing more than a bath. But she wouldn't take off her clothes, not here outside, not in front of him.

The humidity coalesced, the first drops of rain on her head, the large drops warm. She was parched. She closed her eyes and leant back. These were old thoughts, old rules, old Italy. Why couldn't she be free? Why couldn't she take off her clothes? The water offered relief.

She stood, pulled her dress over her head, the under-clothes falling in an uneven pile. Naked, she walked to the shallow, round pool, the air sliding over her skin, slipping between her legs, the rock warm to her soles. The rain tingled her skin, blood-hot drops thrown from the sky, not at all like the sleeting rains of home. He stood, reached out his hand. She regarded it. There was consequence in this palm. She took it. They stepped into the shallow pool, the cool water running over her feet, around her ankles and calves. He crouched, looked at her and invited her to sink.

Any fear she'd felt was gone. Nothing could harm her with his secure hand. She lowered into the water. It nipped her buttocks. She pushed her feet out in front. The cold stung her nipples. He sat back in the water, which buffeted, whirled and swelled and fell. She laid back, the rain dancing on her face, and closed her eyes. How could she feel so unbridled? How could she express this liberation, from clothes, from anxiety, from memory, from distress, from anything? She raised her head, looked at him, his head resting on the side of the pool, his eyes closed, facing the rain. The water took him, wound round him. In the churning, he was erect. He felt as she did. She reached out a hand to his.

'I'm glad you stole the photograph,' he said.

The closing day settled on the small hut. She lay with her back to him. They were the first words spoken all evening. How could he be pleased she'd stolen something? Especially as he'd come to retrieve it.

'Why?'

He exhaled onto her nape, the air far warmer than it should be.

'It showed you care.'

How could he be so cruel? What could she say? Such a simple thing brought the past and the present and the future – the trouble – to the room. She wanted to remain suspended on that edge between great pleasure and tedium, that small instance that, if treated well, danced in the air like a soap bubble. He ran his coarse hand over her belly. She wouldn't have taken the photograph if she'd not wanted a memory. But what did he want?

She removed herself from the narrow bed. She couldn't look at him, didn't want to see that lightness returned to his eye. What was the cost to place that there? She began to dress.

'Don't go,' he said.

'I have work.' Although she had none.

'Let it wait.'

She'd not be dictated to. 'I cannot.'

'I'll come with you.'

She glanced at him. 'What if someone sees you?'

The ramification rocked between them. Was it guilt? Judgement? If the wealthy could absolve themselves of guilt, as Mancuso had done with Emma, why couldn't she? She'd tried so hard to free herself from this iniquity, wash it out, but now, when it was tested, it remained, a three-day-old fish on a platter.

'Stay a while,' he said, getting out of the bed, standing naked in front of her.

So, this was how it was to be: he knew his power and would use it as a weapon. Everything – thought, breath, tissue – wanted only to touch his pearl skin again, wanted the honest scent of his neck. But she turned her back, the strength required depleting her.

'I'll walk back with you,' he said.

'I am all right.'

'Just to the edge of the forest. No-one will see.'

She could stand this no longer, and so picked up her boots and left the hut. In the clearing, she sat on a log by the ring of fire. The tethered horse glared at her. She dusted the leaves and dirt from one bare foot and put on her sock and then her boot. She heard him move about the hut. By the time she had her second boot on, he hurried from the hut, dressed, as always, in khaki shorts and boots. When he saw her, still seated on the log, he stopped in the doorway, slouched his weight over to one hip. He said nothing, his chin down, his eyes tucked under his brow. A chastised boy. He rammed on his slouch hat, the brim turned up to the left side and pinned with a badge.

'Why do you wear it like that?' she said, motioning to the hat.

He looked at her. 'A rifle.' He made as if he held a rifle across his chest, the imagined barrel rising to the side of his head, and she could see why the hat's brim was out of the way. But she resented the hat, that it covered the light in his hair, and he was no longer a combat solider, no longer held a rifle, no longer fought in war, and yet this pin and the habit remained.

She stood. She must go. Too much had happened. He fell in behind her, taking her walk's step and rhythm. Why he thought he had to accompany her, she didn't understand. Italo could leave her alone – why couldn't he? What could she say? She'd shown how much she wanted him, and to say otherwise would be to voice an obvious lie, yet she'd voiced it. The irony was she'd known him as long as Italo but felt something far stronger towards him.

They'd come to the edge of the forest. He looked at her from under his heavy brow. Their pleasure beat, raw and brass, those moments as the water babbled in the smooth pool, his pressure on her thighs, the warm rain on her face, his exertion breathed on her neck. The milk ribbon shot between them, gyred in the water, and was gone.

She wanted that again, to see him naked. She wanted that. She walked the paces to him. She leant and pressed her lips to his, chilled and uncertain. She wanted only this. And she would take it. She pulled away. Walked away. She would count the hours until she saw him again. She would have him, again and again.

Despite the heat, she took her dinner in the main room rather than on the verandah, wanting to be hidden. There was a light knock at the door. She ran to it, unnerved and pleased by Fergus's boldness. But Ben stood in the breezeway. He had never come to the house before, not at night, not like this. He said something, his speech slurred, his mouth restrained by the tight scars on his cheek and neck. He said it again and then she understood – the horse was gone.

She stared into his grey eyes. Italo had asked Ben to care for the horses, and the one she'd ridden to Fergus's hut was still there. How stupid not to have brought it back. There was nothing she could do at this hour.

'In the morning,' she said, 'I look.'

Ben stared at her. What did he know? Had he seen her and Fergus leave on the horse? She wouldn't be scrutinised like this.

'In the morning,' she repeated.

She closed the door, leant back to secure it. There were some moments. And then she heard Ben's laboured step across the breezeway. She felt cold. So soon the outside world had cut. How damn foolish they'd been. She would go in the morning to retrieve the horse, leaving the saddle and bridle with Fergus. She'd tell Ben she found the animal in the forest. She hoped that would put an end to it.

CHAPTER FOURTEEN

What little sleep she took was fitful, dotted with dreams of Italy – Zio Franco's olive oil, so rich it set solid at the first sign of autumn, the gentle sunlight in the morning, so soft it came from a different sun to Babinda's. In one dream she spoke to Emma, the two sneaking a siesta in the far corner of the orchard. She told her all about Fergus. Then the sadness swelled, swirled around the bed, threatening to drown her.

And she dreamt of Fergus, too-vivid images, his body pressed to hers, relentlessly pressing into hers. Even in her dreams, this pleasure lived. He lived. The realisation caused fear, and, against all rational thought, she rose from the bed and searched the house for Italo, concerned he'd returned to find her dreaming of someone else. It was before the dawn, but her day had begun. She'd go and retrieve the horse. She made herself coffee, which she took to the verandah. She heard the cows lowing as they walked the ridge. Ben was about. She'd lost her opportunity to return the horse. He would see her. To her surprise, Ben came to the verandah.

'Horse is back,' he said.

She breathed out. Fergus must have brought it during the night. She was unsure what to say to Ben, how to deal with someone reporting to her. She nodded.

'But ma'am—'

'It all right.'

Ben pulled back. She'd spoken too loudly, but she had no answers to the questions he was going to ask.

Ben regarded her, then acquiesced and turned back to the cows.

Fergus had been near her as she dreamt. How close had he come to the house? Had his scent wafted on the breeze, amplified the intensity of her dreams, acted on her while she slept? Maria said he never slept. Did he roam the whole night?

But had Ben seen him return the horse? And if he had, what would he say? Would Italo mind if Fergus had borrowed the horse? Probably. The horses were his pride and joy. One thing was clear: they would have to be more discreet.

The rest of the day was exhausting, staving off or striving for the moment when the sun descended and she could go to his hut. But as she worked in the garden, she realised the danger she was in. This was folly. It had to stop. She felt a swell of sadness at the loss. But this prospect was right. She was married. Despite any anger she felt for Italo, this was unarguably wrong. She would end it.

Once it was dark, she made her way from the house along the ridge to forest. She carried no torch, walking slowly to keep on the path. Her heart raced at the cries of birds and thumps and calls from unknown animals. Fergus rose from the fire as soon as she entered the clearing.

'I thought you weren't going to come,' he said.

He walked towards her with his hands extended. He wore only his cotton undershirt and shorts. Her eyes caught on his, alive yet with a hint of doubt. She went to protest but knew she couldn't stop. At the sight of him, she was already lost.

On Christmas Eve she heard Maria's truck. She'd not seen her for many days and was thankful she was there to greet her. But perhaps Maria had come while she hadn't been there and would ask questions to which she had no easy answers.

She braved the best open smile she could muster. Maria handed her the mail.

'Would you like to come to our place this evening?' Maria said.

She panicked. She had plans with Fergus.

'That's very kind of you,' Amelia said.

'Then I'll expect you.'

'No.' Had that been too abrupt? 'I have plans.'

'Plans?' Maria stepped two or three paces forward, her face screwed slightly. 'What plans?'

'It's just silly.' She grappled. 'It's been a busy year, a lot of change. I wanted to spend it alone, write some letters. To my parents. And with Italo still away, I don't feel like company.'

Maria scrutinised her and then nodded. 'As you like.' She glared at Amelia. 'Any word from Italo?'

Amelia looked through the letters. But still, there was nothing. 'He's busy,' she said. 'Some legal issue.'

Maria nodded, said goodbye and retreated to her truck. 'If you change your mind, just come.'

Amelia smiled. Was there some pretence in what she asked? She searched Maria's face for some hint of other motivation. What could Maria know? Amelia waved. But what if she did?

For nearly three weeks, no word had come from Italo. She thought he may have got Angelo Rada to write at least a small note. But perhaps Signor Rada couldn't read or write and was dependent on others. Whilst the silence disturbed her, she part relished it. Always he had time for others, for harvests, for planting, for people in far-off cities. Fergus was attentive, generous with his time. Fergus drew something from her, something she'd never felt, not even in passing. But it was unfair to blame Italo. Italo was a good man, entirely good. How couldn't she be fond of him? But Fergus … She thought of him constantly, counted the hours, wondered why she'd left him and craved his slightest gesture.

They passed Christmas Eve together, in the small hut in the forest. Amelia took some fresh damper and a pot of stew to heat on the outdoor fire. He had a bottle of wine, made by the Italian men. When they'd finished eating, the rain stopped beating on the tin roof. They walked out into the clearing to watch the last of the sun. A rainbow, vivid red and blue and yellow and purple, arched over the fields.

'There's a pot of gold at the end of the rainbow,' he said.

She looked at him, thinking she'd misheard.

'A leprechaun hid it there,' he said, nodding his head in all seriousness.

'What's that?'

'He's a naughty little man, all manner of mischief. But if you catch him, he'll show you his pot of gold.'

She laughed.

'It's true,' he said.

'It sounds like a *mazzamuriello*.'

'It's no *mazza*, *mazza* whatever you say, it's a leprechaun.' He looked at her. 'If you don't believe me, we'll go and find him. The future will be perfect.'

She pushed him away and turned towards the hut. The future was frightening, blinding. She was ill-equipped to argue it, given it lurked in many ways in English – *I will go. I will run. I will breathe. Tomorrow, I will exist with you.*

Future tense. Tense.

My love arrives tomorrow. I'm meeting him at the station. I'm going to wear my best dress.

All these ways to refer to the future. How could she ever perceive it clearly? And how long could she push Italo from this future? How exacting such exertion was. She wouldn't have wanted to die without these days. But when she ate, the hunger disappeared, at least for some hours. Though as she walked away from the hut in the woods, she could have easily walked back and spent the rest of the night with him, just as hungry as before. And he'd proved he felt the same, his face above her, his hands softly at her throat.

And so the last days of the year were waved goodbye, waves of pleasure and angst, a year of a kind she was sure she'd never live again. She'd travelled halfway around the world, as far as possible without starting the journey home, left her home and her family and her country. She'd married, learnt a language, learnt to farm sugarcane. And she'd taken a lover. She should call it what it was – Fergus was her lover. How lurid it sounded. How frightening it was. How sensual. She knew that now.

On the last day of 1920, a Friday choked with humidity, she was to go to him in the evening. They planned nothing special. Of course, it would rain. It had rained almost every day since she arrived, and if it didn't rain the day was strung out and lethargic. That afternoon, after she'd completed the most essential chores, she left for the hut. All morning the heavens had rolled with thunder, but it had come to nothing. She had less fear in the forest. The dampness; the seeping, teeming earth; the heavy yet crisp air; the wild screeching of unknown and unseen birds – all were now tied to him, a reminder she'd be with him. He was the forest.

Fergus was lying by the fire on a tarpaulin, asleep, the fire spent. She sat the basket of food on the ground, tried not to wake him. But he woke, stood, glared at her as if he'd not expected her, all care gone from his eyes. It took her breath. With no ceremony and yet all ceremony, he walked to the hut. Her joy sank. She'd not seen him like this, the light gone from his eyes, since her first morning in the village. What was she to do?

Inside the hut, she lit a coil. He lay on the bed and, despite all prompting, would utter nothing. He refused the tin of tobacco she offered. This was one of his bad days, the veil, as Maria described it. How could she reach him? Had he realised their time must come to an end? She must make him talk. She unpacked the carrots and potatoes from her basket. She told him of the food she'd grown and how quickly it grew compared to her parents' crops, which she guessed was a result of the heat and the rain.

He said nothing.

But some of her plants had withered; the zucchini had grown, but the flowers had drooped and fallen. The humidity had rotted the buds, though the precious beans grew pods.

But he offered no opinion.

He'd pinned the photograph from Egypt to the wall.

'When was the photograph taken?' she said.

He didn't respond.

'Who are the other men?'

He looked at her and then slowly moved his eyes to the photograph.

'That was Stephen and Angus.'

Was. Even she understood the stress of that one word. She should veer from it. But perhaps it was better to face it.

'Were they from here?'

His eyes glazed, and a long while elapsed before he spoke. 'We enlisted together.'

She pressed on – 'What year?' – and waited.

'Early in the war. 1914.'

He drifted off, back into thought. It was no good. If he'd not speak, all she could do was be near him. She gathered the carrots and potatoes to wash in the trough outside.

'The army people came to Cairns,' he said. She stopped at the door. 'We went to a meeting. Every able-bodied boy. They told great stories. And made promises. Before I knew it, I'd signed up to defend the empire that gave me birth and nature.'

She sighed heavily, placed the vegetables back on the table and walked to him. 'No-one knew what happened. I remember in Italy—'

'I had no great love for the empire … There was no work. But I had to be away from Oisin. We went to Egypt, at the end of '14. We worked to protect the Suez Canal.'

She thought of the canal, how exciting it was to see it. 'Is where the photograph made?'

He nodded. 'I wouldn't have minded spending the war there, but we were sent to Gallipoli. We were in the 9th Battalion, one of the first onto the beach. I just ran and ran and ran and somehow I missed every bullet and made the dunes. But Angus was gone, and it took me two days to find Stephen's body.'

She said nothing, as no word made any difference.

'We sat in the trenches for nearly eight months. From there we were shipped back to Egypt, patched back together and then taken to France.'

Oddly, the talk of this time had drawn him from the darkness. She offered some of her story, the tale of Emma Veronesi and what she'd seen.

'Of all the things, it's the sound,' he said. 'Even thunder. The thunder scares me. I'm as brave as a cowering dog.'

She moved to him, touched his cheek and then shoulder. He had no interest in Emma, not now at least, and she didn't blame him for not listening to her story.

'You should take the photograph,' he said.

'Why?'

'You like it. I've looked at it too long.'

He looked at her, for the first time that day, in the eyes. His gaze was dull and distant. But then he blinked, and it was as if the veil lifted and he saw her. He blinked again to clear his sight, and then a small light crept into his eyes.

It was then she realised the most frightening thing of all. Fergus loved her.

CHAPTER FIFTEEN

She'd spent the whole night with him. They'd not made love but slept until early morning. At first she panicked and went to leave, but then there seemed no point hurrying. In the late morning of New Year's Day, she walked back to the house. But when she walked onto the verandah, she heard noises, further back in the house. Ben. She gathered strength to scold him, there having been no need for him to take the milk into the kitchen in her absence. He could leave it in the breezeway. It was cooler there anyway. She heard footsteps coming across the main room. She moved forward. The door opened. Italo stood in the frame. He seemed as surprised as her. Her throat constricted. She fought to suppress her surging alarm.

'Where were you?' he said.

'I ... took a walk. Up the hill. When did you return?'

'This morning.'

She breathed out. 'It's so lovely there.' She grappled for more. 'I stayed to look at the view, imagine the house.'

She walked to him and reached up to kiss him but then pulled back. Would he smell Fergus? Would he want her? The thought shot fear through her. She must discourage this. She kissed his cheek.

'Have you had coffee?' she said.

'No.' He raised his eyebrows with interest.

'Neither have I.' She screwed up her face. 'Let me brew some.'

She walked to the kitchen. He remained in the main room. She pressed her hand to her forehead, held her breath, clamped down her jaw. It had been foolish to stay the night. Had Italo returned the previous evening? Surely not. She hadn't left the house till eight, just after dark. And if he'd returned to find her not there, he would have said something, wouldn't have suppressed his anger. Would he?

He came to the doorway, raised his right hand high on the jamb and slumped his weight over to his left hip.

'I wasn't expecting you,' she said. 'What was the trouble?'

'His visa. It was easy to fix.'

And yet he'd stayed in Melbourne for over three weeks, and over the Christmas period. She'd no desire to draw this to his attention and focused on the coffee.

'We have to start planting,' he said.

She breathed out. Of course. That would be his reason to return.

'The gang will be here for a week at least.'

So, she would have to feed all those mouths. How nice to be given some warning. Having fed them once, the second time would be easier. There would be many hands and although the work was lighter, she suspected the men would be just as hungry. She'd kept the menus and shopping lists and could just rejig them.

She poured him coffee and they sat in slightly tense silence on the verandah. Fergus jostled her thoughts, every minute. It was impossible to warn him of Italo's return without some obviously contrived explanation. But he would see the activity in the fields. He would know she couldn't come. But she wanted to.

That night in bed, she dreaded Italo would want her. For some moments, he lay on his side, looking at her.

'I'm sorry I was away,' he said.

She said nothing. He closed his eyes. She braced herself for his hand to move to her. She would say she was bleeding. But he didn't move. He'd fallen asleep, which seemed odd. The Melbourne trip had exhausted him, which pleased her.

On the first day of the planting, the men arrived at first light. She served them oats and eggs and bacon and huge amounts of tea. When they'd all left, she made a cake for morning tea, which she and Maria took out to the fields. First the fields had to be ploughed, a dray horse dragging long furrows into the hundred acres, destroying the roots of the old crop. If they grew ratoons, their yield would be less than the newly planted setts. The men worked along the furrows, laying the small sections of cane in the earth. The other men worked from behind, covering the setts.

The fields took on another hue, another texture, knitted rows of plain stitch. Italo returned to the house exhausted and would fall asleep immediately, almost before his head touched the pillow, leaving her alone.

Each day the men returned for lunch. Most of them had worked for the harvest and Gaetano D'Angelo, the cheeky one, asked her for the minestrone again, though it contained no beans. She'd not planned on cooking it but promised she would. Despite all the commotion, she was lifeless, no energy, no strength. Not seeing Fergus, thinking of him constantly, missing his touch – this agitation had brought with it a malignancy. And Italo seemed to mirror her, dark semicircles under his eyes, more fatigued by the planting than by the harvest.

On the last morning, after a full week of planting, she rose early with Italo and made coffee. But she couldn't bring herself to drink it and left it sitting on the workbench. Soon it was cold and cloudy and bitter. She stoked the fire to cook the minestrone, but when she seared the onion and garlic the smell caught her, a surge of nausea. She ran outside for air. She stood but the nausea wouldn't remit. It came in waves, which became spasms. Maria saw her from the breezeway and came and laid her hand on Amelia's back.

'I don't know what's wrong with me,' Amelia said. 'I've no energy.'

'Are you tender?' Maria touched her own breasts. 'Like you're to bleed?'

Amelia straightened and looked at her. Maria smiled, and she had no idea why.

'Don't you know?' Maria said.

'What?'

'You're pregnant.'

A wave of nausea hit her. She swallowed hard, but it was too strong and she vomited onto the earth. In all her tiredness and occupation, she'd not thought of this simple thing. Maria was smiling. More heaviness and fatigue washed through her. How could this be?

'You're in shock,' Maria said. She handed her a tea towel to wipe her mouth. 'Come inside.'

Once they were in the kitchen, Maria handed her some water. She rinsed her mouth but the taste persisted.

'It must be since you last bled,' Maria said. 'Just before Italo left.'

Amelia glared at her. 'How do you know?'

'A woman notices,' Maria said. 'And with my four it was always just after I'd bled. That's the best time.'

Amelia had no mind to calculate the days. But if Maria thought it was Italo's child, she wouldn't disabuse her. Except she knew the child simply couldn't be Italo's. There had been no union. Just with Fergus.

'What a homecoming—'

Amelia grabbed Maria's forearm. 'Don't tell anyone. Not yet.'

Maria's face coiled in query. Amelia released her arm. But then Maria smiled, raised her eyebrows and nodded. She brought Amelia another glass of water, and once she'd breathed deeply, the nausea subsided. But her mind surged: What was she to do? How could she have been such a fool? What was she to say to Italo? He would know it wasn't his child. Should she tell Fergus? Should she tell Italo of Fergus? She doubted he'd understand. She didn't understand. Why should he?

This curse had come to her. How struck she'd been not to think it would.

But she knew what to do.

CHAPTER SIXTEEN

The weatherboard house in New Farm, Brisbane, stood on its own, back some four metres from the road, raised from the ground like every other building in the street. It was a Saturday, midday. There was a small front lawn, bisected to equal portions by a straight cemented path, six wooden steps leading to a verandah. Someone had recently planted a small citrus tree to one side of the path. Amelia pushed on the picket gate, but it was latched, the wood rough and dry, the flaking paint mostly peeled away. She released the catch and walked the few paces to the tree. The gate slammed behind her. She touched a leaf. It was lemon.

'Zia Amelia. Zia Amelia is here.'

The flyscreen door flew open, banged against the house wall and quivered. Cristiano hurtled down the steps, a smiled pressed over his face but a look near tears in his eyes. He grabbed her as if she were a phantom that may disappear. Amelia put down her portmanteau, wrapped her hands around Cristiano's head and pressed him to her belly. It had been almost six months since she'd seen him, and he was considerably taller.

A silhouette stood in the door, looking at her, illuminated by the light coming from the end of the dark hall.

'Good Lord,' Clara said, as nonchalantly as if they'd seen one another the day before. She opened the flyscreen but remained on the verandah. She wore her hair pulled from her face, a long white apron over her dark-blue cotton dress. Suddenly, Amelia felt calm. No harm could come to anything. Just seeing Clara took her back to the deck of the boat and the last sight of smoking Vesuvius.

Clara pressed her hand to her mouth. Her eyes were pained, filled with tears. Amelia lifted her hands from Cristiano's head and opened her arms. Clara began to walk, slow steps that gathered pace and tapped on the wooden stairs. She embraced Amelia, and Cristiano reinforced his grip around her legs.

'I'm so happy to see you,' Clara said, her voice trembling.

Clara pulled back to look at her. Amelia smiled with her lips and nodded. She *would not* cry. She'd promised herself.

'Why didn't you tell me you were coming?' She looked around. 'And where's Italo?'

Amelia looked into Clara's eyes, taut with concern. Clara embraced her again. There was so much to be said but, in that moment, nothing more needed be uttered. Then, holding hands, they walked back to the house, climbed the stairs. With both hands, Cristiano picked up her portmanteau and lugged it down the dark hall. At the back of the house in the kitchen, without words, Clara set to making them tea. She had a stove. Amelia stood in the doorway. Where was she to begin this story?

'The house is lovely,' Amelia said.

'It's run-down, but anything is better than the hostel.'

'Where's Paolo?'

'He's at work. Overtime.'

Clara ran her eyes around the room. Amelia nodded. The overtime was to pay the rent.

'I'm pregnant,' Amelia said.

Clara looked at her, surprised, and then smiled, put down the teapot and came to embrace her.

'I'm so happy.' She pulled back and looked at Amelia. 'But you're not so happy.'

Once one tear fell, ran and slipped from her cheek, she couldn't stem the flow. She started to sob. Clara led her to a small couch. She curled into a ball, her head in Clara's lap, her soft hand passing and repassing over her head. The sobs wouldn't stop. All these things had been welling and welling.

Cristiano came to her. 'Zia, why are you crying?'

He sat next to her, in the crook of her belly. Clara left them, went to collect the tea. Amelia slowly gained control, her sobs satiating the sorrow and fear and anxiety. Clara sent Cristiano from the room and then sat next to her, passed her hand over her head in soft, comforting caresses.

'I don't know where to begin,' Amelia said.

'You've written many long letters and there's been no hint of this, so I suspect you should start at the beginning. And I suspect that's when you left Brisbane.'

Amelia began to tell – out it poured – how she'd seen Fergus working half naked, how he'd cried at the wedding celebration. How his kiss made her feel like nothing she'd ever felt, that just the press and warmth and scent of his lips had made her aware of another soul. How her heart beat without restraint. How she'd made a mistake with Fergus and then tried to resist, but how Italo had gone to Melbourne and how she was disappointed with him but mostly, and most of all, she was besotted with Fergus.

'I can't resist him.' She was crying, the distress rising and falling in waves. 'I have no control. I think of him constantly. Even now I want nothing more than for him to walk into this room. And he knows that. And now this.'

For moments, Clara said nothing. 'Does Italo suspect?'

She shook her head. 'He knows something's upset me. But after he'd been away, he'd not challenge me on the expense for me coming to you.'

'But does he know you're pregnant?'

'Only a woman who lives nearby.'

'Does Fergus know?' Clara asked.

'I've not seen him since I discovered.'

Clara sighed heavily, lost in her thoughts. Amelia felt calmer just to have voiced this. In many ways, now it was real. Cristiano came into the room. He was hungry so, with conversations only of the mundane, they fed him afternoon tea and walked to a small park. Cristiano refused her offer of help on the swing.

When they returned to the house, Paolo was asleep on the couch. The room was so overheated they threw open the windows. He looked tired and very surprised to see Amelia. Over dinner, they talked of their lives, Paolo full of questions of cane farming.

'You should come,' Amelia said. 'Next harvest.' Was she so sure there would be another harvest? 'We can always use another set of hands. There's good money.'

Paolo looked at Clara, who just raised her eyebrows. 'It's not so easy,' he said.

'Cristiano's had a hard time,' Clara said. 'He refuses to speak English. This year, he'll start school.'

'I have my job,' Paolo said. 'Clara has hers. We must pay the rent. It's not so easy to get away.'

Late that evening, after they'd cleared the meal, the two were alone. It was only then Amelia saw how tired Clara looked.

'If I could split myself in two,' Clara said, 'maybe then I could get it all done and sleep.'

Clara worked at the sewing factory in the morning.

'We hardly see one another,' Clara said.

'Come to the farm. The canecutters make a lot of money.'

'I don't think Paolo is right for it.' Clara looked at the sock she was darning. 'Who do you love?'

The simplicity of the question caught her unprepared.

'I met them two days apart,' Amelia said. 'I don't know either of them. I just happen to be married to one.'

She thought of those days, travelling with Fergus, meeting Italo in the field. How disappointed she'd been. How lonely. How long ago.

'Does Italo treat you well?'

'I can't complain. He's often considerate. I like the farm. But he is as his mother suggested – selfish.'

'Then he's just a man.' Clara went back to her needle, lost in her own thoughts. 'And Fergus?'

'His smile is a spell … But as to his character … He's gentle. But people say he was badly affected by the war. And I've seen his despair. The war is one thing we share, but I don't know much else of him.'

'Except his sweetness in bed.'

Amelia reddened. Even in front of Clara, this was an embarrassing admission.

'We're imagined to feel nothing,' Clara said. 'No red-blooded desire at all. But we do.'

'How can I know who I love?'

'You're right – how can you know?' Clara remained deep in thought. 'And what does it matter?'

'I can't stay with someone I don't love.'

'The world is full of people who do.'

'But you and Paolo.'

'I hardly knew him. He just … swept me off my feet. And then I didn't see him for six years. He's different to what I remember. But what does it matter what I feel? We have a child. And another coming.'

'You're pregnant?'

Clara nodded.

'I'm happy for you.'

'But sad for yourself. Are you absolutely sure the child is Fergus's?'

'Completely. But you're happy with Paolo?'

'What choice do I have? The best I can hope for is we'll return to Italy someday,' Clara said.

'You don't like Australia?'

'Is it a question of that? I have no family here. I miss them terribly.'

Amelia thought of the divide. Here they were on the other side of the world, and she had thought to taste freedom, and look what had become of that? But it wasn't Australia she wanted to escape.

'If I run away with Fergus—'

'Don't.' She put down her work, pressed her eyes to her. 'What you're feeling will pass. I don't think you can trust him.'

'Why?'

'You're vulnerable. He's taken advantage of that.'

'He didn't force himself on me,' Amelia said.

'But he knows you're married.'

'So do I.'

'Do you?'

Amelia breathed out her frustration. 'Then what should I do?'

'What do you feel for Italo?'

'Many things. I was angry with him. Disappointed. He always does what he wants. He always has time for men but not for me.' She considered these negatives, which didn't embrace the whole situation. 'We both want to run the farm well, make an easier life. But there's no passion. He's … familiar, in a way. I married my brother.'

'Then you have only two choices, and for a woman, that's something. You can tell Italo the truth. I suspect this would unleash many problems. His honour would be offended. He would have to act. I doubt he'd just accept it.'

'And my other choice?'

'Go back to Italo and make love. Don't see Fergus. Never discuss it with Italo.'

'Such sharp choices.'

'Being a woman is never blunt.'

Amelia slept badly on the couch in the lounge. Cristiano had offered her his bed, but though it was long enough for her, she refused it.

How could two men be so unlike? Italo was simple and direct. Though all his letters were laced with Dante's metaphors, he was utterly literal. He said what he thought. There was no other meaning. Fergus had some education, but he was wounded, all dark moods and complexity. She laughed out loud. In any other circumstance, the contrast was so great the decision would be easy. But she was to have a child, far from her mother, without any help. And not to her husband.

She stayed the few days she'd intended. They spoke more and more, weighed all the arguments. But Clara wouldn't tell her what to do.

'Only you can decide.'

The last morning, she rose early and packed her few possessions. Cristiano came to the room and saw her portmanteau.

'Why are you leaving?'

She sat on the couch, and Cristiano hauled himself next to her.

'I must go back to Italo,' she said, in English. 'I've something to tell him.'

CHAPTER SEVENTEEN

She caught the North Coast Line from Roma Street Station in Brisbane. The station's name came from the wife of the first Queensland governor, Diamantina di Roma. It would appear, to Amelia at least, there'd been a strong Italian presence in Queensland longer than many cared to admit. The train line wasn't yet completed to Babinda, only to Ingham. But Clara would telegraph to Maria to tell Italo, who would drive south a hundred miles or so to collect her there. Should he not come, she'd find her own way.

On the platform, Cristiano cried, and Clara had to pull him away from Amelia's legs.

'Bello,' Amelia said, 'we should be used to goodbyes.'

But nothing would soothe his red and distressed face.

'We'll just have to practise them more often,' Clara said. 'I'll come to Babinda as soon as I can.'

Amelia's heart leapt again into her throat. She clamped her jaw and nodded.

'Whatever you do, take charge of the situation,' Clara said. 'But good luck.'

Amelia found her carriage. Clara wasn't one to linger, and she and Cristiano waved from the platform and walked away. Amelia tried not to look but kept glancing to them until they were swallowed by the platform's hordes of crisscrossing people. She knitted her hands in her lap. She wouldn't cry. And it wasn't long before they were moving north and soon clear of the city's suburbs.

In the open, she wondered at the sheer volume of land and sky and beauty passing the window. In another carriage, a baby cried and cried and cried. She felt rocked and soothed by the train's motion. What a task lay ahead of her, to tell a man – her husband, no less – she carried another's child. She wasn't the first woman to be in this position and surely wouldn't be the last. She remembered Emma's joy when she told Mancuso. Evidently, his expression barely faltered. He turned his back and she said it again, and he said he had no idea who the hell she was. Poor Emma's broken heart.

Amelia had no great sense of how Italo would respond. She hardly knew him. Would he accept it? Or would he say he wanted no part of her and free her, as hard as that would be? And what would Fergus do? As hard as she fought to balance the extremes, each of her arguments had a counter-weight, and she was left hanging in the balance. But it was the truth, and it shouldn't be denied.

The station in Ingham was small. She made her way along the platform, half thinking Italo mightn't be there, some delay or other, or he may not have received the telegram. She prayed he'd not send Fergus. But Italo stood in the ante-chamber, out of place in his Sunday best on a Wednesday, his stance awkward and unfamiliar. She walked to him, her portmanteau at her side. They looked at one another. She'd left him in such a hurry and without any real explanation, in the middle of the planting, but she was in no mood to start apologising. She reached up, her hand on his shoulder for stability, and kissed his cheek.

'Are you all right?' he said, his brow drawn up to creases.

'Much better,' she said and smiled. 'Everyone sends their love.'

He nodded, and they turned from the station towards his truck. He was quiet, his hands tapping on the wheel, his eyes hardly leaving the road ahead. He knew something was wrong, but she knew him enough to know he'd never ask. She told him small things: of Clara's sewing, of Cristiano's height, of the rented house, of Paolo's construction job. She'd not mention that Clara was pregnant.

'I asked them to come for the next harvest.'

He nodded his approval. And she thought to tell him the truth, then and there in the truck, but it was wrong to do so here and now, so she pushed it off and turned to the view. They continued north. Young canes, short and green, pushed against the breeze. They talked little, each safe in silence. Babinda was a hundred miles away.

They left the main road and drove into the property. She saw their hut, clinging to the hill, humble and broken in a way her parents wouldn't accept. She turned to the land – no sign at all of the canes, no sign of anything growing, just the earth. Italo too looked at the land. But she imagined he saw only what work he had to do, not what the future might offer. They walked to the house, Italo carrying her small case. There was a vase of flowers on the bench on the verandah. She imagined Maria had left them. Italo went ahead, into the hallway with her portmanteau.

Once they were inside the house, she would do what she had to do. She turned one more time to the fields. This was her first homecoming. For the first time in Australia, she felt she had a home. She had everything she'd wanted in Italy – land, space, possibility. And she was to put all this at risk with such a confession?

Italo came back to the verandah door. 'Would you like some tea?' he said.

He was a good man. She turned from the land to him. 'I'll make it.'

It would put off the talk for some more moments. She stepped into the hallway, stopped across the threshold.

She realised then – to tell him the truth was to set a fire. She couldn't. She must be deceitful to survive.

He stood in the bedroom doorway, allowing her space to pass. She stopped, reached her hands to his shoulders. He lowered his face and they kissed. There wasn't that honey, that fire. She took his hand, led him into their room, made him sit on the bed's edge. She looked into those sea-blue eyes, awash with confusion but also a recognisable tide of desire. She removed her jacket. She removed his. And she continued until they were both naked. Then she pushed him back to lie. She'd been schooled. At first her boldness may have confused him, rendered him unsure of his role, unsure how to take her rebuffs of his attempts at control. But as she straddled him, set the rhythm and pace, he acquiesced, left her in charge. She dictated their pleasure; no fire was in it, but this deceit was the only course of action.

The first recognised weeks of the pregnancy passed without great alarm. Italo was joyful, proud, content, a light touch in his step. The women in the village brought her smiles and proclamations of help, and gifts of small blankets and even smaller cotton vests. Amelia remembered her mother had packed the blanket she'd had as a child. It bore stains she'd made. She would ready it for the birth. She did all she could to appear happy, wrote cheer-filled letters to her parents, to Fulvia and Francesca, even to Signora Pina, checking them for any hint of her sadness or fear. Or deception.

She remained at the house, venturing only as far as the vegetable garden, sometimes to the road between the hill and the fields, overwhelmed by her situation, but more to avoid Fergus. Within herself, a discord rose; could she continue this? This lie was another sin. Should she tell Italo the truth? What would he do? But still, this discord swelled.

Towards the end of January, Fergus took her by surprise as she crossed the breezeway. He pinned her against the wall, kissed her, forced himself into her mouth. She summoned all power, pushed flat hands against the dense plates of his chest, but her warmth stoked his zest. All resolve chipped as heat flushed into her cheeks, as she tasted and smelt him. It would be easier to give over. One hand drew the folds of her skirt, his hand searing high on her hip. But she pushed, harder and harder. He ground his hardened groin. Didn't he feel her resistance? She curled her palms into fists, opened some small space between her chest and his. She twisted her knuckles into his chest until his lips left hers. He pulled back. His dark eyes narrowed. He'd felt her change and took his hand away. The folds of fabric cascaded around her.

There was silence as he stared at her, searched her face, her two fists still held at her chest. Did he know she was pregnant?

'You don't want me,' he said, his eyes narrowed.

She stared into those eyes, which so recently had returned to life. But now that life bled away.

'I cannot,' she said. 'Ever. I'm married.'

He moved back two or three small paces to the centre of the breezeway.

She thought of honesty. She arranged the folds of her dress. She couldn't trust him with the truth.

He stood so still. Then she would go, if he couldn't or wouldn't.

She made the few steps towards the main room, closing the door behind her and pressing back against the rough wood. She held a hand over her thickening belly, and tears welled in her eyes. She opened her mouth, but no sound came. She sank, slowly, slowly, slowly until she heaped on the floor. How was she to bear this? How could she have been so utterly foolish?

She remained so for some time. A minute? Ten? She lost any sense of the day. But when she rose and opened the door, he was gone.

For a fleet moment, she thought to follow. But then the thought was gone too.

For the next weeks and then months – those between harvests called the slack season – she busied herself in the house with the accounts and plans for the next harvest. She spun some wool with a drop spindle, as her mother had taught her in their evenings together in the Veronesis' large stable. She knitted the wool to a set of small boots. Determined, she kept herself busy, allowed her mind no folly. She'd made the right decision, assured the child its future.

And cheerful letters came from Italy, full of the requisite words, but this happiness brought sorrow. Why was her mother not here? How could she have left Italy on this madness? But then she was pleased her mother wouldn't see her, detect her sorrow, as she would surely have. What would she say if she knew the truth? And so the chords of discord rose.

Rarely did she venture from the house, and even more rarely from the land. She saw no sign of Fergus, despite scanning the edges of the fields a few times a day, despite turning in the early evening towards the forest for signs of his campfire. There were none, and she hoped after their struggle he'd left the area again. But she could ask no-one. She could show no interest in someone she should have no interest in. He came to her dreams most nights, vivid and warm and real.

By late August, the air was dry and cool, Babinda's version of winter. She'd lived a year in Australia, but there was no celebration. The harvest was in full swing, and Italo was away from the house and busy and tired and distracted. They'd set another cooking fire at the barracks and hired a cook to feed the cutters. He was a British-Australian man, Mal Smith.

'Next time, will you arrange your pregnancy around the harvest?' Tullio Pesaro said.

Evidently, the kangaroo tail soup Smith prepared wasn't to Tullio's liking. But she was sure he wasn't serious, just giving her a backhanded compliment.

Maria came to the house. Increasingly now, the pregnancy was advanced. Amelia, tired and disorientated, had no energy for English and instigated a change back to Italian. But on another level, the new language had brought her no good, and she saw no reason to improve it.

'You're large,' Maria said, her eyes sizing Amelia's belly. 'But you've another month to go.'

'I'm just glad the weather is cooler,' she said.

But by her reckoning, she'd fallen pregnant in early December, just after Italo had left. She was nearly due. But to everyone else, the birth was a month away, having calculated from Italo's return from Melbourne.

On Monday morning, Mal Smith appeared on the verandah. He looked dishevelled, his eyes bloodshot, food slopped over the front of his shirt. He didn't work on a Sunday and would leave food prepared for the men. He'd run out of flour and wouldn't be able to make a cake for the afternoon tea.

'I've to go to the village,' Maria said. 'I can get some.'

Mal Smith glared at her. Had he expected her to make the cake as well? He thanked her and returned to the barracks.

'Why don't you come with me?' Maria said. 'It would do you good to be away from the house.'

The thought wasn't unpleasant. Maria drove and talked – she had a crib Amelia could have. There were blankets too, but she'd packed them away and would have to find them. She sat on her own in Maria's truck, parked on Munro Street. But after twenty minutes, she decided to stretch her legs and allay the discomfort.

It had been some months since she'd been in town. She passed Malouf's General Store, the vacant shop and Mellick's and then the post office. Someone came out, their step quick down the portico's stairs. She placed her arm to steady her belly and stepped aside. But then she caught Fergus's scent and looked. He'd stopped, staring at her, a cigarette hanging from the corner of his mouth. Then he stared at her belly. There was a moment of nothings. He said something. She didn't catch it. He snatched the cigarette from his mouth, pointed at her belly. His eyes narrowed and pierced.

'It – is – mine,' he said.

She turned away, but he said it again.

He'd not spoken loudly. No-one was near them. No-one in the post office seemed aware of the confrontation.

'No,' she said, and met his eyes.

They widened. His fingers trembled. Her pulse quickened and, as hard as she summoned, no more words would come.

'No,' she said, as it was all she had to block him. 'No. No. No.'

She turned towards the truck. Maria came from the general store. Fergus saw her and withdrew in the opposite direction. Maria walked to her.

'What did he want?' Maria said.

'I don't know.' She looked back, but he was walking away. 'I … couldn't understand him.'

Maria looked at her. 'One of his bad days.'

She nodded. No-one had heard him, least of all Maria. There'd been no harm done. But she felt anxious. Seeing him was hard enough. But then to lie to him … She felt his confusion, and it was the last thing she wanted, but there was no longer any place in this for honesty.

Maria started the truck and drove out of the village. Amelia felt a sharp pain in her belly. She'd had these before, almost all through the latter part of the pregnancy, but this was stronger. She screwed her eyes, held her breath.

'Are you all right?' Maria said.

The pain was strong. She ground her teeth. For a full half minute, she couldn't answer. It subsided. She let out her breath, sat back in the seat.

'I'm sure it's all right,' Maria said, 'but let's get you back to the house.'

They drove between the cane fields. She breathed to stay calm. The pain had gone but she felt weak, uncomfortable, as if the heat of the day had suddenly risen. And this had been pain, not discomfort. Even though she was a novice, this was a new type of pain that marked a change.

'The baby is coming,' she said.

Panic spread over Maria's face, and she accelerated a little.

Amelia walked unaided from the truck to the front verandah, but as she walked in the hall the pain struck again. Maria grabbed her arm, helped her to the bed.

'This happened to me,' Maria said, 'with my first. I had these pains, so severe. They'll go. They were on and off for a full month.'

Maria left her to fetch some water.

Within an hour, her waters broke. Maria stayed with her, the contractions stronger and closer and closer, crushing harder and harder. The early evening descended, and Italo came in from the fields.

'My love,' he said. 'It's your time.'

He grasped her hand, and she squeezed it as another contraction gripped her. When it subsided, she opened her eyes to Italo's fear-etched face.

'Don't be scared,' Maria said to Italo. 'I've delivered many early. They come when they're ready.'

Maria suggested Italo leave the room, and she closed the curtains and lit a kerosene lamp.

'The men grow cane,' Maria said. 'They're not used to the sight of blood.'

Maria found towels for the coming blood and the swaddling Amelia had prepared. Maria soothed her, bathing her brow with a tepid cloth. The pain now came in close waves, with little relief between each contraction. Each started as a low throb that deepened and spread, radiating from her belly until her whole body was engulfed. She lost track of time. She moaned. The only way out was to push. Maria stood and laid Amelia's breech across the bed. She wished the mosquito coil wouldn't burn.

'Push!' Maria yelled. 'Harder, harder.'

Amelia pushed, completely involuntarily, completely necessarily. The house rattled and rattled. Maria said a strong wind had come in from the desert.

She looked at Amelia. 'I can see the head. Not long now. Push.'

Despite a reflex to cower from the pain, she bore down and pushed. She felt as though her insides were turning out, but she maintained the pressure.

The child slid from her body. She saw stars.

The child was placed on her chest, warm and wet and heavy, so she couldn't catch her breath. Maria soothed her brow and told her it was a boy. He lay flat, his head turned to his side. She saw his chest expand and contract. He breathed on his own. His hands were curled in tight fists against her chest. She felt exhausted. She felt exhilarated. She had no words. She'd loved him forever and yet he was alien. His face was red. He had a large stock of blond hair, lighter than Fergus's.

And then Italo was with her. Would he question the hair? But she'd never seen him smile so broadly.

'He's a large child,' Maria said, 'especially as he's early, and especially for one as small as you.'

But Italo said nothing, his gaze at the child broken only with quick glances at Amelia.

'How odd the child is fair,' Maria said.

Fear gripped Amelia. Did Maria know something, or was this just an innocent observation?

'Not at all,' Italo said. 'On my father's side, there was blood from Bavaria. We should call him Flavio, the blond one.'

Amelia had no objection to the name. Whatever pleased Italo. She could see none of her features. Maria wrote some instructions and said she'd return in the morning.

'If there are any problems during the night, send Ben for me,' she said, and leant to kiss the child's forehead. 'Many beautiful things.'

There were no words. Italo would look at the child and then look at her, but before she had time to respond he'd look back at the child, almost cooing.

Then she felt the oddest set of sensations. First, it was like a wind had blown her hair from her face. But then it hurt. And Italo's head lurched forward, his chin to his chest. And then a sound, low and very, very loud, rumbled over the room. She gripped the child. Italo curved his arms around them but then stood and ran from the room, out onto the verandah.

'Jesus Christ,' he yelled.

What was happening? She held the swaddled child and, despite the pain, raised herself from the bed and walked the few steps to the verandah. The sound rumbled, rolled and echoed around the valley.

'What's happened?' she said.

'It's some explosion.'

Italo remained staring at the forested hill. And then they saw flames, rising in the forest.

'It's on the ridge. I'll go and look. Will you be all right?'

She looked at the child. 'I'll be …' She smiled. 'We'll be fine.'

Italo smiled, kissed the child and then her and was gone. She could hear men's voices. The cutters had come from the barracks. She could smell the smoke, thick and unctuous, unlike the fire of the fields.

The flames climbed out of the trees, high into the heavens. Fergus's hut was at the inferno's heart. It had a good hold and was spreading, engulfing other trees, leaping to others, fanned by the warm wind. The verge between the fire and the field wasn't so large. Flavio murmured in her arms, and she moved to calm him. If the fire caught the field, with this wind it would be impossible to control and would sweep through all the cane.

The sky showered embers. Large branches, a whole tree, crashed to the forest floor. What could she do? Should she leave? Walk out to the main road? She must think clearly. Spot fires ignited in the field. It took only two, three breaths at most, and the field was engulfed.

An almighty gust of wind, hot and dry and laced with embers, hit the house. The verandah shuddered, resisted, and then ripped, the curved iron roof groaning and gone. She looked to the sky, black and shot with cinders. Was this to be her fate? She'd come too far to die this way. And she held her child.

The hot wind blew hard. Another piece of the roof dislodged. She must leave. With the child in her arms, she walked back to the bedroom. She picked up her dictionary. What else should she take? Clothes? Shoes? There was nothing in the house. And she couldn't carry anymore. Something in the breezeway roof shrieked in pain.

With Flavio held tight in her arms, she walked backed to the verandah and down the stair, away from the house. The hot wind blew her hair across her face, stung her eyes. But the spot fires had picked up in the fields. It wouldn't take much for them to catch and run flames up the hill.

'Italo,' she yelled.

She listened but couldn't make out any sound beyond the rush of wind and fire. She should go towards the main road. Flavio murmured again.

'Holy Mother of God, do not desert me now. I know what I've done is wrong, but you are a woman. You know our choices.'

She looked to the sky. Waited. But nothing changed. What had she expected of the Virgin Mary? She was too demanding, too unworthy of grace. And then she felt it. A drop on her forehead. And then another, and then another, and soon the heavens opened and she remained, these heaven-sent tears streaming her face, onto her clothes, soaking to the skin, baptising the newborn child. And for once, she welcomed them.

She was forgiven. They were safe. They were all saved.

PART TWO

1936

Lust's winter comes ere summer half be done
Venus and Adonis – William Shakespeare

CHAPTER EIGHTEEN

In glossy black ink, Amelia wrote at the bottom of the ledger: 15th of April, 1936.

The accounts were in the black.

Despite an horrific cyclone, the Wall Street Crash and the Great Depression, they'd prospered. The 1934 outbreak of Weil's disease – an illness thought to be transmitted by rats and that left cane cutters with headaches and pains and fevers, at worst with bleeding to the lungs and kidney failure – had stressed the whole industry. But as Italo had always burnt the cane, their farm was unaffected. And despite the bans brought by the Australian Workers' Union and the British Preference League, whereby no-one would handle Italian-grown sugar, the Italian consul general provided the Italian growers support and trade solutions.

Their financial position was less than her projections, well less, but it was black. Her mastery of the double-entry ledger maintained balance. Now she'd discovered this, she judged most of life's situations in a similar debit–credit balance. She blotted the wet ink with a folded wad of blotting paper, her final figure mirrored on the sheet.

Over the entry, she splayed the fingers of her left hand. She'd not removed the wedding ring since it was put there by her brother in 1920. She lifted her hand, the desk lamp's light catching on the apex.

What had it meant to her? A ticket to freedom?

She turned the ring with the fingers of her other hand.

Is that what she'd received?

She gripped it, eased it to the knuckle. If nothing else, sixteen years of cane farming had taken her fine fingers. She spat on the swollen joint, rubbed it around the skin, seized the ring and rotated and pulled. It came, rose to the crest and ceased. She screwed it, felt it budge and budge and budge and then come free.

A band was riven in the flesh, sunless white against her sun-olive skin. That was enough to remind her of marriage. Her hand felt new, light. She placed the ring on her palm, far heavier than she remembered. Wrought in Italy. Plump with gold. She smiled.

She looked over her large desk, over the piles of invoices, past the jumble of ledgers, into the view, golden in the narrowing light. The dark dropped like a curtain on a performance, none of the drawn twilight of home. At the end of autumn, her village held festivals to mourn the season's passing. Could she really remember it anymore, the long, long stretch between day and night? This melancholy had grown stronger of late. She was unsure why.

Italo had been right; the view from this hill was the best in the valley. Spectacular. And how it changed, both day and night, night and day. When the rains swept through the valley it was one thing and when the sun shone with blue sky quite another.

And the house, built to her strict specifications, crowned the view. They'd had little choice but to start to build, in 1927, after Cyclone Willis strew the old house and their belongings over the fields. An ill wind blew no good. Curtailed by the Depression, they'd braced for the worst. But they'd prospered. The ledgers, years of them, lined the bookshelves, a history of the farm, of sorts.

Now the light had changed, the fields dark pools, biding their time to sprout canes. She sighed heavily, set the ring on the desk.

She caught a reflection in the darkened window. Someone had come to her office door, his weight immediately contrapposto to the left hip. Her heart rose, as it had a thousand times. She'd fool herself again: Fergus. He'd come back. With the light behind him, he'd not changed, not in sixteen years. But it wasn't Fergus. It was her son, Flavio.

She turned on the chair. His hair, the same colour of dawn, hung over his forehead. And his eyes, darker than hers, absorbed everything they saw. Although she was his mother, it was as if she'd had nothing to do with his conception, not a trace of her skin, of her hair, of her temperament. All Fergus.

'I'm going to bed,' he said.

Even the timbre of his voice, now that it had broken, was Fergus's. It took her moments before she could speak.

'Where are the others?' She always spoke to him in Italian, but he answered in English.

'Mauro is reading. Marta's helping Meggsy in the kitchen.'

'A five-year-old should be in bed long ago, not helping the cook.' She removed her glasses and stood. She'd no need to ask where Italo was, smoking his last cigarette and tending the horses he kept out of love, those no longer with a practical use.

'What time tomorrow does Zia Clara's train arrive?' he said.

'Midday.'

'Is she bringing Donata and Eugenia?'

'They're in boarding school.' She looked at him. 'She'll be pleased you put off returning to school.'

Not that she approved. Her education had been abruptly ended and she'd not allow her children's to be. He nodded.

'Goodnight,' she said.

She wouldn't kiss him. She never did. He moved from the door.

She too was looking forward to seeing Clara. Amelia had been lonely, terribly, these last years, Babinda a man's domain. She managed the farm and looked after the children and was always busy, but a grey melancholy was never far behind her; their connections with Italy were attenuating, fading. The children spoke Italian poorly, had sparse and fractured knowledge of Italy's history, their attention torn and warped by the distance and time and Australia.

And six months ago, Paolo had been killed on a construction site, crushed by an inadequately supported wall. Such an horrendous death; she doubted Clara could ever get over it. She wasn't working as a seamstress but the children – Cristiano, Donata and Eugenia – were nearly off her hands. This would be the first time they'd seen one another since those dark days around the funeral.

Amelia was keen to discuss a proposal that would suit both her and Clara; she wanted to open an Italian school in Babinda, with Clara as the teacher. Clara would come and live with them. She would have a job in her field of training, everything taught in Italian. Amelia had done the maths. Her budget was viable. She just had to find the right moment, the right mood, to broach the plan with Clara.

And in two days Signor Leandro Chieffi, the Italian vice-consul in Townsville, would come to the house to discuss the project. This struck fear and inspiration in her. She'd never met Chieffi, but some years back, in 1932, he'd attended a celebration in Babinda for the tenth anniversary of Mussolini's March on Rome, organised by the Babinda Fascist Organisation. But Chieffi expressed concern there may be unrest from anti-fascists. In other towns, officials had been spat at. But the Babinda Fascist Organisation acted as other organisations hadn't and beat the daylights out of any opposition and made promises of worse if the celebration was disturbed. But at the time, Amelia thought Chieffi's need for such protection cowardly. Despite the number of fascist salutes he gave, was he unconvinced of the righteousness of the fascist cause?

She looked at the ring on the desk. Since Italy's invasion of Abyssinia, the League of Nations had instigated heavy trading sanctions to curb and chastise Italy. The impotent League couldn't fell the lion, Mussolini. She wrapped the ring in a sheet of tissue paper, placed it in an envelope she'd addressed to the Italian consulate in Sydney, with a letter she'd already written; gold for the motherland.

Living in a foreign land, she wasn't required to do this, but she would send the gold back to where it had come from. These tiny bits of metal would bring a victory in Abyssinia and show the world Italy was a power, an empire reborn. It was an act of faith, a sign of their prosperity. She'd not miss it. She sealed the envelope, placed it on the desk with another letter to her parents.

A step to victory.

She'd go and find Mauro and Marta and put them to bed, one of the sweetest points of the day. Tomorrow, Clara would be there.

CHAPTER NINETEEN

The damn train was late.

Though Amelia knew the others on the platform, by habit she stood apart from them. An Italian couple nearby, the Paduanos, discussed the train's delay in very poor English. What made them so proud to speak English that made them sound like fools? Although vexing, it wasn't unusual for a train to be late. A pair of British-Australian boys ran up and down the platform, yelling and tripping one another. Their parents, the Burkes, sitting on the only bench in the shade, were oblivious to the row. She'd have never let Flavio and Mauro behave in such a manner. And if she had, people wouldn't have held back their criticism. She'd no doubt of that. Italian children were to be seen and not heard, but apparently not Australian ones.

The train was now a half an hour late. Curse them. She had it on numerous reports that since Mussolini had come to power, the Italian trains ran like clockwork. You could set your watch by them. For many years, she'd delivered food parcels to some of the poorer families of the valley, mostly the British Australians, and she'd promised a delivery that morning. Did she have time to do these and return before the train arrived?

Flavio walked along the platform from the stationmaster's office. 'He says another half-hour.'

She sighed heavily. Flavio spoke in English, but she replied in Italian. 'Damn them. I have many things to do, work to finish.'

'Do you want me to take you home?' he said.

'We might miss her.'

A British-Australian man glared at her. 'Bloody well speak English,' he said, not to her, not directly, but loud enough for her to hear. And then he moved out of earshot. Was Italian so offensive? These small exchanges, though petty, were numerous and profoundly bittering. Like water drops on stone, over the years they'd increased and were wearing. She recognised it, had fought against it, but resigned to the breach between the communities.

She unfurled the morning's *Cairns Post*, turning to the Babinda Notes column. Amongst the piffle was another celebration that a British Australian had bought a stretch of land. Why did they never report the Italian land purchases? As if she didn't know.

Flavio raised a hand. He strained his ears and then leant and touched the track. 'The train is coming.'

She stepped back. She could hear it. The fool stationmaster had no idea when it would come. The train rounded the bend, a large plume trailing. Its horn blasted. In the strain of metal and steam and smoke, it squealed to a halt. The carriage doors swung open, and a host of porters scuttled over the platform.

At some distance, Clara stepped down and walked a few paces. They'd not seen one another since those horrible weeks in Brisbane after Paolo's death. She still wore black and had lost more weight. Clara caught sight of Amelia, waved and moved towards her, dodging the people crossing the platform.

'Welcome,' Amelia said.

They embraced.

'It's so lovely to see you,' Clara said. 'We shouldn't allow so many months to pass.'

Amelia held her but pulled back to search her face. There were dark circles and new lines etched about her eyes, her cheekbones far too pronounced.

'You need to eat more,' Amelia said.

Clara looked over Amelia's shoulder. Amelia turned. Flavio walked towards them, that same economical gate.

'I swear, you're taller still,' Clara said.

He came to her. Amelia released Clara and stepped aside. Flavio beamed and kissed her cheeks.

'But you should be away in boarding school,' Clara said.

'I put off returning, to see you.'

There'd always been a bond between them. Clara liked his free spirit. He picked up her portmanteau, and the three started along the platform towards the car.

'Where's Italo?' Clara said.

'It's planting time,' Amelia said.

'And the children, how are they?' Clara asked.

'Mauro is still taller—'

'Not as tall as me,' Flavio said.

'Marta is full of words, overflowing with them. A handful. She just doesn't sleep, but such a joy. They're both anxious to see you.'

Flavio drove the car. Amelia and Clara sat in the back, their talk inconsequential, small snippets of her trip, news from home. Amelia's mother had written, and Aldo's wife had had another baby. Clara spoke of Brisbane and Cristiano, Donata and Eugenia. Amelia skirted anything that might lead to Paolo, a subject she suspected still too raw.

On the way to the farm, they delivered the parcels of food to Betsy Taylor, who lived on the outskirts of the village. Out of the blue, her husband had left her and three children under the age of five and gone to Adelaide. She had no money, no job and no time for one, but she had a fine stitch, and Amelia paid her for alterations and recommended her whenever she could.

Betsy came to the door of her shack to meet them.

'This is my best friend,' Amelia said by way of introducing Clara.

Even Betsy's smile was weary and drawn, one of her front teeth missing. Clara shook her hand. A little girl, two or three, barefoot and wearing a patched dress, came down the hall. Her hair had been washed and combed and pulled back from her face. Clara bent down and picked her up, which made her giggle.

Flavio carried the parcels through to the rear lean-to, which served as a kitchen. The parcels contained some milk and eggs, bread Meggsy had baked that morning, some fresh vegetables from the garden and a large container of chicken soup.

'You'd best eat that today,' Amelia said.

'I can't thank you enough,' Betsy said.

Amelia looked at her. The woman was worn out. Mussolini cared for the poor. If only such care existed in Australia.

'A better way is coming,' Amelia said.

'We'd not survive but for you,' Betsy said.

'I've some mending, the boys' trousers. I'll send them over.'

A small light of thanks ignited in Betsy's dulled eyes, and she nodded. Flavio returned from the rear of the house, and Amelia turned back towards the car. Clara carried the young girl outside and then let her slide down her hip to the ground. The little girl laughed.

'It's very good of you,' Clara said, once the car was moving again.

'It's nothing to have Meggsy cook a little more,' Amelia said. 'No-one else looks after them. Not the state, not even the church. She just needs to earn an income. The trouble of the matter is there are so many people like this in the valley. I can't feed them all, and even then, many have now rejected my help.'

'Why?'

'I'm Italian.'

They drove on with careless chatter until the car arced the small hill on the property and the new house revealed itself.

'Oh my God,' Clara said. 'You've added the second storey.'

Amelia smiled. Clara had last visited some three years ago, and only the lower level had been finished, the large area partitioned into temporary rooms. She'd purposely not told Clara it was complete, the surprise bringing joy to her face, something scant since Paolo's death.

'The verandahs are so broad,' Clara said.

Flavio stopped the car on the flat gravelled area on the lower front side of the house. Clara bounded out, hands clasped to her mouth.

The house sat in the high lee of the hill. Once the land was cleared, Italo dug the foundations with his own hands. He'd not have his new house blown away. Constructed on a concrete slab, the first storey had cement brick walls. People had snarled at Amelia's design, Maria even saying it was absurd to build directly on the ground. But, just as Amelia imagined, the large verandah, over two metres wide, cast broad shadows across all the external walls and windows, keeping the house just as cool as any midair suspension. And they were on a hill; it was hardly likely they'd be flooded.

But at first glance the house did appear much larger than it was, the perceived bulk created by the verandahs, collaring the wooden second storey, a colonnade along both levels. And the height was impressive, made more so by a block tower crowning the centre front façade, which held Amelia's office and an upper observation deck.

Clara's eyes filled with wonder. Amelia took her hand, and they walked through the wide front door and stepped back, inviting Clara into the expansive entrance hall. At the right-hand side, a wooden staircase began a lazy ascent in three sections, first up the right-hand wall of a huge lounge room, then the rear wall and finally the other side wall of the dining room.

'It's so grand,' Clara said.

Amelia smiled. 'Let me show you upstairs.'

They mounted the stairs to the landing, which curled around the staircase with various doors leading to rooms.

'This is your room,' Amelia said.

The room was in the rear corner of the building, and contained a bureau, a double bed, a large cupboard, a washbasin and jug, and a walnut desk at the window.

'I told you not to toss the children from their rooms,' Clara said.

'And I haven't. This is the guest's room, built for you.'

Amelia led her to the window and the vast view of the Bellenden Ker Range. Flavio came with her luggage.

'Let me show you something special,' Amelia said, and reached out her hand. They walked back across the landing to large French doors that opened to the front verandah, as broad as its lower counterpart. Below the rail was panelled, but above the rail the northern sun could be further expunged by a series of plantation shutters Amelia drew across to demonstrate.

'I had them made especially.'

Once they were slid shut, the shutters turned to closed, the sunlight and heat were all but gone.

'The house is beautiful,' Clara said. 'You must be proud.'

'Proud? I don't know …' She pushed back the shutters. 'Just pleased we finally have somewhere safe to sleep. Come, let me show you my office.'

They walked back to the rear of the landing. A door opened onto another smaller staircase, which rose another level to Amelia's office. Clara ran her hand along the edge of the desk, looking out over the fields.

'How can you work in front of this view?' Clara said.

Amelia took her hand and led her higher to the flat roof of the tower, a type of viewing platform.

'You can almost see the sea,' Amelia said.

They looked out to the fields. In the distance, the men worked, the planting machine pulled by a tractor, the small setts of cane dropped into the long lines of furrows. The machine gathered the earth in its wake, closing it over. A cloud of dust, soil thrown into the sky by the machine, followed its path, a few men scampering around like ants.

'So much is different,' Clara said.

Since Paolo's death, in all her letters, Clara pined for the past, buckling at the remotest sign of any change. Amelia supposed it was normal. But at this moment, Amelia could only try to keep Clara's mind away from the past, secured in the present.

'The machines mean fewer men and less pay,' Amelia said.

'More profit. But they must cost a fortune.'

'They paid for themselves in a season. And I depreciated them on the books.'

Clara remained with her eyes on the field but sighed heavily. 'You no longer sound like a Bolshevik—'

'The unions have created no end of problems.'

'Now you sound like a fascist.'

She looked at Clara, her face still turned to the field. 'And what's wrong with that?'

Clara sighed heavily. 'Be careful. We're not in Italy. In Brisbane, if you kept your head down and went about your business, no-one noticed you. But things have changed. Men have been attacked. Women abused on the street for nothing more than a few syllables of Italian.'

'Italy is stirring under Mussolini's hand.'

'Do you really think it will change? A revolution will still leave the lords in control of the land. They'll just wear a different hat.'

'You're wrong,' Amelia said. 'Italy's no longer for the privileged few but the whole nation. Education is for all. The *Cairns Post* reported when Dr Vattuone returned to Genoa from Australia, he was lost, so much had been built.'

'Memory is faulty—'

'Would you know Bologna if you returned?'

Clara was silent. 'By reports, I've heard the fascists aren't exactly lambs. They've bashed and intimidated people, poured castor oil down the throats of any opposition—'

'That's just rumour—'

'They're thugs.'

Should she tell Clara her plan now? No. She was tired, her mood sharp and testy. A noise erupted on the staircase, swift steps on the wooden floor fermented with laughter. Clara turned and crouched. Marta darted onto the rooftop, threw her arms wide and ran into Clara's laughing arms. Amelia laughed, bent down and kissed the top of Marta's head, held tenderly between Clara's hands, with a great smooch. Marta's energy never ceased. And she was pleased Marta remembered Clara. For a five-year-old, time was doubly long.

Clara looked at Amelia and then back at Marta. 'She's the image of you.'

Amelia had sent a photograph of Marta to her mother, who'd suggested the same thing. She and her daughter were both small and doll-like, but beyond that, she could see little likeness.

'Italy awakens,' Amelia said. 'Speed, pace, the roar of machines – they're the future.'

Clara looked back to the field and then back at Marta. 'I should unpack.'

Amelia nodded. She said to Marta, 'Will you go and help?'

'Yes,' Marta said, glee from ear-to-ear.

Amelia looked at Clara and smiled. 'Italo will come in half an hour for lunch.'

She left Clara, and Marta and returned downstairs. Clara's mood worried her, these dour warnings. Paolo's death had cast a pall on everything. She couldn't blame her, but on Italy she was wrong. Marta would work like a tonic to lighten her mood.

The kitchen was at the back of the house, the rear wall part dug into the hill, which helped to cool it. The room was large, excessively so, but set like a hotel kitchen to prepare the copious food for the workers. Meggsy stood at the four-oven Aga stove, central to the back wall. She nodded to Amelia. There were two large metal troughs on the other wall, a huge central work table. Amelia checked the mutton chops and boiling vegetables. Italo would be hungry, as would the other men when the food was taken to them, in the new barracks built away from the house.

She returned to the dining room. Clara was looking at some framed photograph on a side table.

'Marta is a trick,' Clara said.

'You're under her spell.'

'As are you.'

Amelia considered this. 'She's so different to the boys. I appreciate that.'

Clara picked up a photograph of her and Paolo. Amelia had paid for it for their wedding anniversary, some ten years ago. She chastised herself for having forgotten to remove it.

'I'd never say it was a perfect marriage …' Clara looked harder at the photograph. 'We were both so silly and young …'

'You're still young.'

'No—'

'You have another life in front of you.'

Clara looked at Amelia, her face writ over with questions. 'What do you mean?'

The front door opened. Italo stood framed in the archway to the dining room.

Now was not the time. 'Later,' Amelia said and smiled.

In the barracks, Italo had showered and changed, brushed what remained of his white hair. He walked to Clara and embraced her. Amelia went to the sideboard and selected a white damask tablecloth.

'You look well,' he said.

'I can't complain. The house …' Clara turned, her eyes wide.

'It's finished,' he said. 'Thank God. How are the children?'

Amelia unfurled the cloth over the table. Clara helped smooth it out.

'Cristiano will finish in another year. Can you imagine that?'

'A doctor?' Italo asked.

'No less.'

He smiled. 'That's something to be proud of.'

'Donata and Eugenia do well at school.' Clara smiled. 'I'm grateful for every small mercy.'

Flavio came into the room. Amelia turned to the sideboard for the cutlery.

'My son,' Italo said, 'help seat Zia Clara?'

With a faux-gallant gesture, Flavio moved around and pulled out her chair. Clara continued the theatre, sitting in an exaggerated manner. Amelia moved around them, finishing setting the table. Flavio went to pull out her seat, but she waved her hand for him to remain seated. Meggsy served the soup. At first the talk was inconsequential – small news from Italy, small news of the farm and life in Brisbane.

'What's happened with Paolo's case?' Italo said.

Amelia scowled at him.

'It's all right,' Clara said. 'I no longer need to avoid the subject.' She turned back to Italo. 'As he died on a construction site, the union is arguing the company is responsible, that certain precautions hadn't been taken and there should be compensation. But the company have very strong lawyers and have managed to delay all negotiations. They say it could take years, and even then there's no certainty.'

Italo looked at the table and nodded. Amelia took heart that for Clara, her plan to establish a school was viable.

'While you're all together,' Clara said, 'I wanted to thank you.' She looked first at Italo, then Flavio and last Amelia. She placed a hand on Amelia's. 'You've helped me so much. I really couldn't have faced the last six months … and, financially … The union has taken collections, but I don't know what would have happened to us without your support.'

'You're our family,' Flavio said.

'That's right, my son,' Italo said.

'Now Donata and Eugenia are in boarding school, I'll start work again. The sewing factories need women—'

'There's no hurry,' Amelia said, to snuff any discussion before they could talk alone.

'But there is.' Clara looked at her. 'Life has to start again.'

Amelia breathed in. Fortunately, Clara asked Flavio of his studies and was pleased to hear he liked both mathematics and literature.

'What will you do after school?'

'I've not thought about it. Perhaps I'll work on the farm.'

'We can always use more hands,' Italo said.

'You have a good mind,' Amelia said. 'You should think of university.'

She'd not meant an insult to Italo but feared Flavio was like her brothers and saw no good in education. Italo continued to eat. Perhaps he'd not taken it as such. Once they'd finished, Italo stood and excused himself. He would go for a small siesta and then return to the field, once the high heat of the day had abated. Flavio said he would go and change and spend the afternoon with him.

Italo turned to Clara. 'I can't read or write. But your son will be a doctor.' He smiled at her. 'This country has blessed us.'

The two women watched him, heard him climb the stair.

'Would you like to rest?' Amelia said.

'I think a walk.'

Amelia had no time for sleeping during the day, and walking aided digestion. They prepared themselves with broader hats, better shoes and umbrellas for the near certainty of rain. In silence, they walked along the ridge to the forest, the air cool and the canopy with the grandeur of a vaulted ceiling. It was one thing Amelia still appreciated, the rush of life, the spray of ferns and palms and climbing roots strangling the buttressed host trees. This section, just a little from the house, had survived the cyclone almost unaffected and had regrown strong branches where some had been felled. The fan palms looked like unfurled parasols. The unseen birds called their calls, the screeching and cooing and warbling punctuated by the drumming and croaking tree frogs. They arrived at a small clearing.

'Italo wanted to build the house here,' Amelia said.

Clara looked out at the view of the mountains. Low mist clung to the canopy.

'Perhaps the view is a little better.'

'But the forest still stood here. Where the house is built, it had been destroyed; far cheaper to build there.'

'Of course.' Clara laughed.

'Frugality's to be laughed at?'

She shook her head, smiling. 'I owe an immense amount to your frugality.'

Amelia breathed in the cool air. The familiar melancholy came to her.

'Fergus's hut was here,' Amelia said.

Clara turned on her sharply. 'I've not heard you mention him in years.'

'At times, I like to come here.'

Clara nodded slowly, looking around the clearing. Amelia kicked back some undergrowth, the green of ferns and seedlings. The hut's four cement pylons were worn, the forest grinding into them, reclaiming them. She showed the ring of stones that formed his fire.

'You made the right decision,' Clara said.

In all the years, how often she'd pondered this question. 'I had no choice.'

'I only met Fergus once,' Clara said. 'But Flavio—'

'You've no need to say.' Amelia thought of her penance; each day, each minute, each second, his appearance lashed her.

'Does Italo suspect?'

Amelia raised her shoulders and eyebrows. 'You told me never to discuss it. He's never said anything …'

Amelia considered the void. No-one had ever said a word. Only, one afternoon when Flavio was about six, on the old verandah, Maria looked at him, then at Amelia, then back at Flavio and then said she had to leave. From then on, Maria came less often to the house, offered help less often, and asked even more rarely. Amelia realised the nature of her expression – she'd seen something in young Flavio she remembered in Fergus.

Perhaps she'd always suspected and just needed proof. People weren't blind. Amelia knew they talked behind their flimsy, patched-together walls, in the village shops, in the hotels, on other farms. And they'd turned their backs on her, barely acknowledging her, offering no help, hardly the time of day. So, she'd done the only things she could – removed herself, stayed at a distance. And she'd sent Flavio to boarding school in Charters Towers, though there were primary schools in Babinda. If he was absent, perhaps people would start to forget.

'Italo must know,' Amelia said.

'Do you know where Fergus is?'

'I'm hardly in a position to ask. Once Italo said he was in Victoria. Some years later that he'd gone to Ireland.'

'To Ireland?'

'He's Irish.'

'No, he's Australian.'

Amelia looked her in the eye. 'Who's Australian?'

They'd often argued about what an Australian was. Amelia wouldn't allow a person to shake off their extraction, but Clara thought it only a matter of birthplace.

Clara shook her head and turned to the view. 'And his parents still live nearby?'

'Over that hill.'

She pointed in the direction of Oisin Kelly's farm. After the explosion and fire, Fergus disappeared and hadn't been seen for sixteen years. Cyclone Willis destroyed Oisin's crop, most of his property and a whole year's income. Then the Depression caught everyone by surprise. Even some of the Italians had had to sell land. Oisin had put nothing aside, so he sold more land.

Amelia wanted to buy a small parcel away from their main property, but Italo was against it. The land was flat, already cleared, but the idea brought considerable financial risk; they'd have to take a bank mortgage. But Amelia was sure they could. They needed more income and more land to crop. But even this sale – and Amelia would add that the purchase price was more than fair – had aggrieved Oisin. She would hear him in the village, always in earshot, cursing the Italians, ranting they had all the best land.

'There's no-one else to run Oisin's farm?' Clara said.

'Apart from Fergus, he only has daughters. And he couldn't afford to pay a manager. Oisin's old now, bent with rheumatics. God knows what he'll do.'

Clara walked to the edge of the clearing before it fell to the valley. Amelia followed a few steps behind.

'I hope Fergus never returns,' Clara said. 'If Flavio ever saw him …'

Amelia glared at Clara, who continued looking at the view. The mists had lifted, unclouded blue sky backing the dark granite range. But it wouldn't last. Fergus's return was Amelia's greatest dread, another living effigy of their sin. Fergus's absence for sixteen years had made the situation bearable, the stories circulating the village drifting off to folklore. What lesions would his presence lay bare?

'And how's the business?' Clara said, as if she too wanted not to contemplate these consequences.

'The mortgage frightens me. I'd never tell Italo that. But even after paying it, the land makes money.' She looked at Clara. 'No-one ever went broke making a profit.'

Clara tossed back her head and laughed, loud, strong, from the belly. Amelia was pleased to see such a thing and laughed as well.

'This country's been good to you,' Clara said.

'Yes, for greasy dagos, we've done all right.'

Clara turned on her. Amelia felt it may erupt to a disagreement. But then Clara smiled. And together they laughed again.

Amelia returned to the path, not waiting for Clara. When they cleared the forest, she could see Mauro, riding home from school in Babinda. During the day, he'd tethered the horse to the school fence. He was making his way to the new stable, still on the flat near the first field, but when he saw them on the ridge, he struck the horse to a gallop towards them. In one motion, he slowed the horse, tossed a long leg over the neck and slid to the ground. Clara laughed and threw her hands towards him.

'I'd been told you were taller, but this is ridiculous,' she said. The two embraced.

'You're as tall as your father.'

'Not quite.'

He came to Amelia and she kissed his cheeks.

'Perhaps you could slow your growth for a while.'

Clara asked him in English of his day at school, and they started back towards the house, him leading the horse. Amelia dropped behind. It was Mauro's last year in primary school. Next year he would attend the same boarding school as Flavio in Charters Towers. She would miss him.

'You sound like an Australian,' Clara said, in Italian.

'I don't know – I just talk like the others in school,' he said, in Italian.

'Now you sound like an Italian. But you used the wrong preposition. You should use *a* instead of *in*.'

'But *a* is "to", not "at".'

Clara smiled and ruffled his hair. 'It's both in Italian. Prepositions are the hardest.'

'I'll never understand them.'

With that, he mounted the horse and took off down the hill towards the stable.

'They're neither one nor the other,' Clara said.

'They're forced to be Australian.'

'Perhaps that's as it should be.'

Amelia bit her lip. 'I couldn't disagree with you more. They're Italian. Australia reminds them of that again and again.'

Clara walked on ahead. She let her go. She'd not rile her. She needed her to be calm before they spoke of the school.

Dinner was eaten against the cacophony of the children's news for Clara. Having considered her question, Flavio talked about how he wanted to travel after he'd finished school, Mauro said he would do anything not to go to boarding school in Charters Towers and Marta talked on and on about a brand-new dress. After the children were all in bed and Italo went to check the horses, they were alone. They sat outside at a table on the lower verandah, the mosquito coil smoke curling around them. Meggsy brought two brandies, and Amelia told her she could retire for the evening. And they were quiet, not a word between them for some time, looking over the fields.

'You're not wearing your wedding ring,' Clara said.

Amelia looked at the white depression in her finger. 'I removed it last night.'

'Why on earth would you do that?'

'You know why.'

Clara breathed deeply. 'You can't be seen to support fascism.'

'There's no law against it.'

'Not yet.'

Amelia felt chastised and resented it. 'They'll send me an iron replacement.'

Clara drew her face to question. 'What did Italo say?'

'He's not noticed.' She breathed out. 'He wouldn't say anything.'

'You're playing with fire.'

Amelia didn't want to have this discussion. For some while, neither woman spoke, the night air heavy with the shrieking of the bats in the forest, the constant frogs of the fields.

'Widowhood doesn't rest well with you,' Amelia said, by way of opening the discussion.

'Yet by not wearing a ring you choose to feign it.'

Amelia wouldn't respond. Perhaps they should talk of the school tomorrow. Clara still had a sharp edge.

'Does widowhood rest well with anyone?' Clara said at last.

'You need occupation.'

'I have three children.'

'Cristiano will soon finish university. The girls are nearly off your hands.'

Clara raised her eyebrows. 'Ahhh … You've been stewing something. What do you propose?'

Amelia leant towards her. 'I want to open a school.'

'A school? …' She sounded flabbergasted. 'But there are schools here—'

'An Italian school. Everything taught in Italian, to keep the language alive.'

'You never cease to amaze me … why?'

'You've heard the children speak. Their Italian's provincial. You've heard Mauro. Wouldn't you like to teach again?'

'Of course, but in Brisbane, there's no opportunity.'

Amelia leant forward. 'Then move here. Bring the girls. Do what you were trained to do, rather than work in a factory as a second-rate seamstress. You and I are both lonely.'

Clara said nothing. Had Amelia gained some ground?

'Since Paolo's death, I've felt lost,' Clara said. 'And you're right; when I look to the future, just a few years, what am I to become? A grandmother?'

'I've done some investigations. I've done calculations. This is possible.'

'I'm sure you have.'

'Signor Chieffi, the vice-consul from Townsville, is coming tomorrow to discuss the idea.'

Clara raised her eyebrows. 'He knows of this?'

'I wrote to him.'

'Do other people know?'

Amelia sat back. 'I've told no-one.' She wasn't sure how the other Italians of the valley would respond, but the consulate had expressed some interest. Though even this had brought waves of uncertainty; she'd never dealt with someone in such a high position.

'I'm not used to speaking to someone of his class,' Amelia said. She rested. 'The school's necessary and possible. At least help me talk to him.'

Clara was silent. They heard footsteps coming out of the dark. It was Italo.

'It's a touch cold,' he said. 'You two watch yourselves out here.'

He said goodnight and went indoors.

'You mean to do this,' Clara said.

'What greater thing is there than to keep the language alive? Tomorrow. Ten o'clock. He's always sharp.'

Clara laughed.

'Now, what's funny?'

'Punctuality's the newly formed passion of the Italians.' Clara thought. 'You don't need my help to talk with him, but I'm happy to meet him.'

Amelia smiled. 'I can count on you.'

Clara smiled. 'And no doubt you intend to turn a profit with the school.'

'Is that a crime?'

Clara stood, shaking her head. 'I'm tired. And I want to be up early to say goodbye to Flavio.'

Amelia remained seated.

'Don't be so hard on Flavio,' Clara said. 'He'll find his way.'

She nodded. 'Goodnight.'

Amelia remained. She rocked slightly in the chair. She was glad of Clara's support, but they would need much more than that for the school to come to fruition. She had no idea how the people in the valley would react to the school, but hoped they'd not turn their backs on it.

CHAPTER TWENTY

At 10 am sharp, the vice-consul's car came from behind the hill, approaching the front of the house. Amelia stood in the lounge room window. She looked to Clara, seated in an armchair. Amelia flared her eyes with excitement, and Clara raised her eyebrows and nodded quickly. Amelia moved from the window.

'Why are you so nervous?' Clara asked.

Amelia smoothed the front pleats of her dress. She checked her hair, pulled back hard to a band at her nape.

'Come with me to the door,' Amelia said.

'You're the most capable person I know,' Clara said, and laughed. 'You'll be fine.'

The thought struck further anxiety. The car made a wide arc around the flat gravelled yard and came to a halt. She'd not cajole Clara anymore. She must concentrate. She opened the front door and stood at the centre. The car remained, no movement within or without. Should she go to the car? She smoothed her dress, brushed her hands over her hair. Her stomach bubbled. Never had someone of such station come to their home.

The driver's door opened. He was dressed in a grim grey uniform and marched to the car's rear door. Leandro Chieffi stepped to the gravel. He was dressed in a suit, that sheen of finely spun silk, and, despite the heat of the day, wore a dark-blue vest under his jacket. He looked at the house, some twenty metres away, acknowledged Amelia with a dip of his head, and then began to walk. He carried a briefcase, a sign he meant business.

'Good morning,' Amelia said, venturing to the edge of the colonnade. Chieffi was still at the gate, some distance from the house, and possibly didn't hear her, his eyes shadowed by his hat. She retreated from the morning light to the broad shadow of the house. How could she converse with a man of this calibre? She'd no experience of it. Despite her honest intention, she'd pushed too far. She may be capable with a ledger, but these credits and debits she couldn't balance. She wished Clara had come to the door. She knew etiquette. He was only a few metres away. She put out her hand. He squinted, adjusting to the changed light.

'Good morning,' he said, taking her hand in his. 'What a pleasure to meet you at last.'

His hands were those of a bureaucrat, soft and spongy. They'd never felt a hard day's work. Rome rang in his accent – education, status and government. She couldn't reply, her self-consciousness lodged in her throat.

'What a beautiful property,' he said.

He turned to the fields. Italo and the men were at work, the dust trailing behind the planting machine. He raised his flat palm above his eyes to shield them from the light. He was shorter than she remembered, close to her height. He returned his attention to Amelia.

'We're very proud of it,' she said, disguising the taut strains of her northern accent. 'Please, come in.'

She walked ahead to the entrance hall. His eyes rose to the grandeur of the staircase. He smiled. She moved into the lounge room, on the right-hand side, and Clara rose from the armchair to meet him. He seemed startled by her, perhaps the widow weeds on such a young woman.

'This is Signora Clara Sacco.' Amelia's voice quavered. She could draw air only to the top of her lungs.

Signor Chieffi moved to take her hand, and Amelia motioned him towards the long, deep sofa. He waited until the two women were seated.

'I see the harvest is underway,' Signor Chieffi said.

Amelia seized – what was he talking about? And then she realised his error.

'The men aren't harvesting,' she said. 'It's the planting season.'

'I see.'

'The new crop will take a year to grow.'

'That long?'

'We're fortunate. Because of the heat. And the rain. The cane grows quickly. Further south, in New South Wales, it takes up to eighteen months. We can rotate a crop in a year.' She still couldn't breathe.

'I see.'

There was silence.

'When did you arrive in the area?' Clara said.

Bless Clara.

'Yesterday. Babinda holds a special place in my affection.'

Meggsy crossed the entrance hall with a tray of coffee and Florentine biscuits Amelia had baked that morning. She placed them on the table and Amelia thanked her, in English.

Chieffi turned to her. 'You don't keep an Italian girl?'

Amelia reddened. 'There are no Italian women in the district to employ for such tasks.'

'Is that right?'

He sipped his coffee, winced and returned the cup to the table. From his briefcase, he took a small dossier. Amelia looked at Clara and raised her eyebrows. Clara raised her lips to a half smile.

'I'm sorry it's taken time to schedule this meeting,' he said. 'But it was with great interest we received your proposal for the Italian school. From Sydney, the royal consul general, Doctor Vita-Finzi, has instructed me to convey his enthusiasm for the project and to offer you all assistance necessary.'

Amelia smiled, perhaps too broadly, and nodded.

'In this rich epoch, the motherland awakens,' Signor Chieffi said. 'At first glance, at this great distance, Italians living abroad are denied the joy of involvement in Italy's glory. Some, the children of immigrants especially, are disconnected, separated from traditional forms of Italian life and, perhaps more importantly, the new Italy. But you have rightly identified your role in the celebration of the regime: support and promotion of our cause abroad. The notion of education is at the heart of the fascist movement. A community first, but made of individuals.'

Such words, so fluid and complete, as if they'd been rehearsed, caught her breath.

'What easier way is there,' Amelia said, 'to keep the Italian language and culture alive than a school?'

'Quite. What has the interest been from the local community?'

Amelia tightened. 'At this stage, I've not sought that directly. But I've heard many say they despair their children can't speak Italian correctly.'

'And you've devised a schedule of fees?'

Amelia lifted a paper. 'I envisage a fee of five shillings per pupil per month.'

Chieffi wrote the figure.

'And how many pupils do you hope to entertain?'

'To start, about twenty.'

Chieffi wrote more and then looked at her. 'But that's only an income of five pounds a month. You won't pay a teacher for that, let alone other expenses.'

Amelia glanced at Clara and wished she'd briefed her fully on the financial intricacies, so she could help.

'To start, I was considering only opening one day a week,' Amelia said. 'Clara would be our teacher.' She looked towards her. 'What would you consider just payment?'

Clara moved slightly in her seat. 'It's hard for me to suggest what should be paid.'

'And yet you're a qualified teacher?' Signor Chieffi said.

'In Italy,' Clara said. 'I haven't had the opportunity to work in Australia.'

Chieffi regarded her. 'But even so, there's a substantial shortfall.'

Amelia's breath rushed to the depth of her lungs. Clearly, this man hadn't apprehended the subtly of her letters.

'I would like the Italian consul to match the funding,' she said.

Chieffi's eyes grew large. 'To pay half?'

'In other words.'

'I see.'

The idea rocked between them.

'I have other support,' Amelia said. 'Signor Giuseppe Luciano has promised Italian grammar books. I've looked at locations in Babinda and have secured quotes for rent. We may be able to use rooms at the Italian Club for free.'

'I support any patriotic work,' he said.

He returned to his notes. Perhaps she'd misjudged him.

'To be able to assist and protect your effort,' he said, 'it would be necessary for the school to be administered by an Italian women's fascist organisation.'

Amelia hesitated. 'No such organisation exists.'

'Then form one.'

Amelia grappled. 'There's an Italian Women's Association. Last year we donated over two pounds to the House of the Italians Abroad in Rome. We've also sent money directly to the Italian Red Cross in Abyssinia.'

'The Italian government appreciates your support.'

'Perhaps this existing organisation could be pressed to this service?' Amelia said.

'I'm sorry. To support your school, the women's fascist organisation would have to be controlled by the central power in Italy, Fascists Abroad, governing all such groups around the world, under the direct control of Rome. We must move away from the parochial, regional clubs and societies. We are a united Italy. We must have a consistent identity, intent and process. This can only be achieved, especially amongst the diaspora, if things are controlled by a central body.'

She looked at Clara, whose face stretched tight with concern. These direct links to fascism would disturb her. Amelia hadn't envisaged this. And to have other women involved in a committee would exponentially complicate the issue.

'To organise such a group of women would take months,' Amelia said. 'And then to have it endorsed by the central authority in Italy – this could take many more months. It would delay opening the school ... a full year, at the least.'

'The Italian government won't support anything less.'

Amelia breathed out. 'I see.'

'And we would demand that first and foremost, fascist ideology is taught.'

'Of course,' Clara said. 'As an ideology—'

'Not just as *an* ideology. Italian culture and art would be secondary to this.'

'But surely the Italian language is the priority,' Clara said. 'How can children be expected to understand the subtleties of fascist ideology if they can't speak Italian?'

'They'll learn Italian through studies of fascism.'

'Why polarise art and politics?'

Clara looked to Amelia for support, but Amelia had set her face to silence this discord. Clara demurred, slumped back into her chair. Her question hung in the air. If this was to be rescued, the argument had to be Amelia's.

Amelia looked directly at Signor Chieffi. 'If this structure is the will of the Italian government, then it's just. My concern is only the delay.'

Chieffi smiled broadly. 'I can assure you, in modern Italy, Rome *can* be built in a day, should a commitment be seen.'

Amelia was unsure how easy the task would be. There were other women in Babinda who'd been more outspoken in their support of Mussolini and the fascist government. Elena Moretti made it well known she'd donated a five-lire gold coin, along with her wedding ring and other gold jewellery. Amelia didn't have such luxuries to give.

Amelia smiled. 'It's an exciting time.'

'The correct instruction of children is paramount to the empire. On this, Il Duce is sanguine. They're the fascists of the future. And those abroad are under immense pressure to assimilate to their new countries, effectively to disappear.'

Signor Chieffi gathered his papers, signalling the end of their time. While he did this, he reminded the women of what they needed to do; start a women's fascist organisation, gauge the community interest and plan how the school would be structured.

'And raise some money,' he said. 'That will demonstrate commitment. Once this is done, we can proceed.'

Clara said goodbye. He took her hand.

'You have something in common with Il Duce's mother,' Chieffi said.

Clara's face contorted, querulous.

'She was a poor schoolteacher who struggled to provide a good education.'

Clara removed her hand, lowered her eyes, said nothing more and turned back to her seat by the window. Amelia accompanied him to the front door.

'I'll not keep you from your sweet business any longer,' he said, as if this clumsy pun were quick.

He clicked his heels, and she thought he may give the fascist salute. But he turned and walked away. The driver appeared from the side, opened the gate, and they all but marched to the car. He turned before he swung into the vehicle, dipping his hat to her before the car accelerated with that flawless movement of expensive mechanisation.

Amelia remained at the front door. Any work of this nature involved compromise. She'd have to find a way to approach the other women. She returned to the lounge room. Clara was at the window, holding something in her gaze. She made no move to acknowledge Amelia.

'You thought it went badly,' Amelia said.

Clara turned. 'He's stated his terms. Quite clearly.'

'You think they're unjust?'

Clara considered this. 'Not really. Not surprising. But I think he stated something else much more clearly: they just want control.'

'We want the same outcome.'

Clara turned back to the view. 'Why are you so support-ive of this?'

'You've heard the children speak. They need to improve their Italian.'

'You could instruct them—'

'I have no time.' She said this too sharply and moved closer to Clara. 'Don't you see? With the school, you could come and live here, bring Donata and Eugenia, work at your profession.'

'You know how attractive that is to me.'

'And to me. Then why are you against it?'

Clara made no move to answer. Amelia could bear this no more and walked from the room, through the entrance hall and dining room to the kitchen. Clara's attitude peeved her, but she had no desire to cause any discomfort or grief. Meggsy was at the stove, preparing lunch for the workers. Amelia asked her to clear the morning tea, but only because she wanted to be alone.

Why was Clara dour on this matter? It was an offer of employment and to live in Babinda, which was much cheaper than Brisbane, she would wager. Did she want to be like Betsy Taylor, endlessly dependant on handouts? She could find none of Clara's usual zeal.

Clara came to the kitchen. 'I appreciate your idea for the school.'

Amelia gathered herself. 'At first it will only be small but with time and support, it will grow. To have you living close …'

Clara's face contorted in vexation. 'I just don't understand your support for these people. Can't you see? He's not talking about fascism as an ideology; he's talking about indoctrination of children into a regime that runs on utter control, of all aspects of how people live, think and act.'

'I don't *see* he wants me to live, think or act in any way I don't want to.'

'This fury you have goes beyond that,' Clara said. 'Of all of us, all those years ago, you were the first to sound all praise for Australia. Australia is not a fascist country. I see around me the results of hard work and good fortune. You've changed, and I'm not sure I understand why.'

'Don't you remember,' Amelia said, 'when we left Italy, the smoke from Vesuvius? Italy smouldered. The war had snuffed her flame. You said I was a Bolshevik because I pointed out people were poor. These people, as you call them, canvas education for all. Prior to them, there wasn't a way forward.'

'But why do you care about that? We live here. We are Australian. And so are our children.'

'I am *not* Australian. Every day, every time I open my mouth, I'm slapped across the face with it. You know how hard I studied English. Any book I could get my hands on, not a newspaper I haven't pored over. And not a question I haven't asked when I didn't understand the smallest meaning. I slaved, much harder than I work to run this bloody farm. And I'm told by people I speak "so well", as if it's some bloody miracle. I speak English more correctly than half this valley.

'But in some small way, every day I'm told to stay at heel. Stay with the Italians. Stay in my place. They ostracise the Italians and then blame them for keeping to themselves. There'll always be a mispronunciation I'm reminded of. The shopkeeper will make a point of it.' Amelia cupped her hand to her ear, screwed up her face. '"What was that? What did you say? Oh ... flour". How unforgiving they are. How I'm struck for such a sin as a pure vowel, as they diphthong and stretch and torture and strain their drawn, nasally tongues beyond recognition. All because they were born to an English-speaking family.' She breathed out to steady herself. 'I know they call me Mrs Minestrone – and they purposefully butcher the word. And they call me Mrs Kelly. Do they think I'm deaf? Do they think I don't understand? They know. They just don't care. I will not be washed away. I am Italian.'

Amelia stared into Clara's eyes. Clara's face relaxed. 'I experience the same thing, but—'

Meggsy came to the kitchen with the remains of the morning tea.

'Don't you want to work as a teacher?' Amelia said. 'Earn your own living?'

Amelia had been too coarse, referring to Clara's financial situation like this. They'd willingly supported her and the children, but this couldn't go on indefinitely, and nor should it. Perhaps Clara needed to be reminded of that.

Clara breathed out. 'Of course I do. But I just wonder at the cost of doing this. Now. Under these conditions.'

'If there's one thing cane farming has taught me, it's that whatever the conditions, they are the prevailing conditions, and we must act accordingly.'

'And if we want this school?'

'If we want this school we must form a women's fascist organisation.'

Amelia breathed fully and walked from the kitchen, away from Meggsy. Marta had been teaching her Italian, and she was unsure how much she understood. Amelia climbed the stairs to her office and closed the door. She spent the rest of the afternoon working, pushing this upset away. She couldn't blame Clara for feeling uncomfortable with this close association, but if fascism was the way forward, then it was the way forward.

It was after dinner before she saw Clara alone.

'Who will control this women's group?' Clara said.

Amelia pondered this. 'I would be president. You would be secretary.'

'Then to a degree, we could control the school, teach as we saw fit.'

'Of course,' Amelia said. 'Once we have their support, we could distance ourselves.'

'You're proposing a fascist group in name only.'

Amelia thought of this. It would be a balancing act, but everything she'd done in this country had been on a tightrope. If this would win Clara's support, she nodded.

Clara held her gaze. 'All right,' she said. 'What must we do?'

CHAPTER TWENTY-ONE

The telephone machine hung on the wall, encased in a purpose-built booth off the main entrance hall, the large wooden case supporting the two bells at the top, the round piece mounted below, the grim straight line of the lectern a mouth. Marta continually laughed at it, calling it *il uomo del muro* – the man on the wall. The next morning, Amelia placed some notes on the lectern. She lifted the earpiece, wound the lever and waited for the operator to come on the line and connect her to Gino Grossi, the president of the Babinda Fascist Organisation. The line went quiet.

She had a chequered history with Grossi. He was a cane farmer, a Roman, from Rignano Flaminio. She found those born near the capital often bore an arrogance. Many years ago, during a harvest season, Grossi had seconded a gang of men she'd contracted. He was desperate and promised to pay them a higher wage. At the time, he'd left her in the lurch, down four strong men. But if he'd only listened to her, she'd have also let four more men go to him on the proviso that the following week he'd return the eight men plus his men. But Grossi was headstrong and wouldn't listen to a woman's bargain.

Yet in early 1930, Grossi was one of the first to complain publicly about the British Preference League; they were backed by the Australian Workers' Union and stipulated the Italian cane farmers had first to hire their members, all British Australians. Once the British were fully employed, the Italians could employ 'foreigners' to fill any remaining positions. Grossi was infuriated Italian landowners couldn't employ Italian cutters. And the British Australians had set pay and conditions. If these weren't met, the unions could boycott the farmer.

The Italian royal consul in Sydney sent a vice-consul to Cairns, a Count di San Marzano. He toured the area, spoke publicly against the League. The Italian government was willing to help the Italian farmers. Hence the Babinda Fascist Organisation was formed, Italo one of the first to join, now with well over a hundred members. As austere as it sounded, largely it was a type of business league, the manifestation of a communal urge to help one another, as the Italians had always done before the unions and the Preference League came lording to the fields.

Signor Grossi came on the telephone line. She suspected the telephonist would listen to the conversation and so kept it to a minimum. She'd like to meet with him and any other officials of the organisation to discuss a proposal. He had the grace not to ask for details and suggested he and Antonio Burattini, the secretary, could meet with her in three days time. She proposed convening at her farm at ten-thirty on Thursday morning.

When she emerged from the booth, Clara was seated in the lounge room, reading a book. She told her of the proposed meeting.

'He has a high standing in the community,' Amelia said. 'If we can convince him, we'll have a powerful ally.'

'I find it hard to accept he's so against the union movement. A worker has to be protected.'

'It's not like Paolo's situation,' Amelia said, feeling the unintended smite.

Clara was still sensitive. And she had a right to be. Paolo's death was a tragedy, and the way it had been dealt with by the employer, the Australian government, was criminal.

'Farming can't run to such a schedule,' Amelia said. 'When the harvest is ready, it must be done. And a lot of the Italian men didn't want these enforced conditions. The cutting season's short, only twenty weeks. If they got the work done at one farm, they could start at another. They just wanted to make as much money as they could. They'd have worked by moonlight. They might have worked long hours, but they were fed well and paid. The British Preference League just wanted to block the Italians.'

Clara's face turned to stone. Marta came into the room, begging Clara to go and see an excitement in the garden. Clara bounded to attention. She turned back to Amelia.

'I suppose you're right,' she said.

Amelia seethed. Why did Clara reduce everything to an opposition, as if the Babinda Fascist Organisation were a foe, not a potential friend? So she poured out her thoughts to Italo that night, when they were alone in bed.

'Give her time,' he said.

'She's so prone to melancholy.'

'She's had a lot of change.' He was silent. 'We have each other. She's lost that.'

'She needs employment. The school won't happen unless we're totally committed.'

'Then she's your greatest ally.'

She failed to see how he could think this when Clara's opinion vacillated. 'How do you arrive at that conclusion?'

'Her son will be a doctor …'

The statement caught Amelia off guard. 'And? …'

'Could you imagine such a thing in Italy?'

Amelia thought of Cristiano. What would his life have been there? Would he have been able to achieve this? She dismissed the thought. 'He's bright. He works hard—'

'There's no doubt, but Clara has fought to clear the way for him. Such a thing ... at university, a doctor.' He smiled. 'Your school's a noble idea. She'll fight for you.'

'She doesn't seem to share the excitement.'

Italo looked at her. 'She'll come around.'

His face relaxed, was tender. He kissed her. She wanted to sleep. But a flicker ignited a heat she'd almost forgotten, and she returned his enthusiasm.

Three days later, Gino Grossi filled the lounge room. He was taller than Italo, broader and a much heavier set. He had a fair complexion, a reminder of his Roman ancestry, and sharp hazel eyes, but his hair had greyed completely, though he was only in his mid-forties. It surprised Amelia, especially when she'd first met him so many years ago, that he was unmarried. At first she'd suspected some sorrow, a death perhaps, or that he was a difficult man. But it appeared his unmarried status was merely the result of few women in the district, especially Italian women. His voice boomed with authority.

He was accompanied by Antonio Burattini, the secretary of the Babinda Fascist Organisation. He too was a tall man but slenderer. He was accompanied by his wife, Maria, who hadn't spoken to Amelia for many years. Why had she come?

In Clara's presence, an air came over Grossi, something Amelia had never seen before, making him gracious and gentler. There was a falseness to it, as if the gentility he portrayed came with effort.

Once they were seated, Amelia went straight to business and explained the idea for the school. She couched its objectives in succinct terms borrowed from Chieffi: the involvement of Italians abroad in Italy's glory, that education for all was at the heart of the Italian government. She added they'd met with Chieffi, and he was supportive of the idea. Grossi was silent, his attention locked in his thoughts until he breathed out fully.

'Let me first say what an admirable ambition this is. A school such as you've described will provide a service missing from the area, a great addition to our community.'

'Clara would move here to take up the position of teacher.'

Maria Burattini wrote something in a notebook, her eyes beady and withdrawn to avoid Amelia's.

'It's unfortunate you didn't speak with us first,' Grossi said. 'The Babinda Fascist Organisation can't support the formation of a separate women's organisation as you've described. We derive our power from solidarity. Such an act, a separation, would be a dilution.'

'But Chieffi was clear it had to be a separate organisation.'

'I think you may have misunderstood him.' He breathed out fully. 'We've been encouraged to set up a women's organisation but, to be honest, there hasn't been the time or an idea to focus the interest. The school is perfect. We can offer you support and guidance, even financial assistance. But the women's group would have to be under our control.'

Amelia felt out of her depth, but she couldn't bring herself to look at Clara. And that infernal woman kept writing in her notebook. 'What would we need to do?'

'Firstly, you'd need to demonstrate there's interest. The simplest manner would be a petition, signed by people willing to join.'

'This should be an easy matter,' Amelia said. 'Many complain their children can't speak Italian.'

Amelia looked at Clara, her face set stone.

'From the group of supporters, you'd need to hold elections for a president, a secretary and a treasurer. Once these office-bearers were in place, we could acknowledge the group.'

Amelia heard the front door open. Italo came into the room, still dressed in his work clothes. He stood in the lounge doorway. He'd come from the field without washing, and it was only midmorning. He'd removed his work boots. Something was wrong. Amelia's heart rate rose.

'I just heard on the wireless,' Italo said. 'Haile Selassie has fled Abyssinia. The Italian forces have taken control of Addis Ababa.' He paused. 'Italy has won the war in Abyssinia.'

The room froze. This was momentous. Despite the League of Nations' trade sanctions and the world's condemnation, Italy had won. Amelia flooded with pride. Italy was an empire again.

'This is a fine thing,' Maria Burattini said.

Grossi rose from his seat. 'Il Duce is unstoppable,' he said. A smile, spirited and broad, spread across his face. 'Ladies, I hope you'll understand, as president of the Babinda Fascists, there are things I must do. Now this momentous victory is secured, I can say more than ever we support an Italian school.'

He strode to the entrance hall as if there were a fire. Amelia followed him, handed him his hat and coat, and he prepared to leave. Italo opened the door.

'I'll be in touch about the particulars,' Grossi said to her. He turned to Clara. 'How long are you in the area?'

Clara stepped back slightly. 'I'm not sure. But long enough to have this planning underway.'

'Then, I hope to see you again.'

'I'm sure we will, with this project.'

How curious he should initiate this. It was far too early for Clara, and Amelia knew she wouldn't find a man like Grossi interesting. But with that, he left the house, with Burattini and his wife close behind.

Amelia looked at Clara and then to Italo. Both appeared perplexed by the hasty conclusion to their meeting.

'I fear this will make our position in Australia harder,' Clara said.

'What do you mean?' Amelia said.

'Italy can no longer be considered an ally of Australia,' Clara said.

The three stood in silence. Could Clara take no joy from this? Her expression was set hard. Then Italo excused himself, said he must get back to the field.

'This is momentous news,' Amelia said.

'These demands by the Babinda fascist group are too tight,' Clara said. 'The school will be controlled.'

Amelia breathed in. What would ever lift this weight from Clara? She would have to remain calm.

'On the contrary,' Amelia said. 'The enthusiasm for the victory in Abyssinia will help us. It will lend the school the support it needs from wealthy Italian people. And once the school is open, we can establish and maintain a distance.'

'You seem so sure.'

'I know these people. We must do what Grossi suggests, seek out women for the organisation. Once we have demonstrated this, we'll have something to bargain with.'

A flurry of joy circulated the valley. In the market, Amelia saw pride in the Italians' steps. *The Italian Journal* reported something long lost had been regained. And in quieter conversations, people wondered what else Mussolini would achieve.

While Amelia delivered food parcels to the area, she and Clara carried their petition from Italian farm to Italian farm. Amelia had no idea how they would be received, but the women opened to her in a way they hadn't for many, many years. They signed.

And when the word began to circulate, women came to her, seeking out the petition. Within a week, they had the signatures of over a hundred women, pledging to join the women's fascist organisation. As a proactive step, they also took the names of people who would enrol their children. She wrote to Chieffi, affirming they had the interest of at least thirty pupils willing to pay five shillings a week for lessons. Whilst she'd always been hopeful, the warmth of the response surprised her.

When Amelia telephoned Grossi with this news, he was too busy to meet with them.

'This weekend,' he said, 'there'll be a celebration at the Italian Club for the victory.'

'We'll all be there,' Amelia said.

'Perhaps after this glorious evening, there'll be more time.'

Of course, the celebration of the victory took all precedence, but did she detect something else in his voice? Amelia was busy. Always. But if something demanded her attention she would find the time to address it. This tardiness in Grossi carried something else. She wasn't sure what. But she had no way to press him. She would just have to wait.

CHAPTER TWENTY-TWO

The Italian Club was built on a small pocket of land near the bridge across Babinda Creek, which flowed from the boulders around the outskirts of the town and to the sea. The weatherboard building was like a church hall, finished off with a gabled corrugated iron roof. Amelia and Clara climbed one of the two sets of opposing steps leading to a small portico with a matching tiny roof, whereas Italo took the other side. They met in the middle, under the portico.

'What a surprise seeing you two here,' Italo said.

'Go on with your foolishness,' Amelia said, walking directly to the hall, but Clara stopped and laughed.

The hall was long, perhaps thin, casement windows along either side. At the far end, draped across the stage's proscenium, was a large tricolour flag. The stage was set for speakers, a desk and chairs and more flags. Behind them an orchestra was arranged, as dancing and singing were requisite for any Saturday night at the Italian Club. Chairs lined the perimeter of the hall.

A crowd had gathered, the air already close. Clara took Amelia's fur coat, and hers, to the cloakroom. Most of the men wore fascist-black shirts. Italo too. Some of the wives had prepared a supper, which they fussed over to the side of the stage. Although it was a club, it had no licence to serve alcohol, so once it was dark the men would disappear through the side entrance to drink beer at the tray of a truck in the dark of the nearby field.

Amelia introduced Clara to some of the women, Signora Appiani, Signora Guarneri and Anna Nanni. Could these women, on this victorious evening, not give up the aloofness they directed to her? Grossi came from the other end of the hall to greet them.

'I'm so pleased you could make it,' he said.

Whilst he addressed them as a group, he looked only at Clara. Even though she still wore widow weeds, Grossi clearly saw this as no barrier. Amelia wished he would delay an avowal, as Clara was still too raw and would refute any advance. But Clara was an intelligent woman and would make her own way.

'I'm sorry I've not given your school the attention it deserves,' he said.

'We've been active,' Clara said. 'The petition has a hundred signatures.'

Grossi raised his eyebrows.

'And thirty assurances of enrolment,' Amelia said.

'That's quite something,' he said.

Men began to file onto the stage, marking the commencement of the formal part of the evening. Grossi's attention was lost. He slipped from Amelia's fingers again, nodding to the women and walking away. Amelia had wanted to press him for another meeting and felt vexed. He disappeared into a room at the side and reappeared onstage. Burattini and the other office-bearers crowded the stage. Antonio Fontana, the founder of the Italian Returned Soldiers' Organisation, joined them.

Before anything was said, the crowd rose in thunderous applause.

'This evening,' Grossi said, his voice raised over the applause. 'I invite you to cry, *Viva il Duce!*'

Unsynchronised, the crowd spluttered, but soon came to one voice – *Viva il Duce! Viva il Duce!* – with such force she felt as if shoes pounded the floor. Amelia looked to Clara, but she remained tight-lipped. The other women to their side had joined the call. Signora Guarneri looked at her, her mouth opening and closing to the chant. She felt a rush of excitement inhibited only by Clara. It would be unseemly not to join, and so Amelia began the chant. Clara remained mute.

Grossi smiled at the crowd and then at his compatriots on stage. The crowd saw no reason to stop, and Amelia continued as loud as she could. Grossi stepped back from the lectern, as if all that had to be said had been said. When he finally stepped forward, raised his two hands in front of him, the chant wound down.

'The height of this victory, the importance for Italy, cannot be underscored.'

He spoke of the beauty of the strategies in the final battles to take control of Addis Ababa. He spoke of Mussolini's vision, ability and grace.

'The Babinda Fascist Organisation has cabled our congratulations directly to Il Duce and to Marshal Badoglio, the commander in chief of the victorious army.'

Such a thing, that a message from Babinda could be sent to those of such importance. Grossi spoke more, of the role of Italians living aboard, who'd offered support by any means they could.

'The little Italy of the past is not the one of today. New Italy has changed her face. Completely. And not only do Italians know this, but the whole world bears witness.'

The club erupted, out of which grew the chant *Viva il Duce*. Carried away, Amelia joined, shouting with all the force she could find, shouting it too for Clara, who stood mute and steeled at her side. How could she not be moved by this patriotism?

Grossi gave the fascist salute, and the men in the hall came to attention and returned the gesture. A small orchestra came onstage. Even then, as they settled and tuned their instruments, the roar of the crowd continued until they struck the opening of *La Giovinezza*, the fascists' anthem. The noise continued until the crowd settled to its part, a solid, insistent voice. Amelia sang,

> Youth, Youth,
>
> Spring of beauty,
>
> In the hardship of life
>
> Your song rings and goes!
>
> And for Benito Mussolini,
>
> And for our beautiful Fatherland.

The men rose again to the fascist salute, their hands forced proud above their shoulders. The women raised their hands and applauded the anthem.

This state continued as the men left the stage, even while they cleared the tables and lectern. The men came from the side of the stage, out into the crowd, which reignited the din. People shook their hands, these men who represented Mussolini.

The orchestra struck a waltz. Some of the men drained from the hall to the nearby field, but those remaining partnered with the women. Amelia and Clara stood together. Italo wasn't to be seen, but she didn't mind he'd gone outside to drink with the men. Grossi came to them, smiling.

'An inspiring speech,' Amelia said.

'I'm not much of an orator, but Mussolini inspires us to new heights.' He turned to Clara. 'Signora, would you like to dance?'

He offered his arm. Clara flushed scarlet and stepped back.

'I'm sorry,' she said. 'I don't dance.'

'Then let the evening inspire you.'

He smiled again, although an insecurity had entered it, something Amelia had never seen brush his face. Clara stepped back, shook her head slightly and walked away, leaving Amelia with Grossi.

'It's too soon,' she said.

He nodded, and she left to find Clara at the back of the hall.

'Are you tired?' Amelia said to Clara.

'I don't feel like dancing. But I can sit if you and Italo would like to.'

Amelia looked around the hall. Despite the good feelings, she had no desire to be further judged by these people. Italo had returned from the field and was standing to the far side of the hall.

Amelia raised her eyebrows. 'I run a farm. I've no energy for dancing.'

She caught Italo's eye and motioned to her watch, a sign to leave. Amelia went to collect their coats. Signora Guarneri approached her.

'I've heard an exciting rumour,' Signora Guarneri said, drawing Amelia closer. 'The Babinda Fascists are to open an Italian school.'

This woman hadn't spoken to Amelia for years. Why would she choose to tell her something she already knew?

'It's no rumour,' Amelia said. 'If you'd like to sign our petition, I'm in charge of it.'

The woman pulled back slightly. 'But I'd heard the idea was Signora Burattini's, and she leads the planning.'

Amelia stared at the woman. 'Then you've heard most incorrectly.'

Signora Guarneri shrunk back. 'Perhaps I have.'

'If you'll call at my house tomorrow, you can sign *our* petition.'

The woman nodded slowly, as if uncertain. Amelia gathered their coats, but in the hall she could see no sign of Italo or Clara and assumed they were outside. The damn fool woman, a gossip always, and she peddled inaccuracy. Amelia said goodnight, only by nodding, on the way from the hall. In the small portico, Clara was talking with Signora Appiani. She handed Clara her coat and walked down one of the sets of steps. It was past mid-May, nearly to winter, such as that was. The night air was chilled, sharp against the heat of the hall. She pulled her coat in around her shoulders. She couldn't see Italo. She turned back to Clara, who was still in the portico.

'Have you seen Italo?' she said.

Clara looked at her. 'I thought he was with you.'

Amelia waved to Signora Appiani, and Clara said goodbye and came down the stair.

'Where is he?' Amelia said.

'Perhaps he's at the car,' Clara said.

'I wouldn't have thought he'd go without us. Nor his coat.' She looked in the direction of the car, but it was too dark to see anything. 'Let's walk.'

They started in that direction.

'The speeches were so positive,' Amelia said.

'Yes.'

Amelia laughed. 'Only Clara could pack doubt into a word with the opposite meaning.'

Clara huffed and looked away. Amelia linked her arm through hers and they continued to the car.

'A woman just approached me about the school,' Amelia said. 'She was under the impression Signora Burattini was organising it.'

'What did you say?'

'I disabused her of the idea. Such a gossip, and on—'

'What's that?' Clara said, stopping, her arm slipping from Amelia's.

'What?' Amelia peered into the darkness.

'By the car.'

Amelia looked. The cloud-filtered moonlight illuminated little. There was something, like a large canvas bag, lying at the vehicle's rear. She looked closer. It was a man, collapsed.

'Some drunken fool,' Amelia said. 'So drunk he's lost his way back from the field.'

Amelia strained to see more, but it was too dark.

'We should go back for Italo,' Clara said.

The clouds parted, and what little there was of moonlight came through. They turned back towards the club. But as they walked, Amelia heard a groan from the car and glanced back.

'That looks like Italo,' Clara said, taking her arm from Amelia's.

Amelia took several steps and peered. Her heart began to race. She took another step and quickly another. It was him. She could see his face, bloodied around the nose and mouth.

'Italo,' she yelled.

She dropped to her knees beside him. He was unconscious, his shirt ripped open, his tie pulled tight. His left eye was swollen, the skin to the side of the upper lid torn and bleeding. There was the iron smell of blood, but something rank, full of sulphur, like rotten eggs.

'Italo,' she yelled again.

But he didn't stir. She put her hand to his face, felt its warmth, which brought some assurance – he was alive. His chest heaved, covered in a slimy liquid.

He opened his eyes, raised his bloodied hand to her arm. Clara was now by their side.

'What's happened?' Clara said.

'Perhaps he fell,' Amelia said, bewildered, grappling to make sense. 'Did he have that much to drink?'

Clara knelt. She shook her head. Italo breathed and shuddered. Amelia heard something, someone's step on the gravel of the road near them, but in the dark. There was a figure, a man.

'Who's there?' Clara said.

The figure moved forward, just a step or two. At first Amelia thought she was mistaken but was sure it was Flavio.

'What are you doing here?' she said. 'Come and help.'

The figure advanced a little closer.

'Help me get your father to his feet,' she said.

Still crouching, she looked at him. He remained in the darkness. He was dressed in clothes she'd never seen, a white shirt and jacket and long pants. He wore a hat. And then she looked closer. Under some mysterious command, she stood, her legs trembling. She glared into the dark, but he didn't move so she stepped to him.

'Fergus?' she said.

Clara gasped but remained by Italo.

A cold numbness washed over Amelia. This wasn't real. It couldn't be. But she could see his face. He remained impassive, as if nothing of any great significance was happening. She felt no dread. Just sharp inquisition.

'What are you doing here?' she said.

She searched him. In all the years, he'd not changed greatly.

'Let's get him up,' Clara said.

Amelia looked at Italo and Clara. Fergus stepped forward, passed within a few feet. He placed his steady hands under Italo's arms and hauled him, sat him against the rear wheel of the car and then stepped away.

'Italo,' Clara said, still crouched beside him.

'I'm all right,' he said, his voice hoarse and faint.

Amelia stood rooted to the spot, between Italo and Fergus. Italo coughed, softly at first and then more violently. Fergus stepped back. Amelia crouched beside him. His eyes were shut. She looked at Clara, concern on her face.

'I'm sorry,' Italo said, and leant to the side and vomited, a volume of putrid liquid hitting the ground, pooling where he sat.

She passed her hand in small circles on his back.

'The more he can bring up the better,' Clara said.

Once he'd stopped, he sat up, his face raised to the stars.

'I'll go and find a doctor,' Clara said.

Amelia agreed and was glad that Clara had taken command.

'Just take me home,' Italo said. 'Nothing is broken. I'm just sore. Just take me home.'

The two women stood. Fergus stepped forward and squatted in front of Italo, who seemed to be unaware of his presence. In one motion, such was his strength, he pulled Italo to his feet. Italo groaned. Clara found a travel rug in the back of the car and lay it along the back seat. Amelia stood to the side. She wrung her hands. What could she do? Fergus lowered him and then stood and moved back.

Despite the stench surrounding Italo, she could smell Fergus. Italo pushed himself along the seat, but such a tall man had to crumple to fit in such a position.

'Did you see what happened?' Amelia said, without looking at Fergus.

'I was in the village,' Fergus said. 'I heard the noise out here and came to see what was happening. I was walking away when I saw you.'

'Let's just get home,' Clara said, her voice impatient and cold.

Amelia couldn't face Fergus. 'Thank you.'

'Would you like me to come to the house?'

Amelia turned to Clara, who shook her head. 'We can manage,' Clara said.

She looked into his eyes. How many times she'd longed for this. How many questions flickered, but each seemed inappropriate. Why did life tear her between two extremes? She bowed her head and walked to the driver's side of the car. Clara sat in the passenger's and closed the door. Fergus moved around to Amelia's.

'Thank you,' she said again, the only words she could muster.

He raised his closed lips to a half smile and nodded.

Amelia drove from the hall, towards the farm. In the mirror, she caught his frame, still, until the light was too weak and he faded.

'I don't want to talk about it,' Clara said. 'Not here, not now.'

And neither did she. To quell her mind, she concentrated on driving. Italo groaned. She kept the pace as fast as she could. Once they'd curved around the hill, she parked near the gate and hauled him out and between them walked him slowly to the front door. Meggsy had heard the car and opened the door, gasping when she saw Italo's state.

'Take him through to the kitchen,' Amelia said.

Meggsy ran ahead. Italo's gait was strained and uneven, but Amelia clasped him around the waist. Meggsy placed an old chair on the tiled kitchen floor.

'Get him some water,' Amelia said.

She took off his tie, loosened what was left of the black-shirt collar. The shirt and his jacket were covered in the oily, sulphur-smelling yellow liquid. Amelia took the glass from Meggsy and asked her to fetch a basin of warm water, some soap and an old towel.

Italo drank a small amount.

'What's happened?' Amelia asked.

'I'm not entirely sure,' he said. 'I couldn't find either of you and thought you must still be in the club. I thought I'd bring the car closer. I was only a few hundred feet away when I heard someone moving behind me. But it was dark, and I couldn't see anyone, and after such an agreeable evening I didn't think much of it.'

He stopped, took another sip of water.

'The next thing, well … I'm not sure. Someone hit me over the head. It felled me. And then there was a mob, kicking me in the stomach, in the head. Everywhere.'

Meggsy returned with the basin of warm water. She put it on the table, and Amelia dipped the cloth, lathered it from a bar of soap and dabbed at the liquid and blood on his face.

'What is all this?' she said.

'They forced a funnel in my mouth. They yelled, "Take that, you fucking fascist pig". I don't know how much I swallowed. They only stopped because you two came.'

There were rumours for years – everyone had heard them – that Mussolini had coerced his opponents to cooperate with castor oil, 'the golden nectar of nausea'. Amelia had dismissed them. But Italo was a member of the Babinda Fascist Organisation, and clearly he'd been attacked for being at an evening run by this organisation. That much was certain.

Clara glared at her. 'We should get a doctor.'

Italo winced, put a hand to his ribs. 'There's nothing to be done.'

'But you're injured. We should get the police.'

'I'm hurting, but nothing's damaged.'

'Who were they?'

'I only saw them when they were forcing the oil.' He stopped. 'I didn't recognise any of them.'

'They must be Australians,' Clara said. 'Was Fergus amongst them?'

'No …' His face screwed to query. He started to cough. 'They spoke Italian.' He stood slowly, his face wizened. 'I'll go and clean myself.'

Amelia watched him walk from the kitchen. She took the basin to the sink and drained the water.

'He's going to be very ill,' Clara said. 'The castor oil will give him terrible diarrhoea.'

'The oil is rank. Why would Italians do this?'

'We don't all hold the same opinion.'

Clara turned away. The remark slapped Amelia, something callous and chiding in it. Amelia ground her teeth and wouldn't say anything. Too much had happened too quickly. To see Fergus … When had he returned? She'd heard no gossip of it, but the women pursed their lips whenever she walked by. Why was he there? The confusion exhausted her.

She left Clara and went to Italo. He stood naked in the washroom, his torn black shirt and vest and trousers discarded in the corner. Despite the soap and water, the oil stuck to the skin around his neck, glistening in the low lamplight. Even now, the bruising appeared, yellowing purple washes across the skin, around his ribcage and stomach. It was said castor oiling provided a three-way attack: it gave intimate control over another's body, it caused gross humiliation and it imprisoned a person for a week as they recovered. How could someone do this to another?

'Please,' Italo said. 'Leave me.'

'Dry yourself.'

She went upstairs to their room for a robe. When she returned he was bent over, clutching his stomach. When the gripe eased, he put on the robe. She called out to Clara, and together they helped him to the privy at the side of the house.

'This is going to be severe and prolonged,' Clara said. 'I'll move the chamber pot to your room.'

Amelia waited for Italo, and once he'd composed himself she helped him upstairs. Almost at the sight of the commode, the cramps seized him.

They left him in private.

CHAPTER TWENTY-THREE

All night Italo groaned, relieved himself, and for some moments the worst seemed to have abated. But then the cramps flared again: huge amounts of pain, stabbing wind. Within a few hours there must have been nothing left in his system, but the cramps and spasms and what could barely be described as diarrhoea, little more than a frothy mucus, continued.

The morning announced itself, light sweeping into the room, surprising Amelia. She hadn't closed the drapes. The light would rouse him. He needed sleep. She stood, felt faint – having not left his side, she'd not eaten or drunk water. She steadied herself on the back of the chair. He was resting now. She tidied the sheet about his throat and walked to the drapes. The first stains of dawn lifted the sky.

She looked down to the field. Fergus. So long ago, a lifetime ago, he'd appeared in a dream, rather a ghost in a nightmare. But it had only been a matter of hours. Had she just imagined it? He was there, wasn't he? In the car Clara had said she didn't want to discuss it, so she must have seen him. Can an apparition be shared? What was he doing in Babinda? What did he want from her? The years of dread transformed to anxiety.

Across the fields, the day gathered pace. Italo was so attuned to the dawn. She didn't want him disturbed and slowly pulled the drapes.

Clara brought a tray with tea for Amelia and some water for Italo. All night he'd complained his mouth was bone-dry but each time he sipped the water, he kept only a little down.

'He's resting,' Amelia said. 'I don't think we should disturb him.'

'We have to try. He's lost so much fluid.'

They raised his head from the pillow and the glass to his mouth. He sipped some, and they took that as an encouraging sign and gave him more. But once he was resting, he vomited. Amelia sponged the water with a towel. As the morning proceeded they tried again and again but each time he vomited. By midmorning she realised he'd not urinated since the evening before. He would sleep deeply for an hour or two and then rise in an agitated mess, confused as to where he was and what had happened. At one point he called out to Signora Pina. And now he burned, his forehead hot and clammy.

'We need to get a doctor,' Clara said.

Amelia stared at her. How many child fevers had she nursed, but of his she was frightened, beyond knowing what to do. She would give in. Let Clara take charge. She nodded.

Clara telephoned, but it was after midafternoon before the doctor arrived, by which time Italo was awake and complaining of a headache and the next minute saying he felt better. The doctor checked his vital signs; his pulse was elevated and he had a fever.

'Apart from the effects of the oil,' the doctors said, 'he's now dehydrated. Severely. We need to keep his temperature down so he doesn't lose more water through sweating. Remove his bedclothes.'

Amelia unbuttoned the nightshirt and removed it.

'Get some cloths and water.'

Amelia hurried to the kitchen for the water and a cloth. When she returned to the bedroom, the doctor had opened the window.

'We'll moisten his skin. The draft will help cool him.'

The doctor placed some wet clothes in his armpits and groin.

'Now we need to get him to drink some fluid. Boil water and let it cool. Dissolve some sugar and a little salt. But give it to him in very, very small sips. He'll want more, but if you give him too much too quickly he'll vomit, and all will be lost. Just small sips with a ten-minute interval.'

Clara went to boil the water.

'I dare say this will pass,' the doctor said. 'But if not …'

'What?'

His face was stern. Anxiety ripped through Amelia. This was far more serious than she'd thought.

'Let's cross that when we come to it. Do as I've said. Please, let me know how he's faring. If he appears worse, contact me immediately.'

Amelia saw the doctor from the house and went to the kitchen. Clara was seated at the table, Meggsy at the stove.

'What else did he say?' Clara said.

The words caught. 'That he may get worse.' Clara stood. For some seconds Amelia stared at Clara and then began to cry. She breathed in and held the breath. 'He might die.'

Meggsy gasped. Clara, her face held stern, turned to the stove to check the water. 'That's not going to happen.'

'It's all my fault. I made him join—'

'There's no point in thinking like that. Let's get this water to him.'

Clara poured the boiled water into a large jug. Amelia could do nothing. Clara took the sugar from the pantry and dissolved two large tablespoons, found the salt and added a little. She poured some into a glass and tasted it, and then added a little more salt. Just watching her, her practical hand, brought Amelia some calm.

'Thank God you're here,' Amelia said.

'We care for each other.'

Amelia remembered the Gulf of Aden, and how ill Clara and Frau Gruetzmann had been, and the long days she and Cristiano had cared for them.

Together they carried the jug of water back to the bedroom. Italo was lying peacefully on the bed and didn't wake when they entered. Clara poured a glass, wound a teaspoon in the water and left it to draw away the heat. They sponged him again. Clara fanned him with the skirt of her apron.

Once the water had cooled, they raised his head from the pillow. He was only half awake, but he sipped some. He woke then, roused by the fluid, and as the doctor had said, he signalled he wanted more, but they refused him, lay his head down again. Every ten minutes, they repeated this. Even if he was asleep or dozing they woke him. And in between, they sponged him, replaced the tepid towels in his armpits and groin. But his forehead remained on fire, unremitting. By ten that evening, he'd sipped a full litre without vomiting. Amelia telephoned the doctor. He was pleased but still concerned about his temperature.

'Call me if he worsens.'

So the sipping continued. Twice they had to take him to the commode. He would groan and place his hands over his naked belly. He'd not urinated, but the diarrhoea was less.

'It's more cramps than anything,' Clara said.

So they continued all night, aware he needed sleep but more concerned he needed water. And they sat together, not a word between them, just the odd half smile. Amelia felt no need for sleep, none, fear and anger and sorrow and anxiety pushing off this necessity.

Who could have done this? And why? And he'd said these people were Italian but not from the area.

They continued all night, hardly noticing the approaching dawn. Clara stood. 'I'll make us coffee.'

Amelia nodded. She looked at Italo. 'He's resting. I'll come and help.'

In the kitchen, Amelia sat at the table while Clara prepared the coffee. The pre-dawn cold chilled her bones. If Mussolini had employed this castor oiling to coerce his opposition, why had no-one mentioned it in letters from Italy? She'd heard rumours and speculation in Babinda, but nothing at all from Italy. Clara placed the coffee in front of her, its aroma full and inviting.

'It was a shock to see Fergus,' Clara said.

Amelia felt the frankness as a blow. She could no longer push him from her thoughts. Fergus had returned. But in light of the attack on Italo, it seemed minor.

'Worst things have happened,' Amelia said.

'You have to tell him to leave. If Flavio sees him—'.

'What can I do?' She spoke too loud and too strong, but suddenly she couldn't keep the tiredness and stress at bay. 'He's been away for sixteen years. He's free to walk the streets. And yes, tongues will ignite—'

'Then you have to tell Flavio.'

'How can I do that?' She felt drunk with confusion. 'You've always said I can't—'

'What if he sees Fergus? What if someone says something to him? It will destroy him. And Marta and Mauro, if they hear of it. See him.'

Amelia shook her head. 'Don't do this to me, not now.' She began to cry. 'You criticised me for sending Flavio away. Now you understand.'

'All this deceit—'

'You told me never to speak of it.'

'How could I have known the child would resemble his father so closely?' Clara asked. 'It's just more lies to cover old lies.'

'You can't change your mind on this?'

'What happened with Ben?' Clara's tone bore accusation, tremoring her anxiety, which shook Amelia.

'The farmhand?' Amelia said. 'Why do you bring that up?' Amelia sat back in the chair. She wouldn't be interrogated on her past decisions. 'That was years ago.'

After Ben had noticed the missing horse, she'd known he knew of her liaison with Fergus. Ben had moved about the property so silently. When she and Italo had begun expanding the business, she'd justified Ben's removal by arguing they couldn't afford him. She'd found him a position on a cane farm near Innisfail. But despite all the years she felt great remorse.

'He knew something,' Clara said. 'Didn't he?'

'Did Meggsy say that?'

'No.'

Amelia breathed out. 'He'd seen me going to Fergus's hut.'

'You made him leave.'

'There was enough risk,' Amelia said.

'He was a cripple, badly disfigured by a fire. How could you be so heartless?'

'He knew everything.'

'And so does Fergus—'

From the far recesses of the house, Italo cried out.

She looked at Clara. 'I don't know what's to be done, but not another word of any of this. Swear to me.'

Clara stared at her, defiance in her eye. But then it relaxed. 'Of course. You know best.'

'Amelia,' Italo cried, the voice reverberating in the stairwell.

She ran from the kitchen, up the stairs. He was standing at the top of the stairwell, so lifeless he swayed before her.

'Where were you?' he yelled.

'I was in the kitchen. I'm here now. What's the matter?'

He looked at her, steadied himself. 'I must have been dreaming. They were beating me again.'

'You're safe.'

Clara came up the stair. Amelia climbed the last few steps to him. She took his forearm, motioned he should return to the room. He breathed deeply.

'I could drink an ocean,' he said.

Clara took his other arm, and together they guided him back to the bedroom. As they worked, neither mentioned what had passed between them, the argument having leant an automation to their care. Or perhaps Clara wanted to avoid her. By midafternoon he'd drunk another litre of water, and there was no sign of cramping or diarrhoea for some time. He slept, deeply but in short bursts.

'He's doing quite well,' Clara said, finally.

Amelia looked at him. His colour was still greyed.

'I'm sorry we disagreed,' Clara said. 'Why don't you go and sleep?'

Amelia thought. 'As inviting as that sounds, I feel no real need. You go.'

'At least go for a walk, some fresh air. Clear your head.'

This Amelia did find appealing. 'I'll go on the condition you go afterwards.'

Clara nodded.

The evening was just beginning, her favourite hour of the day, where all concern seemed momentarily laid aside. She walked from the house, made her way along the ridge to the forest. A few feet in, under the canopy, she stood still, the cool, moist air pleasing on her skin. She breathed the damp, several times. The scrub hens screamed, the curlews wailed. To the side of the path, a stick cracked, high and sharp. In the half-light she caught a flash of iridescent blue and scarlet, the face and nape and hanging wattles of a cassowary, a 150-pound ground bird, timid unless provoked. The bird hissed. She set off again. Despite her exhaustion, she had energy she sought to burn.

Once in the clearing, she stood to catch her breath, looking at the view across the valley. Why had this happened? Italo had never hurt anyone. All those years ago he'd joined the fascist organisation more at her insistence than out of any desire of his own. And she'd only seen it for what it was – a collective of cane farm owners, an organisation to work against the British Preference League and the unions and their insidious demands. The Italian government promised help. Had the Babinda Fascists accepted women, she would have joined herself, and possibly it would be her now fighting for her life. What could bring such division to Italian people? Couldn't they see the ramifications of Mussolini's triumph? There were none so blind. All reports she'd had from Italy, and all the correspondence from the consulates, saw the new order in Italy as a resurrection. Yet even Clara disagreed with it. But Clara had lost all sympathy for Amelia's position. Amelia didn't need this pressure, not now, and pushed her disagreement with Clara from her thoughts.

But she shouldn't be in this peace and solitude when her duty was at Italo's side. And then the full horror of the attack struck her – this could kill Italo. Her vision blurred. Her jaw shuddered. What would she do without him? How could she continue? She'd taken him as given. For so many years, she hadn't really considered him, no more than she did the leg of a chair.

How had this happened? How could she be so cruel? What did he want? What did he feel? This face she'd looked on for sixteen years was unknown. What lines had she placed there?

She stood, her hands limp at her sides. The sobs rose and rose. She made no move to stem the tears, the mucus from her nose, her mouth jammed in a silent wail. She'd abused his trust in the most profound manner. And it was clear he knew Flavio wasn't his child, but he was such a good man he'd accepted him, without a word, without compromise, with only love for her. And she'd sent Flavio to boarding school when he was only seven and had seen him as an embarrassment, as a breathing, blood-beating sign of her sin, an indelibly embodied memento. Not even as himself.

What good had Australia brought? She had a fur coat and a large house and a farm and mortgages and land and machinery and money in the bank, none of which she allowed herself to enjoy. When had she become so callous, her heart just scars and more cuts? She'd lost herself.

She breathed deeply. For now, she should go back, face what had been done. Italo needed care. Clara needed time. She turned to the path, breathed the cooler air once more. Italo loved the forest. The mountains reminded him of home. If only she could take a pocket back to him. She walked over the remains of the hut and stopped.

A dog ran along the path towards her. It was a medium size, black and white. It stopped and looked back down the path from where it had come. She didn't recognise it. Then in the distance she saw Fergus, walking along the track. She lost her breath. Once the dog had seen him, it turned back and raced to her, its tail wagging furiously, its ears laid down and eyes smiling.

Fergus called out, 'Joey.'

The dog moved from her. Although every instinct said to run, she stood still. He continued, his pace unabated, as if to him there were no shock in finding her there. She thought to move away, but it was her ground and she wouldn't give it. He was within touching distance, less than a metre, when he stopped.

How odd to look at that face. Something she'd craved, wondered about, seen in her mind's eye was now before her, more vivid than she could imagine. Her eyes ran the taut planes of his cheeks, the dark colour of his eyes, the rude roundness of his lips. These things were the same. But there were changes, things she'd not allowed, things she'd forgotten or misplaced. Sixteen years had added wrinkles about his eyes, a furrow to his brow, clouds of grey to the early morning light of his hair, even the first hint of jowls. How they tore at her, the differences between what she thought and what was. She searched his face for emotion, some tell-tale expression, but his dark eyes gave nothing.

What did he see in her? Most surely, sixteen years and three children and all this work had riven lines in her face she no longer saw.

'What are you doing here?' she said, the tone overly aggressive.

'Just walking. How's Italo?'

She paused. 'He's unwell, very weak. Why have you returned?'

He regarded her. 'Oisin can't manage. He's too old and feeble to interfere. He's no choice but to allow me to return.'

'Where were you for so long?'

'In New Zealand. In the south. On a sheep farm.'

Amelia flamed and raised her hand to cool her face. He was robust, no sign of the war shock from which he'd suffered. He looked away, into the distance. Without returning his gaze to her, he said, 'How is our son?'

The question seemed brutal, and she objected to it but couldn't deny it.

'He's away at boarding school. He's grown tall and strong. He's none of my features. Only yours.'

'You don't deny he's my child ...'

'You're unfair. I had no choice.'

'I've never stopped thinking of you.'

She held her breath. Nothing could be said.

'I challenge you to say you have forgotten me,' he said.

How could she make such an assertion? And how could he be so cruel to ask it? He bit his lower lip, rocked back and forth slightly and returned his gaze to her.

'Italo needs me,' she said.

She moved to pass him. He reached out, grabbed her forearm. She couldn't move against his warmth through the thin fabric of her shirt. She pulled away, but he wouldn't let go. She met his eyes, cold and dark but alive. She tugged again, and with that momentum he moved into her as if she'd pulled him. She smelt him, breathed the air about him. The nights without sleep collapsed their full weight on her. She had no more strength. He'd not let go. She sunk to the carpet of ferns and seedlings where once his hut had stood and exploded and burned.

And he followed, with no resistance, to the soft floor, his weight heavy on her. She ran her hands along his spine, felt the hard ridges of muscle. Nothing had changed. No time had passed. She inhaled the scent at his neck. She kissed his cheek, searched for his mouth. He pulled her blouse from the lip of her skirt. His palm seared her abdomen as it forced towards her breast. All shattered. The exhaustion lifted. She thought of Clara's warnings about Flavio and the children. She thought of Italo, bruised and bloodied. She didn't want this.

'Stop,' she said.

But he continued, his mouth at hers so she couldn't speak, his hands at her waist. She fought him, pushed her hands against his chest, beat at it. But he continued. She squirmed, tried to move under his weight. But with just one hand on her shoulder, he pinned her. He lifted himself, freeing his belt and pants with quick jerking movements. He lifted her dress, tore her underpants.

'Don't do this,' she said.

But he wouldn't hear, wouldn't meet her eyes. He meant to have her. While he was still above her, his hand caught in the fabric, and she raised her leg as fast and hard as she could. Her knee caught his groin. He groaned, forced harder on her shoulder, and she thought under such stress it might break. His eyes met her. His other hand came to the earth. She pushed onto his shoulders and he rolled away.

She was on her feet.

'You fucking bitch,' he yelled.

But she was away. She wouldn't look back.

'You've ruined everything.'

Waves of confusion, guilt, regret, disillusion and fear pushed her. She ran, doing her best to rearrange her clothes. When she arrived at the house, she ran to her office and locked the door. She looked in the mirror, straightened her hair. The tears stained her face. Nothing had been marked or torn. Except herself. This would worsen everything. How could she ever ask him to keep their secret? To never speak with Flavio? Perhaps Clara was right, and her only path was to confess it all to Italo and Flavio. Be that as it may, now wasn't the time to consider it.

It was after six when she re-entered Italo's room.

'Where have you been?' Clara said, terror in her eyes.

Italo trembled, a wave passing from his shoulders and chest and through the rest of his body. It was slow at first but then gathered pace.

Clara held his shoulders. 'He's burning.'

Amelia took a wet cloth and wiped his forehead over his chest, along his arms. The trembling increased. His legs began to jump. Amelia held his ankles, forced them into the mattress.

What could she do?

'Telephone the doctor,' Amelia said.

But the tremoring increased.

'Hold him still. If you let go, he'll fall and hurt himself.'

Amelia gripped harder. His body arched and fell. 'Italo,' she said. 'You cannot die. You cannot leave me.'

But he thrashed harder.

'I'm sorry for everything. I love you.'

She'd never said such a thing. She'd never recognised it. It wasn't love she'd never felt for him. It just wasn't what she'd expected love to be. But now it was failing, rising and falling, ripping from her, it was most keen.

His body froze, arched in open spasm, his face screwed till it looked to break. And then the tension released, collapsed. His face relaxed. Amelia breathed to relieve her own heart rate. Italo was peaceful. She looked to his lungs. He no longer breathed. She looked at Clara, who released his shoulders, straightened herself.

Then Italo sighed, peaceful and contented.

And then he inhaled. And exhaled and then inhaled again. 'It's time for the water,' Clara said.

They raised his head. He opened his eyes. He sipped the water.

'More,' he said, his voice a gravel whisper.

Amelia looked at Clara, who nodded. She tilted the glass again. His Adam's apple moved. So they continued, for the hours left of the night. By the first light of morning, they allowed him to swallow three or four sips at a time. The more water he drank, the more his temperature came to normal, as if the water quenched the fire. By midday he'd urinated, as dark as black tea. But he'd turned the corner.

CHAPTER TWENTY-FOUR

With each hour, Italo became stronger. Despite the terribleness of the situation, the utter, utter tiredness and the thoughts – fears, really – of victimisation, Amelia pressed on. Within a day they added salty, clear soups to the regimen and then *ribollita*. He had no appetite and forced himself. But in a sure sign of his returning health, he listed farming chores, which she assured him she'd already done. His worried face eased to a smile.

'What are you laughing at?' she said.

'My aunts chose well.'

She bit her lip and had to look from him to the view. If only he knew the truth. Was now the time to confess to him of Fergus? He was still weak, and she meant him no harm, and she was sure he knew. Perhaps it was a just time.

'Do you think of home?' he said.

She turned back to him. 'What would make you ask such a thing?'

'You talk of your school, but it's a long while since you've mentioned Italy.'

'Is it?' She thought for some moments. 'How strange. I think of it constantly; sometimes the smallest thing tugs at my heart the hardest. The other evening, I thought of the twilight; do you remember it?'

He nodded.

'It would go on forever.'

'All things did when we were young,' he said. 'I'm very grateful to you.'

She breathed in. Now wasn't the time. She went to his bed and kissed his forehead.

For something short of a week, she'd done no work. She wrote to Flavio and told him what had occurred but cautioned any need of return at this stage. And that evening she took Marta and Mauro to Italo's room. In those dark days she'd had little to do with them, but they'd sensed something was wrong and had curtailed their behaviour for Meggsy. Mauro told Italo of his work at school, and Marta danced like a fairy for him, and he laughed and laughed, and they all clapped their hands in time with her. Marta was an angel, a tonic. Amelia would bring her every day to see Italo; she brought life to his eyes.

Amelia and Clara took turns in the nursing, but when Amelia wasn't with him, despite her body's cries for sleep, she had the farm work. She hadn't mentioned to Clara her encounter with Fergus, and nor would she. There was enough to think about. The whole incident was best forgotten. But how do you erase such a thing? And Clara hadn't brought up any plan of action to safeguard the children from Fergus. Amelia was pleased for the quiet.

Three days after Italo had turned the corner, Meggsy failed to appear for work. The first sign of it was that Marta hadn't had her breakfast. At first Amelia thought little of it; sometimes Meggsy had things to deal with in the village but usually arranged the free time. But after she'd fed Marta and left her with Clara in Italo's room, she went to her quarters, a single-room cottage at the base of the hill below the house. There wasn't a sign of her. All her clothes were gone. She'd not asked for leave or said anything. There was a note on the table.

> Mrs Amedeo,
> I can't continue in a house like this.
> Meggsy Dawson

Amelia walked from the cottage. Damn her. She was on a good wicket – her own cottage and each Sunday free. *In a house like this* … What on earth did she mean by such a thing? Amelia had been more than accommodating, and she'd not now be insulted. She paid her far more than Maria Pastore ever had and demanded far less.

When she entered the house, Clara was in the entrance hall. She showed her the note.

'Where would she go?' Clara said.

Despite all the years she'd worked, Amelia had never asked of her life. 'She has family in Tamworth or Tenterfield. Somewhere.'

'We should notify them.'

'How?' She motioned to the letter. 'What does she mean by that?'

Clara gave back the note. 'Can you not see? The rules have changed. We're Italian. She's British. I'm sure she was under immense pressure to quit. Forced, almost.'

Amelia soused her anger. She wouldn't be judged, but moreover, where would she find another girl? In the valley, help was difficult, good help next to impossible. If there was ever a time she needed another pair of hands she could trust, this was it. In her office, she read the note again. Perhaps Clara was right – it was motivated by someone else. Meggsy just didn't have these thoughts. How would she deal with Italo and the children? Thank God Clara was there.

She had just settled to work when she heard a car brake hard on the gravel. She didn't recognise it. Who could it be? But then Grossi walked slowly towards the gate. With Italo being sick, she'd not had a moment for the school. She should have sent a communiqué to Grossi. But surely, he knew of the attack. She hurried from her office and was descending the stair when he knocked at the door.

'Good morning,' he said, and smiled. 'I wonder if we may talk.'

She stepped back. There was gravity to him. She escorted him to the lounge room. He walked with the same stride, indifferent to his surroundings. Without asking her, he sat in a lounge chair near the window, Italo's chair. She offered him tea or coffee, but he refused, which pleased her, as she wanted to know immediately what he was about. She sat. He enquired of Italo's health, and she told him he was still very weak.

'This wasn't done by locals,' he said.

'Italo didn't recognise them. But they spoke Italian.'

'There are Italians who don't see the greatness of what's happening in Italy. Babinda's been free of them for many years.'

'It rather put an end to our celebration,' she said.

'There'll be greater victories, I can assure you.'

Clara and Marta came to the room. Clara greeted Grossi with coldness, Marta with suspicion, but Clara remained on the far sofa with Marta.

'Have you reported this to the police?' he said.

Amelia glanced at Clara. 'Italo saw no point. And didn't want attention drawn.'

'I'm pleased. We can deal with it more sensitively and less … publicly. I've started enquiries. We'll find them.'

Amelia inhaled deeply.

'How will you find them?' Clara said, her features sharp. 'And what will you do to them?'

'We have contacts. We *will* deal with them.'

He stood, this fact the primary assertion of his visit. Amelia and Clara rose and followed him to the door, leaving Marta on the sofa.

'Give Italo my regards,' he said, turning towards his car.

'With all this drama', Amelia said, 'we've had no time to devote to the school.'

'I believe Signora Burattini has been active,' he said, 'collecting signatures.'

So it was true. Amelia occluded her feelings of being slighted. 'All effort helps.'

'It will all be there when you return,' Grossi said. He turned to Clara. 'I was wondering if we may meet.'

Clara stepped back, her face white. 'I'm sorry. Life's busy here. I've no time.'

What a ham-fisted fool he was to make such a demand on a woman in her state.

Grossi coloured. 'Another time,' he said, and left.

Amelia closed the door. The two women stood in silence, looking at one another. They heard his sure tread on the gravel, his car door, the engine start and move away, the strain of the motor fading.

'I'll go and check on Italo,' Clara said, and moved towards the stair.

'I'm sorry he pesters you.'

'His advances are the smallest way he worries me.'

Amelia breathed. She and Clara hadn't really spoken since they'd argued about Fergus. Clara had withdrawn. She saw that clearly now in retrospect.

'Are you all right?' Amelia said.

Clara's gaze was cold, but she nodded and began to climb the stairs. Amelia didn't want her to leave, and said, by way of engaging her, 'Why would he allow Maria Burattini to work on the petition?'

Clara stopped, something impatient in the drop of her shoulders. 'He wants to control it. Completely.'

Clara called to Marta, and the two continued on the stairs.

Amelia remained in the entrance hall. Damn Clara and her damn condemnation. She opened the front door, stepped out into the day, away from the house. She walked down the hill, out into the endless aisles transecting the fields. The earth was ploughed in neat furrows. Fortunately, the setts had been planted before the attack on Italo. She knelt to inspect one section, and then another. Some had started to sprout new growth, small green reeds extending from the earth. It amazed her something so small grew to so much with so little encouragement. But in Babinda, the sugarcane was the only thing that thrived. She and Italo survived, she couldn't deny that, but only with their shoulder pushed hard against the wall of opposition. The cane grew effortlessly.

She knelt. A reed had grown in under a large sod of earth. If she left it, it would continue to grow sideways. It may eventually right itself, but its growth would always be marred. With all care, all delicacy, she lifted the sod. The shoot remained flattened, partly embedded in the earth, sickly, a sunless colour. She righted it, broke the sod and packed the earth around the reed, rendering it erect.

She should be thankful for small mercies. The crop was growing, but nonetheless care needed to be taken. She scanned the exterior of the field. She expected Fergus, but since that day there'd been no sign of him, not even in the village. And she'd had no report, not that she was overly privy to such things, of how he fared taking over from Oisin. Clara's concerns were valid, but there was a good chance an argument would ensue with Oisin and Fergus would leave the valley. Yet Oisin was old, and although she'd not seen him in many years, reports were his fire had gone. It worried her, Fergus staying in the valley. She'd spurned him, no doubt injured more than just his pride. And as Clara had said, Flavio may see him, see himself in him. There could then only be questions. But she was powerless.

She sighed. She'd lost so much time, and lost time irritated her – it could never be recovered. She marched from the fields to her office.

That evening, Italo came to dinner and ate a small meal, his first solid food at the table in nearly a week. Mauro hadn't seen him out of bed and seemed shaken by his frail and gaunt appearance. Marta did her best to entertain him. Italo ate slowly, only the smallest pieces of mutton.

'It's perfect,' he said, 'but I have no appetite.'

'Just eat one more piece,' Clara said.

And he did try, but at the end there was more on his plate than he'd eaten. After they'd finished, Amelia excused herself, leaving Italo and Clara to talk. She put Marta to bed, read to her until she was asleep and then kissed her forehead. In her office, she began to work. If only all of life's equations were so easily solved.

But this evening, despite the urgency, the ledgers wouldn't hold her. She was tired, and her concentration fluttered over the list of what she had to do rather than any specific task. The look on Mauro's face at dinner had said it all – Italo was shaken, so much weight peeled from him. At best, it would take many more weeks for him to recover fully. It was a miracle he'd survived. If only Flavio had finished school. Perhaps he should just leave and return to the farm? But it was wrong to interrupt his education. Perhaps she should hire a manager? But she knew no-one, and trusting a stranger would be reckless. And then the question of how to finance such a position. For the first time in sixteen years, she had no hold on that, the ledgers reconciled far behind the current date. Not knowing their exact financial position frightened her.

There was a knock at the door. She called out to come in.

'I'm disturbing you? …' Clara said.

'These are disturbing me.' She motioned to the ledgers. 'Sit down.'

Clara walked to a lounge chair to the side of the desk. It was covered with books, and Amelia told her to stack them with the rest on the floor.

'I like the silence in this room,' Amelia said. 'What a pity you and Paolo didn't move here when we'd first discussed it.'

Clara nodded. 'Things would be very different.' Clara placed her hand to her mouth and Amelia felt she may have been too bold. 'But Paolo couldn't imagine living in the country.'

Clara retreated into her thoughts, and Amelia left her there.

'How are you feeling?' Clara said.

'Shaken. Exhausted. As you must be.'

'No more tired than usual.'

'I can't thank you enough.'

'Nothing more than you've done for me.'

'My chaperone.' Amelia smiled, but Clara's face remained stern. 'Something's troubling you and has been for days.'

'During those long nights with Italo, I had time to think. The exhaustion brought me … a certain clarity.' Clara breathed out and looked directly at her. 'I won't be part of the women's fascist organisation.'

Amelia stiffened. 'Why not?'

'Italo was nearly murdered—'

'He was attacked by anti-fascists. You heard him say that. And Grossi agreed.'

'But the attack was a result of fascism. It divides people. Violently.'

'All politics divide—'

'In civilised debate. When has anyone been attacked like that in Babinda? They gave a fascist a taste of his own medicine.'

Amelia said nothing. Without Clara, the school seemed hollow.

'How anyone could do that ...' Clara said. 'This has no place in Australia.'

Perhaps it was just her exhaustion, but Amelia felt angered. 'Then you'll not be able to teach at the school.'

'I'm aware of that.'

'You'd give that up?'

'If that's the choice.'

Amelia swallowed. She'd worked hard to develop the school, largely so Clara could live in Babinda.

Clara breathed out heavily. 'To my second point of clarity. The Babinda Fascist Organisation don't want the school. They'll kill it off.'

Clara was now just being provocative. 'They support it.'

'That night at the celebration, Signora Appiani told me she'd heard Grossi wanted Signora Burattini to take control. She's already taken over the petition. Do you think it will stop at that? And Appiani said they have plans to hire a more suitable teacher. She clearly didn't know I was to be the teacher.'

Amelia tightened. 'They can't do that.'

'Those men want their wives to control the women's organisation, and they'll control their wives. It's about long, heavy chains of control. It's not about Italian culture or language – it's only about fascism, and if they don't get their way they'll smash their opposition.'

'So you've crumbled,' Amelia said.

'I won't compete. Fascism's all they want. Chieffi will only endorse the school so it makes him look like he's creating more fascist organisations, all led by Rome.'

'Italy is strong again.'

'At what cost? And why all this talk of Italy? Why have you changed your opinion of Australia so much?'

'I've told you and told you why – I'm Italian!' Amelia shouted.

'And I don't believe you—'

'Italo's attack has made me more certain.'

Clara glared at her. 'There's more than that.'

'And I'm sure you know what it is.'

Clara's face changed to something she'd never seen. 'You've been shunned for what happened with Fergus. You're involved in the school because you want to be part of Italian society. You're doing this to atone, gain favour, stave off judgement.'

Amelia swallowed hard. How could she know such things? She'd never spoken to anyone of these feelings, and here they were splashed at her. Did she bear the birth of Flavio like a scar across her chest?

'You're talking rubbish—'

'You think with patriotic works people will turn a blind eye and forgive you.'

'I'll not stand for this. Not in my own house.'

Clara stared into her eyes, unflinching. 'I'll leave in the morning.'

Afraid they'd crossed a line, Amelia could find nothing to say, either to retrieve the situation from the truth or just to bow down to it, let them cross the line from which they would probably never return. She felt panicked, angered, relieved even.

Clara turned to leave the room but stopped at the door. 'You're not the woman I met in Naples.'

'And neither are you. Or perhaps you are. You were being paid, after all. You're no longer my chaperone. I'll cancel the payments to your bank account.'

Clara closed the door softly. Amelia slammed her hand to the desk. Should she go after her? No. She wouldn't. She'd only ever offered her friendship, and this was an insult she didn't deserve. She too had pride.

The following morning, there was silence in the house as there never normally was. Amelia didn't go downstairs to Clara's farewell. She took refuge in her office, pulled the drapes against the view. She'd thought Clara may at least attempt some last-minute reconciliation, but she heard the car move away. Amelia felt overcome with sorrow. She rose from her desk and ran from the room to the entrance hall. Italo was standing by the gate, Marta and Mauro on either side, watching the car drive before it turned the hill. She stood at the door. He turned back towards the house. He'd taken only a few paces when he saw her and stopped. Amelia bit back on her tears. She wouldn't show them, not even to him.

'You and Clara didn't part on good terms,' Italo said.

'Did she speak with you?'

'She said the girls needed her.'

She was sure more had been said but wouldn't be drawn.

'We argued,' she said, 'about the school.' She looked to the children. 'Mauro, quickly, you'll be late for school.'

Mauro stared at her, and she thought he may say something. But eventually, he turned and sprinted down the hill towards the stable. He was upset Clara had left so abruptly. Both the children were very fond of her. She held out her hand to Marta, but she walked to Italo and took his hand.

Amelia turned back into the house and towards the stair. Italo followed to the entrance hall. She looked down on him. He was so frail she didn't want to burden him. Marta held his hand. And without Meggsy and now without Clara, she would have more work to do.

'She didn't want to be associated with the women's fascist organisation,' she said.

'I tend to agree with her,' Italo said.

'Why take her side?'

'I don't agree with her entirely. But I think you've argued with her profoundly.'

She breathed out. 'What's been said has been said.' She started to mount the stairs. 'Go and rest. I have work to do. I'll bring you lunch.'

Marta and Italo stayed together, staring at her.

At her desk, she placed her head in her hands and began to cry. Just two weeks ago everything had been planned. So neat. Now all was in disarray. She must start again. Start again to place order. Everything would come to order with effort.

She wrote a small advertisement for the *Cairns Post* for an Italian-speaking woman to run the house. She wrote a list of cheques, letters and envelopes to pay their accounts. With that, she went to the kitchen to prepare lunch. Italo had taken Marta to the fields. She placed his soup, a small amount of pasta with meat sauce and a glass of red wine on a tray and took it to the dining room. She went to the entrance hall to call out to them, but then she heard them returning and went back to the kitchen for her and Marta's lunch. The sun and a small walk to the fields had been restorative, given Italo some colour.

After they'd eaten, he said, 'I must go back to the fields—'

'You need your rest,' she said.

'Rest won't run a farm.'

She looked at him. More and more she believed they were made of similar stock. Or perhaps they had just grown together.

'Perhaps a small siesta,' he said.

She agreed and smiled. He turned to the stairs.

'I'll bring you some tea.'

When she brought the tea, he sat in the bed. She placed the tray beside him and turned to leave.

'I've had a lot of time to think,' he said. She turned to him. 'We should go to Italy.'

For some moments, Amelia stared at him. They had never really discussed such a thing. 'What makes you think that?'

'If we were to return, for a period, we could judge all the changes for ourselves. My mother is very old now. I feel guilty, despite how much money we send her. Your parents and brothers – wouldn't you like to see them?'

She felt the heaviness she carried in her heart for her missing family. 'Without a doubt.'

'Then for these reasons alone we should go. As you say, the British Australians don't want us here.'

'They envy and hate the Italians.'

'And now, even some Italians don't. When I first came, I always thought to go back.'

Had she? Had she really carried returning as the end point of her leaving Italy? She thought back to that instant, that split second when her father finally pulled her mother's hand from hers. How she felt it still, the warmth, the adhesion, the friction and the final cold release. How she'd walked, knowing if she looked back she would never be able to leave.

'We should see how life would be there,' Italo said, 'with the new order.'

Amelia stood still. How life would be there … It was easy to lay spare the memories of harsh poverty and injustice. Could those have changed? Was Clara right that no such change was possible? Italo proposed a test – one foot in Australia and one prone lightly on Italy.

'We could go between the seasons,' she said. 'Once the planting's done, we would have nearly a year, time to travel and return before the next harvest. Flavio will be finished school. He could stay to tend the farm.'

He laughed. 'You've planned.'

'Not really, but it's something I've thought of for some time.'

'Then it's agreed. We'll go.'

She stood. Freedom. If they could find their way in Italy, she would be without blemish. No-one would know of Fergus or link him to Flavio. She could walk with her head held high. No scar. She didn't need to run a school. She didn't need to be part of a women's fascist organisation. Her stain would be washed, full benediction. She would escape Fergus.

She went to the bed. She kissed Italo's lips. How familiar they felt. But despite his weakness, he seemed to want something more. She kissed him. And there it was again, an energy, an insistence. She lay next to him. There was none of the hurry or urgency or rush that came with Fergus. This was replaced by something softer, far subtler, gentler and sweeter.

CHAPTER TWENTY-FIVE

Amelia carried the heavy mail sack to her office, upended the bag, the items spilling over her desk. She sorted them into piles. There was a small package – from the Italian consulate in Sydney – she tore open. Something fell to the desk and wound in circles. She slapped her hand to it. It was the metal ring, the replacement for her wedding ring. In all the turmoil she'd forgotten it. She looked at her finger, the white band of flesh now indiscernible, olive from the sun. She sat the ring on her palm. It was a crude contrivance, light, as if the metal were hollow. At what cost had it come? She was unsure she wanted to wear it and placed it at the back of her desk.

She had three responses to her advertisement for a woman to run the house. None were suitable, not even close – this one was too young, this one had no real experience and this one wanted all her travel expenses from Melbourne paid. How had she even seen the advertisement in the *Cairns Post*? The cheek. And none were Italian, though she'd advertised this as imperative. She'd not deal with another British Australian. On that she was adamant. She pushed the letters away.

What was she to do? Day to day, she could cope with the house. Just. But Marta took considerable time, being at an age where she'd discovered decisions. Each day Italo had more strength and spent increased time in the fields. Thank God for small mercies. If the attack had occurred in the planting or the harvesting, it would have destroyed them. With all the expense for the house, the new land's mortgage, they couldn't afford to lose a crop. She looked out the window, across the fields, already sprouting a fuzz like that on a peach, but green. Her running of the business had fallen further behind.

She'd heard Meggsy was working for the Burkes. Good luck to her. She'd find the Irish close-fisted with their pennies. She thought to offer Meggsy more money to return, but her pride dismissed the thought. She just had to find a new woman. Soon the harvest would be upon them. Without help, she wouldn't cope. She may have when she was younger, but not now. Her mother had always complained of being tired. In the last few weeks, something slowing had seeped into Amelia's bones. The concern for Italo, the breach with Clara, the return of Fergus – all these things had robbed her of sleep. That was one thing. But there'd also been such greater demands on her time.

And there been no word from Clara. She'd hoped she'd write. Perhaps she should break the silence, but Clara had caused the falling-out at a time when Amelia could ill afford it. It was up to Clara to salve the wounds. Perhaps she'd just have to employ another British Australian girl. Damn it.

She turned to the rest of the morning's mail. She'd made enquires for their trip to Italy. The Australia-Italia Shipping Company in Brisbane had responded with a quote for their proposed dates. They could sail almost the reverse trip she'd made sixteen years ago, boarding at Brisbane but disembarking at Genoa. The cost for a first-class cabin wasn't as prohibitive as she'd expected, fifty-five pounds each. But the agent stressed to secure the booking they'd need a deposit within a fortnight. Amelia wrote the cheque for the full £110 and an accompanying letter and sealed them. They would sail aboard the *Remo* on the eighth of May in 1937, just under a year away. Before then they would harvest the crop and plant the next to grow while they were away. May they be blessed with plain sailing.

Flavio would oversee the farm, not that there would be much to do, and was excited by the prospect of flexing his maturity. Both Mauro and Marta would be in boarding school. How she'd miss Marta. She would grow so appreciably while they were away. But they couldn't afford to take her. And the travel would be easier on their own. Besides, Mauro had to stay in school. She looked again at the new life in the field. Flavio would cope with it. There was little to be done. The cane just grew. It was a chance for him.

A wave of tiredness came to her. She took off her glasses and rubbed her eyes, such a simple act so soothing. She'd been eating too well, the convalescent's food she served Italo making her put on a little weight.

She collapsed her hands to the desk, seized and tore up the travel agent's letter and the cheque. Who was she fooling? She was pregnant. At thirty-six she'd not considered such a thing possible, but she could deny it no longer.

The irony. Everything had aligned for them to return to Italy, but she couldn't go. The child would be born in March next year. She couldn't make such travel with a newborn, and she couldn't leave the child. This would push back their plans, at least a year or two. Nothing could be done. So be it. There was new life in the field, and there was new life in her. Italo had always wanted another child. He'd be very happy.

She picked up the coarsely forged metal wedding ring, slipped it over her gnarly knuckles and regarded it.

It served a purpose. She'd married again.

PART THREE

1939–43

Love surfeits not, Lust like a glutton dies
Venus and Adonis – William Shakespeare

CHAPTER TWENTY-SIX

Amelia stepped to the rail at the aft of the ship, moving away from the wharf into the Bay of Naples. She placed her hand on the worn wooden balustrade. This, at least, had a ring of familiarity. In five weeks time, four if the sailing was plain, they'd be through the Suez Canal, across the Indian Ocean to Colombo and back to Australia. To see the children would be a blessing. She'd missed Marta as much and far more than she'd expected. And Ilaria would have grown as only a two-year-old can. Exchanges of letters had been drawn out and disrupted, and the Italian newspaper had few reports of anything from home. But she was pleased she'd not brought Ilaria with them. Flashes of wisdom were rare, but at the last minute she'd decided to leave her in the care of Lucia, the Italian housekeeper. She hoped Flavio had tended the cane. She'd had a letter from Mauro's headmaster. He'd been missing classes. Marta had written often from boarding school; she enjoyed it immensely, and her marks were consistently high. And Ilaria ... Would she even remember her mother?

She looked to the receding port of Naples. So much had changed since she stood above these waters with Clara, twenty years ago.

Were she and Italo fleeing Italy?

The thought was unsettling but not without slices of truth. Their time had been expensive. There'd been railways and food, more expensive than she'd budgeted for or letters had suggested. And they'd had to move about more than they'd planned, between their two villages, between her family and Signora Pina. The Italian trains may run on time, but they were costly, a tax for this and for that, just to breathe.

Everything, even the church she'd married in, the main piazza, her parents' table, seemed so small. Her parents were old and hunched, and she believed they'd shrunk. It was cruel to see them, the slow increments of twenty years hurled at her in the most unforgiving manner. And her brothers were now men with their own wives and children and bald pates. Only Signora Pina, despite her protests of failed health, stood rooted to the earth with such force Amelia thought she'd never die.

The first thing Pina said to her after all those years: 'Why have you not brought the children? You've broken your promise.'

Only Pina could see things in such simple isolation.

Within three days of seeing her parents, in hushed tones they spoke of the dark cloud fascism had brought to Italy. People were missing. They lacked all kinds of basic amenities. Yet in the open no-one had a word of criticism, too scared to speak. She saw none of the grandeur of an imperial power, nothing the victory in Abyssinia had portended. And when she pointed this out, that the descriptions in letters didn't match the reality, her parents and brothers bundled her indoors.

'I couldn't risk writing any other type of letter,' her mother said, spitting sotto voce. 'There's a chance the letters would be intercepted. And if I said nothing positive of fascism, they would take that as criticism.'

Her family said she spoke 'old' Italian, and with an Australian accent. Aldo laughed and complained he couldn't understand a word she said. He was only joking, but the fact he could make this a joke meant it was true in part; she was a foreigner in her own land, her own language.

Most regrettably, midway through their time in Italy something occurred they couldn't have foreseen: in September, Hitler invaded Poland and the Second World War began. This she feared the most; who knew where the alliances would lead? At any moment, conflict could flare around them and then Italy would be at war with Britain. And Australia. She felt cut off from the children; the world was changing rapidly, and she could do nothing to protect them.

Foolishly, they hadn't booked return tickets, as they'd left Australia with open plans, perhaps even entertaining the illusion that they had come home and there was no need to return to Australia. But at this outbreak, for the sake of the children, they decided to return much earlier than first imagined. With this decision, though, came an expensive flurry. Tickets to cross the world were harder to book, a rush of people crisscrossing the globe. Tickets, even those in steerage, became far more expensive, but they had to pay the price and deal with the cost later. Even then, though, the earliest available voyage was six weeks away. And with the seas already laced with mines, with passenger steamers converted to troop carriers, there was no certainty in a booking. Here it was, late October 1939, and they were only just underway.

She looked from the water to Mount Vesuvius, lounging over the bay. The volcano's fire had snuffed out, no longer smouldering or prone to ignite. She turned from the rail.

They would be home for Christmas.

This was the last she would look on Italy.

The trip across the globe was contained – no great excitement and no great peril. On the main, the weather was agreeable. From Aden, the ship's portholes were painted black so the ship's lights wouldn't alert enemy planes to attack. The ports they visited were hushed and muted; Colombo had nothing of the vibrancy Amelia had seen only a few months before, the sartorial flair of the men on the streets replaced by military uniforms.

When they finally arrived in Brisbane, Italo suggested they stay a day or two, but she didn't want to tarry; she had this great urge to be home, back with the children, on their farm. And she didn't want to bump into Clara, if that were even remotely likely in such a large city. But they had some hours before their train departed, so they walked about the centre. Brisbane too had hunkered down, nothing on show except large flags hanging from the buildings, both British and Australian. For a weekday, the city streets seemed drained of people. The spans of the Story Bridge had met, but it was still under construction.

That day, the trams weren't working, so despite the heat they decided to walk to Roma Street Station. It wasn't far, and they both agreed their legs could use the practice. But as they walked towards Queen Street, they could hear the noise of a great crowd. The street was lined with people, watching a parade of uniformed men. They stopped, unable to cross the street.

'What is happening?' Italo said to a man next to them.

The man turned, jolted. He looked them up and down, at their latest European clothes, Italo's dark mustard trousers and her shirt made from brightly coloured rayon. The man wore a dark suit, his brimmed hat a mismatched teal. Amelia guessed he was a bureaucrat.

'It's the Second AIF,' he scoffed, as if this were obvious. 'They're leaving Queensland to go south for more training.'

This explained the many flags they'd seen, hung for this celebration. Italo nodded, but the man continued to examine them. Amelia kept the corner of her eye on him, something untoward in his manner.

'There are seventeen hundred men,' the man said. 'Once their training is finished, they'll leave Australia for Europe.'

Italo nodded, turned to Amelia and said in English, 'I guess you're right. We'd best be going home.'

'Have these fools forgotten all the young men who died in World War One?' she said, but softly and in Italian.

To bypass the parade, they were forced to make a long detour, back as far as Creek Street and then across to Turbot Street, but eventually they arrived at Roma Street Station. Amelia was surprised – heartened, in a way – the station hadn't been renamed.

Nothing on the whole journey evoked the excitement she felt as the train came into Babinda. Her heartbeat surged. She pulled down the compartment's window and hung out for a better vantage. She saw the children, three of them standing in a neat row, Flavio and Mauro, now clearly taller than his brother, and Marta between them. But they hadn't seen her, although she waved a bright green handkerchief from the window. Lucia, her long grey hair pulled to a tight chignon, stood to the side, Ilaria in her arms.

But when Amelia climbed down to the platform, Marta spotted her and ran. At first the boys, now both lodged in that time of youthful male reserve, moved forward like old men, but soon Marta's enthusiasm infected them, or Lucia said something, and they ran.

She knelt and caught Marta in her arms and pressed her lips to her forehead. Marta pulled her tighter. She looked up at the boys, who embraced and kissed their father. Ilaria stood beside Lucia, who was smiling, but, despite encouragement, Ilaria wouldn't advance. She just pouted and held her poppet, screwed her left foot inwards. Amelia stood and Marta went to Italo.

She kissed Mauro, then embraced Flavio and turned to Ilaria. She knelt, opened her arms, but Ilaria withdrew to the folds of Lucia's dress. Chilled even in the heat of this day, she knew then how Paolo had felt twenty years ago, this bitter regret, this slap when Cristiano had withdrawn from him. But she had to pay this price, win Ilaria's trust and then love. She went to Lucia, kissed her cheeks. It was only then it occurred to her that she reminded her of Frau Gruetzmann – her age, her blue eyes and her nature.

'How you've all grown,' she said, although Flavio hadn't.

'You all look so well,' Italo said.

Amelia's grave worries lifted. She smiled and then began to laugh, which made them all self-conscious. Mauro asked questions of Italy and Italo began to answer. She stepped back. Marta was nine now, nearly ten, and boarding school agreed with her, refinement and dignity in her posture. She'd almost let go of being a little girl. And Mauro's voice wavered, jumped between alto and basso, but she wouldn't say anything to him about it.

'Let's go into Babinda,' Marta said.

'Bella,' Amelia said, 'we are tired. Let's go home.'

A wave of disappointment passed over Marta's face.

'And I can find your presents,' Amelia said.

Marta's eyes bulged.

Amelia felt calmer. They were all together. Nothing had been broken. Everything would be all right.

CHAPTER TWENTY-SEVEN

Christmas came and passed, furiously hot. Flavio had managed the farm well, tended the growing canes with Italo's care, everything on track for the September harvest. Amelia was pleased, and in the next few weeks she would book the cutters and reserve the mill, well in advance. Despite her absence, nothing had gone awry, and nothing could. At the end of the holidays, Mauro and Marta returned to boarding school but Flavio remained, as Italo still needed his help. And each day Ilaria kept her distance less and less. Amelia knew to give her time; it was all she could do.

And soon the months began to pass again without any clear distinction. Since their return, she'd been unable to sleep well, their time in Italy disturbing, not at all what they'd hoped. Italy had been heralded as much changed, and indeed buildings had been built, and there seemed prosperity, and people were educated, but their views and recollections of events were often at odds with hers. Mainly, people were frightened to express their opinion.

But they were home now, in her own bed, and yet even after six months her sleep was still disturbed, not by any recurring dream or concern, just some minor ill feeling. Instead of lying awake, she would rise and work.

The cost of the whole journey had been high, that of the return voyage extortionate for a steerage cabin without a porthole. But after six months back in Australia, she blotted the wet ink on the ledger. Even after she'd paid out all the pressing accounts, they were just in the black.

In the distance, just before dawn, the dogs began to bark. They were kennelled towards the main road, and something had disturbed them, most likely a possum, the scent alone enough to set them off. To blot them out she turned on the wireless on a small shelf to the side of her desk. As the valves warmed, an eerie yellow light rose from the rear of the machine, blending into her lamplight. The sun would soon be up.

She looked over the figures. She'd even made some small way to paying off the mortgage for the new land. Whilst the finances weren't where she wanted them to be, all the necessary payments had been made. Just none of the extra ones. She dated the ledger – the eleventh of June, 1940.

A mosquito hovered over the page. She slapped her hand down, a slash of blood across the ledger. The insect had bitten her. She took off her glasses, rubbed her tired eyes. It was too late to consider going back to bed and sleeping.

The dogs were still barking. She peered into the dark, her ghostly reflection moving in the glass. The declaration of war between Britain and Germany had made the whole area tense. Major bridges and oil depots were under armed guard. Two months back a young man, only eighteen, had been shot dead for not obeying a command to stop his van for inspection at the wharves in Cairns.

The wireless had warmed. She adjusted the volume, nothing more than static. She laughed. She was too early. They weren't even broadcasting yet. But the dogs were upset. Very upset. Well beyond a possum. She heard engines. At first the sound was like a car's, but it grew into that of some heavier vehicle, roaring. And then it rounded the hill, the headlights swinging onto the road.

She stood. There were two vehicles in convoy, moving at some pace, at least as fast as the narrow road would allow.

Who the devil was that? She put down her pen, took off her glasses and descended to the entrance hall. She could hear an insistent tread on the gravel path, many of them, the groan of the garden gate opening.

She held her breath. The feet continued. They spoke no words. Who the devil? At this hour. There must be an emergency. The boys were in Brisbane. Flavio was making enquiries about enlisting. Something had happened to them. She opened the front door, stepped out onto the verandah. There were five men, dressed in uniforms she didn't recognise, rifles strung over their chests. She lifted the lamp higher.

'Is this the house of Italo Amedeo?' the first man said. He stepped into the light. He was in his mid-forties and of higher rank than the other, younger men, with more colour on his epaulets.

'What do you want?' she said.

'Call him to present himself.'

'What is this about?' she said.

'I am Italo Amedeo.'

Amelia turned. Italo was standing on the lowest landing of the stair, dressed only in pyjama shorts.

'Arrest him,' the man said.

Two younger men barged passed Amelia to Italo.

'Arrest him? …' Amelia said. 'Why?' Her voice was shrill.

'Italy has declared war on the British Empire,' the man said. 'You're now an enemy alien.'

He held some document, a warrant. Italy was at war. It took some moments for her to comprehend this.

'But we're both naturalised British subjects,' Amelia said.

'I have my orders.' He looked to the men on the stair. 'Put him in the truck.'

Amelia gasped. 'I won't allow it.'

'You have no choice.'

'It's all right,' Italo said. He raised an open hand to calm her. 'I'll go with you.' He looked directly at Amelia. 'There's some mistake. I'll go and clear this up.' He smiled. 'No harm done.'

Amelia exhaled. Yes. Clearly, there'd been some mistake. This was the best course of action. The men forced him forward.

'At least allow him to dress,' Amelia said.

The first man looked at Italo and shuffled about. 'Go and dress,' he said. 'You two – don't let him out of your sight.' He turned back to Amelia. 'I have orders to confiscate any firearms. You'll also surrender any torches, wirelesses or cameras.'

'Wirelesses? Torches?'

'Get them.'

The force of his voice frightened her. Why should she surrender these things? But Italo was right. These men were brutes. Now wasn't the time for argument. She went to the lounge room and took the two rifles from the cabinet. She felt their power, that she could take on these men and perhaps drive them from the property. She laid the rifles on the entrance hall table, went to the kitchen and unplugged the wireless. Lucia would miss it, her companion all day while she worked. She'd not surrender her wireless. She needed some contact to the world. Thank God the boys weren't home and Marta was at boarding school. Only Ilaria was upstairs, asleep in her cot. The man stood glaring at the landing of the stairs. Two other men blocked the front door.

'Why are you doing this?' she said.

'Where are your financial records?'

'What?' A new wave of panic passed through her.

'You can either show them to me or we'll tear the place apart to find them.'

She stared at him. Her father had always said to know when you were overpowered. Without a further word, she mounted the stairs. The man followed but then more steps started, three others carrying empty boxes. In her office, she positioned herself in front of her desk to obscure the work she'd just completed. The wireless glowed on the shelf behind her. She pointed to the old ledgers, which were largely obsolete. One of the men packed them into a box.

'I can't run the business without them,' she said, as a distraction.

'Where do you file your correspondence?'

This had now entered the realm of farce, though she made no attempt to discourage him, just pointing to a filing cabinet. He nodded, and again a man opened the drawers and loaded the files into a box. Once this was done, he ordered the men to remove them to the truck. They marched from the room. The man left too, and she followed them onto the landing, closing the door behind them, and down to the entrance hall. She'd saved her current work. And the wireless.

'When will they be returned?' she said.

'You'll be issued with a list of what's been taken.'

'You've no need to do this.' Italo's voice came from above them. It was booming in a way she'd never heard. 'I've lived thirty years in this country, and now you put me in chains.'

The men started to descend the stair. Italo was dressed in corduroy pants and a shirt and vest. But his hands were fixed behind his back.

'Look what they've done to me,' he said. 'I'm no better than a slave. The Italians are just the Kanaka. We've worn out our welcome and now we should be dealt with.'

'Mamma, Mamma.' Ilaria stood at the top of the stair, looking through the posts.

'*Va a letto*,' Amelia yelled to her.

Ilaria started to scream.

'Just put him in the truck,'

'My sons are in Brisbane, one applying for the Australian army,' Italo said. 'How can I be your enemy?'

They pushed him forward. He passed her. Their eyes met. He was scared. She'd never seen Italo scared. What could she say? What could she do to release the handcuffs? Ilaria screamed, high and piercing, but remained at the top of the stairs, clinging to the posts, propelling herself forward and back, her cheeks reddened and wet. Italo stumbled, his balance gone from his restricted hands. One of the younger men pushed him through the door, out into the dark. She followed, the group of five men now encasing him as he walked. She could hear Ilaria's screams, but she had to help Italo. There were more men standing in the gravel yard. They shone torches in his eyes. One pulled up the rear canvas of the truck.

'In there,' one yelled.

But there was just a single metal step, and without his hands he couldn't pull himself up. Two men stepped forward, picked him up and placed him in the rear of the truck. It was only then torchlight illuminated the interior. There was Gino Grossi, Burattini, Manny Pellegrino, Enrico Garofalo and many others of the Italian men of the area. Their faces were white, their eyes held wide. All their hands were behind their backs. The guards chained Italo's bound hands to the truck. Amelia gasped.

'Where are you taking them?'

'I'm not at liberty to say.'

'You can't just take him.'

But the men were done. They closed the flap of the truck. The dogs barked on. The engines started. She heard the truck's doors slamming, the gears engaging as the trucks moved. She stood still. The truck carrying the men came at her, but she wouldn't move to help them leave. The truck stopped inches from her, the heat of the engine foul on her face. The gears ground to reverse, the truck moving back and then pulling away around her.

She watched them, the sound fading, the headlights dancing on the hills. She could hear Ilaria. Once there was nothing to see, nothing to hear save the barking dogs, she turned towards the house. She crossed the entrance hall. The telephone rang. Ilaria screamed.

'*Cara, stai zitta,*' she yelled, but it had no effect.

She walked to the telephone cupboard.

'Tell Italo to run,' a woman's voice said. 'Hide.'

'What? It's too late. They've been.'

The line went dead.

She stood, unable to hang off the line. Who was that? What was happening? Ilaria howled. She dropped the receiver, ran up the stair and swept her up.

'Signora Amelia.' The voice came from the entrance hall. Lucia stood, her long grey hair dishevelled, her body crouched and tense. 'What's happening?'

'Italo's been arrested.' She must go, follow them, find where they'd take him. 'Take Ilaria.'

'Nonna,' Ilaria said.

Lucia mounted the stairs and embraced Ilaria, familiarity calming the child. There were voices, from her office. She ran the stairs to the room. The wireless had come to life. Italy had joined the war.

This news was new.

She turned off the wireless. She should have surrendered this, but it now had a value far outweighing its purchase price. She unplugged it and hid it at the back of a cupboard.

She drove out to the main road. There was no sign of the trucks. She got out of the car and looked at the mess of tyre tracks, some peeling off towards Babinda, some to the south. She couldn't read this. It was impossible to tell which tracks were which, and which way they had gone. She'd go to the Babinda police station and demand information. She drove as fast as she dared. The day had only dawned; blushed chintz scrawled across the sky. Was the riddle of this day written there?

She drove into Munro Street and slowed. From the police station a crowd of people spilled – Italian women, some children, no men of any age. She left the car, walked to the group. In silence, she joined their ranks. The building, this inert object, would offer no answer. She looked for Maria but couldn't see her. It took some silent moments until she realised she stood next to Teresa Garofalo. They hadn't spoken for years.

'What's happening?' Amelia said.

'No-one has any answers.'

Amelia stood in silence. All her questions were unanswerable. She moved away from Teresa, skirted the outside of the crowd towards the station's door and managed to slip through. Inside were more people, more noise. She joined a queue, inched forward until she approached the sergeant on duty. He was a British Australian, Irish, she suspected.

'Your husband is a member of the Babinda Fascist Organisation—'

'This group hasn't been active—'

'We're at war with Italy. Under regulation 20 of the Defence Act, he'll be interned.'

'Interned? Where will he be taken?'

'At this stage, I'm not sure.'

'How long will he be here?'

'Who knows how long the war will last?'

'And who will run the farm?'

The man looked at her and raised his eyebrows. He turned away from the broad counter, back into the depth of the station. She waited for him to return.

'He has nothing,' she said. 'Can I bring him some clothes?'

The man sighed heavily, as if it were him who was bothered. 'You can bring two small cases. I'll try and get them to him.'

When she left the building, people were still outside. She didn't stop and drove back to the house. Lucia was full of questions, but she ignored her and went straight to the office. Italo would be interned. He was a prisoner of war. A prisoner. But there were no grounds for this. This was a mistake. For the rest of the morning, she wrote letters, to the Italian consulate, to Vice-Consul Chieffi in Townsville, pleading for information and help. She sent a telegram to Flavio and Mauro at their hotel in Brisbane and ordered them to return immediately. She gave no detail and hoped they wouldn't hear of the arrests, but no doubt there would be reports in the newspapers and on the wireless. There'd have been such arrests in Brisbane. And then it struck her – what if they'd been arrested? They were Australian, surely, born in Australia, but were there such borders anymore?

She made telephone calls, to the mayor of Babinda, to the police station, but no-one with any seniority would offer any information. And the Italian women of the valley telephoned her, just to tell what they knew, which was nothing of any great consequence except their fear.

She heard a car approaching and went to the front verandah. It was Maria Pastore. They hadn't spoken for many years, beyond the most perfunctory salutations in the village.

'I just came to see if you were all right,' she said, walking through the gate towards the house.

'Italo's been arrested. Has Dante?'

Maria looked her in the eye. 'Yes.'

Amelia gasped. Maria was born in Australia. Even that hadn't exempted her Italian-born husband.

'They've arrested all the members of the Babinda Fascist Organisation,' Maria said.

'These arrests had been planned.'

Maria nodded. 'They've just been waiting for a reason to act.'

'What will happen to them?'

'No-one will say.'

Maria had to leave, as there were other women she wanted to check, but she would telephone if she heard any news.

'Thank you for coming,' Amelia said.

Maria turned back to face her. 'We only have ourselves. It's best to forget our differences. We should pull together, as we used to.'

Amelia could bring no response. There it was, all out in the open as if nothing had ever covered it over. Despite all the ill feeling Maria had towards her, in this desperate hour she was generous. And so should Amelia be, forgiving. There was now a greater threat. She tried to raise a smile, but there was little of it. Maria nodded and turned to the truck. How could they have come to this?

She packed two suitcases with Italo's pants, shirts, under-clothes and shoes, left Ilaria with Lucia and returned to the police station. Many people, mainly the Italian women and their children, spilled over the road. The officials refused to let her speak with Italo. They refused her any information, just presenting her with the blankest faces they could muster.

But they accepted the suitcases, marking them with his name and a number, PWQ 7082. Outside, she stood in the distressed sea of people, stern faces meeting her eye, a small nod the only mark that they were united. No-one spoke. What was there to say? They remained in some silent vigil.

From the other side of the street, Amelia looked to the police station. It was only small, a weatherboard building on stilts. If they'd arrested every member of the Babinda Fascist Organisation, they'd arrested over a hundred men. They couldn't hold them at the station for long. There just wasn't room. And there was no other facility in Babinda they could press into service. They'd have to transfer some of the men, if not all. The trail of logic turned Amelia's stomach. Where would they take him? North to Cairns? She doubted there would be any substantial building there. But it was late in the day. It seemed unlikely anything more would happen. She must leave him, much as she didn't want to, though her presence there had no effect on him. She returned to the farm. She didn't sleep. She hadn't heard anything from Mauro and Flavio, so first thing in the morning she telegrammed again. And the telephone rang, over and over, with calls from the worried women of the valley. Aware the telephonists would listen, they were careful, always speaking in Italian. But no-one knew anything. What could they do? Who could they contact? One woman had heard that Vice-Consul Chieffi had already left Townsville for Sydney. He and the other Italian consular staff would leave Australia in the next few days.

'There goes all the support they promised.'

Amongst the snippets of news, that piece cut her. She'd not heard of Chieffi for over three years, since she'd abandoned the idea of the school. She'd never really liked him, found him far too proud, puffed with authority. And he'd judged her for keeping an Australian girl to work. But she'd forgiven him these sins and had sought his help, no matter how much he offended her. Why had she done that? What end had she been seeking? An Italian school. All his small promises of help were only made for his own promotion. And now she knew the picture he'd painted of new Italy was far, far from the reality. She'd been a fool.

Clara had been right. She had sought to expunge her guilt over Flavio, carve herself a secure position in the Italian society of Babinda. But she hadn't, and she'd lost Clara.

The day passed in a blur. Around three, the telephone rang, and she thought not to answer but hoped it might finally be some word from the boys.

'Come to the police station.' It was Maria. 'They're moving the men.'

'Where to?'

'I don't know. Hurry.'

When she arrived at the station, a crowd of people had gathered. The police were keeping them at bay, but she could see at the back of the building the men were being loaded into large transport trucks. They were handcuffed. She saw Italo in the middle of a pack. She called out his name, but he didn't hear, didn't respond. So much shouting – how could he hear her? The trucks pulled away. The crowd followed on foot down Munro Street, then towards the train station, and when they arrived, the loading – herding, as if these men were cattle – had already begun. She called out his name again. She wanted to touch him, kiss him, but an angry sea of people separated them, and the train's windows were barred like a prison's.

'Where are you taking them?' people yelled.

The police were well briefed to say nothing, or perhaps they were simply uninformed, their faces blank.

Once the men were loaded, the train started moving to the south, towards Brisbane. Amelia's heart sank. Distance between them would make everything more difficult. But that, in the new Australia, seemed to be the plight of Italians.

'Don't come back,' an Australian man yelled at the train.

And indeed, Amelia had no idea if Italo ever would. Above the crowd's heads, some fool turned a broad and long cane knife in slow, menacing circles in the air, the blade occasionally reflecting the electric lights.

CHAPTER TWENTY-EIGHT

She returned to the farm at almost five in the evening. Once in the entrance hall, she made for the stair but stopped. She sensed something, another scent in the house, earth after rain. Flavio was home. Mauro too. They came from the kitchen to the dining room.

'We came as soon as we could,' Flavio said.

She felt made of stone, unable to move. Flavio walked forward. For most of his life, as he grew more and more to resemble Fergus, she'd resented him. And here he was; he'd come to her when she needed him. She raised her hands, embraced and hugged him. Mauro came and held her. She cried. She kissed both their foreheads. Mauro helped her to the lounge room and Flavio went back to the kitchen to ask Lucia to make tea. Ilaria returned with him and sat on her knee as she explained everything, every small detail she knew.

'Don't they see the irony?' Flavio said. 'I'm enrolling in the army.'

'You must not do that,' Amelia said.

'But I want to join. I must now. Even more so.'

'Who knows how long your father will be away? You don't have any debt to this country. That's been cancelled. You must both stay to run the farm. I can't do it on my own.'

'The family must come first,' Mauro said.

Flavio swallowed hard, squared his jaw. He looked at Mauro and then back at her.

'I'll withdraw my application,' he said. 'What have you done to free father?'

'What can I do?' Her desperation was clear in her voice. 'I've telephoned everyone I can. No-one will give me any information. The vice-consul has left Townsville. They've all fled.'

'We should contact a solicitor,' Flavio said. 'Surely, he'd know how to free him.'

She breathed deeply. When had Flavio gained insight and wisdom? How could she have not noticed?

'Thank you,' she said, looking into the depth of his dark eyes. 'I'd not even considered this.'

Lucia had prepared dinner and they ate it together. They left Italo's place at the head of the table unset.

'Where is Papa?' Ilaria asked.

Amelia looked to the boys, to Lucia, but no-one could answer.

'He's away,' Amelia said.

But this answer was wholly insufficient, and Ilaria began to cry. It was late in the evening, after her bedtime, and she was overwrought. Amelia lifted her, took her to her room and prepared her for bed. She read to her, stroking her hair, but the child resisted until she could no more and fell asleep.

Flavio met her as she descended the stair.

'Will you come with me, to the solicitor?' she said.

He regarded her, that same unreadable face of Fergus, but said nothing.

'You speak English better than I ever will,' she said. 'It would help me to have you there.'

'Of course.'

He walked the two steps to the landing on which she stood. They were at the same level.

'We will survive this,' he said.

Would they? What had happened was unfathomable. But she wouldn't destroy his hope; she needed it. She nodded, reached out, touched his hair, still that colour of first dawn.

'I feared your hair would darken with age,' she said. 'But you remain Flavio, the blond one …'

He leant towards her and kissed her cheek.

And she didn't flinch or shy away. She accepted it for what it was.

The following morning, Amelia and Flavio went to the solicitor's office. Mr White was a lean man in his mid-fifties. He'd dealt with the contracts and mortgage for the new land, and Amelia had found him knowledgeable, trustworthy and efficient.

'The men have been arrested as the government is concerned for actions of a fifth column. It's happened all over the state, all over the country. My guess is they've been taken to Gaythorne concentration camp, just outside Brisbane.'

It had been built during World War I to house German merchant sailors arrested in Australian waters, but recently he'd heard it had been reopened.

'It's the only facility that can house the number of men they've arrested,' he said.

'How long will they be there?' Flavio said.

'They have a right to lodge an appeal. But unless we can establish a good reason for his release, he'll be there for the duration of the war.'

'He has a business to run,' Amelia said.

'I'm afraid that's not enough.'

Amelia reeled at the bleak remark.

'Don't be discouraged,' he said. 'We must build with what's possible. Italo is well-liked in the community, not just the Italian community. I advise you to obtain as many character references as you can, from people he's dealt with in business and people he knows socially. If we're going to free him, we need a broad base of support.'

She agreed to this and said she would start with Mr McDonald, the bank manager, and Henry Ling, the Babinda chemist and druggist. They would both speak well of him. At least it was something positive to do, rather than the endless hours of powerlessness.

That evening she wrote a letter to Marta, explaining all that had happened and that she was to concentrate on her studies, as her father would hope she would, and not to worry herself, as this wretched matter would soon be resolved. She searched a map of Brisbane and located Gaythorne. It wasn't so far to travel. They couldn't divide a husband and a wife. She would go, soon, demand to see him. But first she had to stabilise the farm and plant the seeds of his release. Whilst the boys had been involved in all aspects of the business, she couldn't leave it to their giddy-headed-ness. She needed a plan for them, an explicit schedule, and to book the mill and the cutters.

And then she thought of Clara. They'd had little com-munication since their break, four years ago. Amelia's pride hadn't allowed it. The boys said they hadn't seen her while they were in Brisbane, but she suspected they had. Perhaps Clara could go and visit Italo? Gaythorne wasn't far for her to travel, and Clara had no argument with Italo. If anything, she saw him as a pawn, and his arrest proved everything Clara had heralded, primarily that Australia wouldn't abide their involvement in fascism. And despite everything, Amelia trusted Clara to tell the truth of Italo's condition.

She wrote a short letter, direct and to the point, telling what had happened, asking what she wanted, without emotion, no admittance of blame, no cadence of guilt, no appeal to anything but their history.

And so they began to wait. The solicitor kept them informed – there were no developments that would free him. She wrote a long letter to her parents, detailing the troubles that had befallen them, complaining of all the problems with the farm and the injustice of the situation. She placed the letter in an envelope and addressed this to her parents, but then placed this in another envelope and addressed it to a cousin in Switzerland. Before they left Italy, they agreed on this method of communication if Italy were to enter the war, to send the letters first to neutral Switzerland. Direct mail services between Italy and Australia would likely be interrupted.

And fortunately, there was one thing free of politics: the fields. Despite Italo's absence, caught in its automatic cycle, the cane grew. And she thanked God with every prayer she could muster. If this were to fail, every difficulty would be magnified. And the boys hadn't failed her; in fact, they continued to surprise her. They applied themselves to the tasks in a way she'd never seen. It was her first sign of hope that perhaps they could survive Italo's absence.

CHAPTER TWENTY-NINE

Amelia received a letter from Clara. At first it was confusing, but then Amelia realised Clara had already been to the camp without Amelia's prompting. She knew the Italian men had been taken to Gaythorne, guessed Italo would be amongst them and had taken it upon herself to go to the camp. Although the officials wouldn't confirm he was there, they did say she wouldn't be allowed to see him, as she wasn't a relative.

'So you see, they've admitted he's there. I've tried.'

The letter was both settling and unsettling. Clara's letter contained no prelude to reconciliation and no emotion. She spoke of Italo as if he were an object to be found. And she gave no impression of the condition of the camp – how large it was, did it feel as if it was permanent or would he be moved again? Was this just her still holding a grudge, or were the conditions at the camp so horrendous she couldn't report them?

Amelia wrote a brief note, thanking her for her trouble. If she heard more, she would write to Clara and perhaps she could go again to Gaythorne.

She also received a letter from the bank. It contained her cheque to pay their monthly account at Northern Builders Supplies. It was stamped in red, *No Funds*. A wave of anxiety lashed her. The cheque account always had funds. And it had an overdraft, which she'd never used. She'd not wanted such a facility, but the bank manager, Mr McDonald, had demanded she take it. She flicked through the ledger. There it was, the balance of two pounds, six shillings and four pence. More than enough to cover this piddling cheque. This was a mistake. Her anger rose, not so much at the error but at yet another item she had to put right.

She telephoned the bank.

'There is no error,' Mr McDonald said, immediately. 'There are no funds.'

'There's a balance of two pounds, six shillings and four pence.'

There was a long silence. 'We had to remit all funds of enemy aliens to the taxation department.'

Her breath slipped. 'What?'

There was another long pause. 'This isn't something I wanted to do.'

The floor of the telephone cabinet fell away as if she was floating, falling.

'We have no money?' she said, finally, more as a declarative.

Again there was silence. 'I'm sure once these arrests are resolved, the money will be reimbursed. I've written letters maintaining there should be interest.'

'How am I to run a business?'

Still more silence.

'What about the mortgage on the new land?' she said.

She could hear him breathe heavily. 'The repayments will need to be made.'

Frustration rose into her voice. 'How am I to do that?'

Again, silence. 'I've written a character reference for Mr Amedeo. I'll leave it at the counter for you. Please, if there's anything else I can do, don't hesitate to contact me.'

She continued to stare at the telephone's mouthpiece, although she knew Mr McDonald had rung off. It was only when she removed the earpiece that she realised the force with which she'd pressed it to her ear, the cartilage hurting as it buckled back to shape. She hung the earpiece on the brace.

They would be ruined. To not have money was one thing, but to have to make payments was completely another. For some time, she sat in the lounge. How were they to survive? This was unjust, grossly so. They'd worked so hard. She'd kept them well in the black. Their tax returns were prepared by an accountant and lodged on time and paid in full; she'd never wanted to draw the department's attention. And now it was all gone. Was there no goodwill? How could she be expected to run a business? Without Italo. Without capital. And a business with an annual period of income and debts all year? Had the other women of the valley been reduced to this?

She took stock. They must survive with what they had. She'd survived with far less. At present, they owed Northern Builders Supplies and the mortgage. Lucia would have to go unpaid. She had free board and keep. This matter would be resolved in the next few weeks with Italo's appeal. It couldn't go on. She breathed. She'd kept a wad of cash in the house, bundled behind the shelves of her office. Her insurance. Perhaps she'd known this day would arrive.

The harvest was coming. She would try to book the mill a little earlier. If the crop was slightly immature, they may lose some of the yield, but they'd have some money. But the mill would pay by cheque, and if she cashed this it would surely be seized by the taxation department. How futile. More than ever, this harvest was their future. Then she found an answer – she'd open a bank account in Flavio's name. They couldn't touch him or a cheque in his name. As much as they may not like it, he was Australian.

This country wouldn't beat her.

Two days later, she retrieved the mail at the post office. One of the letters was addressed in a hand she didn't recognise. But she saw the postmark – Gaythorne. On the post office step, despite her trembling hands, she tore at it, a huge wrenching sound in the quiet of the office. A man glared at her. She ran to the safety of the car. It was written by someone Italo didn't identify. He was at Gaythorne. Everything was all right and they were treated and fed well, although through the first few days of the internment they'd been housed like pigs. He was unsure how long he would be there. He'd received the two suitcases and thanked her. He knew other men in the camp. He was all right. She wasn't to worry and must put all her time and thought into running the farm with the boys. His appeal against the imprisonment would be held soon, and all would be set right. He thanked her for the references she'd organised.

She reread and reread the letter. She had more errands to run, but she wanted to be at home and started the car. Despite the letter's cheery tone, it worried her. Were these the words he'd spoken, or were they just what whoever had written the letter thought she would want to hear? And what could he say except that everything was all right? If he was such a risk to the country, the letter would be read by some official before it was sent. He could hardly list the faults of this Gaythorne.

Gaythorne. The sound of such a place. How could a thorn ever be happy? Such sarcasm.

She called Flavio and Mauro to the lounge room and read them the letter. They shared none of her concern regarding its authenticity and were pleased he was safe and well.

And the telephone rang all afternoon. Other women had received letters, theirs expressing similar sentiments.

Perhaps she should trust the letter? But trust had been cast away, a blood-blotted handkerchief.

The weeks of his internment swelled to months. Clara went again and managed to see him. She confirmed he appeared in good health and, although extremely concerned and agitated, of sound mind. And he sent letters often, always in another unknown hand. Each letter said he kept well and affirmed she had to make whatever decisions she thought just.

'Survival is all that counts.'

With so much else to do, Amelia fell behind with all the correspondence, a pile of mail on the side of her desk. At three o'clock one morning she sat to start work on that alone. The harvest was booked to go to the mill in mid-September. This was the easy part. This they'd done many times. The hardest part was going to be the cutting.

All the Italian men from the gang she usually employed had been arrested. She would have to seek other men, but the only available were British Australians. She resented this. Whilst all the men, including the Italians, were unionist, the Italian men had always done the job as quickly as possible. She was sure, if she could employ them, these British-Australian men wouldn't be so helpful. They would work to rule, which would ultimately take more time and money, raising the cost of harvesting when they could least afford it.

She worked this into her calculations. Even with this, they would at least cover costs and leave a small profit. But the mortgage on the new parcel of land was onerous. She cursed the money they'd spent in Italy. And for what? The time had been nothing short of a waste. Pina complained and demanded they send her more money each month to compensate for not having brought her grandchildren. The war broke out. But Amelia valued seeing her family, who were so old. Aldo and Giuseppe ran the orchard together with their own families. God knows how they made enough money to survive, and if she and Italo weren't sending so much to Pina she'd gladly send them some.

She looked into the dark outside the window. Down by the road at the base of the hill, she saw a small orange light, just a pinprick that a less-sharp eye mightn't have seen. It moved, swayed and disappeared and then ignited and danced again. Someone was walking along the road, smoking. Neither of the boys smoked, and as far as she knew they were both in bed. Who could it be? The thought made her shudder. Did people move about the house in the dark? It was the first time she'd ever thought such a thing. She'd grown used to the unlocked doors. But now she walked all the way downstairs and locked the front door and went to the kitchen and locked the rear door. But what good did that do? There were so many open windows. When she returned to her desk, she peered again into the dark. There was no sign of the smoker. But she must remember to check the doors last thing at night.

She returned to her work. Perhaps she should consider selling the newer parcel of land. Whilst not a perfect long-term solution, the lack of the mortgage would alleviate some financial stress. Italo would be horrified at such a suggestion, but he wasn't there. It wasn't his fault; she offered no blame, but it was the reality. She had to make decisions. But she wished she could discuss it with him. Perhaps Flavio would have some opinion. But Italo had told her to make the required decisions to survive. He would just have to accept that. But the land meant so much to them, and to the business. It was dire to consider selling it. She would think of this more, but there was no-one left in the area whose counsel she trusted. Perhaps the boys …

Outside the window, the dark night was replaced by the first seeds of the new day. What was that – in the distance, at the far edge of the field, in the remaining dark? She stood. She was sure of it – flame, orange and bristling, a straight line along the field's edge, like a cane gang would light. Why would they light the field now? The harvest wasn't for another month. The boys knew that. The cane would rot if it was burnt and not harvested. But as she watched, the fire gathered pace, tore along the northern boundary in two directions, as if pushed by a dry, hot wind. And then it came to the eastern boundary and began to move along it. To the west, the same happened. And then, under some unseen power, the golden light flared along the aisles between the fields.

She turned from her desk, knocked over her chair, which thudded on the floor. She ran to the landing.

'Fire,' she called out. 'Fire. Fire.'

She ran down the stair, tore at the locked door, and dashed to the front gravel yard. Soon Flavio was beside her, dressed only in pyjama bottoms, his eyes as wide as buttons.

'What the hell's happening?'

She looked to the sky. Although it was written over with smoke, it was blue.

Mauro came from the house. They stood in the gravel yard on the hill, the whole field in front of them alight. The ash, golden and joyous in the air, rained around them.

'What can we do?' Flavio yelled.

There was nothing they could do. The fire was dispersed. They could only watch.

'It won't get to the house,' Flavio said. 'But it might get to the barn. Mauro, come with me.'

Flavio started down the hill, and his brother fell in behind him, disappearing into the opening day and the amber fire. Flavio was wise to do this. With petrol being rationed, the horses were valuable to the farm.

'Lucia,' Amelia yelled to them. 'Wake her.'

Her hut was near the barn, and she slept like a stone.

Amelia turned back to the house. She wasn't so sure the fire wouldn't reach that far. The grass on the hill hadn't been cut, and a small spark would flare. She ran upstairs to Ilaria's room. The fire's stink had permeated the whole house. Amelia swept the sleeping child from the bed and, with her still half asleep, continued higher into the tower. She sat Ilaria on the office floor.

'What's happening?' Ilaria said, perplexed.

'Just be quiet, darling. We have to leave the house.'

Amelia went to the bookshelf to the side of her desk and squeezed her small hand behind it. The purse was there, with what remained of the cash. She pulled it free. At her desk she looked at the blazing field, which undulated and seethed, waves of heaving flame. Had it all come to this?

She picked up Ilaria and ran to the lower levels of the house. The child jarred in her arms and started to cry, and she tse-tse-tsed in her ear as soothingly as she could, out into the gravel yard, but Ilaria now sobbed. Lucia strode up the hill, dressed only in a long flannel nightdress, her grey hair unpinned and tangled, a madwoman.

'We should leave,' Lucia said.

Amelia handed her the child and stepped forward. Flavio and Mauro led the five horses away from the stable, towards the main road. Spooked, they shook out their manes, one raising its front feet from the ground. If she got Lucia and Ilaria to the main road, they would be safe. It was wise to leave while they could. She looked back at the house.

'Come,' she yelled, waving them towards the car. They drove from the house, around the curve of the hill. Once on the straight road, she could see the boys and the horses ahead and slowed, not to scare the horses any more. At the main road, the boys tethered the horses. Lucia and Ilaria remained in the car.

'There's nothing we can do,' she said.

Flavio looked back towards the field, an orange glow catching on the belly of the clouds.

'There must be something,' he said, and started back to the field. Amelia commanded Lucia to stay in the car with Ilaria. If the fire came closer, they were to walk towards the village.

With Mauro and Flavio she ran to the field. What the boy thought he could do she had no idea, but she'd not dampen his confidence. Once at the barn, he stopped, his hands on his hips, glaring at the fire as if he dared it. The air was unbreathable, laced with smoke and ash and heat and crackling.

'If it crosses the road, we can try and put out the spot fires.' He ran into the stable and returned with some hessian bags he threw into the horse's trough. 'We'll be able to smother it with these.'

It would gain them some time, moments, but they couldn't keep the fire from the house for long. The first fire flared some seventy feet back up the hill, and Flavio sprinted to it, slashed at it with the bag until it died. Another erupted near Amelia, and she did as he'd done until it was gone. Mauro too began. But soon it was clear the fires were lighting quicker than they were being exhausting.

And then God answered her prayers – a drop of rain on her cheek. The boys felt them too and turned to her. She looked to the sky; the smoke was so thick she couldn't see it, but the rain – large, heated drops – fell to her face. The rain had come. The single thing she hated most about Babinda had saved her again. She would never curse it. It gathered pace to a downpour. They walked to the fields. The water hissed and spat as it hit the ground. Together, for some time (who could measure it?) they stood and watched. When the flame had subsided, Flavio waded into the fields.

'It was savage,' he said. 'How would it have started?'

She described what she'd seen, the flame speeding along the borders. 'It was unnatural, the way it spread.'

'Someone's used petrol,' Flavio said, 'but they spread it all over the field.'

'But who?' Mauro said.

God bless his innocence. Amelia had no idea who it was, but knew it was linked to the arrest of the Italian men. Another form of castor oiling.

'It's all right,' she said. 'The crop was nearly ready. If we can harvest in the next few days, there's no real harm.'

'But we'll need men to do that,' Flavio said.

'And the mill,' Mauro said. 'They won't take it. It will rot.'

She breathed deeply. They'd taught the boys well. She would have to offer the mill more money to take their crop early. She would find a gang. Even if she had to pay more. Amelia eyed the sky. The rain set in. Sheets of water fell, unusual in their ferocity for that time of year.

CHAPTER THIRTY

Flavio reported the fire to the police, but it was late morning before they came to look at the smouldering mess. They agreed it may have been arson.

'It was probably the blacks,' the policeman said, writing something in a notebook.

'I saw someone,' Amelia said, 'from my office.'

The officer looked at her.

'When?' Flavio said.

She told them she'd been working, around four in the morning. She pointed to the window. 'I saw the glow of a cigarette,' she said. 'Someone moving along the road.' She pointed to the edge of the field.

The officer turned to Amelia. 'What did he look like?'

'It was dark. I just saw he was smoking.'

The policeman smirked. 'The blacks smoke.'

Flavio shook his head.

The officer wrote something more in his notebook and said they'd look around the field but doubted there'd be anything to identify anyone. But they would also ask the other farmers in the area if they'd seen anyone unusual moving about, if anyone else had had a fire. They would report back to them.

After they'd gone, Amelia telephoned the mill and explained a fire had gone through the main crop, and she wanted to shift the milling forward.

'We're fully booked,' the man said.

She thought he answered a little too quickly, and far too bluntly.

'Kelly's crop starts today,' he said. 'It'll take the next few weeks. Then you're booked.'

Her skin prickled. 'Perhaps he's delayed.'

'He's on schedule. He'll burn today, start cutting tomorrow.'

She could contact Fergus, ask him to hold off. It wouldn't harm his crop to wait. But they'd hardly parted on good terms. And she wanted nothing to do with him.

'I'd be prepared to pay considerably more,' she said.

'It's not a question of money,' he said.

He stopped at that. She left the silence ringing.

'You know how it is,' he said. 'It's just how it's booked. Do you want me to keep your booking?'

'We will have the cane from the new land. It will be on schedule.'

If there was any change he'd be sure to let her know, but he doubted there would be.

What was she to do? When had it not been a question of money? She flushed with anger. The mills had shuffled in the past. It was to everyone's advantage to run as smoothly as possible. But the outbreak of war had brought such swift change, the collegial, the communal, gone.

She gathered her options. If she didn't harvest the crop immediately and mill it straight away, it would rot. And if she took a gamble and paid men to harvest it, and then it couldn't be milled, it would rot. There was nowhere to store it undercover. And now it was raining, it was wet. It would be a substantial loss to pay to cut it and then let it spoil.

But if she left it in the field, ploughed it all back into the earth, she'd have at least saved the money needed for the cutters. They'd lose the major part of their income, though, having only the little from the new land for another year.

The thought appalled her. She couldn't just let it rot in the field. It was a waste. She telephoned to organise the cutters, but hardly any were available, and those she could get weren't available until a week later, when it would be too late. And at short notice, they were double the price. The unions, so strident on a minimum wage, had no opinion on a maximum. She simply couldn't afford to harvest without some assurance it would be milled. Through all these negotiations, it rained.

So she did as they'd never done before – they left the whole crop to rot. They would lose most of a year's income, raising just a small amount from the new land. Already they had no money. The cash reserve was eroding, no more than five pounds. Could they possibly get by with fewer provisions? What more could she cut back? Already their food came from the garden, the cows and the hens, what the boys could hunt. They spent nothing. She wouldn't allow repairs. In the short-term, they would just have to make do – the machinery, the buildings, the fences. Nothing could be touched.

Marta would have to come home from school. It was wrong to interrupt her learning, something she'd never imagined, but she couldn't afford the fees, and she'd not ask for charity. She breathed out. It would only be for a short time. It just had to be. And another pair of hands on the farm would help. There was no choice, and an odd relief at the realisation of such a saving. She wrote a letter to the headmaster, explaining their new circumstances and that Marta must return home.

But how could she make the payments for the new land? She had no option and met with Mr McDonald at the bank the following morning. He was a quiet, guarded man but he welcomed her but avoided her eye, moved around the office like a sheepdog. Once they were seated across his broad mahogany desk, she explained the situation, without rushing, without fawning.

'What an undue time for this to occur,' he said.

'We still have the new land. This crop will give some income, but it's some way off and … Well, it will barely meet our expenses.'

'What do you need from me?'

He sat back in his chair, removed himself. She would have thought it was bloody obvious what she needed.

'I don't want to have to sell the new land. You know how hard I fought for it. And as you can see, at this point it's our saviour.'

He remained impassive. Wouldn't he intervene? Did she have to say it all?

'But I need some time,' she said, 'without having to pay the mortgage. I'm aware you must charge interest, and I'm sure once the small crop is harvested, I'll be able to resume.'

Something cold swept over his countenance. 'These are troubling times, for all. My hands are tired. In the face of such controls, there's little I can do.'

He linked his hands and placed them on the desk. What was she to do? Accept this? If this was his answer, she wouldn't give him grace and thank him for his time, excuse it, say she understood. She met his eyes, that steel blue of so many Irish-born men.

'How long until you harvest this small crop?' he said, emptying out his lungs.

She'd gained a foothold. 'A month.'

He sighed. 'I'll suspend the repayments for a month—'

'Two?'

He glared at her. 'All right, two. But no more. And you are correct, the interest will accrue.'

She breathed out. She stood. She stretched her hand across the broad desk, as perhaps a woman shouldn't. He rose slowly from his chair and met her hand.

'Thank you,' she said. 'You of all people know Italo and I have always met our duty.'

'You have a fine son to help you.'

She studied him, knew what he inferred, that Flavio was a better son because of his heritage. She took the comment on the cheek, although she seared with heat.

'I have two sons,' she said. 'And my daughter will return from school. We shan't fail, you or ourselves.'

She marched from the office before the anger jelled on her tongue. His was no casual remark. It was pointed and barbed and callous. Would she never work this stain off? But she'd got what she wanted. If this insult was the price she should pay, it was cheap.

Flavio, Mauro and she spent the afternoon in the field collecting good canes from the rubble to cut setts to plant for the next crop.

'There isn't much here we can use,' Flavio said.

'We'll save some from the other field,' she said.

They carried the few they found into the barn, laid them undercover between trellises to dry. She heard a vehicle and went outside. It was the police. She was surprised to see them; even they'd expressed doubt they'd turn up any information. Perhaps there'd been another fire in the valley? She met them outside the barn.

But it was only one of the officers from the morning, and he was accompanied by an older man. They both bore stern, fixed expressions, colourless, showing unease that hadn't been evident before.

'Mrs Amedeo?' the older one said.

He knew who she was. She just nodded.

'I have some rather bad news …'

He stopped as if he expected her to give him permission to go on. Something had happened to Italo, she was sure, but he said something to do with Marta. Why the hell was he talking of Marta? She'd been killed. In a car crash. On her way from Herberton. The headmaster survived.

'You're wrong,' Amelia said. 'She's not coming home until Tuesday.'

The officer looked at Flavio, who stepped forward, took both her arms and looked into her eyes.

'It *is* Tuesday,' Flavio said.

'No,' she said. 'It can't be. It's not her. It can't be.'

A numbness rushed into her heart. She'd go back to the barn where, a moment ago, this hadn't been. She would cut the setts. No. It would be there now. How could she undo this? Take this back, reverse such a thing? As little as a moment ago … Flavio held her arms. She looked into his eyes, so full of fear and pain. What could she do? She could take no more.

'Come back to the house,' he said.

'Back to the house …' she said. She looked at him. 'Of course, Fergus.'

And she stepped and stepped and then gave way and collapsed in his arm. With all marks of gallantry, he swooped her up as if she were nothing more than air and carried her, started up the hill.

Mauro ran ahead, calling and calling, 'Lucia, Lucia, Lucia, Lucia.'

His strength. Would this carry her? Would this crush her?

'I'm sorry,' she said, her throat so dry. 'I'm sorry. I'm so sorry.'

'There's nothing to be sorry for,' he said.

But she kept saying it as if it made sense. He carried her over the threshold, through the hall to the lounge room. Lucia screamed, tumbling over and wailing at a higher pitch. Ilaria cried out. But she could do nothing. He laid her on the soft couch.

She could take no more. Some part of herself curled, a flame-coloured leaf, let go of the bough and drifted away, further and further. And died.

CHAPTER THIRTY-ONE

Amelia wouldn't leave the house. She couldn't. She didn't want to see anyone she didn't want to see. Moreover, she wanted no surprises. Nothing unsettling. Nothing unexpected. No sickly condolences and no-one to snub her. She stayed in the tower office – the curtain pulled against the view – or her and Italo's bedroom; at most, she ventured to the lounge. Lucia ran the house, cared for Ilaria, cooked for the boys. She couldn't face the boys' dull stares. Ilaria didn't understand – Marta was just away at school – and she continued to laugh and sing and dance. Amelia couldn't cope with Ilaria's play and removed herself. She ate little and brooded. She wrote a sad letter to her mother, the news old when it would reach her. Would Amelia feel across such a distance the moment her mother knew? They should have taken the children to Italy … But that would have made all their problems worse.

In her office, she regarded herself in the mirror. Dark clouds hung under her reddened eyes. She looked gaunt. Her black cardigan hung from her shoulders. In these last days, she'd aged a lifetime. Someone knocked at the door. She froze. She was in no mood to talk. But the person knocked again and then pushed open the door, stepped into the room.

Clara. She thought she was seeing things and blinked. But tears had come to them, and this vision before her blurred. Neither woman moved. The ten or so feet between them remained, unbridged, unmanageable.

'I came as soon as I heard,' Clara said.

She stepped into the room, but Amelia could find no words.

'Flavio telephoned me.'

Clara looked the same, her hair no more greyed, her weight remained, dressed still in black as she'd been the last time they'd seen one another, as if nothing had changed. Amelia was unsure she wanted to see her. But these were changed times. And Clara had always remembered Marta's birthdays. But in many ways, it all seemed a natural corollary of Clara's dire predictions. Clara came to Amelia and, though her eyes were lowered to the ground, took her in her arms and held her. Amelia's arms hung limply at her side. She had no volition, no energy, no certainty, with which to return the embrace.

'I'm so sorry,' Clara said. She released Amelia.

Amelia remained some glassed exhibit in a museum, unable to speak. Clara took her hand and led her to the small office lounge. For long moments they sat together in silence, for what could they possibly say of any consequence? Lucia brought them coffee, which neither of them touched.

'Have you contacted Italo?' Clara said.

'The authorities have. I've written to him.'

'Can he come to the funeral?'

Amelia glared at her. 'He's a prisoner of war …'

Clara recoiled. Amelia had been too harsh.

'The solicitor has asked,' Amelia said, 'but he's not hopeful.'

Clara looked away, towards the closed curtains of the windows.

'She didn't suffer,' Amelia said, almost by way of amelioration. 'The police assured me.'

'And the headmaster?'

'He's in hospital, in Cairns.' Amelia could hold herself no longer. 'Why *her*?' The word tore. 'Why has this happened?'

'I don't know.'

'She was just a girl. Why has she been taken?'

'We're not born to understand.'

Amelia breathed deeply. She'd not wanted to show these emotions to Clara.

'Did Flavio tell you?' Amelia said. 'We have no money.'

'He said you've lost a crop.'

'The tax department took all our money. All of it. I had to cut spending. Don't you see? I couldn't afford her school and boarding fees. It's all my fault. I made her come home.' These words screeched. 'I should have sold the land and left her in school, and this wouldn't have happened.'

'It's the authorities' fault, not yours.'

'But I made Italo join the Babinda Fascist Organisation. All this ill fortune began with that.'

Amelia fought to withdraw, covered her face with her hands, shut her eyes. She'd lost control and said more than she wanted. Clara let her sob, made no move to soothe or belittle her emotion.

'Who knows how long these chains of fate are?' Clara said. 'This isn't the time for analysis. And it changes nothing.'

Ilaria ran into the room. Clara clasped her hand to her chest. Clara had never met her.

'You've seen a ghost,' Amelia said.

'She …'

'She's the image of Marta when she was young,' Amelia said.

Ilaria remained staring at Clara, until Clara motioned to her. But the child sat next to Amelia. For the first time since the news of Marta's death, Ilaria appeared lost, robbed of confidence.

'The funeral is in the morning,' Amelia said. The words set her heart to break. 'What a thing to speak of.'

'To bury a husband is one thing,' Clara said. 'But a child ...'

Had she meant this?

'I'm sorry,' Clara said. 'For everything that's happened.'

Clara coaxed her to come downstairs. At first she refused, but then together they walked the stairs, the sound of their heels heavy and slow on the wooden stair. People came from the lounge, and Amelia turned back to the stair to escape. But Clara took her hand and gently turned her towards them.

Cristiano, tall and lean and wearing a dark-blue silk suit, stepped forward. Donata and Eugenia followed. Cristiano had matured, groomed to refinement. And the girls had bloomed. Something poor Marta would never do. Amelia fought off the emotions.

Cristiano, as tall as his father and as handsome, hugged her, just said her name, 'Zia Amelia', and released her. How he'd changed, his face now without any of the plump of youth, the planes bold and sharp and proud. Donata and Eugenia hugged her, their wordless eyes lowered to the ground. Both had inherited their mother's poise.

The following day was hot – as if it could have been anything else. Amelia and Clara, both dressed in black, sat in the front row of the church, their children on either side. Some of the Italian women came, but largely the church was empty and echoing. She could afford only a pauper's grave, just a wooden cross with her name and dates painted. Once they'd recovered financially, she would put it right with something stone.

They invited people back to the house, but few came, just the priest and two of the Italian women. Amelia sat in the lounge and said little to anyone. Clara did her best to play hostess but was cold and perfunctory. Amelia was unsure of its source – did she still bear their argument, a break between them even death couldn't overcome? Or was she just calloused by death?

The morning after the funeral, the Sacco family prepared to leave. Cristiano had to return to work at the hospital in Brisbane, and the girls to school. Clara and Cristiano called Amelia, Flavio and Mauro to the lounge room.

'Because of Italo's incarceration,' Cristiano said, 'you have deep financial problems. We'd like to take over the payments of the mortgage. At least for the coming months.'

'I won't accept charity.'

'It's hardly charity,' Clara said.

Amelia said nothing.

'When Paolo died ...' Clara said. 'I've never forgotten your help. At the least, couldn't you see this as repayment?'

'I won't accept it.'

'Do you remember,' Cristiano said, raising an open palm, 'when we first arrived in Australia, those last few days on the ship?'

Amelia looked at him and nodded.

'I remember calling you *zia* for the first time. You looked so surprised. But from the moment we went ashore in Fremantle, I knew I'd never have a *zia*, not one like you. As an immigrant, I was lucky. I could choose my *zia*.'

Amelia remembered that moment. The simple word had shocked her, surprised her, enchanted her. The possibility of choice in such a matter seemed reckless, against the natural order, and yet it was thrilling, like a highwire, something particular to this new country. And she'd embraced it.

His eyes glistened. 'Let me do this for you. If it means that much, when you're back on your feet, you can repay it. Then it's not charity.'

Despite herself, tears, more tears (where did they all come from?) rolled her weary cheek. Whilst she'd staved off the bank for two months, beyond this time seemed bleak. This was good fortune, not charity. And perhaps it would salve some of the cuts between her and Clara.

'How could I resist my favourite nephew?' she said. 'But it will be returned, in full. And with interest.'

Cristiano smiled, and for a moment she stood with him in the arrival hall in Brisbane, twenty years ago, a trembling boy meeting his father. What strange states this country brought, what odd moments it induced. What an unknown country.

The rest of the morning was pleasant. For the first time, Amelia enquired of their lives. Both Donata and Eugenia were studying teaching. Clara worked in a factory that specialised in quilting. They lived in the same house, in New Farm. Cristiano was in love and soon to marry. He invited Amelia and the children to the wedding in the new year. Amelia doubted they could attend, but murmured appreciation.

But even death doesn't stop the blood surge of time. In the coming days, she remained inside the house. She received a letter from Italo, written in another unknown hand. He spoke little of his feeling for Marta and hoped only Amelia, the boys and Ilaria were safe. He wished he could be with them.

Late that evening, she took her first walk, through the ruined field and out to the new parcel of land. She pulled a cane towards her, gave it a sharp twist. They needed income. The harvest of the small parcel of land was to begin.

The boys took care of it all, which pleased her, as she had no mind for it. Lucia cooked for the cutters, not that the land required many. And the cane was hauled to the mill and ground of its precious syrup. They would have some money. With Cristiano's relief of the mortgage, she could spin it out until the next full harvest. She would see to it.

Only the young can believe in miracles. She reminded herself of this, time and time again as she read and reread the letter she'd just received. Italo had been taken from the camp at Gaythorne to Brisbane, to the Bankruptcy Court, which had been pressed into this new service. He'd been questioned in front of an advisory committee of three men, but he'd had no lawyer to represent him. If only she'd known, she'd have gone to Brisbane. At least asked Clara to go. Or sent Flavio. How would he have fared with his English so poor? The result of the appeal wouldn't be known for some time, but nonetheless Italo was to be transferred from Gaythorne to another camp at Hay, in the Riverina of New South Wales.

This was another blow, a gush of anguish and regret and anger that tore at her heart. He was so far away. She should have gone to Gaythorne, but she had put it off because of the harvest and then Marta's death. What good had it all done?

And now he was so far away, in another state. Why was he taken there? The answer was immediate: they just wanted to cause as much pain and suffering and anguish as they could. It was part of his sentence. It would take her more than three days to travel there. Her anger bore no calibration. How was she to run a business and take so much time away? But she had to. For herself, she had to. For Italo, she had to. For the remaining children. She must see him and ask what he needed, if he was fed or neglected. And who knows when or if they would transfer him even further afield? She'd heard some men had been taken to a camp in South Australia, even further away.

But first they must plant the new crop. So she explained it to the boys.

'We can handle the planting,' Flavio said. 'Just go.'

Could she trust them to do this without her overseeing it? It would mean she could travel immediately to Italo, but if they failed, it would be their complete ruin.

'There's much to be done,' she said.

'You don't trust us,' Flavio said.

'How can you say such a thing? Of course I trust you, but you'll need other men and they have to be fed and housed. Do you think that just happens with no effort?'

It was then she realised she must stay. Whilst the boys knew their job, they had no idea of hers, of what staging the planting involved, let alone the financials. For them, it was only the work in the field. She couldn't run the risk of this not being done.

'I have a suggestion,' Flavio said. 'Given it's hard – well, near impossible – to find men for the harvest, wouldn't it be wise to plant only the fields in front of the house?'

'Not plant the new fields?' Amelia said.

'That's right. Whilst we won't make as much money, wouldn't we be able to reduce our costs as well?'

'And wouldn't that reduce our risks?' Mauro said.

They had clearly conferred on this plan, and she could see the logic.

'I'll do some calculations, based on what you're suggesting.'

That night, she worked through the figures. There was solid truth in their proposal. Whilst it would reduce their income, it would also reduce their costs. And with a small amount to harvest, it would mean they would need fewer men.

In a month, they could start to plant. They were late. Once this was done, she would take her long journey to Hay in the Riverina, and to Italo.

The new crop was planted by the end of November, a little later than she would have liked; the lack of men had made it slow and arduous and expensive. The boys worked hard, and even she'd spent some days in the fields until her back ached, reminding her she was neither young nor supple, and she'd retreated to the house.

And following Flavio's idea, they'd planted less, not even attempting to cultivate the newer fields. Leaving them fallow wasn't an unsound idea, but she would get the boys to plant lucerne to plough back in at the end of summer, to improve the condition of the earth. With clearer planning, next year they would plant all the fields. By her calculations, they would be able to harvest the main fields and would yield just enough income. It was a fine balance but with all these conditions, it was the best she could do.

Months after Italo had fronted the appeal hearing, he was told his objection wouldn't be upheld. Despite all the letters of support of his good character, nothing could be changed. He would remain in the camp till the end of the war. All legal means had come to no ends, the law unyielding to the demands of a family, the needs of a business, the declarations of good character. And yet she was sure the taxation department would still demand its cut of any profit she may declare in the time he was away. But she would put off these thoughts. They must pull ahead. There was no other option.

One afternoon she heard a vehicle approaching the house. She looked from her work to where the road rounded the hill. Her pulse quickened. Who would be coming to the farm? She descended the stairs and peered from the loungeroom windows. Fergus. She hadn't seen him but had heard he was doing well now he'd taken over his father's property. Fortunately, Flavio and Mauro were in the village. What the hell did he want? She hurried to the front door. Lucia was coming from the kitchen. She waved her back and said there was no need for refreshment.

She opened the door. He walked from the truck towards the house, no longer wearing khaki shorts and shirt, although he'd maintained the slouch hat, dressed now in long pants and a check shirt, as if he'd made some sartorial overture to seeing her. If anything, time had buffed some of the sharp edges. She tightened. She could no longer call it desire. She bore no ill will towards him.

'Good morning,' he said.

Such words. How odd they were. He gave her some moments, but she glared at him. She could find nothing inconsequential to say.

'Could we talk?' he said.

He looked over her shoulder. She turned. Lucia stood in the door with Ilaria at her side, half hidden in the folds of her dress. Lucia's brows rose, though Amelia had no idea why – the presence of a man? The absence of other men on the property? Or had she heard talk and now, seeing this man, had had every rumour confirmed?

'Privately,' he said.

What on earth was there to discuss? This was farcical, but he had intent. It was best to take him out of Lucia's earshot.

'We can walk,' she said.

He seemed perplexed and then nodded, stepped back to allow her to pass. She turned to Lucia, told her to take the child inside and assured her there was no concern.

They started together, him slightly behind her but his step in time. From the gravel yard, she started down the hill and then along a path into the field. He said nothing, which had always been his way. The fields had no sign yet of new growth.

'I hear you're managing well,' she said.

He nodded. 'There's a lot to repair. Oisin had let a lot fall away.' He paused. 'I'm sorry for the loss of your daughter.'

The spasm of her heart shook her. She looked at him. Was this all he'd come for? She nodded, unprepared to reveal the chafed-raw sorrow.

'It must be hard, without Italo,' he said.

'You of all people know the difficulties of cane farming, but we're better off than others. It's all we can do.'

'I meant without your husband ...'

'I know what you meant.' She had no desire to discuss her imprisoned husband.

He looked away from her, out across the fresh fields. 'You've not planted the new land?'

'We don't have enough hands.'

He stopped walking. She stepped forward and then turned to face him.

'I'd like to buy that land back,' he said.

She answered without thought. 'It's not for sale.'

'I'd pay what you did, plus some, for the land's improvement.'

She considered him.

'We know one another too well not to trust,' he said. 'It's an honest offer.'

She looked across the land. Heat blared to her face.

'You could never match the price I've paid,' she said.

He pouted. Did he think himself a sorcerer and her so fey? Her sorrow for Marta slackened the anger.

'That may have worked on me once,' she said, 'but I'm older now. My eyes are open. You have no power.'

He narrowed his lips. 'I mean to have it back.'

She tightened her face. 'Your father sold it. The land is legally ours.'

They stood, their eyes locked, until he looked away, looked at his feet, put on his slouch hat and walked away.

She stayed in the field, looked to the deep sky. What a proud fool she was. How much easier it would be just to sell the land. Was her refusal only pride? She knelt, ran her fingertips over the imprint in the soil of Fergus's boot.

Did she still love him? If she were honest, she did, in some part. At least, she loved the person she thought he was. But his love had evaporated, vaporised. She pressed her fingers into the soil, pulled the sod free, Fergus's footprint destroyed. She flung the soil at the sky, straight up above her, felt it rain down on her. She had come too far. The soil was worth having. She would keep it at any cost.

CHAPTER THIRTY-TWO

Three wire-mesh fences at least fifteen feet tall, set ten feet apart, tatted with barbed wire, bound the perimeter of the Hay internment camp. A hot, dry wind pulled off the desert and whipped dust into eddies or just plain blew it into Amelia's eyes, lashing her legs. Most of Italo's life had been passed in the soupy air of Babinda, and now he was in this desiccated place. She'd no doubt it had been chosen for this, because with this air and wind and dust came isolation. Despite the three wire-mesh fences, few would dare to escape, and those foolhardy enough would soon perish.

The gate was marked by two upright pillars of wood, nothing more than a guarded break in the wire cage. Small sentry towers stood at each corner. It was a city of large rectangular huts, endless, as far as she could see. Each day, she was allowed only a half-hour visit. She would stay a week, at the Commercial Hotel on Lachlan Street, so it was only a short walk to the concentration camp just beyond the small town's limits. Seven visits, three-and-a-half hours after months and months of separation and gruelling days of travel.

Once through the outer layers of wire, she was shown to an administration building, the air inside considerably hotter. She loosened the collar of her shirt and followed the officer through a maze of corridors to a small room, bare of artifice – a table and two chairs, a single high, viewless window cloaked in bars. She sat, placed her bag at her feet.

After some time, she heard two sets of footsteps in the hall, and Italo appeared at the door. She stood. He looked at her. What was she to do? He was a good weight, not as she'd suspected. This heartened her. But his clothes, the same ones he'd put on the morning he was arrested, were worn, stained and tatty. And he wore a beard, dark but heavily laced with grey, long and full like those of the desert Muslim men.

He came to her. They embraced. Her heart raced. With closed eyes, she kissed his mouth and tugged at the beard.

'It must be hot to wear such a thing in such a place.'

He smiled, that extra blue coming to his eyes. 'We've no razors.'

They sat at the table, their hands laced.

'You look better than I expected,' she said.

'You look like an angel.'

She blushed profusely.

'How are the children?' he said.

She spoke of them, that the boys had been a tower of strength and had applied themselves to the farm in a manner she thought beyond them. And Ilaria grew. Marta hung between them, unspoken.

'I keep busy,' he said, breaking the silence. 'I know a lot of men here. We've started a small garden. The food is tolerable.'

'Where do you sleep?'

'In the huts. Twenty-eight men in each. We have two-tier bunks. I can hear the men all night. I've grown used to it. I have a high bunk.' That brought a smile to his face. 'The stuffing falls from the mattress onto the lower man. Straw and dust.'

She smiled, even though she was appalled, the conditions worse than she offered the canecutters.

'It's so dry and dusty,' she said.

'There's a bad drought, the worst in years, apparently. But there are still bloody mosquitoes, even when the temperature drops quickly at night.' Suddenly, sadness swept over his face. 'I've become nothing but a number, seven-zero-eight-two.'

They sat in silence, despite the heavy presence of time. She refused to look at the clock on the wall, or the watch at her wrist. These guards would tell her soon enough when their time was finished, and she was sure no protest from her would have any effect. He asked, and she told him of the day of Marta's funeral. He held her hand and they wept. She told of Clara and her family's kindnesses and of Marta's poor grave she would rectify in time. He asked, and she lied, about the state of their finances and the condition of the farm.

'Don't lie,' he said. He looked directly into her eyes. 'No longer.' He pulled his hands from hers. 'We can't survive this without the truth.'

She recoiled. She'd only ever lied to him of one thing. And now, with these simple words – 'no longer' – he'd told her he knew of Fergus, he knew of Flavio, and yet he'd never spoken of it. What could she say? Any justification was pointless, rude in such circumstances. Tears came to her eyes, tears for her sin, tears for his generosity, tears for Marta, tears for this frightful condition that her insistence on faith in fascism had engineered. But this was unjust, too harsh a penalty for their supposed crime. She should be here in jail. No. Neither of them should be. She didn't want to speak of Fergus, or Flavio, not here, not now. But before she could gather her thoughts, he pressed on.

'I know they've taken all our money,' he said. 'I know about the fire.'

'Then there's little I can tell you.'

'Except how you are.'

She lowered her voice. 'I had some cash, not a lot but enough, hidden in the house.'

'I suspected you would.'

'That's covered our needs. The staff agreed to stay for board and keep, and a promise they'll be paid when this is over.'

She told him of the bank account they'd opened in Flavio's name, which gave them some security, and that Cristiano was paying the mortgage. To her surprise, he made no protest.

'Have you made up with Clara?'

'To some degree. But she's cold. With time ...'

'And the fire?'

'I've no doubt it was lit. It was unnatural, the way it ran. We set about to harvest what was left, but the mill wouldn't take it. And even then, we couldn't get the men to harvest it. There are no men.'

'Except the British Australians.'

She nodded. 'And they can pick and choose, and they chose not to help the Italians. And the rains came and just wouldn't stop. The cane rotted in a few days. The boys ploughed it back into the ground.'

A wave of dark sadness swept over his face. 'The earth will appreciate it.' He conjured a smile. 'This year will be a good crop.'

She breathed out. She could lie no more. 'We've planted a much smaller crop. Flavio thought we'll need fewer men to harvest, and there's more likelihood we can take what we've grown to the mill.'

Italo withdrew. 'There's sound thinking in that. So you've not planted the new fields?'

'We thought it best to leave them.'

He considered this. 'As you see fit.'

Their time was gone, half an hour in smoke. She'd no need to tell him of Fergus's offer to buy back the new land. She'd not accepted it. It could lie fallow.

She saw him for the allowed half-hour each day. Everything that needed to be said had been said that first day; the rest they talked of the children, talked of older, happier times. And they shared their sorrow at Marta's death, both often sobbing. And she visited any of the other men she knew there – Maria's husband, Dante Pastore; D'Angelo, Garofalo, Lucchesi, Tedesco – the men who had worked in communal gangs with Italo when she'd first come to Australia. She wrote to their wives, even those who didn't speak with her, to tell them that, all things considered, she found their husbands well.

In the small town of Hay at a well-stocked general store, curiously called the Ringer, she bought him warm clothes she could ill afford, clothes he'd never needed. And she arranged to send him parcels of food and clothes.

'I would stay longer,' she said, the last time they met. 'But I must get back ...'

'There's something I must tell you,' he said.

She had no idea what he wanted to say, but in these days she'd been exhausted with emotion and seized. 'Italo, whatever it is can wait.'

He shook his head, raised an open hand. 'That first Christmas, when I left you to go to Angelo Rada in Melbourne. We had a long tradition of meeting two women in Melbourne after the harvest was finished. It was a ruse. It was wrong to go, but it was the last time. I never loved her.'

She breathed in. Why had he told her this? Of course, he'd had other women. Signora Pina had told her as much. But did this attenuate or amplify her sin?

The guard said their time was up. Why had he said this now? What was she to say to such a confession?

'I must go,' she said.

A smile, broader than she'd seen during all these meetings, relieved of great weight, bloomed over his face.

'All those years ago,' he said, 'when you first came to Australia and I wasn't there to meet your boat – you thought I was some uncouth oaf, choosing a harvest over meeting you.'

She nodded.

'Now you understand why I didn't. Go. Run the farm.'

They embraced. He kissed her. 'You've still not told me how *you* are,' he said.

And indeed on purpose she had avoided her doubts, her fears and mostly her hopes. What were her troubles compared to his?

'Take all care,' she said. She smiled.

'And you.'

She pulled away, walked away, each step at increasing cost.

She recognised it then – a cruel trick had been played on her, set in motion by the strength of Fergus's back, his bold thighs and his broad shoulders. It had never been love she felt for Fergus, not like she felt for Italo. Her and Italo's love had grown slower than the canes. Only now had it flowered the white brushes. She just hadn't recognised it for what it was.

Over the following months, Amelia realised she had never so appreciated the farm's rhythms. Despite anything else in the world, the cane grew, automatic, oblivious of Italo's absence, unfazed by war's shifting borderlines, unconcerned by the petty plights of many men. She pulled a cane away from the others, taller than usual, thicker. She smiled. With the ploughing of last year's crops, Italo had predicted the cane would grow well. Even in his absence, his presence was felt. She sliced the cane, a single swing of the blade freeing it, and twisted it between her hands, placed her lips to the fold. The juice dripped and ran. Such sweetness.

Soon after she saw him, Italo was moved further south, to another camp in South Australia, a place called Loveday. All her unsure feelings flowered again: What were his circumstances? Was he well fed? How was he housed? Why had they done this? Only this last question had a certain answer: it had been done to make their suffering worse. Loveday was at least another two days travel, even more remote, bounded by desert, completely loveless. In Hay he'd known other men. They'd started a small garden. Italo needed occupation. Did he have this in Loveday? Would he know men there? Or had the authorities split the men so they couldn't plot, Mussolini's meddling fingers in the Australian pie?

From Loveday Italo sent a letter. All was well, and the family weren't to worry. She doubted he could say anything else. But she accepted those words, whomever had written them, whomever had read them; other Italian women told similar stories of this Loveday.

She dropped the cane to the earth. In November, when the harvest was complete, she'd travel to see him. It would take her many, many days and cost money she could ill afford, but as the war showed no signs of remitting – in fact, it was worsening, lurching closer and closer to Australia – she could see no other choice. She had to see him.

One must push forward. She returned to her office.

With Flavio's help, they planned the harvest with an attention to detail she'd never deemed necessary. Flavio said, time and time again, 'Nothing can go wrong.' And indeed, her lists and sub-lists were excessive: the number of men, the field they would cut first, the food stores, the contractors for perishables and non-perishables. Fear drove her. If they didn't earn a decent amount, she'd have nothing more to do than sell the new land. Whilst Cristiano had paid the mortgage, she had this on the ledger as debt. At some point, it had to be paid. And she was sure that now it would be clear to all she was desperate, any price offered for the land would be subpar. And she didn't want Fergus Kelly to make good his threat. That would rub salt into the wound. The crop had to be good.

A vehicle approached from the main road. The sound was light, so she presumed it was a car and not a truck. She blotted the ledger's red ink and rose from the desk. By instinct, she closed the door behind her, more to keep Ilaria's busy fingers from the room than anything. She walked one flight from her tower to the upstairs verandah as the car circled in the front yard, coming to rest with the passenger's door facing the house. A man stepped from the rear, dressed in a military uniform. On the far side, a policeman alighted. She knew him – Sergeant Boyle, from the Babinda police station.

'What do they want?' Lucia said, behind her.

Amelia prickled. She'd had no warning of this visit, but it wasn't social. Her pulse quickened. She had seen this before. Something had happened to Italo. For what reason would they send two such men?

'Will you go and prepare tea?' she said, pressing herself to sound calm. But Lucia remained. 'Quickly.'

Both the military man and the policeman looked to the verandah, raised their hands to their hats' brims and nodded. She made no sign and withdrew into the house. The morning was already warm, but the shadows of the house were cooler.

She walked to the lower level and opened the front door. Both men stood facing her, their faces set grim.

'Mrs Amedeo,' Sergeant Boyle said. He carried a square portmanteau case.

'Good morning.'

'This is Captain McLennan.'

She regarded him. He was middle-aged and, although military, from the size of his midriff, clearly not engaged in active service. She put out her hand and thought he mightn't accept it. His grip was not unduly firm.

'I'd like to have a word with you,' Captain McLennan said.

'Has something happened?'

'If I may.'

She checked his eyes. No trace of sorrow, but apprehension. The policemen had been distressed by Marta's death, but she could find no such emotion in his eyes. But something concerned him. She moved from the door, across the entrance hall to the dining room without turning to check their progress, though she could hear their steps.

'Would you like tea?' she said.

'We've not the time,' Sergeant Boyle said.

This abruptness gave her heart. Surely the bearers of bad news wouldn't speak so. They were here on business and nothing would change this. She motioned to Captain McLennan to sit and walked around the table to face him. Sergeant Boyle sat next to him. From his briefcase, Captain McLennan took a folder. He laid it on the table, set his locked hands on top of it. He looked deep into her eyes. She had to meet this self-possessed glance or she would be lost to whatever he was to say. Without shifting, he opened the folder. She wouldn't look away.

'Something has come to our attention,' he said.

She remained impassive. He was the one to look away, at the folder of papers. He singled one item, lifted it from the folder, made to read it. It was an envelope, the type she used. Involuntarily, she gasped and clasped her hand to her mouth. She could see the front and recognised her own hand, familiar and yet foreign. He wrote something, noting her concern. How dare he? With some considered manner, he placed the envelope on the table, tapped it with his fingers and slid it to her.

She recognised it, a letter to her parents she'd sent less than a month ago. What had she written? Surely, it was inconsequential. Maybe some ranting about the injustice of Italo's arrest, but she'd voiced this in many forums. And even this hard McLennan would have to admit the arrests had brought great hardship to many families.

The sound of running feet trammelled the stair. Ilaria rushed into the room. Amelia turned and spoke to her in Italian, told her to go to the kitchen and play with her dolls. Captain McLennan smiled at Ilaria.

'What's your name?' Captain McLennan said to her.

Ilaria looked at him and said nothing.

'She doesn't speak English,' Amelia said. Again she told Ilaria to go to Lucia in the kitchen.

Captain McLennan twisted his head towards her. 'Why not?'

Lucia came to the room. Amelia spoke to her in Italian, asked her to remove the child. Lucia hesitated until she assured her there was no concern. She faced Captain McLennan.

'We are Italian,' Amelia said.

She felt damp. Damn her arrogance. She shouldn't have said this, a grave error. But this fool and his dallying maddened her. Lucia gathered Ilaria into the folds of her dress and walked her from the room. She breathed deeply.

'Yet you live in Australia,' he said.

'It is possible to be Australian and speak Italian.' She sighed. 'Since my husband's arrest I've been very busy. Do you imagine it's easy for a woman to run a farm?'

She waited, left him a space to deny the ramification of Italo's sentence, but he elected to remain mute. She took his silence as a point won.

'She spends most of her time with Lucia, who speaks little English,' she said. 'With all these horrors, I've not had time to teach her. It's simply easier for me to speak Italian.'

'And yet your English is remarkable. Quite faultless.'

No matter what she did, she was set apart. 'Do you speak another language?'

Captain McLennan raised his lips to a smile and a small laugh. 'I speak English, the language of Australia.'

'If you spoke another language, you'd know it comes at great cost, especially when I'm tired.'

He paused. 'You'd do well to teach your daughter. Others may misconstrue your … motivation.' He wrote something and returned his attention to the envelope. 'Did you write this letter and sign it?'

She looked at him. He wasn't smart, dullness in his eye, his voice thick and slow. She opened the envelope, addressed to her cousin in Switzerland. Inside was a second envelope, addressed to her parents in Italy, which had also been opened. With some caution, she removed the letter from the second envelope. It was her letter, her handwriting. She turned the pages, just to be sure even this was as it had left her. It was her letter. How did they come to have this? Her anger boiled. Was there no end to this harassment? She couldn't deny her handwriting, her words, her signature on the last page.

'I wrote the letter to my parents. I signed the letter.'

Sergeant Boyle wrote something.

She looked at McLennan, his hands clasped together, his thumbs pressed to his lips. He released them.

'Did you place this letter in the envelope addressed to Italy?'

'Yes.'

'Did you place this in the envelope addressed to Switzerland?'

'Yes.'

'Why did you do this?'

She paused. She wouldn't allow his momentum to bamboozle her.

'Before we left Italy, my brother's wife suggested if there was a need we could communicate in this way, via a cousin in Switzerland.'

'Why?'

'We are at war ...'

'Aren't there other ways of communicating with Italy?'

'None that I know of.'

'And yet, in your letter you mention ...' From his folder he took a typed page, which she presumed to be an English translation of her letter. '... the Vatican and the Red Cross as possible methods of communication.'

She looked at her letter. Her face flushed. 'Perhaps,' she said.

'You see, what you've done could be ... misconstrued.'

She breathed deeply. 'I've not read this letter as recently as you. I don't recall its exact contents. But my memory is that it was inconsequential.'

'Yes ... inconsequential. But what did opening this line of communication prefigure?'

Perhaps she'd misjudged this man, and he was brighter than she suspected. 'I had no intention of committing a war offence.' She did her best to smile. 'I hope I'll not get into trouble over this.'

'I'll need you to sign a statutory declaration, stating these facts we've discussed.'

She nodded. He conversed with Sergeant Boyle, who took a portable Corona typewriter from the case and began to type.

'If you can be quick,' she said, above the battering keys. 'I have a harvest to oversee.'

Sergeant Boyle typed the declaration. Whilst it contained no direct accusation, she feared the language was hostile. What would they do if she refused to sign? What would Italo say? A letter, a bland letter at that, addressed to her parents ... Was this so condemning? She had no choice. She signed the declaration.

Once the men had left, she did her best not to be prey to thoughts of the possible ramifications. Surely, the visit meant nothing beyond intimidation, which women were prone to. But there was a war on. Weren't there more serious matters to attend to? Evidently not.

CHAPTER THIRTY-THREE

Over the next few days, the harvest began and proceeded. The British-Australian cutters were pleasant and worked hard enough but wouldn't extend themselves beyond anything their union representative prescribed. But they appreciated her food, even the minestrone for which she'd been so derided in public for so long with her nickname, Mrs Minestrone. They all asked for second helpings.

What a sense of achievement they felt as the cane was transported to the mill. Flavio said again and again, 'It's a good crop.' Despite all the interdictions, they'd succeeded. And the yield was very good. And despite the increased costs, the profit was fair, the mill's cheque, written in Flavio's name, banked into his account. With tight economy and no more problems, they could survive another year. She wrote to Clara, saying she'd resume the mortgage payments. In a few months, when her financial position was clearer, she'd start to repay the debt.

She'd heard reports of women on other farms, plenty far worse off, some women left with daughters, others with husbands in concentration camps and sons away at war. Flavio and Mauro helped these families, as much as time allowed. Where women had been unable to harvest a crop, British-Australian men had come onto the land and taken the cane to the mill and been paid for it. Some had sold land. Some had simply left. Thank God that wasn't her fate. She had two sons who knew their business.

At Flavio's insistence, without rest, they planted the next year's crop. With a good growing season, they may be able to harvest within the year, which would only help their cash flow. And they planted the new land, a victory, nothing less, a testimony to their organisation. Amelia could see it in no other terms. She wondered what Fergus would make of it, this fallow land he coveted put back to use. But she was too tired and preoccupied to waste time thinking about it and had no control over Fergus.

The months passed without Italo and took their new rhythm. Her economy held, frugal and vice-like, and the war far worsened. The Japanese attacked Pearl Harbor and the USA entered the war in Europe and the Pacific. She bade goodbye to the prospect of an easy end to the conflict. Italo wouldn't be home soon. The farm passed through the gaunt Christmas of '41 into the brand-new year of '42.

There were good days and bad. Good was when she missed Italo, often for something so inconsequential, like the way he would turn down only his side of the bed or the way he would announce in the late evening that he would check the horses he loved like it was the first time he'd ever done it. The memories of what had annoyed her now brought her pleasure.

A very bad day was the February morning when Maria arrived at the house. Amelia saw her from the second-floor verandah as she rushed through the garden and banged hard on the front door. Something was surely amiss, and Amelia ran downstairs to be met by Flavio coming from the kitchen. Maria stood on the doorstep, her face reddened and feared.

'The Japanese have attacked Darwin,' she said.

'No,' Amelia said. 'It's Singapore they've taken.'

'That was four days ago. This only just happened.'

Amelia stepped back, inviting Maria in. She closed the door and looked at Maria. Surely, she could trust Maria.

'Follow me,' Amelia said.

Together the three climbed the stair to her office. She knelt into the alcove behind her desk. From behind the drawers, she hauled out the wireless she'd hidden from the police. Flavio picked it up, placed it on the desk.

'Good for you,' Maria said. 'I was too honest, and all ours were taken.'

No-one said a word while the machine warmed to reports of waves of planes having strafed the most north-eastern city of Australia, destroying a swathe of the town, the port and the airfields.

'What does this mean?' Maria said.

Amelia shook her head. 'Dante and Italo won't return home soon.'

In the coming days, newspapers and people on the street spoke again of the yellow peril, the olive peril now safely tucked away in concentration camps and seemingly forgotten. In the coming weeks, people renewed their war efforts, braced for more attacks, night and day scanning the skies and seas for any sign of the Japanese. Australian soil was sacred. The battle for Australia had begun.

Lucia was away to visit her son in Brisbane, and Amelia took over the cooking for the month. She didn't mind. The farm was quiet, in the growing phase. The boys busied themselves with other chores – the vegetable patch, the citrus orchard and pineapple and pawpaw trees, some overdue maintenance to the barracks – and helped the men-less Italian women of the area.

This part of the day had become her favourite, when the day's work was done, when the evening first settled; they'd survived another day. The boys loved her *pizzoccheri*, even though the recipe came from Valtellina and a much colder clime. Perhaps for these memories, she liked to cook it. She liked the feel of the buckwheat, soft but gritty, as she kneaded an egg and warm water and milk to a pasta. Once this was done, she left it to rest and simmered cabbage and potato in seasoned water. She rolled the pasta to a sheet, cut it to long ribbons and added these to the cabbage and potato. In three separate pans, she fried in butter onion, garlic and sage. It was a hearty dish and would keep the boys hunger-free for at least a few hours. Although the evening was warm, they still loved the dish, which she'd let cool a little before she served.

She took the pot of vegetables and pasta from the Aga. With this simple movement, she was taken over, taken back to the first house, taken back to the open fire on which she'd cooked for so many years, in an instant taken back twenty years. How had they survived in such a place? But despite all the inconveniences, the draught cracks in the floors, the thin walls of the kitchen, she'd always loved the front verandah, with its long view out over the fields (and the tap! The letters she'd written to Italy about the wondrous tap). They'd survived the house. They'd survived its destruction by a cyclone. They'd survive Italo's absence.

She drained the vegetables and pasta and placed them in a large dish. This was the metamorphosis of the recipe, where things were brought together and something else developed. She poured the three pans of frying butter into one, mixed all together. She substituted a local cheddar for the dish's usual *Valtellina Casera*, the mountains' pasture milk whose delicate flavour she could still remember. The cheddar bit at her tongue – too strong, no sweetness at all – but there was nothing she could do. Then in another dish she layered this mix, sprinkling the cheese and then layering and sprinkling till all was used. She cut thick slices of bread baked earlier in the day and took the board and the bread to the dining room, sung up the stair to the boys that dinner was ready.

But there was a knock at the front door. A young man, British Australian, stood with a box of vegetables in his arms, overflowing with light and dark greens and whites and orange and even darker greens.

'What do you want?' she said.

He stepped back. 'I'm James Harrison. Jim. We live out Happy Valley way.'

She nodded.

'I brung ya these.' He looked at the contents, the beans, zucchini, cauliflower, carrots and spinach. 'Thought they might come in 'andy.'

Amelia rose – what was this charity? 'We've more than enough—'

'Ya mightn't remember us. Years ago, ya brung over a stew. Bloody good it was too. When me mum was crook.'

Amelia remembered Anne Harrison. She'd died a horrible death in the early 1930s – breast cancer, they said. She had the softest smile in the valley. Amelia could see a trace of it now, in this young man before her, Anne's son. His awkward manner, his clipped speech, amused her. His honest desire to help comforted her and she let a trace of a smile grace her face, the first in so many weeks.

'Well, it must have been good,' she said, 'if you remember it.' Her smile bloomed.

And he smiled too. 'Mum always said you eyeties knew 'ow to cook.'

'She was a kind soul.'

He breathed deeply. 'I'm sorry for your trouble. They shouldn't judge everyone the same.'

She suddenly felt suspended, unable to speak. Tears came to her eyes. She felt no embarrassment, no ability to stop them, and let them roll onto and down her cheek.

'How are you keeping?' she said.

He lowered his eyes. 'Dad died a few years back.'

'I'm sorry. If I'd known ...'

He raised his lips to a smile. Flavio and Mauro descended the stair behind her.

'Better get going,' Jim said. He handed the box to Flavio.

'Thank you for these,' she said. 'I'm most grateful.'

'No worries. I'll bring ya some more.'

She hesitated. 'We're just about to eat. Would you like to stay?'

He licked his lips. 'Would I! But I can't. Gotta get back to the little ones.'

He was now father and mother to his younger siblings.

'Another time?' she said.

'Yeah, I reck'n.' He looked to his feet. 'All things will pass, Mum always said.'

She nodded. 'I'm sure she was right.'

He turned, that same loose gait so particular to this country, which seemed that evening to reiterate his claim there was nothing that wouldn't pass.

Flavio carried the box into the kitchen.

'What kindness,' Amelia said. She breathed deeply and served the pasta onto large open bowls to help it cool and carried these three on a tray to the table. She'd only just sat when they heard a car approaching.

'Who's that now?' Flavio said.

She looked at her watch. It was after eight at night. Peeved, she rose from her chair and marched to the door. She heard the car stop in the gravel yard, the gate open and close. Perhaps young Jim Harrison had changed his mind.

That would be it. How lovely. Flavio came to her side. She opened the door.

But two men stood before her. They were police officers. One was Sergeant Boyle. Her pulse quickened.

'Good evening,' Boyle said.

'How can I help?' Amelia said.

'Are you Amelia Amedeo?'

She winced. 'You know I am.'

'I have a warrant for your arrest.'

The words fell on her. He handed her the document. Flavio stepped between them.

'What for?' Flavio said.

Boyle ignored him. 'You've been charged as an enemy alien. Will you come with us?'

'Now?' Amelia said.

'Yes.'

'I've just served dinner,' Amelia said.

'I can't help that.'

'I have a business to run.'

'That's of no concern.'

'I have a five-year-old child. The housekeeper is away. I have no husband. I can't just leave her.'

'Then, if you insist, you'll have to bring her.'

She looked at the two men. 'You must allow me some moments. You *will* wait outside.'

The two men stood their ground, as she did. But she won. They retreated, allowing her five minutes, which she told them would be ten, at the least. She closed the front door.

'How can they arrest you?' Mauro said.

'They have a document.' Anger lodged in her throat. 'I'll not be dragged out of here. I'll go with them.' She turned to Flavio. 'In the morning, contact the solicitor, tell him what's happened. I'm sure this will be resolved. But it will take some time. Lucia will be back in about three weeks.' She swallowed hard. 'You'll just have to cope till then.'

Flavio turned to her. 'Then leave Ilaria with us.'

She shook her head. 'You can't care for her.'

She went upstairs, took her small portmanteau and a larger case and in a fevered state packed clothes, some changes for Ilaria. What would they need? She ran to her turret, grabbed her dictionary, some pens and ink and paper, envelopes and stamps. Her only defence would be the written word, and she would damn well exploit them to the fullest.

She went to Ilaria's room. Tonight, of all nights, she'd fallen sound asleep, unaware of anything. Should she leave her? But they were boys, only boys. They'd be hard-pressed to care for themselves. It was dangerous to leave Ilaria. And how long would she be away? Italo had been in prison for nearly two years, and there was no sign of his release. She pulled back the covers.

'My little one. We must go.'

Ilaria raised her sleepy head, screwed up her face.

'Where?'

If only she knew. 'Somewhere special. Come.'

She dressed her, the child a floppy doll. But she didn't cry. They were both too stupefied. She carried her downstairs, the child's legs clutching her waist. The boys carried the two cases to the entrance hall. She turned to Flavio.

'You must run the farm. You know what to do. You've done it before.' She turned to Mauro. 'Help your brother. Do as he asks, without question. Contact Maria. I know we have differences, but she'll help you. And continue to help the other women. They'll help you in return.'

She looked from one boy to the other, their faces full of concern. What else should she tell them? They would need to do their own cooking and washing, and they had never done such things. They would find food, somehow, when they were hungry. The men banged on the door.

'Your father and I love you. And we trust you. God bless you.'

She took Ilaria's coat from the hall cupboard and then her own. She hugged each boy, inhaled their scent. They kissed their sister and then her. She opened the front door and passed the men with no acknowledgement, straight on to their car.

At the Babinda police station, many Italian women had been arrested, possibly ten. The women stood, guarded in the corner of the station's antechamber.

'What's your crime?' Amelia said to Elena Moretti.

'I sent too much gold to Italy.'

There was Teresa Garofalo, Anna Nanni, who had both signed a pledge to join the women's fascist organisation. Maria Burattini was there. In fact, the school was the most condemning issue. But she was most surprised to see Maria.

'But you're Australian,' Amelia said.

'I'm suspected of having fascist sympathies.'

She stared at Maria. She couldn't help herself. If Maria had been arrested on such a charge, the gravity of the situation was worse than she'd imagined.

After at least two hours, during which Ilaria sat quietly at her side, it was her turn to be interviewed.

'You have publicly demonstrated your support for fascism,' the police officer said. 'You canvassed women to join a women's fascist organisation.'

'That was to facilitate opening a school.'

'An exclusively Italian school.'

She breathed. 'Be that as it may, the internal squabbling laid all the plans to rest. It never happened.'

'You sent your wedding ring back to Italy. You helped raise considerable amounts of money to support the Red Cross in Abyssinia and the house of Fascists Abroad in Rome. You've communicated with Europe via another address.'

Ilaria whined. 'Be quiet,' she said. 'We will soon go home.'

But she spoke in English and Ilaria didn't understand. It would be foolish to speak Italian in front of this man. Ilaria, perhaps stressed by the harsh tone of her voice, continued to whine.

'We spoke of this misunderstanding,' she said to the officer, 'and even so, the letter was innocent.'

'But it established an illegal line of communication. What was the purpose of your travel to Italy?'

She would be careful with her words, not let her anger speak. 'We have family there. We wished to see them.'

'How long have you lived in Australia?'

'More or less twenty years.'

'And your husband?'

'He came fifteen years before me.'

'Why, after all these years, would you pick such an inopportune time to travel to Italy?'

She knew what he was alluding to, but she persisted. 'It was between the planting and the harvest—'

'Don't be smart with me. The whole world was on the brink of war. It could be misconstrued.'

'To what?'

'A show of your support for Italy. Do you deny you've sent large sums of money to Italy?'

Her anger, laced with fear, rose. 'What are you talking about? I have no money to send since the Australian government took it from our bank account.'

He handed her a list of dates and transactions. They went back many years, almost the full time of her life in Australia, money sent to Pina. She tried to calm the agitation.

'Is that a crime now – for a son to care for his mother?'

'You deny they were sent to buy Italian government bonds to support Mussolini?'

She paused. Did he know something she didn't? 'What she did with the money was her concern.'

'There are reports you visit poor British-Australian households.'

'As far as I'm aware there's no segregation.'

'What were you doing there?'

'They're poor. I take food.'

'We have reports you attempted to persuade them to fascism.'

Her face contracted. What an accusation. She had no ready response. 'I …'

'Your English is perfect. You could communicate with them, coerce them to your way.'

The bitter irony overwhelmed her. If she hadn't learnt English so well she'd be accused of being a separatist. Because she had, she was accused of indoctrination.

'We believe you've been sending messages to the Japanese,' he said.

Her mouth fell open. She felt dumbfounded. 'What? How?'

'From your house. From the roof of the tower. During the night. Flashing lights have been seen.'

'Who said this?'

'There have been reports.'

'I work to run a farm. I can't sleep because of the stress. How could I be signalling to the Japanese?'

'The roof has a clear view towards the coast, to the ships offshore. Lights were seen flashing. A relay.'

'This is ridiculous. Am I to bear responsibility for the Japanese attacks on Darwin?'

'You support Italy. You support the Axis. It's been noted your child doesn't speak English.'

She suppressed an urge to laugh, nervous as it would have sounded. What could she say to such absurd accusations? He looked at the papers on his desk, wrote something.

'You don't deny this support?' He narrowed his lips.

She glared at him. 'Aren't you Irish?'

Boyle looked at her.

'Even to my coarse ear, there's still an Irish lilt to your voice, that lovely sing-song I've always enjoyed in your countrymen, that talks of leprechauns, of ghosts and forest queens. You cling to it. It reminds you of your father, who was surely born in Ireland. It's part of who you are. Why shouldn't I feel about Italy as you do about Ireland? You're just lucky the Irish haven't entered the war on the side of fascism.'

He regarded her. 'You're true to the reports.' He tapped his hand on a pile of documents. 'A shrewd, cunning woman.'

This was madness. But she saw no escape. 'And that on its own would be enough to condemn me. Where will I be interned?'

A half smile crossed his lips. 'I'm not at liberty to say.'

She was taken to a cell at the rear of the building, with a single pallet bed with a hay mattress and a blanket, a can for a toilet, nothing more. She sat on the bed, placed her head between her hands. Ilaria stood in front of her, looking at her, her brow creased with confusion as a child's should never be. Fortunately, the child had eaten. She hadn't, but the nausea and stress quenched any appetite. She folded Ilaria into her arms. Her warmth was pleasing, soothing.

Nothing she could say would change anything. The course was set by people far away.

Fully clothed, she laid Ilaria in the bed and lay next to her. She covered them with the thin blanket. How these people could destroy lives with such flimsy evidence. She'd not quench her anger to sleep. A mosquito, lazy and loud, turned around their heads. She lay awake, waving it from Ilaria. It wasn't a cold evening, but it would be long. Ilaria was exhausted and soon asleep, the one boon.

CHAPTER THIRTY-FOUR

The next few days were a series of claims and refusals. She asked to see her sons and was refused. She asked for information – how long they would be held, where they were being taken – and was told there was none. She asked to speak with the solicitor but was told it wasn't possible. And in the evening, with no warning, the women and children were loaded onto a truck. At least their hands weren't cuffed. Anna Nanni also had a young child. Ilaria paid her no attention. God knows where some of the other women's five-year-olds were? Once the flap of the truck was pulled, the dark engulfed them. She held Ilaria tighter. Maria sat next to her. Amelia could see nothing outside the truck but had a sense of their movement.

'They're taking us to the station,' she said.

Maria raised her eyes to the truck's ceiling, felt the sway and the jars against the road. 'You might be right. We've just turned out of Munro Street.'

After more turns and stretches, the truck came to a halt. The canvas flap was pulled back. They were at the station, unloaded from the high truck, stepping down a ladder. Amelia left Ilaria hanging onto Maria. When she was halfway, Maria guided her into her arms. None of the guards offered any help, not that she'd have accepted.

'Where are you taking us?' a woman on the ground called to a guard, but he refused to acknowledge her, refused to answer her.

'*Porca miseria*,' a woman yelled.

They were left in the stationary train for over an hour. No-one could move from their seat. There was no food, no water and little air, the barred windows sealed, and no access to a toilet. All the Babinda women were held together in one carriage. Perhaps there were other women from other towns in the other carriages.

The train jolted to motion, moving south. Ilaria sat on her lap, her eyes wide, devoid of any notion of sleep. Maria looked out the window, into the darkness.

'I don't judge you,' Maria said.

Amelia glared at her. Were they to be honest on this journey? 'But you have, for so long.'

'That's true.' Maria sighed. 'But I was wrong. You'll have to forgive me.'

They rocked with the train's motion. 'I won't deny what happened,' Amelia said.

'You wouldn't be the first to fall for a good-looking man. Nor the last.'

Amelia looked at Maria, who paid no heed to her glance, her eyes fixed on the dark outside the window. What had passed between them was no more than a shopping list, the fewest of words. But with no more words (because what good did they really do?), Maria took Amelia's hand. Hers was rough and work-swollen, but the warmth allayed a small part of Amelia's fear. And Amelia understood the meaning of the intimacy – in some unspoken part of Maria, there was a similar story.

They travelled in the dark until they arrived in Townsville and then were offloaded and transported to Stuart Creek Prison. Maria carried their bags as well as her own, while Amelia carried Ilaria. It was a grim place, cold and without relief. She wanted only to leave there. They were shown to a walled yard. Ilaria's eyes bulged at the height of the sunless walls. They were to sleep in the open.

The next morning – if there was a clean division between night and day – they were moved again. For two whole days, they travelled to Brisbane and then to the camp at Gaythorne, a hulking place with mounds of barbed wire. Having visited Italo in Hay, she was forewarned what these places looked like, but this was brutal. They were housed together in a long hall, rows of beds and small dressers. Ilaria refused to eat and fought off sleep.

'Don't leave me,' Ilaria said.

'My dear, I'll never leave you.'

Ilaria glared at her as if she too understood that nothing was certain. Eventually, guided by the rocking motion in Amelia's lap, she gave in to exhaustion. Amelia laid her in the bed, covered her.

'Everything we feel, she feels more keenly,' Maria said.

'I shouldn't have brought her.'

'You had little choice.'

If she'd had little choice at the farm, her options were now more reduced. But later that evening, Amelia wrote to Clara, asked her to come to the camp and take Ilaria. Whilst it would betray Ilaria's wish, she would be happier with Clara than here. But the next day the women were moved again. Even if Clara had received the letter and came to the camp immediately, she would have missed them.

In the coming days, they travelled through a relay of camps, all through New South Wales, the further south, the lower the temperature, especially at night. She swathed Ilaria in layers of thin clothes, but still she shivered. Bewildered, in the middle of the night they changed trains at Tocumwal and crossed the Victorian border to Shepparton, then on to Rushmore. They were then loaded onto buses, heavily armed soldiers everywhere, and driven away from the train.

They were even more bewildered when around midday the buses drove through the gates of Tatura Camp 3, a large barbwire cage, but flimsy like all the others she'd seen. They wouldn't keep a cow at bay but for the guns. The perimeter was much like at Hay, snarling wire fences separated by fifteen feet of no-man's-land, coiled with endless large loops of barbed wire. High towers stood around the perimeter, all manned with armed guards. Amelia wondered at the regular spacing of the towers, a fixed rhythm, but then realised they were probably set apart the distance someone could shoot a gun with any accuracy.

A roar went up as hundreds of men crowded close to the fence to see the new female arrivals, so fierce it was as if there'd been some warning women were arriving. They glared at the women, some waved and some blew lurid kisses, clutched their groins with a free hand. How could they behave in such a lude manner? She felt a new level of fear; surely, these men could overcome these flimsy gates? The noise frightened Ilaria and she began to cry. Amelia picked her up, tried to cover her eyes and ears. For the first time since her arrest, raw fear swamped her anger.

'This is no place for children,' she said to the welcoming official who processed her documents.

He stared at her, his face a mix of ennui and contempt. She shouldn't have spoken.

'There are many children here,' he said, and waved her through.

The camp was isolated, inland, dry and dusty, like the other camps. The women were to be housed in long rectangular huts, iron in construction, fitted close together, regular stamps across the field. Camp 3 contained whole families

– men, women and children. The newly arrived women were walked the paths stretching between the buildings like the rows of the cane fields. Along the paths, there were small flowerbeds. The sprays of colour calmed Amelia's heart – somewhere in this place, someone cared for beauty.

The other women were shown to one hut, but Amelia and Ilaria were taken to another, across the other side of the path. She didn't want to be removed from the others, but Maria pointed out the distance wasn't so great. To her surprise, the long rectangular building had been divided with flimsy partition walls, so she and Ilaria had their own, small room. Ilaria sat on the bed and watched Amelia survey the room: a rough cupboard made from wooden packing cases stuck to the wall, covered with thin fabric.

There were two small tables, one she could work at in front of a rectangular window and one with a washbowl and jug. It was small, sparse but clean, and she hoped this was their home, that they wouldn't be moved again.

'Do you like it?' she said to Ilaria, injecting as much positivity as she could. Amelia opened the window, hinged from the top, and secured it with a pole between the sill and the window frame. The child wouldn't look at the room, only at her.

'Relax,' Amelia said. She hugged her, this limp doll, kissed her brow. 'It's quite comfortable. We'll make it our home.'

She would keep busy and impress order by unpacking their few clothes and placing the two empty cases on the shelves above the packing-case wardrobe. Still, Ilaria sat on the bed, her eyes never leaving her. There was a knock at the door. A woman came, blonde nearly overrun with grey, and in her mid-fifties, tall and a strong build. She carried a small plant, the pot fashioned from a jam tin.

'Welcome,' the woman said, handing her the plant. 'I am Gertrude.'

Never had yellow daisies looked so homely. Amelia thanked her and introduced herself and Ilaria, who stared at the woman with no reaction. Gertrude was part of a German religious group, the Temple Society, who'd lived in Palestine. At the start of the war, the British had interned them and transported some to the concentration camps in Australia.

'Did you plant all the flowers?' Amelia said.

Gertrude nodded. 'I refuse to let them beat me.'

'They're very welcoming.'

'The flowers are civility,' Gertrude said. 'These *dummkopf* men, they have no idea. We women must create life.' She smiled. 'It's not so bad. There are many interesting people here. And we run a little school.' She looked at Ilaria, who frowned and turned away. 'If you would like to attend.'

'Perhaps,' Amelia said. 'But she's only five and she doesn't speak English.'

'That's not a problem. The classes are in German.'

Gertrude began to laugh, hard and from the belly. Amelia froze. It was the first time she'd heard someone laugh in days. Ilaria's eyes bolted wide. And then Amelia was taken over by the utter carelessness of Gertrude's mirth and began to laugh, but Ilaria remained stern-faced.

'We live in the Babel Tower,' Gertrude said. 'Communists and fascists of all creeds, cheek to cheek.' She smiled. 'There are Italian children too.'

Amelia placed the plant on the windowsill. Gertrude asked if they would like to see the camp's facilities. Amelia liked this woman and agreed, but Ilaria whinged and didn't want to go.

'Come and see all the flowers,' Amelia said.

Ilaria may not have wanted to go, but she didn't want to be separated from Amelia for a second and shuffled off the bed with great reluctance.

Oddly, the camp was built on a mild slope, which gave something of a view and provided a walk to relieve the flat monotony of the rest of the day. Some of the other women had come into the air. The camp consisted of two main roads that met at right angles, dividing the camp into four compounds, A through to D. They were housed in A. But the perimeter fences formed a diamond. Each compound had its own set of amenities: a large kitchen and store, two large mess halls, a small triage room and separate toilet blocks for men and women, with only cold water. Gertrude took them to the communal buildings: a small library and schoolroom, a canteen that supplied an array of goods at fairly cheap prices.

'It's no paradise,' Gertrude said.

'We'll make do.'

'Boredom's the devil.'

Gertrude was right. Amelia was used to being active, engaged in the business, always stressed for time. Here the lack of any purpose would bring another type of stress.

That evening, the food was bland but plentiful, although Ilaria refused to eat. Despite all coaxing, she drank only a small amount of milk and ate a plain biscuit. Once they'd finished, they went to the toilet block and then returned to their room. The thin metal walls would be hot in the day and cold at night. Ilaria had been put to bed but lay watching Amelia.

'I'll not leave you,' Amelia cooed.

But there was no reasoning with her, so Amelia went about her chores under Ilaria's unerring watch. She unpacked the paper and pens, the dictionary, the envelopes and stamps. In the morning, she would start writing letters. This would fill her time – to write herself and Ilaria out of this detention, use their language against them. But to whom would she write? And what was she to say?

She would have a right of appeal, but even this, as she knew from Italo, was only a show trial. The emergency laws under which the country operated in war gelded the judiciary. A judge couldn't free anyone, no matter how unjust the internment. They could only advise a prisoner be freed. The accusations were stacked against her. No good would come of an appeal. She picked up a pen to write this. It would guide her in expressing her defence.

She was plunged into darkness. She gasped. It was nine o'clock – lights out.

In the dark hush, Ilaria began to cry. She pulled the child from the bed and looked out the window. The floodlights along the perimeter wire fences glowed cold, the light hung like sheets. Ilaria glared at them, whimpering.

'Hush, hush, hush,' Amelia said, sotto voce.

Armed guards patrolled the fence. They were there, roaming with intent, every time she checked through the first sleepless night.

The morning began with rollcall, the process not so much about making sure everyone was still present (How could a woman with a small child escape this barbed wire?) but to remind them there was no escape from what they were – prisoners, with all its connotations of criminality. They would eat when they were told, not when they wanted, and not what they wanted but what they were given. And they would answer a rollcall each day. They would shower and toilet when they were told. Their lights would be shut off at nine at night.

'But that's where it stops,' Gertrude said. 'Don't accept what they say you are. You're no more a prisoner than Mussolini or Hitler.'

What had they come to? Ilaria shouldn't bear such a stain, an innocent child paying for Amelia's support of fascism, her alliances, her decisions, which now seemed remote. Had all this been groundless? Flippant? Wrong?

After breakfast – plenty of eggs, bread and tea and coffee – they returned to their room. Ilaria lay on the bed, listless and withdrawn. She had hardly slept, so Amelia left her there and hoped she might now drift off. Amelia wrote to the boys, telling them they were safe and giving them the address through which she could receive mail. She wrote to Italo, telling him what had happened, although she suspected he'd already know. She wrote a small note to Clara.

Gertrude had told her there were whole families in Camp 3. Could Italo be transferred to Tatura? What harm would that bring? They could be reunited and temper some of the anxiety. She would make enquiries. And she wrote to Mr White, the solicitor in Babinda, although the boys had already contacted him, giving a detailed account of the accusations against her. She was sure the letters would be read before they left the camp, but she added it was inhumane for Ilaria to be held there. She considered this a statement of fact.

Apart from the morning and evening rollcall, there were some small cleaning duties, but the rest of the day was hers. Boredom was the devil. She wrote letters of injustice, pleas to be released, to businesses and important people in Babinda for character references. She read what she could find, although there were no newspapers and the library was limited. And she tried to improve Ilaria's mood, but she would weep without reason, clutched by a halo of sorrow.

'She must miss her brothers and Lucia,' Maria said.

'She misses everything about the farm,' Amelia said, 'except her father, whom she no longer remembers.'

At night Amelia could hear men shouting, laughing and carousing around the camp as if they were drunk. The noise kept Ilaria awake.

'They've made a still,' Gertrude said, 'out of jam tins and whatever they could lay their hands on. It's whiskey they've made.'

The men howled like dogs.

'Don't the authorities know about it?'

'They must. But I guess it's not causing them any harm.'

It may not be causing them harm, but the noise was frightening. Amelia could stand the camp no longer and the following day made an appointment to speak with an official. She enquired if Italo could be transferred from Loveday to Tatura.

'It isn't possible,' he said, without much delay. 'Too much bureaucratic red tape.'

She bit her lip, but she couldn't help herself. 'And it would bring happiness?'

His face drained to ashen. She shouldn't have been so tart. She apologised and left the man to his work.

One afternoon a child of about seven or eight, who spoke German and a little English, came to their room. Amelia thought it was unwise to allow her and Ilaria to play. This little girl was the enemy. Would Amelia be misjudged, again, if she left them together? And then it occurred to her: Amelia and Ilaria were both the enemy. She smiled. And the little girl smiled and came in. On the bed, Ilaria and she sat together. She gave them some of her precious paper and some pencils, and the little girl drew beautiful pictures of the room, details beyond her years, the common daisies, the objects on Amelia's desk. But Ilaria remained at a distance, unengaged, looking at the girl as if she wished she would just go away.

Clara wrote. She'd been interviewed by the police, questioned about her involvement in the school, but had managed to avoid arrest thus far. Amelia understood; the interrogation would have been filled with wild accusations and have frightened Clara. Amelia had embroiled Clara in the school, and Clara resented these ramifications. She knew her hand well enough to see her anger in the writing. Any apology she could give would be incomplete. And given all the mail was most likely screened, it would probably further fuel the case against Clara. And herself.

One morning Ilaria said she would take herself to the toilet block. Greatly encouraged by this act of independence, Amelia said she could go on her own. With no great accord, Ilaria set off. But when she was perhaps sixty feet away, Amelia was seized with anxiety and decided to follow, at a distance. To get to the females' amenities block, the women had to pass the males'. Ahead of them there was a great commotion, men yelling and some running up to the building and then away.

Ilaria stopped a few feet from the men's building. Amelia ran to her. A man had been brought outside. He was bleeding. Cuts at his wrists. Another man called for help, over and over. Someone strapped a white shirt around the wound, but the blood was profuse, pooling, darkening, congealing on the ground. The man's face was cold and white as marble. Amelia covered the child's eyes with her hand and tried to pull her away. But she resisted, rooted to the spot, slipped her head from Amelia's hand and looked again on this dreadful sight.

'Come away,' Amelia said.

She carried her off, pressing the child's face into her breast. Ilaria made no noise, no sound at all. Amelia felt the warm wet on her hands, felt it splash down onto her bare lower legs. Ilaria had wet herself.

'He was German,' Gertrude said, standing in the door of their room. 'He just found out the SS shot his brother in Dresden.'

'Why would they do that?' Amelia sat Ilaria on the bed.

'He was helping Jews.'

She pulled off Ilaria's wet smock and her underclothes.

'So he was held as an enemy internee,' Amelia said, 'and his brother shot for opposing the Nazis. No-one can win.'

Gertrude looked at her for some moments and then nodded.

'The British can't see there are Germans who love Hitler and those who hate him.' Gertrude continued to observe her. She met her gaze, which narrowed to some accusation. 'As there are Italians who hate Mussolini.'

Gertrude continued to stare. She knew something of Amelia, had spoken with someone, somehow knew of the willing support she'd offered Mussolini. She wished Gertrude would leave. Ilaria made no sound, just sat still, her eyes transfixed on the middle distance, as Amelia poured water into the washbasin and began to clean her. She wished the child would cry and thought to pinch her. She wished she could cry.

Finally, she looked at Gertrude, who then turned in the doorframe to leave. Something in her coat, a small tear in the side, reminded her of something, someone long forgotten. Signor Gregorio. He would be long dead, and she'd never thought to ask her mother of him, never thought of him when she'd walked across his piazza. How far she'd strayed from … what? Some ideal; herself. She rushed to the doorframe, called out to Gertrude. 'Is there anything I can do, for the man?'

Gertrude turned, her face perplexed. 'He's dead.'

Once a week, a priest, Father Owens, and a group of Brigidine Sisters came from the nearby town of Echuca to hold Latin mass, one of the dining rooms pressed to impersonate a church. The Latin linked those in the camp of the Roman faith. Amelia and Ilaria attended, and as the weeks passed Amelia came to enjoy the small ritual. And it drew Ilaria from her shell, her eyes wide with wonder. She loved the smell of the incense, the candles, the rich purple and cream in the priest's gowns. These were some of the few moments in a week when Ilaria would let Amelia move more than a few feet from her, still within sight, and walk to the makeshift altar to take communion. One of the nuns, Sister Helen, would encourage Ilaria to sit with her. While she took the bread and wine, Amelia would hear Ilaria laugh.

'This is no place for children,' Sister Helen said to Amelia.

Sister Helen was Irish, in her mid-forties, and spoke with a strong brogue. Amelia looked at the Sister.

'I can't seem to reach her,' Amelia said.

'Does she play with the other children?'

'I've tried, but most are German. She doesn't speak English.'

'Then you must change that.'

'I speak to her more in English, but she withdraws and responds in Italian. She says she doesn't want to speak the other way. And her Italian is deteriorating.'

'I can speak no Italian,' Sister Helen said. 'Leave her with me for an hour after mass. But you must speak to her only in English.'

Amelia smiled – that in such a harsh place there were acts of kindness. But no matter how hard or softly they tried, each word of English seemed to conjure quiet in Ilaria. She would refuse to leave Amelia's side, sobbing softly if she tried. She refused to eat, or at best ate very little and had lost a considerable amount of weight. She repeated over and over that she wanted to go home. She missed her brothers.

'I don't like it here,' she said.

And how could Amelia argue with her? Amelia tried to get her to help with Gertrude's flowerbeds, but when Amelia wasn't looking, Ilaria scuffed the coloured flowers into the earth. If only Lucia were there. Amelia wasn't blind – Ilaria loved her. She'd left her with Lucia when they'd travelled to Italy. Ilaria spent her days in the kitchen around Lucia's feet and called her 'Nonna'. But Lucia wasn't there. And neither was Lucia in Babinda, having stayed on in Brisbane to help her son and his family. Amelia couldn't blame her for wanting to be near her kin, but it had left the boys to fend for themselves. And there was no possibility of trying to return Ilaria to Babinda. Only Sister Helen could bring Ilaria from herself, and only for the shortest time.

One afternoon, while Amelia was writing letters, Ilaria lay in her listless state on the bed. She said something that Amelia didn't quite catch. She asked her to repeat it.

'I want to go to Marta.'

The words sent chills through Amelia. The child wanted to die. She had no answer except to pick her up and carry her to the sunshine, surrounded by Gertrude's flowers. Ilaria stared at them. She had no colour in her face, grey heaviness under her eyes, her dress hanging from her shoulders.

'This place is bad for her,' Amelia said to Sister Helen.

'I can't see it's good for anyone. How does she know of death?'

Amelia told her of Marta. 'At the time, Ilaria seemed ... unaffected by it. I didn't think she understood what had happened. Marta had been away at school – Ilaria just thought she was still there.'

'Even a child's mind works to defend itself.'

'She's so unhappy, and as brutal as it sounds, I do nothing to lift her spirits. I've failed her.'

For some moments they sat in silence.

'I was misled,' Amelia said. Sister Helen said nothing. 'The letters from Italy, they spoke of the great good the fascists had achieved. Who was I to doubt that? And here, the Italian consulate offered support to the Italian workers when all we'd received from the British Australians was condemnation. They invited us to work. but when we were a success ... They didn't like that.'

'These are extreme conditions. No-one can see in this fog. You made decisions you thought were just.'

Just decisions ... Amelia could barely scrape up the meaning of these words.

'With you, Ilaria smiles,' Amelia said. 'I've even heard her laugh.' Sister Helen couldn't refute this. An idea came to Amelia. Although she fought it, it glimmered as an answer. 'Would you take her?'

Sister Helen sat back. 'I'm not sure she should be separated from you.'

'Could she go with you, just for a week, and see how she fares?'

Sister Helen focused on the middle distance, considering this proposal. 'We run a boarding school. She could stay with us. But I'm still not sure—'

'If she's unhappier, if that's possible, she can come back here.'

'But you'll miss her.'

'I miss her now. But my needs are nothing to hers.'

Sister Helen breathed out. 'I'll speak with the camp authorities. And the school. I can't promise anything.'

'She whimpers when she sees the barbed wire. She must go from here.'

The following week, Sister Helen took Amelia aside and told her she and Father Owen had spoken with the school and they'd agreed to take Ilaria. And she had permission from the camp. It just needed Amelia to sign some papers, and it could be done. Amelia breathed in, held her breath to tighten her resolve. Although Ilaria would find the separation distressing, it could only be better for the child to be away from that infernal place. Amelia fought back the tears. She would miss her, as she did Italo and the boys. But she would worry less for Ilaria; in her absence, she would be safer.

She smiled when she told Ilaria she was going to live with Sister Helen for a week at the boarding school. Ilaria glared at her, that stony, blank expression that had become her state. Then she smiled, small, just a lift to the edges of her lips.

Her hand slipped from Amelia's. She walked away, holding the fringes of Sister Helen's cloak. She didn't look back, not once, leaving Amelia heartbroken but resolved. She remained watching, sorry she'd not return, pleased she'd gone, until there was nothing left to see. Maria came to her side.

'I'm burning,' Amelia said. Despite the settling cool of the evening, she pulled at her grey scarf until it came free of her neck. 'No tears will put out the flame. If only ...'

If only what? What else could she have done?

They stood together, side by side, for over an hour. Maria said nothing, her silent presence everything Amelia needed.

And then the evening's cold descended and Maria said the evening meal would soon be served, and they should prepare themselves.

CHAPTER THIRTY-FIVE

The days without Ilaria were drained and drawn long. Amelia forced herself to be busy. As they cleaned the camp, helped in the kitchen, Maria assured her she'd made the right decision.

'The hardest decision for a woman,' Maria said. 'But the child had lost her light. She'll find it again there.'

In the next fortnight, Amelia had her appeal before the advisory board. This gave her much to think about, something to work for, and something more to fear. It was wrong to stake too much hope on release, but stories circulated of people who'd secured their release one way or another. Surely, she had good cause – a child, a farm, a business – but she'd been labelled a threat to the country's security, and this opinion would take something to change.

At the appeal, she'd have no legal representation. Her solicitor in Babinda had sent some arguments with some legal weight. She'd written back for clarification of points, but the mail was slow. Of course, when it did finally arrive, it had been opened, which no doubt slowed the progress and alerted the authorities to her arguments. This surveillance prompted even further feelings of alienation, more disorientating than the camp itself. But that was the intention. Despite all her requests, no businessmen from Babinda had vouched for her good character.

And she'd wake in the night and strain her ears for Ilaria's breathing. But there was nothing. How could she give up her child? Was she reckless? No. This was the best she could do.

Italo wrote to her at least once a fortnight, always a different hand. He'd been concerned for Ilaria in the camp and thought Amelia had made the right decision. It would be hard for Amelia, but Ilaria would be safer. He made no mention of himself, of how he was keeping, even when she wrote back asking explicitly.

When a week was over, Sister Helen brought Ilaria to the camp. She was still quiet and sullen, but Sister assured Amelia she'd been livelier during the week.

'She's even started to speak a little,' Sister said. 'She knows a lot more than she lets on.'

Amelia had to decide. The child looked better, brighter, the dark circles gone from her eyes. And Sister reported she was eating well, which was obvious in her ruddy cheeks. She and Ilaria walked the grounds in silence, although Ilaria had to be coaxed from Sister's side.

'Do you like living with Sister Helen?' Amelia said, once they were away from her.

But the sullen veil had slipped over Ilaria again, and she wouldn't be drawn on her feelings.

'Where do you sleep?' Amelia said, attempting a more general discussion.

'With the others,' Ilaria said.

'Are they nice girls?'

'Their parents don't want them.'

Amelia breathed in. The child had learnt implication and blame.

'Can we go back to Sister Helen?' Ilaria said.

Amelia kept her gaze for some moments. What could she say? Her position was far too complicated to justify to Ilaria. Would she be safe? Marta had died away from her. Could Amelia protect her in this place? She was nearly at an age for school. The nuns would school her and, most importantly, in

English. She nodded, and Ilaria turned and skipped away to Sister Helen, which said all that needed to be said.

'Then it's decided,' Amelia said to Sister Helen. 'She'll stay with you.'

'I'll pray to Our Lady to watch over her.'

'Don't bring her here again. It upsets her.'

'But you'll miss her …'

A knife slid into Amelia's heart. Sister Helen was a good soul. Amelia was right to trust her. Something Italo had said came back to her.

'Until I leave this place,' she said. 'I've ceased to exist. I'm just a number, QF 8788.'

Now it was Amelia's turn to walk away, not to look back, to be casual, as if it were Ilaria's first day of school. How could steps, so common in a day, be so heavy?

The morning of her appeal, she received a letter from Flavio. She ripped it open, apprehensive for news of the farm, hopeful of something good. They were preparing for the harvest, but he'd been unable to secure men to cut the crop. On the street in the village, Fergus Kelly had given an impassioned speech about boycotting any work on the Italian-owned farms to protest the enemy aliens' crimes.

At first Flavio had doubted such a campaign would have any effect; ultimately, the canecutters had to work to earn a living, and there were so many Italian-owned farms that if they boycotted them all they'd not be working. The mill had accepted his booking unequivocally for mid-November, but when he tried to engage cutters, they turned away in droves. He had no idea how he'd get the crop from the field to the mill.

She looked from the letter. It was dated the thirteenth of October, 1942. It was now the tenth of November, the letter almost a month old. The agitation lodged in her throat. It was only a few days before the cane was due at the mill. Had Flavio found men? She had no way of finding out. If he hadn't, men would come onto their land and harvest the crop, take it to the mill and claim it as their own.

They would lose another year's income, which would make their lives impossible, unable to continue the mortgage payments. The pressure built in her. She wrote a quick letter back to him, encouraged him not to give up and that a solution could be found. But she knew the letter was useless. By the time it arrived, all would be laid to rest. But the boy must feel abandoned and needed some words of support in whatever dire situation engulfed him.

There was a long chain of appeals, many desperate women trying to find a way home. She was the last in the day, ushered in by an armed guard as another woman left in tears. Two long desks faced each other, a judge and two other official men. Another man, the stenographer, sat to the right. She arranged her papers and dictionary in front of her. She breathed deeply to keep the spasm in her heart at bay.

It began in a cordial manner – they asked of her life, her family. Then the judge asked if she had anything to say.

'I am innocent,' she said.

They asked so many questions, of her allegiances, why they'd travelled to Italy, what they'd done there, why she'd wanted to start an Italian school, what she had been signalling from the house's tower at night to the Japanese. What did she speak of when she took food to the poor? Over and over and over, they recounted the details of her crimes, hopping from one to the other in no seemly order, hoping, no doubt, to muddle her. Everything was typed by the clerk, the machine pounding into the small silences between their demands and her responses. And as they talked at her, she realised something as plain and simple as day and night.

Fergus Kelly had been watching her.

It was a habit he'd begun so many years ago and couldn't cease. But whereas once it was driven by desire, now it was fuelled by hate. She'd refused him, denied him, injured him. He would think her his wife, that he was a cuckold. For years, he'd not betrayed her because he sought to destroy her. He'd played this game far better than her. She was the victim of a jealous lover and greed and spite. He'd turned her over to the authorities.

'Would I be able to speak?' she said.

The judge looked at her. In the void, the banging typist ground to a halt.

'I want to show you something,' Amelia said.

After some seconds, he nodded and she moved towards him. She flicked through the leaves of her dictionary, the fluttering pages stopping in the centre. From between the pages, she pulled two photographs, stored there, far from Italo's eyes.

She presented them. He glared over the rim of his glasses at the first. It was Flavio, standing in front of a newly planted field. It was early evening. He was stripped to the waist, smiling, no shyness of the camera. Flavio's happiness glowed. She'd taken it when the fields were planted after Italo's arrest, after the fire. She sent a copy to Italo as pleasing proof the work was done.

No comment flickered over the judge's face, no words. He looked at the second photograph. It was Fergus, smiling and falling from the back of a mule in Egypt.

'Since my husband's arrest, we've suffered great deprivation. We lost the major part of a crop to a fire that even the police agreed had been deliberately lit. Can you imagine the strain on our finances?'

His face remained steel.

'Look at these two photographs,' she said.

The judge squinted at the two images. 'What of them? I see no connection.'

'This is my son.' She motioned to the one on the judge's left. 'The older photograph is of Fergus Kelly. Oisin, his father, owns the property next to ours. My husband bought our land from him.' She breathed in deeply, the typist pounding. 'Fergus wants our land back. Inch by inch, he's instigated this. He burnt the crop. But we survived. He has misconstrued my actions. I was working, trying to save the farm. Perhaps my pages moved in front of the lamp, causing the light to flutter, but there was no signal. I had no time to signal to the Japanese. But he was watching me. He's reported the light in my window at three in the morning. And in the last few weeks, he has incited the men not to harvest our crop. This morning, I've had a letter. In the next few days, when the crop isn't harvested, he'll come onto the land and take it. Without a crop, the bank will close on the mortgage. Then the bank will appoint a farm manager, and no doubt it will be him and—'

'I fail to see—'

'Do you see some resemblance between these two photographs?'

The judge glared at her and then narrowed his eyes, looked from one photograph to the other and then back to the other. He nodded.

'Soon after I arrived in Australia,' Amelia said. 'After I'd married Italo, Fergus Kelly was my lover. Flavio was conceived with Fergus in the last weeks of 1920. He was born in September 1921.'

The stenographer's rhythm broke, a small silence. The judge, an old man who she'd wager couldn't remember passion, glared at her.

'Maria Pastore,' she said, 'who is also held here, will vouch for this story. Fergus Kelly seeks revenge, means to have our land. This is the real reason I'm here.'

The judge looked again from one photograph to the next.

'These are serious allegations,' he said. 'What proof do you have?'

'Just the photographs. And with this confession, I've destroyed what shreds of honour I have left. Your typist has written it all. It's on the record. I'm a whore.'

Amelia turned away.

'Stay there,' the judge said. He rang a bell. 'Bring Maria Pastore.'

He put the photographs together and handed them back to her. He looked at his notes, asked if there were any further questions from the other men who sat on the bench. Amelia stood, so close to these men she could hear them exhale. But no-one looked at her.

'When Maria Pastore enters the room, you'll look at me, not at her. Do you understand?'

Amelia nodded.

The wall clock tick-tocked. She looked at her feet. She counted the seconds, tried to bring them to minutes, but she lost count of the reckoning when she heard the door behind her open. Two sets of steps.

'Are you Maria Pastore?'

'I am.'

It was Maria's voice.

'Who is the father of Flavio Amedeo?'

She heard Maria's breath catch. And then there was nothing. No sign of breathing.

'Do you not have an answer?'

Again there was silence, and the pound of the typist made way to the tick of the clock and the beat of her heart.

'What is the purpose of such a question?' Maria said.

'Just answer it.'

There was a drawn silence. 'Italo Amedeo.'

Amelia stared at her feet. She couldn't meet the judge's eye.

'Thank you,' the judge said.

She heard Maria taken from the room. The judge told her to return to her seat, but she couldn't. He advised her, sarcasm lacing his tone, all comments would be taken into consideration. The men stood to leave as she still stood before them. They straightened their papers, picked them up and filed from the room.

The typist packed away his equipment. She couldn't take back the pages. He looked at her then lowered his eyes and left.

She'd said aloud something she'd held within her heart for over twenty years. It was over. Her darkest secret told, written and soon to be filed away. But there was no sense of having lightened a burden.

Despite Maria's profuse, profound and often repeated apologies, which she accepted, in the coming months Amelia distanced herself from her and the other Italians in the concentration camp. She wanted nothing to do with them, nothing to do with her compatriots, nothing to do with the homeland or her chosen land. The reasons for such isolation were nebulous, complex and included embarrassment at her confession. But she found solace from her anxiety in letters, in Gertrude's flowers, and in reading.

> The language in which we are speaking is his before it is mine.

Never had she read something so profound, written by an Irishman of English.

CHAPTER THIRTY-SIX

In July 1943, almost a year after Amelia's failed attempt to be released, after many First Holy Communions in the camp's makeshift church, through births and deaths, the Allied forces invaded Sicily. The beginning of the end had begun. The forces inched their way through the south of Italy, insistently further north towards Rome.

In the camp, accurate information was hard to obtain, but by the end of July, the internees had heard the king of Italy had arrested Mussolini. For Amelia, this news had a hint of betrayal; Italy had imprisoned its saviour. Bittersweet. This thought caught her by surprise, and she wondered at herself and how she could still think such a thing. Her support of Mussolini had placed her in a concentration camp. But above this, she felt an optimism; the tide of Italy's involvement in the war was changing. Perhaps she could see the end of it. She cared not for right or wrong. She wanted peace and to return to her home.

On the eighth of September, Italy surrendered to the Allied forces. The Italians in the camp were no longer the enemies of Australia. The news sent waves of speculation crashing through the camp: What would happen? Would they be released? Amelia looked at these women, drawn to exhaustion and nervous collapse by months of inactivity and worry. It almost made her laugh; what threat had they posed? Yet they weren't free.

The camp had reports great confusion followed Italy's surrender. Germany invaded, freeing Mussolini, who then fled to the north. Though she'd written many letters to her family, they remained unanswered, not a single word about them for over two years. Now their village was under German control, and she prayed they would go unnoticed.

At the morning rollcall on the twenty-sixth of November, 1943, there was no rollcall. The Italian women were told they were free to leave. Amelia felt confused, as if she'd misheard, except that the women looked at one another, their faces full of blighted wonder. It must be true. They were free to leave.

Fearing the authorities may change their minds, the women returned to their huts and pitched their few belongings into whatever cases they had. Amelia had little worth taking, all in one portmanteau. She gave back the jam tin of common yellow daisies to Gertrude, who was still an enemy and wouldn't be released.

'*Auf Wiedersehen, Schatzi*,' Gertrude said, smiling, singing. Gertrude made no concession to hide her heritage, which Amelia admired.

'I'll start writing letters for your release,' Amelia said.

'Thank you, but they won't listen.'

Gertrude started to laugh. And Amelia could do nothing but join in. The two embraced.

Outside the hut, the other Italian women had begun to walk, streams of them coming from the rows of huts, gathering to a river on the broad central road. No-one smiled, or frowned. They looked straight ahead. What a ragtag bunch of 'enemies', who had now again become friends of the nation. At the gate, the officers gave them money for their passage home.

Amelia walked out through the flimsy barbwire fence and the cage gate with only one portmanteau, twenty months after her arrest. With each step, she felt guilty for those left behind, happy for those who were leaving, angry at the wasted time, but above all fearful of the time ahead. What would she find in Babinda?

A fleet of buses waited for them.

'Do you want me to come to Echuca?' Maria said.

Amelia considered it. She had no idea how to travel to Ilaria's boarding school or even how far it was and how long it would take. She hadn't seen Ilaria for over a year. But now she would. She felt a surge of excitement and thought perhaps Maria could help her. But that was selfish.

'Go home,' she said to Maria. 'Your family needs you more than me.'

They were taken by bus back to the Rushworth train station, not an armed guard in sight. With rapid waves of tears and promises to stay in touch, the women said goodbye to one another.

'When we are home,' Maria said as they parted, 'all this will be forgotten.'

'What I've said here will never be forgotten.'

Tears crept into Maria's eyes, and she assured her again that she felt no animosity for what had happened. 'When the judge asked, I had one chance in two,' Maria said. 'I chose the wrong person.'

Amelia had no desire to remonstrate Maria. The situation was impossible. None of the women were to blame for anything.

'Go home,' Amelia said. 'We will see what the future brings.'

Amelia would take a train that branched in another direction, further inland to Echuca. But now the fear and anxiety were too much, and she steeled herself to react to them as little as she could. On the train, the people in her compartment stared at her, eyes steady and narrowed. She smiled. They remained fixed, unembarrassed by their stare. Why were they looking at her? She realised she was wearing a dress only marginally better than rags. And it was obvious what she was. She moved from the compartment to stand in the antechamber at the end of the carriage.

She watched the flat, dry land slipping along, stretching to the limit of the eye. What a different scene to her home. How would it be? The world was still at war. In the camp, she'd had a roof and food and security. They'd been overcrowded; now she was alone, the move from certain to uncertain unsettling. What would she face now? Italy may be an ally, but how many years would it take to salve all this hostility?

And now she would go back to Babinda after she'd confessed everything of Fergus. She could only imagine how the tongues rattled in the town. She shook her head. What a useless act it had been. She'd learnt from letters that her predictions in front of the advisory committee had all come true: when Flavio failed to harvest the crop and defaulted on the mortgage, the Kellys had harvested the crop and been paid by the mill. The bank appointed Fergus Kelly as manager, and he bought back the new land. But somehow Flavio had held onto the original land. God love him. He'd fought off his own father. She had no idea what Faustian pact he'd signed. And she was too tired to care of it.

At the Echuca rail station, she asked a woman the direction of St Joseph's College. It was only a short walk, half an hour at most; she'd just to follow Annesley Street to the end and then turn left to the river esplanade, and she would see a sign. The day was already hot and there was little shade. She passed the Murray River, the tall gums languid in the hot sun, a paddle-steamer passing on the slow river, others patiently tethered to wharves along the bank.

The college was an impressive edifice, two storeys, filigree brick details, arched, deep verandahs and a horseshoe drive. At the office, she asked for Sister Helen and waited and waited in the long hall, its high ceiling cooling the air, echoing any movement or sound.

After some time, Sister Helen bustled along the hall, her dark wimple and gown fluttering, her smile wide and strong.

'What a sight,' Sister Helen said. 'We'd heard rumours but nothing official.'

'We had no idea.'

'Let's hope it's a first step back to normality. Have you heard of your husband?'

Amelia shook her head.

Sister tightened her mouth and nodded. 'I'll make enquiries. Let's get Ilaria.'

'How is she?'

'She's much loved. She celebrated her first communion last week. She'll be pleased to see you.'

'Will she?'

Sister Helen wouldn't countenance such a question, waved it away with her hand like a bad odour. 'The other girls are very fond of her. They'll miss her.'

Sister Helen walked into the college. Ilaria was in a class of girls older than her, as the school had no preparatory classes. Sister Helen went inside. Amelia waited. She could see through the classroom windows that opened onto the hall. Sister Helen spoke to the teacher and Ilaria came to her and took her hand. She was so much taller but dressed like a little doll, her hair in tight pigtails. Clearly, she trusted Sister Helen completely. The other girls' eyes followed Ilaria to the door.

She jolted when she saw Amelia. Possibly, she'd not seen many women out of the order, their hair uncovered, but possibly her dress of rags shocked her. She clutched Sister Helen's robe.

'It will take her a while,' Sister Helen said.

Reticence was a curse of this country. In silence, Sister Helen took them, Amelia on one side and Ilaria on the other, to a small garden. They sat together on a stone bench in the sun, where Sister Helen left them. Amelia couldn't bring herself to look at Ilaria. Instead, she looked up at a gum tree, peering over the building. From the high roof, a magpie warbled.

'We can go home now,' Amelia said, in Italian. But clearly Ilaria had forgotten it, and she repeated it in English.

Ilaria looked at her. 'But this is my home.' She spoke in English.

'Don't you remember the farm?'

Ilaria thought and shook her head. Amelia felt tired and drained. How could she not remember her home? But why would she? It was all so long ago, a third of her life.

'Don't you remember the fields of cane?'

Amelia raised her arms in the air and moved her hands slowly and slightly from side to side as if a light afternoon breeze cajoled them.

Ilaria shook her head. 'I remember Nonna.'

The child sat back, tired from the strain of thinking.

Again, Amelia felt a stab of pain that she'd failed her. 'Don't you remember your brothers? And your father?'

She shook her head. 'I want to stay with Sister Helen.'

Amelia looked up at the clear sky. What right did she have to uproot her again? None of this was Ilaria's making, and yet she had paid for it. But Ilaria was her daughter. And she was her mother.

'I can't tell you this will be easy,' Amelia said. 'But we must try again, to be a family.' She looked at the child and wondered how much she understood. 'Otherwise, we will have lost everything.'

For some moments Ilaria considered this, her expression scrunched in concentration. And then she relaxed, opened her face. 'Will Nonna be there?'

'No, but your brothers will. And I hope your father.'

Ilaria nodded.

The following morning, there were many tears in the main hall from all the girls who'd come to say goodbye. They hugged Ilaria, gave her a posy of flowers and some boiled lollies, handed her about like a precious doll. But Ilaria remained clear, focused, as if she'd resolved this was to happen.

Sister Helen accompanied them to the station. Amelia was unsure if Ilaria knew exactly what was happening, but when the time came to part, Ilaria hugged Sister Helen.

'May the Holy Mother care for you,' Sister Helen said.

The Sister's face was unerring, giving no extreme emotion away.

Ilaria turned away, took Amelia's hand, and together they boarded the train. Once they found their compartment, they saw Sister Helen walking into the station, disappearing into the shadows, no parting glance. For some moments, Ilaria stared from the window. Did she expect Sister Helen to return? But when there was no more sign of her, none at all, Ilaria hoisted herself up and sat back in the too-large train seat. Amelia left her to her thoughts, partly from fear that any question might cause the child to shatter, partly as she felt no reserve to resolve any of these feelings.

Each morning, despite the fact it was another bed in another unfamiliar hotel, Ilaria woke at the same time, six-fifteen, made her bed, the sheets and blankets expertly tight, dressed, prayed and waited to be told to eat. Amelia had her own rhythm, different but as precise, and at times on the trains as the long hours rocked away, they were both paralysed, waiting for some instruction, roused only by the train's tooting or the stationmaster's whistling.

Over a week of dusty travel later, Amelia stepped to the train platform. Babinda held blue skies, dotted with cotton-white clouds. The platform hummed with voices. Some faces she knew, but all failed to acknowledge her. She looked around one last time. She'd half hoped Italo would be there, but there was no sign of him. She didn't know if he'd been released from Loveday. She had no idea where he was. And Flavio and Mauro had no idea of her return. She'd not written.

She turned back towards the train door, shifted her portmanteau to her right hand and stretched her free hand to Ilaria. Ilaria waved her hand away and walked the steep stairs on her own. Amelia stepped back but the child remained fixed, glaring at the surroundings. The poor child had been shunted from bed to bed, through Victoria and New South Wales and into the far north of Queensland. And Babinda, of all places, was foreign to her. Amelia tugged at her hand, but she remained.

'We're going home,' Amelia said, in English.

She tugged again and with some reluctance, Ilaria stepped forward. She missed Sister Helen and the routine of the school. It would take them all time to adjust. They approached the stationmaster. He nodded, but made no more overture to recognising her, intent on his clipboard and the mail bags and luggage from the train.

'Would you be so kind to telephone my home?' she said. 'One of the boys can come for me.'

'I could try,' he said. He looked from his clipboard and scowled. 'But the line's disconnected.'

Amelia jarred. She should have thought of this. Flavio had been unable to pay so many bills; of course, the telephone account would have been one of them. The man returned to his clipboard.

She'd not show her embarrassment. 'It's such a lovely day. We'll walk.'

'It's a long way,' he said. 'I'm sure if you wait, someone will pass who could give you a lift.'

Amelia looked at the people leaving the station. She was sure the man's tone suggested this as a kindness, but she doubted these people would help her.

'I've not been able to walk a long way for nearly two years.' She looked at Ilaria. 'It will do us good. Could I leave this suitcase with you?'

He nodded.

They started in the direction of the farm. Ilaria pulled her hand from Amelia's. They were soon away from the village, passing along the high fields of cane, their white flowers swaying in the light breeze.

'I remember seeing them for the first time,' Amelia said.

But Ilaria remained with her eyes turned down, no interest in the cane or Amelia's memories. Amelia couldn't reach the child and looked to the sky. A dark wedge-tailed eagle reeled slowly, round and round above the patchwork field, then strafed onto some hapless prey, rising again and gone, a mother fetching for her young. What a poor job she'd done as a mother, forced to circle over fields she'd never intended to. But still, the guilt remained.

They continued in silence. For so many months, every day Amelia had walked around the camp's perimeter, but her legs had no sense of this distance and grew tired. It would take an hour, at least, to arrive at the farm.

'Would you like to rest?' she said, in Italian.

Ilaria stopped and looked at the road ahead. 'Why do you speak that funny language?'

Amelia was conscious of this switching. 'We should speak English, like everybody else, when we're in public. But when we're alone, don't you think it might be nice to speak Italian?'

'I don't like it.'

Amelia breathed out. 'You used to speak it so well.'

Ilaria shrugged her shoulders.

Amelia had forgotten how quickly the rain could come, unheralded, untold. She cursed it. But she'd not felt it for so long, not rain like this, large drops, almost bath-warm, not piercing and biting and cold. What fortune rain had brought her. What a change to have rain, rather than tears, running down her cheek. She closed her eyes, leant back to face it. She remained so, unaware of anything but the beating. When she finally opened her eyes, Ilaria stared at her as if she'd lost her mind.

Amelia smiled.

Ilaria stayed so stony, but then looked away and started to laugh. And then dance. Did she remember this style from Marta? That wasn't possible, but there it was, as if their limbs reacted in the same manner to the rain's rhythm.

And Amelia started too, holding both Ilaria's hands, the pair turning and turning, soon wet to their skins. People driving by glared at them, these two fools in the rain, but no-one stopped. And she wouldn't have accepted their approach. They were wet. Sodden. Nothing more could touch them. And she was independent. She needed no help.

By the time they'd reached the farm turn-off, the rain had eased.

'This is our home,' Amelia said.

Ilaria looked at the road with no sign of any building. The boarding school was grand, and Ilaria had expressed wonder at living in such a place. But the entrance to this home was just scrub, no wrought gate.

Amelia started but Ilaria remained fixed. She walked back the few paces and took her hand, and so they walked along the road curving around the hill. Ilaria seemed uncertain, not a flicker of recognition on her face. And there it was, the land for which so much had been fought and lost. The fields were bare, overgrown with high weeds, no sign of cane. If the fields weren't tilled, so quickly the forest would reclaim the whole farm. The impermanence thrilled her. It would take work to clear them, to ready them for planting. But what did it matter? They'd lost the new fields to the bank and then to Fergus. They still had the main field, something to be grateful for.

They walked towards the house, past the stables, the barn and the barracks. There was no sign of life, the horses sold and gone. What a pity, as with petrol rationing they'd come back into their own. The gravel yard crunched under their feet. Amelia pushed the gate, which cried in pain, the garden unkempt and overgrown, destroyed by neglect. Amelia sighed. Simply another thing to put right. She looked to the house, to the second floor, the beautiful broad verandah, to the tower and her office. The sun flashed in her eye. A woman in crimson and sapphire robes stared down at her, her face so open and tranquil. Amelia had no idea who she was. Amelia raised her hand to shield the muted sunlight. And then she heard the bell-beat of wings. A cloud of red and sapphire eclectus parrots rose into the sky. Amelia smiled. The woman was a trick of the light, the colours from the birds, a memory. The vision, from so long ago, meant this was home.

She looked to the lower level. A man stood in the open front door. She stepped back. He wore dark woollen pants and a white cotton shirt draped from a painfully thin frame, not a hair on his head, the last worn away by worry. Italo. He remained so framed, not moving, so like him, and Amelia in the open space stood still too, still holding Ilaria's hand. Across such a distance, such an expanse, she looked at him, and he at her, into each other's eyes, neither smiling nor frowning, laughing nor crying.

She searched his face.

As he searched hers.

And then the sun, warm with delight, came from the cloud. The shadow of a parrot whirled over the ground between them. Amelia looked to the sky. The bird circled into the sun and disappeared. All things would pass. With time and effort, everything would be set right.

EPILOGUE

Many years later, as far forward as 1991, three nuns from the Loreto Sisters spent the June long weekend south of Berrima, in the New South Wales Southern Highlands, in a small cottage, a sparse place: two small bedrooms, separate dining room with a long refectory table and a lounge room and kitchen with nothing more than a cold open fire. It rained and rained and rained, and Sister Mary Margaret thought it the wettest place on earth. Until she remembered Babinda.

She'd not thought of her home, not in these close terms, for many years. Memories – no, that isn't close enough; sensations – faded in and out with each wave of water lashing the corrugated iron roof, some drops crossing the broad verandah to thump against the windows. She felt the feathery waving heads of the cane, the sounds and vivid colours of birds in the forest canopy, her Nonna Lucia's firm but gentle hand.

When it was clear the rain had set in, when too many card games and rounds of Monopoly and Cluedo had degenerated into squabbles (yes – nuns cheat and squabble) Sister Teresa suggested they tour the nearby Berrima Gaol. Sister Mary Margaret was opposed to it. A part of the prison's life was interning German immigrants during World War I, and she felt no need to gawk at the dregs of sorrow. Sister Agatha suggested the nearby Berkelouw Book Barn. In an instant, Sister Mary Margaret agreed and hoped they could lose one another for an hour between the shelves.

The others scattered into the book labyrinth, but she warmed herself by the huge stone fire. The rain beat on the high vaulted ceiling. But once her fingers had thawed and there was no sight of the others, she walked along the shelves with no real purpose, just happy to stretch her legs. And indeed it was a barn, filled with books of all station: old, rare and antique, trashy murders and any number of cast-offs.

But Babinda held her thoughts. Her mother said a decade after she'd arrived in Australia she'd read every English-language book she could find in Babinda. How she would have revelled in this barn. If there was a word she didn't know, even the slightest, she chased it. If someone in the village annoyed her – God help them – she would use some obscure word – calumny, arrogate, ersatz, badinage – and leave the recipient reeling in the void of their ignorance. When Sister Mary Margaret looked up the word, it was perfect, as if her mother had painted a fine highlight on the dark canvas of disagreement. In her working life, as Sister Mary Margaret urged her students to understand something as basic as 'to be', she'd think of Amelia, marvel at her.

Sister Mary Margaret heard Sister Agatha – who never stopped talking, even in her sleep – and ducked into another aisle and hid at the apex. She turned to the spines, held in strict attention. A beaten copy drew her, the dulled red leather spine creased and cracked, the size of a paperback but with a good two-inch spine. She reached for it, an old and well-worn Italian–English dictionary, the gilt of the page edges worn to patches. She fluttered through the leaves until they stopped flowing, jarred open. Two photos, pushed hard into the binding, stood erect and required some force to free. They were old, black-and-white and fading and creased, wedged among English words beginning with *f*.

The first was of three uniformed soldiers, seated on a mule, tethered by a dark-skinned man in a white galabeya and kufi. The man at the back was skylarking, smiling broadly as he feigned falling from the animal. The second wasn't nearly as battered, of a young man, as young as sixteen, standing on a path between two ploughed fields, stripped to the waist. He wore a round straw hat, larger than a dinner plate, at a rakish angle, pushed off centre, his face open in a mild smile. His chest was full and firm, his abdomen tight and strong, not a hint of age.

Then she saw it: her brother Flavio. The thought came to her unburnished but not unwelcome. She flooded with heat. How did this photo come to be there? She sat on one of the low padded leather stools at the apex of each row, laid the book on her lap and flicked through every fine page lest there were more. And then she settled on the front flyleaf. The words took her breath, raced her heart.

Amelia Durante, 1920.

Un regalo da sua madre in occasione della sua partenza dall'Italia.

You can imagine her shock. How could this be? And what force, except Our Lady's hand, had moved her eyes, her cold fingers, among those thousands upon thousands of spines? And why? Sister Agatha bowled down the aisle towards her. She closed the photos in the book, held it to her heart and made in the opposite direction. She paid for it, seven dollars for such a fortune, and made certain nothing fell from it as the smiling assistant placed it in a thick paper bag.

She said nothing to the nuns, just that she'd bought a penny dreadful about a mass murder in Second Empire France, but urged they should go back to the cottage. They left the barn along the dual rows of bare poplars – the rain had calmed to drizzle. She locked herself in the bathroom and took out the photos. In the light above the sink, once she'd seen it, the image was indelible: the man on the back of the mule was Flavio. Despite all contradictory sense, she was convinced. When had Flavio been in this situation?

The family anniversaries flooded her. Amelia died in late 1978, living the last years of her life with Mauro in Rockhampton. Her body was cremated, but her possessions ... How her dictionary came to be in a book barn in Berrima, and how these two images were still embedded, and how they related to one another, Sister Mary Margaret had no idea.

She returned to Sydney and placed the image of Flavio in Egypt under a strong magnifying glass. She was convinced it was him. He was sixteen when she was born. What did she know of these years of his life? Her first memory of him was when they returned to the farm, of a broken and shattered boy, no enticing smile, no hat pushed back with mirth. He'd suffered so badly while Amelia and Italo were interned, making many decisions well beyond his age, and in the years after was racked with guilt and depression. Who knows where he may have travelled? He was smiling, something she didn't remember.

Italo died in 1953, a decade after his release. He was sixty-eight, a fair but not great age. Sister Mary Margaret had such a short time with him, but he'd been softly spoken, relentlessly polite, always appreciative. He never got over the melancholy, clinging to him like sump oil. He'd been imprisoned for three-and-a-half monotonous years. He was a man of the fields, not of proximity to others. On one occasion he spoke of that time, he said it had changed how his mind worked, and no matter how hard he searched he couldn't find his old self.

After their release, for the remaining two years of the war, Amelia and Italo lived under tight restrictions, each week having to report their movements to the police. In the streets of Babinda, Italo could never look people, his old friends, in the eye without thinking they distrusted him. It wore him away. And he stopped eating, slowly and surely, a little every day, despite all Amelia's best cooking and cajoling. He died of a broken heart and stomach cancer. One way or another, he never recovered from his dose of the 'golden nectar'.

For a decade or more the dictionary and the entombed photos and the mysteries they held stood on Sister Mary Margaret's shelf, visited by her now and again as she searched to see something she hadn't seen at first. On the back flyleaf, Amelia had written all she knew of the family tree: their names, their dates of birth and the dates they died. The last two entries were Marta's and Italo's.

Sister Mary Margaret wrote to Flavio's wife, Greta. After he'd left Australia he lived most of his life in Chicago and had died there. But Greta wrote that he'd never spoken of any travel to the Middle East and had never enlisted in any army. Mauro and Sister Mary Margaret weren't close. He never accepted her joining the order. He knew nothing of these things, but she knew he wouldn't tell her even if he did.

In 1975 the documents pertaining to Italo's and Amelia's arrests were declassified, thirty years after the event. Sister Mary Margaret didn't learn of this until the early 2000s, and soon applied to have copies made. The bundle of papers contained letters about the Italian school, letters intercepted on their way to Italy, letters between the police advising caution – Amelia was described over and over not as intelligent, but as a shrewd woman (Was this a crime?

Clearly.) How awful to read her old name, Ilaria Amedeo, among these papers, singled out to go to a boarding school in Echuca, which singled out her life, as if the Madonna had had a hand in it. The papers held the transcript of Amelia's appeal against her incarceration.

Deep in the heart of any family there are names, muttered from time to time, skeletons spoken of once or twice, but few are discovered in such a manner. Amelia's confession of her affair with Fergus Kelly was made under palpable duress. Sister Mary Margaret felt such horror from the written word. And Maria Pastore denied it.

The relationship between the images was explained. Such quivering emotions Sister Mary Margaret felt, shocked to read these documents, but without judgement. Was the mother she knew a lie? Why had she not told her? Why should she have told her? Poor Amelia, living under this threat of discovery. How did this change the past?

She remembered meeting Fergus Kelly, only once. She must have been ten or so. He was older then, much older than this photo, and she'd been too young to draw out what Fergus would have looked like as a younger man, as a photo does with ease. Amelia wouldn't let him in the house. She welcomed all people, often to overcompensate for Italo's distrust, but to this man she was rude, which had left Ilaria confused and made this meeting noteworthy.

But this explained something the family had always skirted, that Flavio looked neither like Italo or Amelia. The family skeletons were out. Had Amelia ever loved Italo? Had she instead loved this man? Why had she loved this man, this Fergus Kelly?

Flavio never got over the stress of running the farm during their internment, nor his feelings of failure. He moved to the United States, as far as he could from the small cane farm in Babinda, and he never returned. But now she understood. At Flavio's conception, Fergus's genes had won every battle, in the collision of ovum and sperm beaten all of Amelia's traits into recession. He knew. Perhaps he'd recognised his father in the street. Perhaps Fergus Kelly's final act of retribution had been to present himself to Flavio for this purpose. Flavio fled his past, fled all that was coded in him, fled his mother.

Without Flavio, Amelia and Italo continued to farm. Mauro had no interest in it, and Ilaria married Christ. But once the war receded, more people came to the district, some from Italy, and if they worked hard Amelia employed them and fed them very well, and most would return the following season.

After Italo died, Amelia continued, no small achievement. She bought more of the adjacent land. Now Sister Mary Margaret knew this had been Fergus's family land, which in the years after the war had gone completely to ruin. Fergus drank until he could drink no more.

Amelia sold the farm in the late 1960s for an impressive amount. She left the area for Brisbane. She renewed her friendship with Clara, but there was always a distance between them. Sister Mary Margaret had lost touch with Babinda and didn't know who owned the farm. But in 2006 she heard the unheard-of hurly-burly of Cyclone Larry flattened the crops, toppled Amelia's tower and ripped the broad verandahs from the building. But the base still stood. Italo would have smiled.

Sister Mary Margaret continued her search of this trove of declassified documents. Every name she could remember, every name mentioned in a set of documents, she chased. In Maria Pastore's file she found a letter from Amelia, written in 1941 when Amelia was visiting Italo in the Hay concentration camp. Amelia had seen Maria's husband, Dante, and wrote to assure her of his health. But in this letter about Dante, something surprising rested.

> I found Italo quite anxious to see me. Now that we've seen each other we're both more contented and again resign ourselves to the future and what it will bring. Certainly, the separation is again painful. I would like to be near him, but as I've other obligations, I force myself to be resolute and strong.

Such intimacy in a classified file. She married a man she'd never met, never seen, never touched, just as Sister Mary Margaret had. She loved him, grew to love him, of that Sister Mary Margaret was sure. She remembered them happy. When she was in bed she'd hear their feet as they swirled around the living room floor to the gramophone. She held no anger for Amelia, only sorrow, only understanding.

People talk of the horrors of World War II. They'll never, must never, be repeated, but they have been, are, will be. Every day someone is encased in sorrow and suffering. Over twelve thousand people, of so many castes and creeds they can't be listed here, were interned in Australian concentration camps. All that lost time and vitality. All that sorrow. Once these forces turn and gyre, are loosed on the world, once such feelings of nationalism are evoked, ancient grudges break to new mutiny. Innocent people where interned for years on unsworn testimony. Who knows what private vendettas the combatants then pursue in the name of nationhood? No official apology has ever been issued.

In her moments of despair, when she was old and frail, Amy (she changed her name by deed poll) dismissed herself as an 'ignorant old wog' or a 'stupid dago'. Would you hear such things today levelled at Italians and Greeks and Maltese? Perhaps in jest, as we gobble the pizzas and yiros and golden pastizzis. But this country holds little of its history; it relishes the palatable and scorns anything in need of stern mastication, sucks the jelly and leaves the bone.

On the back flyleaf of Amelia's dictionary, Sister Mary Margaret filled in the details of Amelia's death, of Flavio's death – including his biological father's name – and of Mauro's (he had died six years ago), neither with issue. Only Sister Mary Margaret remained, her name to take its place on this list.

Sister Mary Margaret's tranche of documents of her mother's life, a brave life, culled from memories, snippets of recalled conversations and cold declassified papers, sat on her shelf. Broken hearts mend, stronger and wiser. The past is riddled with untold-of women. Ilaria's time was nearly over and with that her chance to fashion the full-of-grace papers to a manuscript, weighted by Amelia's dictionary, heavy with two photos that tell, in equal quotient, of lies and truths, and lust and love.

END NOTE:

Dearest Reader,

So ends Amelia's story. If you have enjoyed this novel, could I please, please ... please ask you to review it on Amazon or Goodreads or any other review platform. These reviews are the lifeblood of a novel, the gush and surge. Only you, dear reader, have the power to stimulate the heart. Please give it a good dose of adrenaline. The review doesn't have to rival those of Julia Kristeva, Umberto Eco or academic Maud Bailey, just something heartfelt and pithy like *Fabbo!* would do. One more time, with affection – please. *Please.* I'll cook you dinner. I'm thinking pecorino truffle souffle ...

ACKNOWLEDGEMENTS

So many people have helped along the way. On closer inspection, what initially seemed a swinging and swift writing period ended in a long and, at times, dragging adventure. Mr Plod.

Firstly, I must thank my former neighbours, Gloria Nilsen and Philip Gallagher, who one evening invited Miss Mia and me in for a whisky and, you know, we got to talking … A few hours later we swerved home with a folder of fascinating and tragic documents. Between these loose pages, and many more conversations, this novel was born.

The first draft of the novel was delivered in Dickens-like serialisation to my writers' group – Karen Vegar, Avril Carruthers, Mara Tisci and Srinath Mogeri. Meetings with them applied pressure to hone the text and resulted in a swag of good insights. Elisabeth Storrs and Lauren Chater read later drafts with great encouragement. Kim Kelly provided me with an exhaustive swathe of scathingly-good suggestions, and good humour, and help with the final edits. Gianfranco Cresciani was very generous with his thoughts, research and ideas. Many years ago *The Italians in Australia* seeded the first inspiration for this novel. Abby Mellick's passion carried me over the dark, fluttering pages of years of redrafts.

Nicola O'Shea's enthusiasm for my writing and for this project took the editing to a most enjoyable level – www.nicolaoshea.com. Tony Ryan's clear, bright eyes and unbridled generosity honed the copy to great effect – www. tonyryan.net.au. And so much discussion about a comma.

Ian Thomson's cover design work was precise and incisive – www.ianwthomson.com. John Bortolin's cover photographs are glorious, and it was nice to see something in his work other than a seemingly endless stream of taut, naked men - johnbortolin@soupa.net. Ella King played Amelia on the cover. And Evan Shapiro performed a stylish Shapiro-ette and did a slick formatting job – www.greenavenue.com.au.

And as always, the biggest thank-you possible to John Watson, who puts up with all these crazy characters who come to live with us for a few years and rattle and roam around the house at all hours of the day and night, delaying and burning dinners, causing tantrums and bedlam and mayhem and frustration. Despite the drama they cause, John, you always have clear insights into their characters.

The line Amelia reads towards the end of the novel is of course James Joyce, from *A Portrait of the Artist as a Young Man.*

And lastly to you, dear reader – it's always such an honour and surprise when you arrive at these last words. Thank you for reading. Please stay in touch and register for news-letters contact via my website, www.gsjohnston.com, on Facebook at @GSJohnston.author, or on Twitter at @GS_ Johnston. Fabbo.

BOOK CLUBS

If you are in a book club looking for an author to meet with you via Skype, I never sleep, so I'm on all time zones, truly global. So please get in touch via the contact page on www. gsjohnston.com. Or Facebook at @GSJohnston.author.

Here are some pithy discussion topics to get you going:

Does this situation have relevance to a modern situation?

How does the novel's title relate to the novel?

How well would this story unfold if it was told through another character's point of view?

If the events of this period were considered a history lesson for the present day, has anything been learnt?

If you were to write fanfic about this book, what kind of story would you want to tell?

What was your favourite quote/passage?

How did Amelia change through the story?

If the book were being adapted into a movie, who would you want to see play what parts?

PREVIOUS PUBLICATIONS – AVAILABLE THROUGH AMAZON:

Consumption: A Novel (2011)
The Skin of Water (2012)
The Cast of a Hand (2015)

If you've enjoyed *Sweet Bitter Cane*, you may also like *The Skin of Water*.

CHAPTER ONE

At the height of the Hungarian summer of 1943, Zeno Czibula saw a woman in the forest.

She strode along a trail edging the sheltered verge of Lake Balaton. Even at this distance, her white diaphanous dress stood out against the deep forest. Diamond light bounced from the silver lake, picked out the dress flowing behind her slight frame, a dress not built for walking in forests. Zeno guessed she was staying at The Hotel Hungary.

She stopped. He held his breath. She looked right, left, over her shoulder. She may have seen him, sensed a set of eyes piercing her solitude. He moved behind a tree. He felt a small stick beneath his left foot and feared it would snap, echoing in the forest's damp quiet. So he stood, one foot raised, peering out from behind the tree. Then he did what he always did: lifted his Cine Kodak Eight Model 20 to his eye, released the wound mechanism, and began to film.

A nervous gazelle, she tilted her head this way and that. She looked down at her shoes and scuffed them off, kicking them clear. She stood facing the path towards the hotel. Her brown hair, straight and strong, bounced about her shoulders. She'd return to the hotel. He moved his lens in that direction and she slipped from his view. She'd hesitated.

The camera's mechanism clanged in the quiet forest. He should reveal his vantage. If she caught him spying he'd be fired and despite being only seventeen he needed this job. As he stepped from the tree's cover, the camera still to his eye, the stick snapped under his left foot. Nearby turtle doves took fright and flight, fluttering across the camera's field of vision. Through the lens, he saw her begin to run—away from the hotel, a sprinter from the blocks, barefoot now.

He switched off his camera and left it at the base of the tree. Once his legs began to race, following the narrow trail, the heat and humidity took hold. Sweat gathered on his upper lip and under his arm pits. He picked up pace anyway, his foot sure but silent. He found her abandoned shoes at the side of the path and scooped them up. The leather was soft, the slender heels not made for running.

The path led to a small bluff at the lake's edge. If he left the path and cut through the forest, he'd beat her there but alert her to his presence. He decided to follow her unnoticed, staying on the path. Her bare feet made no sound. He followed blind.

As the path rose, he stopped. He could hear nothing save the lake's low lapping and the drone of a distant powered boat. His senses sharpened. Was she now in hiding, watching him? He scanned the dappled forest but saw no trace of her. Perhaps he'd lost her. Or she him. No birds called. He breathed deeply, as if the air were robbed of oxygen. He shouldn't have followed a guest this deep into the forest.

He heard a sound, thin at first, then stronger, insistent with a timpani finish. A body hit water. He scampered up the remains of the path. Her dress lay discarded on the earth. On the western side of the lake, the afternoon sun glistened back at him, scorching his sight. No ripple, nothing broke the surface. He counted. One. Two. Three. Four. His heart pumped harder. Why had she not surfaced? His eyes darted about. She wasn't there.

He dropped her shoes, threw off his own along with his shirt and shorts, leaving only his underwear. He scanned the surface. Nothing. He dived, a grace-filled arc. As he descended those five metres, arms outstretched for balance, he glimpsed something breaking the surface. He hit the water, blessedly cool. His downward momentum dissipated and he pushed his arms up towards the light.

Once at the surface, he ran his hands over his face to clear the water and that flop of dark golden hair that hung down over his forehead. She was swimming, freestyle, away from him, her stroke firm and regular.

"Hey! Are you all right?"

She stroked on. He started strong freestyle strokes, his body a plane on the water. He could hear her limbs beat ahead of him, see her ruffle the water. He swam alongside her, slowed to her rhythm. And then she stopped, abruptly, as if she refused competition. He stopped, his legs caving in below him.

She brushed her hair from her face. Her pink nipples and small breasts blinked in the water. He couldn't look lower. Aware of his gaze, she glared at him, her hyacinth-blue eyes cold and penetrating.

"What do you want?" she said.

She was older than he expected, perhaps even in her mid 30s. Like her shoes, her accent was foreign and soft and expensive. Working at the hotel, he'd taught himself to mimic these accents of wealth.

"I was worried about you."

"There's no need."

"But you were swimming out into the lake."

"I didn't know this too was forbidden."

She was French, her accent light but noticeable.

"Well…" He was out of his depth. "I'll leave you, then."

He lingered a moment but she said nothing. He turned towards the shore, poised to swim.

"Young man, are you a guest at the hotel?"

Shit! A bellboy on his day off was forbidden in this part of the forest, reserved for paying guest. She could report him.

"Yes," he said.

"Then I'd appreciate you don't mention any of this." He nodded. "To anyone."

"Of course." He trod water. He should be away from her. "Enjoy your swim."

"And you yours."

He reached his arm again towards the shore.

"Your shoes…" he said, immediately regretting it.

"What of them?"

"I left them by your dress."

She raised her right eyebrow and nodded.

Slowly he turned away. He dug his hands hard into the water but as he began to plane, the turbulence caused his underwear, tied to his hips by string, to slip, then slide into the dark, dark water. He panicked, caught between escape and exposure. He couldn't stop. He continued his strokes towards the shore, slipping easier, his round buttocks white and glistening in the late afternoon sun.

With no difficulty at all, he hauled himself up on to the rocks and looked back at her over his shoulder. He hoped she'd resumed her swim but she was stationary, about seventy-five metres from the shore, treading water and staring in his direction. For a moment, neither of them could turn away. He was sure she continued looking as he climbed back up the side of the bluff to his clothes, abandoned near hers, but he couldn't look while she was looking at his bare ass.

After he'd dressed, he made his way back to the hotel, slowed by the heat and the lack of underwear. How embarrassing. It could've been worse if he'd chosen to keep an eye on her and backstroked away. And what else could he have done except keep swimming? Stop? Duck-dive around her looking for his smalls? What a grand sight that would've been.

And he'd lied. He'd have to avoid her. The hotel was large, over five hundred guests. He could just avoid her room. But in order to do this, he'd need to know her name.

As he reached the end of the path, the Hotel Hungary rose seven stories out of the surrounding gardens. At this time of day, that breathless afternoon hollow, even the main building looked sleepy, the window box plants drooping, the eaves seeming to sag, quiet, no laughter, no signs of the activity soon to erupt as the hotel guests lurched towards cocktails, dinner, and dancing. Indeed, no hint of the war raging across Europe to which, through part good management and part good luck, Hungary had remained immune. German troops had marched through Hungary's streets and roads to the north and the south but no bombs had fallen, nothing had torn open its jewel, Budapest.

Something twinkling at the side of the path caught Zeno's eye. It was an ornate golden chain, fine weave, caught in the twigs of a low shrub. He knelt down and carefully pulled. As if he'd caught a fish, a weight resisted at the end of the chain, small but heavy. A sturdy gold crucifix. With great care he unraveled the chain and held it in his palm. Not really beautiful, plain flat surfaces, no Art Nouveaux curves. What should he do with it? He was no judge but thought it was gold and worth a fortune. Turn it in to the concierge? He heard voices. Two women, guests of the hotel, were coming. He clutched the crucifix in his palm and stood aside.

"Lord only knows where she's got to," one of them said.

They were looking for the woman. Should he go back and warn her? How stupid! He wrapped the chain around the cross and placed it in the button-down pocket of his shorts, the metal through the fabric cold against his skin.

The employees' quarters were at the rear of the hotel buildings, a group of small chalets scattered at a discrete distance. Zeno's roommate lay on his single bed, enervated and naked as usual.

"Hey," Zeno said. "I didn't think you'd be here."

"They want me to work again tonight."

Tibi was a deal older that Zeno, already twenty-five, blond hair with a film star's looks: a strong lantern jaw, full lips, fine blue eyes. His body, like Zeno's, was all chest and lung and broad shoulders. Listless by nature, he lived in Budapest but each summer came down to the lake to work.

Zeno pulled off his soaked shirt.

"Do you know a woman–"

"I know many women."

"Listen. She has dark hair. Slim. In her thirties? A hotel guest."

Tibi face soured. "It could be any of the women staying here. Why this one?"

"I saw her in the forest, near the lake."

Tibi sat up on the edge of his bed. He pulled a towel over his groin, took up a box of cigarettes, and lit one.

"But why would this old woman attract you?"

"Attract?"

"She's stirred something up in you."

"She seemed…"

Why had he started this? He didn't want to tell Tibi, the joker, how he'd embarrassed himself.

"I might have known you'd go for someone older," Tibi said. "You're such a sly, silent type…"

"Just because I don't paint my conquests across the sky."

"Exactly."

"She just seemed unhappy."

"And Zeno, the swashbuckling hero, must swoop in and rescue her." Tibi laughed, then said, "Does she have a foreign accent?"

"French, I think."

"And wearing a white dress with a faint leaf pattern?"

"Yes. Yes, she was."

"Steiner. It's Catherine Steiner. Very rich. What time did you see her?"

Zeno sat on the room's other single bed and faced Tibi.

"An hour ago..."

"This afternoon I took drinks to a table of women on the terrace. She left abruptly and said nothing."

"What'd happened?"

"That's it — nothing. She just stood and left."

"What had they been talking about?"

"Same as usual." Tibi stubbed his cigarette in the ashtray and lay back down on the bed, arranging the towel and placing his hands together behind his head. "What was in fashion, what wasn't. Nothing. After she left, the women talked about her. That something had upset her."

A sharp knock at the door heralded Kovács, the head waiter of the hotel's restaurant.

"Zeno," he said. "I was hoping you'd be here. We need you to work tonight in the restaurant."

Zeno sighed. He was only a bellboy but twice before in emergencies he'd been pressed to help wait tables. The war stayed out of Hungary but it had robbed the hotel of staff, especially of the itinerant workers on which it was so dependent for the busy summer period. Zeno hadn't really enjoyed waiting tables, embarrassed by his inexperience. But the money was better and the tips could be good.

"Tibi can partner you," Kovács said.

Still Zeno hesitated.

"It's Thursday night," Tibi said. "The men are all in Budapest working. It won't be so busy."

Both Tibi and Kovács looked at him. Zeno wanted to move to Budapest and he needed extra money. He nodded.

"Good," Kovács said. "Both of you, get ready. I'll send up a uniform for you."

Kovács nodded in his military manner and left the room, closing the chalet door behind him.

"You'll do fine," Tibi said. "Don't worry."

"This war will kill me."

"Better to die as a waiter at the Hotel Hungary than on the Russian front."

Perhaps he'd be okay as a waiter. But first he needed to wash off the day's sweat. He walked over to his dresser and removed his shorts.

"Why aren't you wearing underwear?"

Zeno blushed, covering himself with his shorts.

"Long story."

Tibi raised an eyebrow and lay back on his bed.

Zeno and Tibi walked from the kitchens into the restaurant, smooth in their white dinner-suit uniforms complete with white gloves. The restaurant was empty of guests. In the hotel's bars, the sculpted guests took bitter aperitifs to stimulate their appetites. Kovács, already busy, merely inclined his head towards the pair.

"Just don't be seen for a while," Tibi told Zeno. "Stand over there and wait."

Zeno stood alone near the kitchen servery window while those more qualified buzzed about. The restaurant curtains were drawn apart. The open higher case windows above the line of French doors that looked onto a large terrace allowed something of the evening's cool to enter the room. But the humidity persisted. He felt it on his skin. The very last of the day's sunlight glistened on the darkening lake. One by one, the room's two dozen electric chandeliers ignited, but the room still felt dark, a side effect of the dark wood-paneled walls. A violin player drew a bow across strings that were quickly tuned. The trio sprang to life for a few bars, then rested.

"All this fuss," Tibi said, as he passed by Zeno. "These pigs will never even notice."

Zeno followed Tibi. He thought it was fine no trouble or fuss was spared. Did it matter no one noticed? The dinner guests began to file in. His stomach gurgled with first-night nerves. The whole staff breathed in together, became individual cogs in one machine. Quite quickly, the restaurant swarmed with the hum of conversation and peals of mirth. The trio played Schubert's String Trio in B Flat but the heat zapped all the brightness from the piece. Over two hundred people to be fed.

Kovács came towards them.

"The entrees are ready for table ten."

Tibi and Zeno and four other waiters took up six plates from the servery window. As they approached the table, Zeno's nerves jangled—three men and three women, one of the men a German SS Officer who'd stayed at the hotel before, a lieutenant colonel Müller whose round face looked generous until he curled the edges of his mouth in something of a snarl as he spoke.

The officer was seated next to László Fehér, a man Zeno also knew only by sight. He was a local member of the Arrow Cross Party, the Hungarian fascists, a rotund little man, always at the hotel for dinner and always with guests who seemed to outstrip his rank. Next to him were György Földes and his wife. Zeno had taken their luggage to their room and received a hefty tip. Földes was an industrialist from Budapest, a neat, quiet man.

Two women, both weekday widows, completed the party, seated together like maiden aunts, their backs turned towards Zeno, facing the magnificent view of the lake. The taller, Ilona Rákóczy, the wife of a big industrialist, sat on the left. The other was Catherine Steiner, her dark hair now dry and shiny and straight. Zeno, panic-stricken, moved as if he were an automoton.

"And where's your husband tonight?" the officer Müller asked her.

"He's in Budapest," she said. "He's working."

She drew out the second sentence. The officer smirked. The waiters moved to their places around the table.

"Such a large factory must never sleep," the officer said. "You're not Hungarian."

Zeno was close enough behind to hear her breath.

"At what point," she said, "does one cease to be something and become something else?"

"Mrs. Steiner is French," Földes said, bowing his head towards the officer.

"I was born in France," Mrs. Steiner said, "but I've lived here for over twenty years."

Zeno carried her soup. He positioned himself at her left side. He took a moment, to survey the setting, anticipate any sudden change.

"Steiner..." the officer said suddenly.

Zeno began to lower the plate, slowly at first.

"They're an old Hungarian family," Földes said, his tone firm. "They converted to Christianity in the late days of the empire."

"I think Herr Müller has me wrong. I am a French Catholic." Swiftly, Catherine lifted her left hand to her chest, fumbling in the folds of fabric. Gripped by a kind of seizure, Zeno shook, just enough to cause a little soup to spill to the side of the under plate. The other waiters perceived this tremor and halted their advance. Like a magician, Tibi produced a cloth and removed the droplet. Zeno breathed out.

"That was a liberal time for such things," Müller said.

"One has to wonder," Fehér said, "how much conversion was sincere or forced or simply pragmatic."

"What rot are you talking?" Földes said. "The Steiners are a model Christian family. They maintain The Lady of Charity Orphanage in Budapest. They've received the Pope's benediction."

Without shaking, which required strenuous effort, Zeno lowered the plate to the table. The other waiters lowered theirs. Catherine Steiner made no acknowledgement. Zeno stepped back.

"Vichyssoise," the SS officer said. "You remain true to your cuisine, at least."

"You misread me yet again," Mrs. Steiner said. "The soup may be French but the coolness is an American touch. The evening is warm."

The waiters withdrew to the side servery.

At that moment, Kovács motioned. Food was ready for other tables. While he delivered these meals Zeno worried about returning to serve Catherine Steiner. But what choice did he have? And after all, she'd not noticed him. She was occupied in countering the officer. It was worth the risk. He'd say nothing to Tibi.

His serving at other tables was without fault, and with each plate his confidence rose. And when he returned to Mrs. Steiner's table, he did what was required without incident. She never looked at him. The table's conversations were inconsequential, talk of the opera in Budapest, of some marriage scandal, of the war. The officer defended Germany's dwindling position in Russia, especially since the January fall of Stalingrad.

"The Hungarian Second Army suffered terrible losses," Földes said.

"There'll always be troop losses," Laszló Fehér said.

"The Soviets crushed the remainder at the Battle of Voronezh."

Müller breathed deeply. "You must realize the loss of Hungary's troops is our own loss. New machinery, modern machinery is needed." He looked directly at Catherine Steiner and she returned the intensity of his gaze. "There are moves to secure these things. Perhaps your husband would be interested in such contracts?"

Catherine glared at him. "Perhaps."

"Perhaps we could discuss this, later this evening?"

Catherine looked quickly at the others. "I'm sure there's nothing we can't discuss here. My husband will return at the weekend. He'd be happy to meet with you."

"How ironic!" His open palm struck the table. "I must return to Budapest at the weekend. To work." He roared with laughter and returned his eyes to Földes. "Once this work is completed, the war will proceed as the Führer intends."

When the waiters approached later with desserts, no one was speaking. Ilona Rákóczy's stern expression turned into a welcoming smile. Földes banged his hand hard on the table and argued that Hungary had taken considerable action.

"Then why has Regent Admiral Horthy so resisted deportation?" Müller said.

"The men are working in labor camps. For years, we have restricted the number of Jews in different areas of business. They are completely forbidden from government office. And we have made this tighter by defining a Jew as more than one grandparent of Jewish extraction. They are a race, not a religion. And we've legislated against marriage between a Jew and a non-Jew. Any such intimacy is illegal."

"Then why not deport them as we have asked?"

The dessert plates were lowered to the table.

"They're restricted," Földes said, "identified and controlled."

Catherine Steiner stood, abruptly pushing back her chair. She turned to leave the table, turning directly towards Zeno. He'd no time to retreat. She looked into his face. Both froze. He felt his heart fall away. Her blue eyes flared violet, remained impassioned but not, he thought, with recognition. All eyes at the table were on her, but as this standoff extended, the eyes drifted to him. He stepped sideways. She looked down, away, and began to walk.

The fleet of waiters peeled from the table. All Zeno had to do was fall in line. As he moved back into the depths of the restaurant, he saw Catherine Steiner, her step brisk over the restaurant foyer. She'd bid no farewell, no explanation. She'd just left, much as Tibi said she had earlier that afternoon.

CHAPTER TWO

Zeno arrived for work at 6 a.m. in the reception area, comfortable again in his bellboy uniform. The concierge moved about, put his half glasses on, read something, took them off, and moved about some more. He barked a command at his assistant, sending him into a similar flurry of motion.

"What's the matter?" Zeno asked.

"Catherine Steiner has lost a gold crucifix."

Zeno froze. The concierge took off his glasses and glared at him. The crucifix. God damn it. And damn his inattentive memory to hell. It was lying on the floor in his shorts pocket. Zeno closed his mouth, tried to brush his expression clean.

"She thinks it's been stolen," the concierge said.

Damn, damn, damn.

"We must go to the Steiner suite," the concierge said, "and see if we can find this thing."

"But I can't."

The concierge swung back around to him. "You can't?"

"Someone should work here." He waved his hand at the reception desk. "There are people checking out this morning. Someone should be here."

"You don't seem to realize the gravity of this situation." The concierge's voice hissed on the "s" in the last word. "If it can't be found, Steiner will call the police and we'll all be under suspicion. Move it!"

The Steiner suite was on the top floor of the hotel, seven stories up, five bedrooms, a lounge and dining area, a large balcony with an uninterrupted view across the hotel grounds to the lake. The entrance hall had parquet floors, the lounge a higher ceiling and larger chandeliers, the furniture was plumped with a little more down than counterparts on lower floors.

Already a fleet of black and white uniformed maids fluttered about the room, the drapes pulled back, the weak sun spilling onto the floor. The apartment's electric lights were still turned on. A maid, Magda, who normally worked on a lower level of the hotel, rolled her eyes as she passed Zeno.

Catherine Steiner was seated on a sofa, wearing only a long sky-blue silk dressing gown pulled in hard at the waist. With her was Ilona Rákóczy, also in a robe and looking as if she'd just been pulled from bed to this drama. Despite the panic he felt, Zeno stared at Catherine. She wore no makeup. Her face, although still handsome, bore no trace of a girl and yet no real trace of age, no undue creases, the skin lucent despite her time at the lake. Her dark hair carried no gray. As she looked about the room, her eyes flashed. She was beautiful. He knew it then, as he'd suspected at the lake — beautiful beyond any face he'd ever seen.

"It was a recent gift from Sándor," she said. "Thank God he's not here to witness all this."

"You're not here to stand," the concierge said, sotto voce, to Zeno. "Help György lift the furniture."

"I remember wearing it yesterday afternoon," Catherine said. "I put it on before I left."

"What time was that?" Mrs. Rákóczy asked.

The concierge motioned Zeno close to Catherine to help lift an armchair.

"I don't know. . . . When we met for a drink, in the afternoon."

"Around three, then?"

"I imagine so."

Mrs. Rákóczy thought for a moment.

"I believe I saw you wearing it. I think I saw it. But you left us. Where did you go after that?"

Despite his heart rate, Zeno glanced at Catherine. Her face darkened. Did she now think of her swim at the lake? Imagine the crucifix at the bottom of the lake? Did she now think of him? His bare ass. He turned his back on her.

"Where did you go?"

"I walked in the forest — "

"But we looked for you there."

As they stooped to lift the armchair, the quick motion caught Catherine's eye. She looked first at the chair then directly at him. He could feel her gaze. His face burned. Magda ducked down under the chair, twisted, and looked up into the underlying springs and lining.

"I... noticed it was missing, last night at dinner."

"At dinner?"

"I hadn't put it on."

Shouldn't he end this silly game, this waste of time? No. He couldn't speak directly to Catherine Steiner. He'd lose his job for that alone. He looked at the concierge. He couldn't trust him, and anyway, she'd sworn him to secrecy.

Magda found nothing in the springs of the chair. She stood up, looking at Zeno.

"What a farce," she said quietly.

Zeno and György lowered the arm chair and lifted another for Magda to inspect. The fruitless search continued for an hour, every item in every room moved, turned, parted, shaken, or pulled apart. Once it was clear nothing could be found, the hotel manager, who'd arrived halfway through the search and taken control, asked Catherine what she wished.

"I'd just like it found. Perhaps I dropped it in the hotel grounds."

"Of course. Now there's good light, I'll instruct a thorough search of the grounds." The manager looked towards an assistant and nodded. He left the room. "Would you like tea brought up?"

"No," she said. "Perhaps it has been stolen."

"If you'd permit us to search the grounds, before we contact the police..."

"Yes. Yes, of course."

At the manager's instruction, the workers drained from the rooms. Zeno made his way back to reception, the area completely unmanned and the lobby empty of patrons or staff. He ran to his chalet.

The room was dark save for a shaft of sunlight, the air close and warm. Tibi was still asleep, his naked back turned to Zeno, the bed sheet pushed to the base of the bed. Zeno closed the door. In the dark, he fell to his knees and patted his hands on the floor, searching for the discarded shorts.

"Are you looking for this?"

Tibi rolled over, cocooning himself in the sheet. He pulled his hand free. The gold crucifix rested in his palm, the chain laced between his fingers.

"Why have you got it?"

"Stubbed my toe when I went to relieve myself." Tibi frowned. "Where'd you get this?"

"I found it in the garden. It belongs to Catherine Steiner."

Tibi bounced the crucifix in his palm. "Why didn't you hand it in?"

"I forgot."

"You forgot to hide it?"

"I forgot about it till I got to work and everyone was looking for it."

Tibi looked at him, pulled his mouth sideways.

"This must be worth six hundred pengő. How much will you earn this summer?"

"Four hundred."

"We could sell it."

"That would be dishonest."

"You're not convincing me. What's going on with you and her?"

"Nothing."

"Yesterday evening you asked about her. Last night at dinner you were nervous around her. What are—"

"Nothing happened. They're searching the grounds. Fast. Help me find it in the garden, will you?"

"These bourgeoisies have too much already."

"I have to give it back, dammit."

"Don't swim out of your depth." Tibi allowed the crucifix's chain to unravel from his hand. It fell to the bed. "If there's a reward, I want half."

The hotel grounds swarmed with maids and butlers and gardeners and any other spare set of hands, arse-up in flower beds, hedges and potted plants, others picking about in the well-tended hedgerows like workers in a field of tea. The Italian, Giovanni, waded in the murky waters of the main fountain, his trousers rolled up knee high, laughing and flicking water at one of the maids.

"I'm sure Catherine Steiner didn't swim there yesterday," Tibi said. "Where did you find this?"

"Over there." Zeno motioned with his eyes. "At the path."

At the entrance of the path, two maids half-heartedly brushed aside the bushes.

"We should go there," Tibi said.

"But they'll see us."

"You can't find this where she wasn't. Unless you know somewhere else?"

"Shut up. What about on the terrace?"

"You said that woman saw her leave with it."

"Right."

Tibi was right. It had to be found somewhere credible to her, some place she wouldn't dispute. Zeno breathed deeply. They walked towards the start of the path. Unobtrusively, they mixed with the others. How long should he wait? What was a fair time to search? He made his way towards the exact spot, but there were so few shrubs in which to hide it, really only the ones in which he'd found it. He held the crucifix in his palm. The maid, Magda, stood up in front of him, searching the same spot. He rammed the crucifix back into his pocket.

"Nothing there," she said. "Not that it's any great surprise."

She moved off to another area. He looked over at Tibi, who nodded to him to advance on their plan. Zeno began to act. He looked at those around him and tried to reproduce their slightly heavy brows, their eyes moving quickly, side to side, up and down. He checked if anyone was near and slipped the crucifix from his pocket and allowed it to fall. The chain caught in the branch. And there it hung, entangled, the sunlight catching on the gold. For a moment he thought he should just leave it for someone else to discover. But how long could this whole charade continue? What if no one found it? And what if someone did discover it and didn't turn it in and the police were called?

"I've found it," he said. No one but Tibi looked at him. How would a voice sound in such a situation? Elated? Surprised? Relieved?

"I've found it," he yelled, with all three qualities entwined in the words. Bodies straightened, heads and faces appeared from all manner of positions. Tibi ran to his side.

"Well done," Tibi said, squatting down to unravel the chain from the bush. People congregated around them.

"Thank God," another maid said. "Now we can all go back to work."

A senior worker arrived, took the crucifix from Tibi's hand and walked back towards the hotel. The other workers dispersed.

"What were you worried about?" Tibi said. "They only want the crucifix. Now they're satisfied. There's no scandal. No questions asked. No reward."

"Back to your places," a duty officer announced.

"But I searched here," Magda said. "I didn't find it."

She looked at Tibi and Zeno and then again at Tibi. Zeno shrugged his shoulders slightly and looked away.

"What one eye misses," Tibi said, "another sees."

"But I looked here."

Her eyes were determined.

"And you didn't find it," Tibi said. He screwed up his face at Magda and tapped Zeno on the back to make him walk.

The other bell boys were already in the reception area, the concierge back in place and working at a decidedly smoother pace. The morning proceeded. Bags and guests arrived and were processed with speed, dispersed to the various corners of the hotel. And from these corners bags were collected and brought back to the foyer, out to the waiting army of taxis and cars. Amongst all these comings and goings, there was no sign of Catherine Steiner. She must have stayed all morning in her apartment. Zeno could melt away again.

"Which one of you found the crucifix?"

Zeno blushed. It was the hotel manager.

"I did," he said.

The manager glared at him as if he wasn't capable of such a thing.

"Then you must smarten yourself and come with me."

"Why?"

The manager spun with great gusto towards him.

"Because Catherine Steiner wishes to thank you. Personally."

People may say I can't sing, but no one can ever say I didn't sing.

Florence Foster Jenkins (1868–1944)

Made in the USA
San Bernardino, CA
26 April 2019